STAR-CROSSED

THIS IS A BORZOI BOOK PUBLISHED BY ALFRED A. KNOPF

Published in the United States by Alfred A. Knopf, an imprint of Random House Children's Books,
a division of Random House, Inc., New York.

KNOPF, BORZOI BOOKS, and the colophon are registered trademarks of Random House, Inc.

www.randomhouse.com/teens

Educators and librarians, for a variety of teaching tools, visit us at
www.randomhouse.com/teachers

Library of Congress Cataloging-in-Publication Data
Collison, Linda.
Star-crossed / Linda Collison. — 1st ed.
p.   cm.
SUMMARY: Having been discovered as a stowaway as she tries to reach Barbados in 1760 to claim her father's
estate, teenaged English orphan Patricia Kelley struggles to survive by learning to be a ship's doctor and by
disguising herself as a man when necessary. Includes map and glossary of nautical terms.
ISBN-13: 978-0-375-83363-2 (trade) — ISBN-13: 978-0-375-93363-9 (lib. bdg.)
ISBN-10: 0-375-83363-3 (trade) — ISBN-10: 0-375-93363-8 (lib. bdg.)
[1. Seafaring life—Fiction.   2. Sex role—Fiction.   3. Survival—Fiction.   4. Orphans—Fiction.
5. West Indies—History—16th century—Fiction.]   I. Title.
PZ7.C69758Sat 2006
[Fic] — dc22
2005035826

Printed in the United States of America
November 2006
10 9 8 7 6 5 4 3 2 1
First Edition

LINDA COLLISON

STAR-CROSSED

ALFRED A. KNOPF
NEW YORK

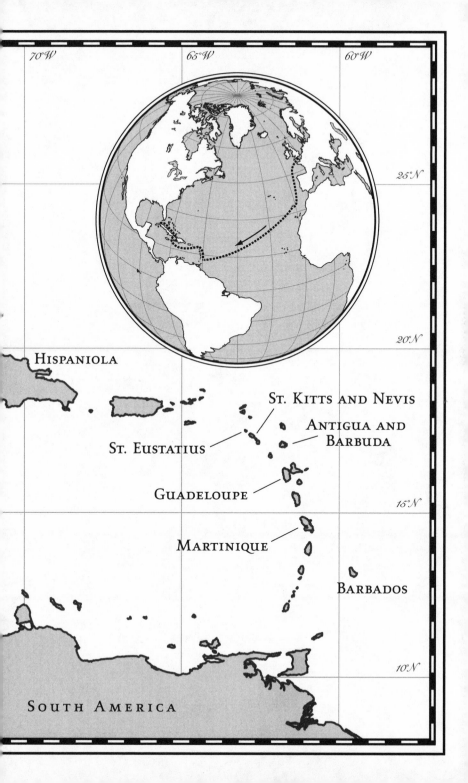

70°W   65°W   60°W

25°N

20°N

HISPANIOLA

ST. KITTS AND NEVIS

ANTIGUA AND
BARBUDA

ST. EUSTATIUS

GUADELOUPE

15°N

MARTINIQUE

BARBADOS

10°N

SOUTH AMERICA

I am possessed by the fierce noise
all around me
of the purple, tormented sea.

—Simonides

PREFACE

November 1760
Portsmouth, England

I came aboard with the prostitutes the night before the ship set sail. It was a rash scheme, but I was a brash girl with nothing to my name but a promise.

Half of Europe was at war, but the grappling among kings held little interest for me. Though the conflicts were far-flung across the globe, my troubles were of a much more personal nature. My fear was not that England might lose her place in the world, but that I might lose mine.

I had spent the last ten years of my life at the Wiltshire Boarding School for Gentlemen's Daughters. It had been just three months since my father died, leaving me alone with no means of provision. He did leave me one hope—his remark that

I would one day inherit the Hatterby Estate in dowry. The very West Indian sugar plantation where I was born and where I lived the first six years of my life. The estate where he died (in reduced circumstances; he was too fond of the horses, I fear). This wish he expressed in a letter he wrote to me when I was thirteen, a faded and oft-folded leaf of paper that I now kept in my pocket along with a bit of hard cheese.

I had so much to gain. The West Indian isles were the richest little mounds of earth on the globe, a string of emeralds in a tropical sea. Britain had laid claim to her jewels, the French to theirs. The Spaniards, the Danes, and the Dutch had grabbed their share too—and all guarded their possessions jealously, for men were making great fortunes there from sugarcane. All the civilized world was mad for West Indian sugar to sweeten its coffee and tea.

As for me, I wanted not wealth so much as a home. I was single-minded, yet quite naive. I held a girlish conceit that if only I could get to my destination, everything would somehow work itself out. With Father dead, I had not a penny to my name. But I was willing to sell my last favor if it would get me aboard a ship bound for Barbados to claim what he had promised me.

PART ONE

ONE

"God's blood, Henry, can't you row any faster? If we don't get there soon, they'll be too bloody drunk to lift our skirts."

The old trollop smelled strongly of spirits. In the darkness I couldn't see her features, just a moon face beneath a wind-lashed bonnet. There were perhaps a dozen of us in the open boat, though I never bothered to count.

The oarsman's oath was lost on the wind.

"Take us alongside the nearest vessel, that little merchantman just ahead," the old woman said.

The ships in the roadstead stretched like a forest; hundreds of masts swayed on the Channel's black swell. Lanterns winked from the portholes and disembodied voices carried across the water. The wind scattered the clouds, spilling a weak wash of moonlight on the vessel we were headed for. Shivering, I pulled my cloak close.

"That's a collier, I'd wager," the woman next to me said, her elbow sharp against my side.

"All the men-o'-war in Portsmouth and we have to climb aboard a dirty little coal barge," came a girl's thin voice from up in the bows. A very young girl, by the sound of it.

"Do we care what she carries as long as her men have specie in their pockets and are randy to spend it?" The old tart laughed, but no one else did. "Besides, I know this boat, I know her well. She don't carry coal, she's been converted to a West Indian trader and is off to the Caribee at first light. You'll make some money here tonight, girls, mark my words."

I knew nothing of ships or their cargo, though this one did look rather tubby and blunt-nosed, the closer we came. And not so very large. I wondered with a sudden panic where exactly I would hide.

A gust snatched my hat off my head and I reached for it, too late. It flew away, tumbling on the wind. It was only a bonnet, and an old one at that, but it tore my heart to see it go. My head felt naked without it, and I covered my ears with my hands.

We drew up alongside the vessel, bumping into her hull on the choppy swell.

"Ho! What's this?" a voice called out from above us in the ship's waist. "Why, it's a bumboat full of sweethearts, lads! Our wives have come to bid us farewell!"

A deep huzzah rose up from the belly of the ship. I followed the girl ahead of me, taking hold of the rope with shaking arms and scrabbling up the footholds in the hull of the vessel, catching my foot in the hem of my petticoat. I was almost to the top when a pair of strong arms grabbed me and lifted me over the rail and onto the deck, bussing my cheek as he did. I couldn't bring myself to look at his face, but his breath reeked of liquor. We were then herded like goats down the companionway.

In the flickering candlelight below I couldn't see how many men there were, but by the sound of it, all of them were drunk. They leaped toward us like a pack of dogs, knocking over sea chests, scattering dice and tankards.

Everything was happening too fast. Molls spreading themselves out on the sea chests like higglers displaying their wares.

Fear rose in my throat; I couldn't go through with it. I bolted for the companionway, but a sailor blocked the steps, a bawd on his lap. Her shabby dress was bunched up, and her bare legs flashed white in the candlelight.

"Come here, girl," a man's voice purred in my ear. "Come give old Earnshaw a taste of your pudding."

His toothless face leered at me in the yellow light, his eyes rheumy, bloodshot, and unfocused. His breath stank like rotten cabbage. I backed away, but his hand grabbed my skirt and the seam ripped. Like a mole, I scurried for the darkness, stooped behind a hogshead on the larboard side, then crept forward along an iron firehearth that was still warm from the evening meal. I had no idea where I was, only that it was dark here.

"Why, the devil, I say! Come back here!" the old goat bellowed. "Who took her? Who stole my sweetheart?"

"Lost your molly already, Earnshaw?" Another garbled voice. "Or too bleeding drunk to find 'er!"

I spied an open door ahead, near the bow, away from the glow of the wicks. A short door, as if to a dwarf's cottage. Lifting my skirts, I scrambled for it, ducked inside, and felt my way among damp casks, heaps of hempen sailcloth, and bundles of rough cordage until I reached a place so small I could neither stand nor stoop but had to lie down and wiggle myself in.

A perfect little casket it was, black and airless, but padded with sails. I hunkered into it, losing myself in the stiff folds. A hot panic rose in my chest, the panic of being trapped in a small space, yet I managed to quell it by counting my breaths. After thirty I lost count, but the sound of my own breathing soothed me. Like the whiffle of sugarcane on a balmy night, the memory of a sound from my earliest childhood.

The darkness, at first so flat and featureless, began to take on dimension. My sensation of confinement gradually reversed itself; now it seemed I was on the edge of a cliff, inches away from falling off into the blackness. My head spun and the illusion was so real I dug my fingers into the canvas, holding on. And so I lay awake, heart knocking, until the debauchery ceased and stillness crept in like a fog. Somewhere a cock crowed.

I awoke to stamping feet, groaning hawsers, and the rough singing of men as they worked to raise anchor. Knowing we were getting under way cheered me, and the busy sounds were a welcome distraction from my discomfort.

I had never in my life known much discomfort, at least not the physical sort.

Until my father died my biggest hardship was having to sit indoors for hours, fumbling at French grammar or banging at the harpsichord when I would have preferred to spend the entire day on horseback, cantering over the Salisbury Plain. I had always been happiest when out-of-doors with no other company than my horse. Riding like a banshee, leaping over stone enclosures, breathing the smells of bruised grass and warm horse lather.

At Wiltshire Boarding School few girls sought my friendship. The teachers told me I was too abrupt in my speech, too aloof toward my classmates, and far too hoydenish to attract the attentions of a marriageable gentleman. A lady may learn to ride horseback, yet she wasn't supposed to relish it. But I convinced myself I didn't care what anyone thought of me. Only my father's opinion mattered.

We were daughters of privileged gentlemen, all. Yet we measured one another with a keen yardstick to determine who was higher-born, who had more worth, who could make the best match. Every year my position hovered just beneath the mean, for although my father was the son of a baron and not some grasping merchant-made-good, I was not his legitimate issue; he didn't give me his name. To my chagrin and everlasting dismay I was born Patricia Kelley, not Patricia Hatterby. I was what people called a "natural child." A bastard.

There were plenty of natural children in the Wiltshire Boarding School for Gentlemen's Daughters; after all, secluded country boarding schools were exactly the place to put such inconvenient offspring, if one had the means. So I wasn't the only one without her father's last name.

Perhaps if my mother had been well bred herself, instead of a servant girl from Ireland, I wouldn't have felt as disadvantaged. Or if I had been a great beauty, charming and demure. I wasn't. I had too much height and not enough bosom. Too rash a temper and too sharp a tongue, I'd been told by my schoolmistresses. Yet my temper and tongue seemed to work of their own accord; I could manage neither. Hot words sometimes burst out of my mouth, scalding even me.

Early on I decided that England held nothing of importance for me. The Caribbean isles made allowances for quirks of nature and winked an eye at society's rules. I'm certain that's why my father got on so well there. I always believed that someday I'd return to Barbados and live on the estate, though the idea of a husband never seriously entered my mind. I was complacently virginal, an eighteenth-century Artemis. Father's *little Patra*. During my years at boarding school I spun an imaginary cocoon and waited, for I knew the day would come when my father would send for me. Never did I dream he would die before I could get there.

I slept, woke, and slept again. I knew not what day it was nor how much time had passed, only that I had boarded the ship on the night of November 21, 1760. The long moments were marked by the rhythmic slap of water, the creak of the pumps. Regularly a bell would ring, some sort of timekeeping system, but I couldn't work it out.

Hunger cramps tormented me. I nibbled at the cheese I had brought aboard, tied up in a bundle under my

petticoat. It tasted salty and smelled as bad as my surroundings. Tang of pitch, moldy flax, the acrid piss of rats. My
clothes were damp, my skin itched, my legs twitched. Feeling around my immediate surroundings, I discovered a
small cask filled with nails that I emptied into a heap. A perfect chamber pot.

On occasion the fiddle sawed and the men sang, and it
cheered me. I hummed with them softly, just to hear my
own voice. Once I heard the trill of bagpipes, a forlorn
sound that seemed to carry all of the world's heartbreaks in
one thin tune.

I tried to sleep, to dream the time away. Recalled my
early years on the sugar plantation but did not know if the
memories I held were real or not. Vague images: a ticking
clock on the first-floor landing, the creak and hum of the
windmill, the strong rot of bagasse. Perhaps they were only
fancies my father fashioned for me in his letters. *My dearest
little Patra* . . . Alone here in the dark I began to wonder if
anything was real, anything but this blackness. I slept, I
woke, I slept again.

A sudden rustling beside me—I gasped as something
jumped onto my bed of moldy canvas. Good Lord, a cat!
Merely a cat. My heart hammered for several minutes.
Peering into the darkness, I found I shared this hole with
not one cat, but a tribe of three. I was glad for their company, however mangy and flea-ridden they might be.

"Here, kitt, kitt, kitty." I unwrapped the dwindling block
of cheese. They devoured the crumbles I gave them—and
later brought me the heads of rats they had dined upon. To
pass the time I whispered to my feline companions in

French. I was never very good at pronunciation and grammar, but they took no notice of my deplorable accent. They curled their paws underneath them and blinked.

Above us the men went about their work. Scraping the decks, hauling on halyards, their voices calling out in lusty rhythm. Hearing them thrilled me deeply in a way I did not understand. They made a powerful sound—vibrant, masculine—and I longed to be a part of that sound. The same way that looking at a masterful painting made me want to enter it.

I slept again, and when I woke it was to a new motion. The vessel was pitching and slamming into the waves with such force it seemed it would break apart. The wind shrieked in the rigging, amplified by the wooden hull; it must've been blowing a gale. The cats retched, heaving up the vile contents of their stomachs on my bed of sails. I was flung about and became so sick I thought I'd die—indeed, wished for death. Miserable, frightened, I longed for sleep so as not to be awake when the final moment came.

Amazingly, I did sleep. When I awoke the seas were calm and the cats were gone. Had I dreamed the storm? Close at hand I discovered a flask of water and a bowl of porridge. No dream, these. Apparently I had been found.

TWO

A blade of light penetrated the darkness.

"Awake? Thought ye might sleep to Madeira."

With the light behind him I could see only a silhouette. His voice had a roughness to it, like a cat's tongue. His northern accent was of the poorer class. My nose detected a whiff of tobacco, tar, and warm sweat.

As I scrambled to sit up, my head banged on the overhang.

"Who are you?" My voice was shrill and I struggled to control it.

He seemed bemused. "Nae, that's my question to *ye*."

"Patricia Kelley," I said with as much aplomb as I could manage.

He waited, as if expecting more.

"I'm a passenger. Unaccounted for, perhaps."

"One of the wharf girls, are ye?"

"Certainly not. I only came aboard with them."

"If ye're not a molly, what then are ye?" He inched closer, as if for a better look.

"I am Sheldon Hatterby's daughter," I said proudly. "The late Mr. Hatterby. Of London and Barbados."

"Never heard of him."

"No, I suppose not," I sniffed with as much indignation as I could muster. "He was the third son of Baron Avebury of Whiteparish."

"Well, now I suppose ye'll want me to bow and scrape." He grinned.

"Please don't mock me." Apparently my father's name had not impressed him in the least. "I'm not royalty, but I'm not a streetwalker either."

"How old are ye, miss?"

"Seventeen." I stretched the truth a wee bit, for my seventeenth birthday was still a fortnight away.

"Brian Dalton, at your service," he said, touching his brow with exaggerated deference. "Neither lord nor gentleman am I, but bosun's mate of the merchant ship *Canopus*. And this would be the bosun's locker ye're holding court in."

"Was it you who brought me food and water?"

Brian Dalton put a blackened finger to his lips. "I'll not admit to it. Ye'd best lay low if ye wish to stay with us."

Though grateful for his kindness, I couldn't bring myself to thank him. My pride seemed to be the only force keeping me together. "This ship is going to Barbados, is she not?" I demanded.

He laughed. "A fine time to be asking that. Aye, we're

going to Barbados. But if the Old Man finds out there's a stowaway on board, he'll likely put ye off in Madeira."

"No." I refused to entertain the possibility. "He cannot."

"Aye, miss, he can. But no one wants to go to the West Indies. At least no one in his right mind."

"Why?"

"Too bloody hot. Full of fevers and disease."

"For some, perhaps, but I was born in Barbados," I said. "I lived there on my father's plantation until I was six."

"Is that so?"

He knelt down so that we were nearly face to face. I realized he was about my own age, perhaps a bit older; it was hard to determine in the dim light. He had a sturdy nose and wore his dark hair pulled back in a tail, save for one damp lock that had come loose and fell over his eyes. Thick, dark lashes. Dark eyes, and shining, but with pleasure or mischief?

"A Bimshire princess, are ye?"

"You are mocking me still," I said. "I tell you I was born there, I have property there, and if you'll keep me on I will eventually pay for my passage and make it worth your while. Perhaps you'd like a position. Are you handy with horses? Can you manage the servants?"

"Nae, Princess, I'm no farmhand. Ships' ropes are my business, not horses or servants. I was sort've thinking the reverse. I was thinking ye might like a job on the ship."

I met his sparkling eyes.

"What sort of work?"

"Oh, there's no end to the work aboard a ship. The

rigging, for one, always needs tarring," he said, scratching his stubbled chin. "My lady, how handy are ye aloft with a bucket of pitch?"

I shot him the most withering look I could manage under the circumstances.

The bosun's mate's smile flashed across his face. "Princess, I like your spunk."

He then picked up a coil of rope and backed toward the door. "With your permission, my services are required on the fore t'gallant yard. G'day."

As suddenly as he had appeared, he was gone.

In spite of his teasing, I felt the dark-eyed sailor was on my side. After all, he had fed me and emptied my chamber pot. I hoped he would not change his mind and reveal me.

Hours passed, I have no idea how many. Someone opened the small hatch almost above my head and a bit of light and fresh air flooded in. I could better hear the men above me on the foredeck, their good-natured swearing and boasting. Singing as they worked, with ribald words and unforgettable tunes. When the hatch was closed again, I felt more alone than ever. Time crept.

The door opened and the bosun's mate appeared, tossing a bundle of clothes at me.

"Don these," he whispered hoarsely.

"What? Why?"

"Hurry now and I'll take ye on deck for a breath of good air."

"Are you mad? I can't go on deck, I'll be discovered."

"Trust me. It's after midnight. Most of the watch has nodded off and there's no moon to reveal ye. But just in case the Old Man pops his head up on the quarterdeck, ye'll be less of a sore thumb. Dressed as a Jack."

"Jack?"

"Jack, Johnny—a common sailor," he said impatiently. "Now step lively, we haven't got all night."

He turned his back while I crawled out of my hiding place and undressed, changing into baggy trousers stiff with tar, a well-worn flaxen shirt, a canvas jacket, and a woolen cap. They smelled of him, the bosun's mate. Tobacco, tar, and sweat.

"Lively," he urged.

I followed him out of the cramped locker and up on deck, where a wet wind filled the sails, driving us through the darkness. The moon and stars were not to be seen. I leaned against the rail, breathing in the spray in deep, grateful gulps, dizzy with my newfound freedom.

The bosun's mate took me by the elbow, for I had no sea legs and felt wobbly in the knees. He bade me hold on to the rail while he tugged on ropes as thick as my wrist. Tightening the braces and lifts, he explained. I wondered how he could be so familiar with each rope in the darkness, for there were so very many; a maze of them snaked overhead. They all seemed to terminate on the rail of the ship, where they were coiled in tidy loops, hanging from pins and timberheads. The ropes were the domain of the boatswain, or "bosun," as he pronounced it. The bosun and his mate reeved, tarred, and mended the miles of hempen rigging that supported the sails that drove the ship.

I liked the grand orderliness of it all. The complexity, the strength, the beauty of it. She seemed a living being, *Canopus*. I could hear her breathe and sigh, I could feel her joints creak as she moved. A ship was a thing built by men but bigger and better than any man. Able to transport me, to fly me home.

Looking around me, I saw another man leaning against the foremast. His arms were folded across his chest and his head bent forward, bobbing with the motion of the ship.

Dalton put his lips near my ear. "That's Earnshaw. He's a fine one for sleeping on his feet. Sets the standard, he does. But he's a good topman, even if he is getting up in years. And he can lead a fine chantey."

"Where are the others?"

He jerked his thumb astern. "Cunningham is at the helm, Quixote's aloft. Doughal and Hans are on the fo'c'sle having a game of cards, and Mr. Kent, the first mate, is down below."

"So few men to sail the ship?"

He laughed, a soft sound through his nose. I could feel his breath, warm against my cheek.

"Only seven men to a watch. We're a merchantman, not a bloody naval warship."

We crossed to the starboard side of the ship. I was glad for his arm, for I lurched like a drunkard.

"Look, do ye see that light way out there? That's one of our convoy, the *Godspeed,* I would wager."

"How many ships are we?"

"Ten and three. All merchantmen but chartered by the navy for this run."

"All going to Barbados?"

"Aye. Barbados, then to Antigua, then back to England. That is, if the French don't catch us."

"What would they do to us?"

He shrugged. "Rob us of everything and send us to rot in a French prison, most likely."

"Do you always assume the worst?"

He laughed again. "That's not the worst, Princess. They could save themselves the bother and feed us to the sharks."

Dalton made me stay in the ship's waist by the cannon while he went aft to the quarterdeck to check the mizzen rigging. I heard him speak to the man at the helm, heard their low, easy laughter. Heard the groan of timbers, the rattle of blocks and rigging, the steady rhythm of water against the wooden hull. I would've loved to have curled up there on deck with a blanket until dawn, but Dalton sent me below to my hiding place, where he shared with me the remains of his supper, a lump of tough salt beef and a moldy biscuit. I was much too hungry to refuse.

He left without asking for the clothes he had lent me. I kept them on; they were much more comfortable than my petticoat, corset, and silk gown.

The bosun's mate came for me the following night and every night after that. I looked forward to his arrival; knowing he would come back kept me from going mad or giving myself up. Each night the air grew warmer and clearer, revealing the heavens as I had never seen them in England. Dalton introduced me to the sky as a map, a gigantic storybook. He pointed out bright stars and constellations, the characters who played their part on the midnight stage overhead. I learned to recognize Orion the hunter, rising in the east, and Taurus, the red-eyed bull. To the south, Argo Navis, a great ship with its brilliant star Canopus, for which our own vessel was named. These were things I'd never learned in school.

The ship *Canopus* was another world, with more working parts than I'd ever imagined. Even before the moon rose, the stars shone brightly enough to illuminate the sails. Courses, tops'ls, t'gallants, stays'ls, sprits'ls—Dalton taught me the names of each one and explained the puzzle of sheets, halyards, clews, and buntlines that worked them. I wondered at how much he knew, for I had always assumed that sailors were an uneducated lot—all brawn, no brain.

It was only with Dalton's help that I was able to endure the dragging hours hidden away. I lived for those fifteen minutes each night when he took me on deck to breathe the clean sting of salt and gaze up at the geometry of canvas against the ink sky.

THREE

The locker door opened with a crack, startling me out of a sound sleep. I knew immediately it was not the bosun's mate. The door was flung wide and the harsh light of day penetrated my hideaway. The cats fled.

Footsteps grew closer. I closed my eyes, like a child in hiding, and my heart beat so hard I thought it would be heard. A hand touched my face and I gasped. It was a small hand. I felt hot, quick breath upon me.

"Pray tell, a dead man!"

I said nothing.

"Identify yourself immediately," the little voice commanded. "If you are alive. Or I shall call my superior officer!"

I opened my eyes and saw a fair face with round, wide eyes peering at me. A little boy.

"I am quite alive, thank you," I said. "Although nearly expired for the want of a decent meal and a proper bed."

The child gasped. "Why, you're a girl, aren't you? A stowaway girl!"

"I beg your pardon, sir, but I am a lady, a gentlewoman. Traveling incognito."

"'Incognito.'" He said the word slowly, as if tasting it.

"It means to be in disguise," I said.

"I know what it means. Of course I do. 'Incognito.'" The boy regarded me with intense curiosity, as if he were examining a bug or a toad.

I thought of what I might say to keep the impertinent little whelp from revealing me.

"My name is Patricia, what's yours?"

"William Young," he said, puffing himself up. "They call me Young Willie. Lieutenant Molesworth is my uncle, and he's in command of this old coal carrier. But did you know? We're not carrying coal at all; we're carrying cannons and powder! We've got enough powder on board to blow up a fleet of ships. Kaboom!"

"Gunpowder?" I hoped I wasn't lying atop it.

"The hold is packed with it," he hissed in my ear. "Gunpowder and shot. Crates and crates of muskets, all for the West Indian forts."

"Indeed?"

"Did you know, miss, that someday I'm to command a ship? A man-o'-war with a hundred guns. I'm going to be an admiral, my mama said."

"Admiral Young," I said. "Yes, it has a nice ring to it. Master Young, you are destined for greatness, I am certain."

Willie sighed, my sarcasm over his head. "Yes, but right now I'm just the cabin boy."

"A cabin boy. Well, one must start somewhere, I suppose. And how old are you?"

"Nine. Well, nearly so. I say, are you armed, madam?"

"Armed? No."

"I didn't think so. Neither am I. Although Lieutenant Molesworth says I may wear a dirk on Sunday."

"That must be quite a sight."

"You remind me of my sister," he announced with a childlike leap in thought. "How old are you? Emily is sixteen but wishes she were eighteen so she could marry Mr. Longley."

"Is that so? Listen, Master Young, I beg you, please don't tell anyone you've found me here. If you keep this our secret, when we get to Barbados—"

I was just about to make a wild promise when the door opened again.

"What the devil is keeping you, Willie?" a man growled, hunching over as he stepped inside the locker. It was definitely not the bosun's mate.

"Where are you?" The figure approached us. I held my breath as Willie stood, mouth agape, unable to speak. "I asked you to bring me a sack of oakum— Why, what's this? By Jove, a stowaway?"

Before I knew it I was hustled out of my dark hiding place by two red-coated marines and dragged up the stairs into the blazing light of day, straight to the foot of the quarterdeck to face Lieutenant Molesworth and the shipmaster, Captain John Blake.

Lieutenant Hugh Molesworth of His Majesty's Royal

Navy was a finely chiseled man with a nervous tic that
caused his face to contort in spasms. He was perhaps five-
and-twenty, and dressed in fine clothes and silk stockings.
His kid shoes, just inches from my face, were immaculate.

In a blatter of words I rushed to explain myself, to convince him I wasn't an ordinary stowaway but a gentleman's
daughter fallen upon hard times. The lieutenant interrupted me with a stamp of his foot. "I will not coddle ille-
gal passengers of either sex, Miss Kelley, and I do not care
who you claim your father was." His left eye winked in
rapid succession. "Where did you get those clothes? Have
you stolen them?"

"They were my brother's," I said. It was the first thing
that entered my head.

"A likely story," the lieutenant snorted. "You say you are
a lady and your father the third son of a baron, yet your
brother is a common sailor?" He pressed his forehead between his hands and squeezed his eyes shut.

"Until we make Madeira you'll be confined. Please see
to it, Captain Blake."

"The hold is completely full, sir, and every cabin occupied," the man called Blake said gruffly. Though he apparently held a position of importance aboard the ship, he
wore no wig and did not powder his iron-gray hair, tied at
the nape of his neck in a Hessian tail. "We have no place to
confine her."

"Find one," the lieutenant said.

Blake's weathered face, ploughed with creases, deepened in color. "With all the cargo and your entourage on
board, we've nary the room to imprison a cockerel."

Lieutenant Molesworth turned on him, his eyes

glittering. "Then what do you suggest we do with her? Put her in the hen coop?"

"I'll see if my wife can look after her," Blake grumbled.

"Make certain your wife keeps her out of mischief." Again the officer's well-formed face collapsed in a violent twitch. He sighed deeply. "Here we are in the heat of a great war that could guarantee my career, make me a post captain. Instead, I am cursed with a raggle-taggle converted coal shuttle and a convoy of merchantmen." Molesworth stopped his tirade, pursed his blue-tinged lips, and looked at me again with disdain. "Give the little tart something useful to do. See that she is kept busy and out of the way."

I was handed over to Mrs. Mary Blake, a woman past her prime but big with child. Her lying-in must be near, I thought, for her condition was quite apparent beneath the brown serge gown she wore; a plain dress, rather out of fashion and worn shiny at the elbows. Her eyes lit up when she smiled and her face seemed to crack into a hundred fine lines like an old porcelain plate. Mrs. Blake was kind to me and treated me graciously, inviting me to have tea with her. As if I were a guest instead of a stowaway.

I changed into my own clothes, damp and soiled though they were. Pinned up my hair as best I could. Sat down at her table and looked around the simple, sparsely furnished wardroom.

Mrs. Blake poured from a silver pot almost as nice as the tea service I was accustomed to at boarding school. This was a welcome improvement from my previous accommodations in the bosun's locker, and I was glad for the ritual and the small talk that accompanies a cup of tea.

The captain's wife stirred a lump of sugar into her cup,

explaining that her husband owned the ship in partnership with his brothers.

"*Canopus* was built to carry coal but the Blakes are merchants and drapers, not colliers. We bought her in need of repair and refurbished her. She serves our purpose well."

"Don't you miss your home?"

Her eyebrows shot up in surprise. "My dear girl, this ship is my home. I have no other."

I asked if it was unusual for a female to accompany her husband to sea.

"Not if you love your husband and want to be with him," she said with a conspiring smile. "Lots of women set up housekeeping afloat. And believe me, most men want the company of a female no matter what they might say to the contrary. Why, even the navy allows its men to have their women, though they are given no extra allowance, not so much as an extra weevil-infested biscuit." Mrs. Blake sipped at her tea, her eyes twinkling over the cup.

I thought the navy was cruel and said so.

"Ah, but they don't see it that way. The navy must answer to the Victualing Board." Still, the smile. A wise and superior smile, as if she thought herself not just a captain's wife but a woman of some importance.

"Women aboard ship aren't listed on the muster books, you know."

"And why not?" I demanded.

"Too costly. To the navy we're not souls, just seagoing chattel. Little luxuries a man brings aboard at his own expense. Jack's warming pan at night." She winked as if sharing a great secret. "But my lot is better. My husband is part owner of this ship and he commands it, not the navy.

Though for this run the navy has chartered us and we must do as they bid."

"Why would the navy charter a private vessel?"

"Why, my dear, what warships and transports they have are spread thin. All over the globe, they are. Protecting our shipping routes and our colonies from the plundering French. 'Tis rumored the Spanish are about to declare war against us too."

Britain had been at war with France for several years now, fighting over colonial possessions. But beyond these most basic facts, I was woefully ignorant of political issues. A young lady's schooling did not include topics like warfare or the workings of governments.

Mrs. Blake laughed. "I'll admit, Miss Kelley, I'd much rather be carrying linens and woolens, but money is money and the British Navy pays well."

The pregnant woman was full of surprises. She wasn't just the merchant captain's wife, his warming pan at night, but she acted as the ship's purser as well. It was she who provisioned the ship, kept records of stores on board, and sold the sailors their tobacco, rum, and slops, which was the seaman's word for work clothing.

"I've never heard of a female purser," I owned.

Mrs. Blake waved her hand, a red hand with ragged nails. "'Tis no great thing. I know how to stretch a shilling like any good housewife, and I've a good head for lists and figures. Although I must say, I have saved the Blakes a pretty penny over the years. You see, they don't have to pay a man to do the work I do for nothing." Though she was modest there was a gleam of satisfaction, nay, pride, in her eyes.

"You're in need of a decent meal, I'm certain," she said. "You'll sup with my husband and me tonight. Mr. Kent, the first mate, and Dr. MacPherson will be joining us."

"I've caused you trouble enough, I shouldn't intrude on your meal." Though ravenous, I was afraid to face Captain Blake again in such an intimate setting.

Mrs. Blake seemed to understand this intuitively. "He'll have a soft heart for you, don't worry. But we must find you something clean to wear. And your hair, we must do something about your hair."

I was mortified. After ten days in the bosun's locker my mane of hair was a tangled, salty mess and most likely infested with fleas. My best feature was my hair—red-gold, thick, and curly.

Yet I had never been a beauty, never even dreamed of it. A Viking of a girl I was, with broad shoulders and great long legs. My fair skin had been ruined early on by freckles, which seemed to multiply of their own accord, and my chin had already developed a firm set to it, giving my face a stubborn air. I had been told many times by my schoolmistresses to smile pleasantly and often if I ever hoped to attract a man. But I scorned their advice, for I had no need of a man. I had my father, after all.

"More tea?" Mrs. Blake offered.

"Lieutenant Molesworth, he seems hateful of me," I said as she refilled our cups. "Do you think he will put me off the ship in Madeira?"

The captain's wife pursed her lips and the smile left her eyes. "I cannot say, but you should prepare for it, yes."

My stomach churned. I simply had to stay with the ship. Perhaps Mrs. Blake would know how this might be accomplished. I felt I could trust her, she was so kind to me. But at that moment there was a clattering on the companionway and Young Willie burst panting into the wardroom.

"I've come for the captain's glass. Madeira is in sight and it was I who first spied it from the masthead."

Madeira, so soon? It was only after Willie left and I felt Mrs. Blake brushing my hair so determinedly, so patiently, so thoroughly, only then did I feel my veneer of strength begin to weaken. My eyes stung but I held back the tears.

Supper was a simple meal of boiled beef and pudding, served with claret and quickly eaten. We sat at a dimly lit table rimmed with wooden edges to keep our plates from sliding into our laps, which they surely would have. I had to wedge my foot against the table leg for balance; the table itself was bolted fast to the deck. I was famished but ill at ease, worried about my fate.

Conversation was kept to a minimum; Mrs. Blake and the three men seemed intent upon their food, for which I was glad. I could hear the creaking of the tiller ropes that connected the wheel to the great rudder that steered us, and the clatter of the nanny goat's hooves as it scampered across the deck above.

Mr. Kent excused himself and left the table. It was then Captain Blake cleared his throat and fixed me in a penetrating glower.

"Tell me now, Miss Kelley. Why have you sneaked aboard my ship? 'Tis unlawful and the consequences are grave."

I hung my head. "Sir, I beg your forgiveness but my situation was desperate."

He forked the last bit of meat on his plate. "How so? I'm told you are a gentleman's daughter."

"Yes, but my father is dead, these three months."

"I am sorry to hear that. But he made no provision for you?"

The ropes groaned as the helmsman made a correction. I wondered how to begin.

"He left me no money. But he gave me a promise."

"A promise?" Blake's voice was skeptical.

"Yes, sir." I managed to choke down a bite of meat with a sip of claret. "His estate in Barbados."

"A marriage portion, then? A dowry?" He continued to chew, and I could hear the clicking of his false teeth.

I nodded. "Of sorts."

"And have you any suitors?"

I gulped some more wine. "Not presently. No."

"I see." He cleared his throat. "And what of your mother?"

"I hardly remember her. She died when I was six." I didn't elaborate, for I was ashamed to admit my mother was but an indentured servant from Ireland. My father's housemaid.

"Hmmm. A pity. Was there no one you could turn to? No interest anywhere?"

"None."

"Then how have you been keeping yourself?"

"I stayed on at the school in Salisbury for as long as I could, but they had no permanent place for me."

"And you had no influence through your father or his family? No relatives to take you in?"

"No."

I did not say that my father had died in greatly reduced circumstances. That he had fallen behind in his financial arrangements for my keeping. Very far behind. And although I was his *dear little Patra,* I was not a legitimate heir in the eyes of the law. My father never married my mother, for he had a proper wife back in London. A lawful wife; a wellborn lady who would not acknowledge my existence.

Captain Blake chewed and chewed. At length he swallowed, wiped his mouth with his linen, and cleared his throat.

"Lieutenant Molesworth has chartered this vessel, and he intends to put you off in Madeira," he announced, his gray eyes boring into mine.

"My father's estate is my only hope. If I can just get there."

"We should make landfall tomorrow," Blake said gently. "You should prepare to disembark."

"John, this is your ship, is there nothing you can do?" Mrs. Blake touched his arm with her hard, worn hand.

He sighed. "I'll speak to Molesworth, but I don't know what good will come of it. Until we deliver the goods he is commander of this vessel, not I."

For several long minutes there was nothing to be heard but the noises of the ship and the scraping of spoon and fork against plate.

I pushed the remainder of my food around, unable to swallow another bite.

The ship's bell rang three times and Captain Blake excused himself to go on deck.

My hopes sunk.

"More wine, Miss Kelley?" Dr. MacPherson, the ship surgeon, asked.

MacPherson was a big Scot whose once-red hair was now bleached, like a frock left hanging too long on the line. I wondered if mine would be that colorless someday. His eyebrows, though pale, were thick and straight, giving him a rather fierce expression.

As he poured the wine, I saw his pink, splotched hand, the size of a country loaf. I marveled that he could manage a lancet without maiming the poor patient. I judged him to be old; in his thirties, I would guess.

MacPherson was one of Molesworth's retinue. Because the lieutenant preferred to dine alone in the great cabin, the ship's surgeon had been taking his meals with the merchant officers in the wardroom. MacPherson's proper title was "Doctor." Besides being trained as a surgeon, he had a degree in medicine from the University of Edinburgh.

There was quite a difference, for a surgeon was but a tooth yanker, a blood letter, a bone sawyer, a seamstress of flesh. A handyman as opposed to a learned man. Surgeons were good enough for most navy ships, but Molesworth insisted on having a physician, a medical doctor, and he paid for the difference out of his own purse. Although his job was mainly to attend the lieutenant, MacPherson was required as part of the contract to treat anyone on board who needed his services.

As there were only the three of us left at the table, Mrs. Blake attempted to engage us in conversation, but to no avail. The doctor wasn't one to waste words and I wasn't in a sociable mood. He excused himself and left the two of us alone.

"It's a lovely evening," Mrs. Blake said. "Would you care to join us on deck? Dr. MacPherson pipes the sun down and the men all sing. 'Tis the best part of the day."

"No. But thank you for the invitation," I added lamely, seeing her disappointment.

"Are you certain? Lieutenant Molesworth is taking his supper in the great cabin," she added. "He won't come up."

"I'm tired," I said. Though in reality I was uneasy because of my tenuous situation.

"Poor child, of course. Why, you must be exhausted," she said, her kind face nearly causing me to crumble. "Let me help you hang a hammock and you can get a good night's sleep."

I hadn't been called a child in some time. Did I really look so young?

Apparently I was to sleep in a seaman's hammock in the same cabin where Captain and Mrs. Blake slept. She stood on a sea chest and showed me how to lash the hammock to the timbers. Then she gave me a pillow, a blanket, and one of her own muslin shifts to sleep in.

"Try and get some sleep. Perhaps Providence will intervene for you." Mrs. Blake pulled the door shut, leaving me alone in the darkening cabin. Above I could hear the bagpipes whining and the men singing in unison. It was a poignant sound, too true to bear.

The clanging of the ship's bell woke me. Eight bells. The ringing every half hour was a rhythm that I had become aware of while hidden away in the bosun's locker, and Dalton had explained the code. Beginning at noon the bell was struck every thirty minutes, each time once more than the last. Every four hours—eight bells—the watch changed and it began all over again. Eight bells; midnight. The middle watch.

I slipped to the floor and pulled the shift over my head. Stepping into my canvas trousers and man's shirt, I felt a thrill in my gut. This was the time of night I was accustomed to going on deck. The Blakes' hanging bed rocked with the ship, as if on a breeze. Quietly I opened the cabin door and went out, up on deck, into the night. I was hoping to find the bosun's mate.

He was waiting for me at the lee rail. We stood there awhile without speaking. He packed his pipe with tobacco.

"Molesworth is putting me off in Madeira," I said.

Still he said nothing. Just lit his pipe and took a long draw.

"They say we make landfall tomorrow."

"Aye, that's true. And then what will ye do?" He turned his head to blow his smoke.

Suddenly I was angry with him, unreasonably angry. That this man who had once looked out for me, brought me food and water, now did not have a plan. But Brian Dalton was only a seaman of the poorer class. He had no influence, no more than I. How could he possibly intervene? My life seemed to be falling like a net around me. I looked up to the sails, stiff with wind.

"I want to go up there."

He nearly choked. "Aloft? Why? Are ye daft?"

"Take me."

I felt a sudden need to escape the confines of the ship. It was as if I was trapped, pinned down by some invisible force.

"But ye can't climb."

"I can," I said recklessly.

"Ye're a girl. A lady, I should say."

"And what of it?" I challenged.

"Do I look like a fool? Do I look like a simpleton? No, I won't take ye. Ye'll fall to your death."

"I won't, I promise. Show me how." I caught his eyes, felt the spark between us, and knew then he would do as I bid. At last he looked away and sighed.

"Bloody hell. Take your shoes off."

"My shoes?"

"Do as I say," he commanded. "Ye can't go aloft in shoes, ye'll have no purchase. Ye'll climb in bare feet or ye'll not climb at all."

I fumbled to remove them and hurried after the bosun's mate to the windward chains.

"Watch me and do as I do." He sprung up the ratlines, fast and sure as a gazelle.

Taking a deep breath for courage, I grasped the tarred shrouds in my hands and followed. The ratlines dug deeply into the soles of my feet as I climbed after him. I didn't dare look down. Above me the mast swung like a pendulum.

Dalton was already on the platform called the fighting top, grinning down at me. He looked so at ease up there. *So this is what it's like to be a boy,* I thought, my legs moving freely in their loose seaman's breeches. No stays to constrict my chest, I could breathe deeply, fill my lungs to the brim. I've always been a hale sort, strong and sure-footed, more suited to riding than to needlework and conversation.

"What do I do now?" I stood at the base of the futtock shrouds, where the rigging supporting the upper mast jutted out at a frightful angle, around the fighting top. Well above the deck now, I could feel the wind pressing against the backs of my legs.

His laugh was merry and made me bold. "Go back down, I suppose. Or cheat and come up through the lubber's hole."

"How did you get there?"

"Like any red-blooded sailor does: climb the futtocks. Much too hard for a princess, I'm sure," he taunted.

"Why, you devil!"

Spurred on by his challenge, I reached for a new handhold and continued to climb, almost upside-down now, like an opossum or a tree sloth. The ship rolled as if to toss me off, but I held on tightly and pressed on, heaving myself over the edge of the fighting top and flinging myself onto the relative safety of its platform. Dalton stood there grinning at me.

"Well now, ye've gone this far. But ye're only halfway. Do ye want to go higher still? To the top of the mast? The t'gallant?"

"Of course," I panted, frightened yet elated. My fingertips tingled and I could hear the blood pounding in my ears.

Now the ratlines narrowed to barely the width of my foot. The higher we climbed, the greater the arc the mast made as the ship rode the swells. Dalton waited for me at the crosstrees, where there was barely room for one of us, much less two. Yet I squeezed onto the timber beside him, my arms entwined in the rigging. Looking down at the deck, at the sea, at the courses and stays'ls awash in moonlight, I felt sharply aware. My throat was raw; each breath stung.

So this is how a bird sees the world. How easy it would be to fall. Merely let go the ropes and wait for the next roll of the ship to carry me. This was not a fright but an epiphany. That someday I would die, yes, but right now I was quite alive on the edge.

"I must be off my head," he said.

Standing so close, I could feel his chest moving as he breathed. That we were both alive at this moment, and knew it, seemed a remarkable coincidence.

Halfway back down, on the fighting top's platform, we sat to catch our breath.

"Ye did well," he said. "But I shouldn't have taken ye. 'Twas foolish of me."

"No." I touched his arm. "It was magnificent. Thank you for taking me. And for befriending me."

A smile broke through and spread across my face; I couldn't hold it back. Grinning at the bosun's mate, all breathless and wind-whipped, I felt like anything might happen.

"'Tis my pleasure," he said, pulling me close to him. I offered my mouth to be kissed and found his lips eager.

Above us the wind sang in the rigging, a keening dirge, reminding me of my fate. Tomorrow I was to be put off the ship.

FOUR

Madeira loomed, a dark mountain robed in mist.

The foredeck was a busy place as the men readied to anchor. The bosun's mate was out on the larboard cathead preparing to drop the bower. Two other sailors were faking down the hawser, pulling it up from the locker below and laying it in a long, back-and-forth fashion along the starboard deck. They laughed and cursed as they worked; their forearms rippled and glistened in the sun, which was just now breaking through the morning clouds. The old sailor started a chantey and the rest joined in. There was an excitement among them I could feel, and at that moment I wished that I might trade places with one of them. Any one of them. Though a sailor's life was rugged, it seemed to be without complications.

This was the hour I'd been dreading. The lieutenant

sent Young Willie to fetch me to the quarterdeck. Willie
swelled with self-importance and had I not been so distraught I would have pulled his little queue or pinched his
pink ear for being the smug messenger of my fate.

The deck was crowded, everyone busy with the task of
coming into harbor and anchoring. Captain Blake had a
folded chart in one hand, a spyglass in the other. He and
Mr. Kent were discussing the approach they should take on
entering the harbor. Dr. MacPherson stood at the rail, gazing at the mountain. He had his bagpipes under his arm, as
if he were preparing to pipe us into port. Each man was busy
with his own concerns, yet I was sure all eyes were on me.

The morning sun shone brilliantly. Even under his fine,
three-cornered hat Molesworth was squinting, his face
twitching. I looked away quickly, down at his polished
shoes. Noticed his perfect stockings, not a snag or a pill or
a stain. His slender, well-shaped calves.

"Gather any tawdry belongings you might have brought
aboard," he said to me. "You'll go ashore in the second
boat. A marine guard will escort you."

"Escort me where, sir?"

He glowered at me, the spasms of his face reignited.
"To the authorities, Miss Kelley," he said with dry disdain.
"Where would you presume to be escorted—to a ball,
perhaps?"

I dared to look into his dancing face again. A face that
had a life of its own.

"What will become of me, sir?"

"I suspect you'll be treated as any vagrant," he sniffed.
"Sent back to England on the next mail packet, most
likely."

"But—"

He stamped his well-shod foot. "It is none of my concern what happens to you, let me make that perfectly clear. You chose your fate when you came aboard, and I'll not have stowaway strumpets on this ship."

I burned with shame and anger. Could not move, could not see a thing but the hot, white sun.

"Lieutenant Molesworth, might I have a word with you?"

It was Dr. MacPherson's voice, booming across the quarterdeck.

Molesworth joined him at the rail. I couldn't hear what was said, just the tenor of their voices, back and forth, like a duet. I remained where I was, on the steps of the quarterdeck, rooted like a turnip. I felt my fate stripped completely out of my hands. Long minutes passed and I sweated like a sailor in the heat. I could hear their voices, but a teasing waft of air snatched the words away like scraps of paper.

After a time the lieutenant's footsteps approached, quick and sharp on the quarterdeck. I felt his black eyes boring into me, as if nailing me in place.

"My physician has intervened on your behalf, Miss Kelley. He has taken a liking to you, it seems."

My eyes flew to his.

"The good doctor requests a loblolly and so I shall indulge him. By serving Dr. MacPherson you can pay in kind for your passage and to some small extent for the trouble you have caused us. Do you accept the terms?"

"The terms?"

"Do you agree to be indentured to Dr. MacPherson for

the remainder of this voyage? I'll warn you, it's the only way you can stay on this ship. Will you serve him?"

Serve him! What was I, a commodity to be bartered?

"Yes," I hissed like a cornered cat.

"Oh, aren't we a saucy tart," Molesworth sneered. "I'd advise you to quit your high-and-mighty act and give Dr. MacPherson a hand. Not to mention a little pleasure in his bed."

My face flushed hot with indignation. "I'm not a tart, sir. I am a gentleman's daughter."

He rolled his eyes. "Oh, save your false modesty for someone more gullible than I. If you were a gentlewoman you never would have come aboard this ship with a bevy of harlots, at least not if you had an ounce of good sense and self-respect. But here you are, and if you wish to stay, you will do your time under my physician. Serve him well, Miss Kelley."

FIVE

I was immediately thrust into the ship doctor's care, and he wasted no time but put me straight to work.

We were in his cabin, a small space that also served as his office and dispensary. My first task was to learn what every instrument in his box was called, the name of every powder and herb, and the proper place for everything so I could fetch it in an instant. This was a daunting assignment and I told the doctor so.

He laughed, his voice rich and sonorous. "Come now, Miss Kelley, ye're not just a pretty winklot with batter for brains. Ye must put your mind to it. Apply yourself."

That, of course, was precisely the problem. I had no interest in scalpels, lancets, and other sharp objects, nor in jars of powders and salts and the compendiums that explained them. If I had to be a servant, I'd rather it be some

other sort of work. And the idea of giving the doctor pleasure in bed, as Lieutenant Molesworth had suggested, was
absolutely out of the question.

My distaste for the job must have been clear, but he was
not easily put off. "I am preparing to bleed a patient in just
a few minutes," he said. "And ye, Miss Kelley, shall be my
assistant. No time like the present to begin your training in
earnest."

"Now?" I said defiantly.

"Why not?" He looked at me quizzically. "Ye aren't a
squeamish sort, are ye? Don't faint away at the sight of
blood, do ye?"

MacPherson's eyes were keen and blue. They held mine
in his own and I could not speak.

"Now, then, are ye willing to work for me or not?"

I fought to keep the tremble out of my voice. "Yes, in
order to stay aboard ship. To get to Barbados."

"Ye're a bold lass and I admire that, but ye've much to
learn if ye're to be of use to me. Ye shall be my loblolly girl,
nurse, and clerk all rolled into one, and if ye're any good I'll
promote ye to surgeon's mate." He smiled as if he were of-
fering a child a bauble.

I shook with revulsion. If that great hulk of a once-red-
headed old man thought I was going to share his bed, he
was mistaken. If that was what a loblolly girl was, some
sort of sailor jargon for a prostitute, then I refused. True, I
had been prepared to sell my favors to get to Barbados on
the night I came aboard, but that night was past and I
didn't care to remember it.

"Yes. But—" I stopped.

"But what?"

"I won't sleep with you," I blurted out, feeling the flush creep up my neck.

His eyes fairly popped out of his head. "Ye what?"

"I'm willing to help you, I'll carry your kit and hand you instruments, but I refuse to be your—your loblolly or whatever you call it." My voice was shaking but I was determined to stand my ground. "I will not sleep with you, Dr. MacPherson."

He looked away, scratched his head. Reached into his pocket for a handkerchief and wiped the back of his neck. A long moment passed.

At last he spoke, his voice matter-of-fact. "Let me explain a loblolly's duties, Miss Kelley. A loblolly boy, or in your case loblolly girl, is a surgeon's assistant. Generally loblollies have charge of feeding the patients. They help with the bathing and the fumigating. Sort of like a sea-going nurse, a loblolly is. That's all." His eyes were kindly.

So it wasn't a prostitute he wanted! What must he think of me? Humiliated, I covered my blazing cheeks with my hands.

"'Tis all right, lass," he said gently. "I won't harm ye. I won't molest ye, I swear it. But I really could use your help."

I couldn't tell him how relieved I was. Couldn't say thank you. I stood like a post, and all I could do was nod.

MacPherson cleared his throat and straightened the stack of books on his desk. "Now, then, Miss Kelley. Your training shall begin in earnest. We have a patient to bleed. Can I count on your assistance?" He looked at me with his keen eyes.

Indeed, how could I refuse?

He picked up his instrument kit. "Where did they go?"

"What, sir?"

"My spectacles."

"Pardon me, but who are we bleeding?" My curiosity got the best of me.

"Lieutenant Molesworth. Now where did they go? I just had them."

"Is he ill?"

He scratched his head, scanning the small, cluttered room. "I don't believe so."

"Then why are we bleeding him?" I persisted.

"Because he requests it." MacPherson bent down to look under his desk.

"You mean he actually wants us to pierce his vein and collect his blood?"

"Lieutenant Molesworth believes frequent bloodletting will prevent him from coming down with the fever."

"Will it?"

"Perhaps. Ofttimes what a man believes is the most powerful nostrum of all," the doctor said, straightening his great frame prematurely and knocking the top of his head on one of the low beams. "Ouch, damnation! Pardon my language, but where are they? They can't have just walked off into the deep blue!"

"There they are, sir. On top of the stack of books on the chair."

"Aye, of course. See there, lass, ye're a help to me already." He smiled a friendly smile that put me at ease.

Molesworth's cabin was the largest on the vessel. It took up the full breadth of the ship, nearly thirty feet across, and was furnished with a large walnut table where at one end Young Willie stood polishing the lieutenant's swords and cutlasses, spread out before him like a set of fine silver. He looked up and smiled at me, a winsome, boyish face. I couldn't help but smile in return.

Molesworth paced the floor, dictating to his clerk, who sat at a secretary writing furiously. "That will do for now, Mr. Simmons," the lieutenant said imperiously. "Leave them for me to sign as soon as I am done here." Then, sitting down at the table, he held out his left arm. "May we get on with this procedure, Doctor? I wish to go ashore."

"Ashore? Sir, I'd advise you to rest afterward."

"How I should love to rest." Molesworth's lips curled into a humorless imitation of a smile. "But I am expected ashore."

The lieutenant looked at me, but I saw no flinch or snarl; indeed I saw no sign that he recognized me, although of course he did. *Perhaps it is easier for him,* I thought, *if he pretends I don't exist.* To him I was invisible.

"Why do ye have me aboard if not to heed my advice?" MacPherson groused.

"I have you aboard to bleed and purge me at my discretion. To attend me should I fall ill or become wounded. Not to coddle me like a mother hen." Molesworth rolled up the cuff of his well-tailored sleeve.

Red-faced with anger, MacPherson said nothing but moved quickly, wrapping a piece of whipcord above the lieutenant's elbow.

"Lancet."

I realized it was to me he was speaking. I opened the bag and withdrew the silver case that held the blade. My hands trembled in spite of myself. I watched as MacPherson felt for the blood vessel, his huge fingers pressing gently on the pale flesh.

The lieutenant's face was composed. Absolutely serene. Now that it wasn't twitching with the tic, I could appreciate his fine features, his delicate lips. Like violets, his lips.

MacPherson took the lancet from me without taking his eyes off the vein he was about to tap and inserted the sharp blade quickly, expertly, with the nonchalance of stabbing a bite of beefsteak. I watched the blood escape down the valley of his elbow and into the silver bowl, a deep purple stream. Molesworth's face relaxed even more. He closed his eyes, his dark lashes fluttered, and his lips parted slightly as if he were waiting to be kissed. The blood ran.

SIX

Safe at anchor in the Funchal harbor, our convoy of ships awaited an armed frigate to escort us across the Atlantic. We would make quite a prize should the French capture us, laden as we were with gunpowder and cannon.

Meanwhile, the doctor kept me busy polishing instruments and learning what they were used for. And I was given the lowly task of cleaning and fumigating the sick berth. MacPherson expected more of me than any of my schoolmasters or mistresses ever had, and now that I trusted him not to molest me, I was anxious to please him lest he change his mind and dismiss me.

Unlike most indentured servants, I took meals in the company of my employer. And I was given a new sleeping arrangement; MacPherson insisted on giving me his cabin, while he strung himself a hammock just outside the door.

A young lady needs her privacy, he said, and I welcomed his generosity.

Still, I spent every free moment at the rail, gazing at the isle and sniffing the air for the heady smells of land. Grass, leaves, flowers, the mineral tang of soil all wafted out to the boat, tempting me ashore. Though I was wild to get off the ship, I dared not ask permission for fear the lieutenant would change his mind and leave me here in Madeira.

On the third day I was given the task of going to market to purchase fresh produce, Mrs. Blake's condition being too advanced. She gave me a list and a purse of coins with which to bargain. Though pleased to go, I couldn't shrug off my fear that the lieutenant would change his mind and leave me behind.

Tibbs, the lieutenant's personal servant, accompanied me in order to acquire delicacies for Molesworth's private table. We went ashore in one of the boats, along with Dalton and three other sailors assigned to load barrels of water for our passage. I hadn't seen the bosun's mate since the night before we made landfall, the night we climbed the rigging together. Though it would not have been quite proper for us to converse, I glanced more than once in his direction. He tended his oar and did not look my way, but the air seemed charged with his presence.

The surf was rough, and as we approached the beach, the men worked hard at the oars to keep us from broaching. A broad-shouldered Portuguese waded out and lifted me from the boat as if I were a sack of onions, carrying me safely to shore. Tibbs scrambled to follow and lost his footing. His arms flailed as he reached for the gunwale. The next wave knocked him to his knees and swept the wig from his head. Dalton dove to retrieve it, but the uppity servant snatched it away without a word of gratitude. With a huff he replaced the peruke, but it looked more like a dripping muskrat crouching on his head than a proper hairpiece. The sailors and I burst into laughter as Tibbs stomped off toward the tents, mad as a cat who has run afoul of a pail of dishwater. I hurried to catch up, but he was soon lost in the crowd.

The marketplace was a gaudy dazzle of color. Sudden smells, a jumble of incongruous scents, hit my nose. Jasmine and lemon blossoms confronted the odor of steaming horse droppings and the stench of fish entrails rotting in the gutters. A chatter of different languages filled the air. English and French, I knew. But there were others I could make no sense of—Portuguese, most likely, and the strange patois of the Africans.

Hucksters hawked their goods; guinea fowl scattered underfoot, screeching. A woman wearing a red-and-gold-striped turban held out an exotic-looking fruit and said something I didn't understand. Her beautiful skin was black and shimmering, her palm as pink as the fruit she offered. I longed to taste it, but walked on, unsure.

After I'd spent ten days on a rolling sea, the ground beneath me seemed to dip and sway under my feet and I tottered like a drunkard among the makeshift tables, the colorful awnings. My head reeling, my legs refusing to cooperate. Land sickness, they called this. I didn't care. Let the world spin. This place was alive and I wanted to experience it.

First on the purser's list was pomegranates, yet I had no idea what one looked like. I found a brown-skinned grocer who spoke the King's English. She sold me not only pomegranates but everything on the list—oranges, lemons, walnuts, cabbages—and arranged for it all to be sent to the ship's tender. In return I gave her every penny in my sack, for which I was later chastised. (Mrs. Blake said I might have bartered and bought the lot for half the price, but I was not accustomed to haggling. I had never before purchased anything on my own, as marketing was not a task for proper young women.)

My errand now completed, I should have gone back to the landing to wait for Tibbs and the boat that would return us to the ship. But, itching to explore this colorful place, I wandered from the marketplace to walk along the waterfront, keeping a sharp eye out for Molesworth's man. I passed the chandlery, the apothecary, numerous warehouses, rum shops, and taverns. I saw donkey carts heaped with produce and driven by grim-faced black men. I was passed by sedan chairs carrying fat Englishmen, toted by sweating, swarthy Portuguese. Groups of sailors stumbling from one public house to the next, swearing goodnaturedly. The only women I saw were servant girls and slaves. And molly girls looking to sell their favors.

I knew the waterfront was no place for a lady to linger, yet I couldn't bring myself to quit it so soon. There seemed to be no particular danger, at least not in broad daylight. A young woman's life was entirely too restrained, I felt. If I were a boy, I could enjoy the sights and sounds without people giving me curious glances. In a pair of breeches and with sturdy shoes on my feet, I could've walked faster and covered more distance. I could've gotten out of the boat and ashore on my own.

Reaching the end of the waterfront, I turned back and

headed for the beach. That's when I spied our ship's boat, loaded with water casks, making its way across the bay. And there in the bow was Tibbs, his ruined wig askew on his head.

"Wait!" I called in a panic, thinking they were intentionally leaving me behind. "Come back!" I picked up my skirts and ran toward the beach but the oarsmen held their course, in spite of my cries. Had I kept my wits about me, I would've realized the boat would surely return, as there were many more barrels of water still on the shore.

A burst of laughter, a familiar voice. I turned to see the bosun's mate in the company of two strumpets dressed in shabby finery, their lips and cheeks unnaturally rosy. I felt like I had been shot in the heart with an arrow. Seeing my distress, Dalton broke away from the girls and approached a fisherman mending his nets under a nearby tree. Pointing out across the water toward *Canopus,* he reached into his pocket and gave the man a coin. The girls waved their fans and called to him to return.

All this was done quickly, without a word between us. In fact, we hadn't spoken at all since that night we climbed aloft. Up in the rigging, in the private web of ropes that was the sailor's domain, it had been easy to talk to the bosun's mate. The words just tumbled out. But by the light of day, with me dressed as a lady and all eyes upon us, it was much less so. Besides, what could I say to him just then? What could he say to me that would erase this feeling of betrayal?

As the fisherman rowed me across the bay, I dared not look back. But I remembered very vividly how he looked with his hair pulled out of its Hessian tail, his neck scarf undone, his jacket slung over his back. A shadow of whiskers on his face, and smears of scarlet paint. I should have been overjoyed to be back on *Canopus;* instead I was miserable with jealousy.

The bosun's mate could keep whatever company he liked, I reminded myself. He had done me a kindness, to be sure. And we had enjoyed a passionate kiss on the fighting top the night he took me aloft. But he had no place in my future; he was not the sort of man my father would have wanted for me. Brian Dalton was just a sailor and sailors consorted with prostitutes. I vowed to put him out of my mind for good.

I needn't have worried about the ship leaving, for we remained at anchor off Funchal for another week. Dr. MacPherson had plenty of lessons for me, and plenty of work to take my mind off the bosun's mate. He insisted the instruments be cleaned and polished daily. Soon I was intimate with each tool. I could have identified them blindfolded, which the old red-haired Scotsman said I should be able to do, as the lighting belowdecks was very poor. I hoped my newfound knowledge would not be put to the test on our next passage.

The days dragged and still no frigate appeared to escort us. If I had to be aboard this cramped ship, I wished we were at least sailing toward Barbados. Lieutenant Molesworth spent most of his time ashore in the taverns. Mrs. Blake said he wasn't a drinking man, that he was there to learn about the comings and goings of French vessels.

"He's gathering intelligence," Willie whispered, eager to show off his knowledge.

"Oh, what do you know?" I teased. "You're only nine."

He wagged his tongue at me and I chased him across the ship with a bone saw, for which I was severely reprimanded. We were both of us like pent-up puppies, shipbound too long. Though he could be an annoying little whelp, Young Willie was what I imagined a little brother would be like. I was growing fond of him, almost in spite of myself.

I didn't see much of the bosun's mate that week. Perhaps he was ashore with those girls, and I didn't want to think about that.

SEVEN

"You'll need a hat," Mrs. Blake said, pinning the last loop of hair to my head.

Dr. MacPherson had asked me to accompany him to a dinner party that evening, the fifth night of our stay in Funchal's harbor. Although MacPherson was an honorable man, I didn't fancy the idea of being escorted to a party by my master, a man on the other side of thirty. Still, the chance to go ashore, to see what a party in Madeira was like, was tempting. I accepted his invitation.

Mr. Farber, a well-to-do British wine factor and friend of the Blakes, was having a dinner party at his quinta on the mountainside overlooking the town and harbor. All the gentlemen aboard our ship had been invited, but the captain and his wife had declined due to Mrs. Blake's advanced condition. Mr. Kent, the first mate, and Henry Blake, the

bosun, were to represent the Blakes. Mr. Kent was a soli-
tary man who kept his own counsel and wore the shadow
of some long-ago grief most noticeable on his face. I suspect he didn't relish an evening stretching his smile thin in
the name of commerce, but he was a dutiful man.

Henry Blake, Mr. Blake's nephew, was in charge of the
watch opposite Dalton's. A tall yellow-haired man of nine-
teen, the younger Blake had hands that looked far too
smooth and white for the likes of a bosun. Why, I had more
tar buried under my nails than he did. Though Henry Blake
drew a bosun's pay, he did little to earn it, from what I could
see. He put on airs, as if he were a nobleman instead of a
bosun, ordering the men about, yet not lifting a finger himself if he could help it.

Molesworth was attending the dinner too, although not
in uniform. Here in Madeira he was presenting himself not
as a lieutenant but as Mr. Molesworth, a passenger en route
to the West Indies to see to the family plantation. This
story had something to do with our secret cargo. From
what I knew of Molesworth, he was certainly not attending
for the pleasures of social discourse but to gain what news
he might of the French.

Mrs. Blake had spent the morning cleaning and repair-
ing my only dress, the one I had come aboard wearing.
Amazing, what she was able to do for that green silk sacque;
except for some water stains about the hem, the gown
looked nearly new.

Dr. MacPherson gave me the afternoon off so that I
might ready myself for the night's event. Mrs. Blake helped
me wash my tangle of hair and I dried it on deck in
the bright sunshine, under a mild blue sky. We sat on the

ventilation hatch above the wardroom, where she combed and dressed it for me. Willie played in the rigging above and dropped small bits of oakum to annoy us.

"Don't you have something useful to do, you little deuce?" I called to him.

"No," he squealed delightedly. "Uncle has given me the afternoon for my leisure. He says I may have a parrot or a monkey. I'm thinking a monkey would be more of a companion. What do you think?"

"I think I would like to come up there and tweak your ear."

Willie giggled and dropped another bit of oakum, which the wind carried onto my hair.

"Stop that, you little moon-curser," I shrieked, shaking my fist at him.

"Make me, I dare you."

"Children!" Mrs. Blake scolded. "Behave, the pair of you, or I shall send you to your cabins." In spite of her threat she laughed when I jumped up and started for the ratlines.

Our caterwauling was interrupted when the doctor returned from town, clambering over the gunwale with a box under his arm.

"For ye, Miss Kelley." The look on his face was the look of a boy, pleased with himself, yet self-conscious.

My first thought was that he had brought more tools of his trade. A bleeding bowl or a lance. I untied the string and opened the box, revealing a bonnet of the latest fashion. It was a pretty little thing and set well on my head.

"Why, it's lovely, sir. A fine hat." I fingered the silk ribbons. "I'll reimburse you when we get to Barbados."

MacPherson looked at me oddly. Probably thinking I was delirious. Here I was, a destitute stowaway, indentured to him, promising to pay him on arrival. With what? A puncheon of raw sugar? It was a silly thing to say and I regretted it immediately. That's the trouble with hastily spoken words; they can't be taken back and they linger too long in the air.

"'Tis a gift, lass. I expect nothing in return but to see ye wear it."

I looked to Mrs. Blake for help. She nodded, smiling her approval. But I didn't know how to graciously receive a gift. Other than my father, no one had ever given me one.

"Ye need suitable attire for the party, do ye not?"

I nodded. "My old bonnet blew away the night I came aboard."

"Well, then," he said, almost gruffly. "No more talk of reimbursement. 'Tis yours."

"It's very nice, sir. Most thoughtful of you."

"And what a lovely color," Mrs. Blake said, adjusting the hat and tucking in a rebellious curl that had fallen forward over my face. "It brings out the green in your eyes." The captain's wife kept a straight face but her eyes gave her away. My suspicions were right—she *had* planned this whole event.

"Aye," the doctor said. "A bonny hat for a bonny lass."

I squirmed under the praise.

"We leave the ship at two bells. Don't be late, Miss Kelley," MacPherson said, as if it were an order, before disappearing down the companionway.

"It was your idea, you put him up to it," I hissed, squinting at Mrs. Blake from beneath the hat's brim.

"Dr. MacPherson is a fine and honorable man. Besides,

you did need a new hat, didn't you? And such a hat it is." She handed me the looking glass. "See for yourself, you're ravishing."

"Hardly." I glanced at my red-faced reflection in the mirror. "But presentable, perhaps." It *was* a stylish hat. If only I didn't have such horrid skin. If I wasn't so long and lanky. As tall as many a full-grown man, I was.

"Look out for seagull poop," Willie cried, dropping another bit of rope on me. I ducked my head and laughed. If only I'd had on trousers, I'd be up those ratlines to teach him a lesson.

Just before sunset six men from the starboard watch rowed us to shore. We were a taciturn lot for a group on their way to a party. Yet Molesworth was unable to ignore me as we sat knee to knee in the crowded longboat. He acted as if we had just met and seemed to regard me not as a stowaway, harlot, or indentured loblolly, but as a brand-new thing entirely. He touched the edge of his hat politely and spoke a few clipped words of acknowledgment. Perhaps I was legitimized by the fine new hat I wore or by my elevated status as the doctor's guest. Perhaps I was just a character to him; a *gentlewoman.*

The sailors ran the boat as far up the beach as they could so that the gentlemen would not get their breeches wet, and a husky boatman swept me up and carried me over the rocks, for which MacPherson tipped him a farthing. From the shore we took sedan chairs a mile up the side of the mountain, the chairmen huffing, sweating, and swearing in Portuguese as they hauled us up the steep, stony road.

The Farber estate was an elegant baroque-style house overlooking the harbor. Dozens of sedan chairs and carriages crowded the courtyard. From inside the great house, the yellow glow of a hundred lamps and the din of dozens of conversations. A land breeze stirred the air and I was glad Mrs. Blake had given me her lace wrap for the evening. Although the breeze was still warm, I hugged the shawl tightly for a sense of security.

In spite of my upbringing I was anxious; I had never been to an event quite like this. The school I attended was tucked away on a country estate in Wiltshire, where the biggest social event of the year was the headmistress's birthday party. Although I had been well rehearsed in the arts of conversation, etiquette, and dance, it was all just playacting with the other girls and the school dames. Now that I was faced with real society, I felt awkward. I was grateful for Dr. MacPherson, who sat beside me at the dining table and put me at ease throughout the long, lavish dinner.

The talk was of England's new king, another George. George II had died just last month and his grandson now reigned. George III. Truthfully, I cared little who governed the country, for I was consumed with thoughts of my own future. *Would I remember any of father's house servants? Would they remember me? How many riding horses did father keep? Was the cane crop ready for harvest?*

After the coffee had been served and the last morsels of fig pudding eaten, our hostess announced it was time for the women to retire to the garden. Curtsying to the gentlemen, I took my place in the train of rustling silks and brocades as the ladies, all twenty of us, trooped after Mrs.

Farber. Back at the table the men lit their smokes and discussed governments and taxes.

Outside the air was drenched with the scent of night-
blooming jasmine. I sniffed, my nose in the air like a
pointer, nostrils flaring, until my lungs and head were full
and I could smell it no more.

We had only the light of the lanterns to see by, as the
moon had not yet appeared, though it would be rising
shortly. Back in England I never knew the phase of the
moon nor where in the heavens to look for her, as the
gloomy clouds, the trees, the pointed roofs of houses obscured much of the sky. But at sea the sky is unavoidable; it
refuses to be ignored.

Now in feminine seclusion, the women fairly exploded
into chatter. Apart from the men, their talk was less restrained than it had been around the dinner table. Laughter
escaped in giddy peals. Mostly they discussed people—
people I had never heard of. Meanwhile the men's words
flew from the open windows, out into the garden, dropping down now and then like bats. . . . *war profits* . . . *the cost
of war* . . . *smuggling* . . . *alliances* . . . I couldn't follow any
of it.

Strangely enough, I found myself wanting to return to
the ship—the very ship I had been eager to escape just a
few hours ago. I had a compelling urge to climb to the top
of the mast, as I had done that night with Dalton, less than
a fortnight ago.

Remembering the adventure caused my breath to
quicken and my fingers to tingle. My innards squeezed
like a fist as I relived both the fear and the elation that
came with overcoming it. To think, I had climbed to the

crosstrees. To the t'gallant yard! My very own arms and legs had carried me there. I was proud of them, disguised now beneath yards and yards of delicate fabric. Proud of my ragged, freckled, unfeminine hands that stuck out from the lace-trimmed sleeves. Trembling and unsure, they had taken me where I wanted to go. I knew then that I would climb again.

Tangled up with the memory of the climb was the recollection of Dalton's embrace, an indiscretion that shouldn't be repeated. We were of different worlds, he and I. Still, I cherished the memory of our brief intimacy: the exhilaration of climbing, his nearness, the strength of his arms, his pressing kiss. One vivid half hour lived fully, between the ringing of the ship's bell.

The musicians began tuning their strings, bringing me back to the present moment. Feet firmly on land, at a dull party, my escort a stuffy old ship surgeon. And now it was time for the ladies to rejoin the men in the great hall for a few hours of dancing. The other women pulled out pocket mirrors, patted their hair into place, wiped the shine from their noses, readjusted their hats.

The orchestra struck up the processional, a servant flung wide the doors, and down a grand staircase we traipsed, one by one, into the cavernous ballroom. All eyes were on us; I could feel them more than see them. I held my head high and walked with all the poise I could muster, though I felt ungainly. Much too large and my face a brilliant red beacon.

"Ye've turned everyone's head," MacPherson whispered as I took my place beside him, relieved to be out of the spotlight.

The doctor's eyes gleamed in the candlelight. He had powdered his hair for the occasion and looked rather distinguished in his coat and cravat.

"One can't help but notice a five-foot, ten-inch red-headed freak," I quipped.

"Hold your tongue, I'll hear none of that. A bonny lass ye are, Miss Kelley. Especially tonight."

I made a face, wrinkling my nose. "It must be the hat."

The orchestra began a minuet and couples flocked to the floor.

"May I have the honor?" he asked, his face so grave I wanted to laugh.

I was happy to dance, glad for the chance to get up and move. Conversation was not my strong suit and I had never mastered the ruse of being coy. However dainty, at least dancing was physical, a sort of game played in motion.

I took MacPherson's arm and followed him to the dance floor. He towered over me, so I didn't feel so awkward about my height. We must have been a sight, the raw-boned Scot and the flaming-haired Amazon mincing across the floor, yet I found I was relaxed, comfortable, as I had not been all evening. He danced well and was easy to follow.

The next dance was an allemande, which I gave to the eager Henry Blake, who presented himself before the minuet was scarcely over. The young Blake danced well enough but nearly talked me to death at every opportunity, going on about the importance of this run *Canopus* was on and how one day he would be in partnership with his father and uncles and own a share of the ships and wouldn't have to stoop to climbing the rigging anymore like a common sailor. To hear him boast one would have thought he was a baronet instead of a bosun. It was all I could do not to yawn in his face.

I danced next with the laconic Mr. Kent, who moved listlessly across the floor, wincing all the while as if his shoes pinched him and heaving a sigh when at last the lugubrious song came to an end.

I was glad to go back to MacPherson for the next minuet, and I stayed with him for the rest of the evening. The doctor did not try to impress me, flatter me, or flirt with me, and I felt no need to boost his ego or to simper and smile, stretching my lips unnaturally. We simply moved to the music. His big hands were warm and he smelled of bay leaf and lime.

EIGHT

At daybreak on the ninth day of December *Canopus* weighed anchor, the seamen singing as they pushed the capstan that winched up the great iron weight. *Since rovin's bin me ru-i-in, we'll go no more a-rovin' with you, fair maid. . . .* As always, the sound of their husky voices singing a working song stirred me, but this time doubly so; our next stop was Barbados and now I was almost certain I would make it. Only four weeks to endure, perhaps five. Then my real life would begin.

Canopus and the convoy of merchantmen would continue from Barbados to the island of Antigua to deliver the remaining troops and armament to the fort at English Harbour. There Lieutenant Molesworth would leave *Canopus* to take command of his frigate, *Eos*. A frigate, Willie told me, was a far worthier ship to command than a merchantman.

A frigate was a small battleship, after all. But I didn't care what sort of ship Willie and his uncle Molesworth would be on, since I was disembarking at Barbados. I bragged to Willie that I was going home to my sugar estate, and good riddance to vessels of any sort.

Captain Blake set the course, though the breeze was light and the sails hung forlorn. One by one the other ships in our company weighed anchor and pottered along behind us. We had no armed escort—there was none to be had—but Molesworth said we could wait no longer. The wind, he promised, would freshen by nightfall.

Suddenly the ship seemed too small and inconsequential for this immense body of water, the Atlantic Ocean. Pacing the deck, I discovered it could be covered from bow to stern in forty-eight long steps, and the beam in just twelve. Four weeks to cross the ocean—it seemed a lifetime. I fought a feeling of confinement, as if the ship were a prison, and belowdecks the dungeon. The only thing that kept me sane was knowing that I could escape aloft.

Dalton and I had resumed our nightly conversations, though not our embraces. The thought of those girls I'd seen him with on shore still piqued me, but an intimacy with the bosun's mate was unsuitable. My goal was to obtain my father's estate and to that end Dalton was no asset. Still, I followed him up the rigging at night, where we talked of things nautical. Sails, tackle, the state of the sea, the sky above us. Cloud formations and the weather they foretold. The paths of the planets and stars and how to steer by them.

★   ★   ★

The ship fell into her accustomed routine. The day officially began at noon, when the sun climbed to its highest point in the heavens and the captain brought his brass quadrant on deck to measure the angle of the sun. From this he deduced our position on the chart and corrected the course as necessary.

"Sou'west by west, one-quarter west," the captain called.

"Aye, sir. Sou'west by west, one-quarter west," the sailor at the helm repeated, making a minor adjustment to the wheel.

At one bell—half past noon—the cook called us to dinner, the main meal of our day. Molesworth dined alone in the great cabin, attended by Young Willie, his manservant Tibbs, and Simmons, his clerk. Captain and Mrs. Blake considered this rather queer behavior but didn't make an issue of it, for the lieutenant had paid for the luxury of the great cabin as well as the adjoining private cabin. If he wished to be a hermit at mealtime, well, that was his business. No one much wanted his company anyway.

Captain and Mrs. Blake, their nephew Henry, and Mr. Kent all dined together in the wardroom, as did Dr. MacPherson and I. The sailors took their meals with their kind in the forward part of the ship, where they also hung their hammocks at night. But as the days grew warmer they often took their meals topside on the foredeck.

The six marines of Molesworth's retinue messed, that is to say they took their meals, in two shifts so that half of them were always on duty. I never actually saw them eat, nor did I know where they ate. The marines were a class unto themselves, scorned by the sailors and ignored by the gentlemen. I felt rather sorry for them, for they seemed not to belong to any world but their own.

Every person aboard a ship had his duties but it seemed to me the fourteen sailors had the worst of it. In addition to sailing the ship and keeping a lookout, they were required to clean, maintain, and repair the vessel. Seawater and salty air seemed to be constantly nibbling away at us. The tapping of hammers filled the air every afternoon, for rust accumulated quickly on the deck hardware and had to be knocked off before a fresh coat of black paint could be brushed on. The anchors were kept coated with fish oil.

The best sailors climbed the ratlines with buckets of tar to blacken the rigging. This was done to protect it, and to keep it tacky so that a topman might have a better grip on a wet night. To attach new gaskets or replace a cringle, the sailors walked out on the yards with the easy balance of starlings hopping across a clothesline. I admired them for their grit and their grace aloft.

And so the day was worked away. Always there were sails to mend, new reef points to braid. If any man looked idle for a moment he would be set to work picking oakum. This meant unraveling pieces of old rope in order to salvage the fibers, which were used for caulking, patching, stuffing, and the like. Living afloat, nothing was thrown away but was instead used again and again, often in new ways. Although the seamen considered picking oakum to be a lowly task fit only for inept landsmen ("lubbers," they disdainfully called them), I would as soon sit on deck in the fresh air and pick oakum all afternoon than be cooped up belowdecks polishing surgical instruments, tearing cloth for bandages, or weighing out musty herbs and vile powders, which were just a few of the many tasks MacPherson found for me to do.

Canopus was sailed on a two-watch bill, meaning there were only two groups of seamen to sail the ship. These were referred to as the starboard watch and the larboard. The starboard and larboard watches took turns on deck; four hours on, four hours off. The ringing of eight bells meant the end of one watch and the beginning of the next. Somehow the sailors got by on snatches of sleep, and then only if the winds remained steady. If the weather turned and a change in sails was needed, or if extra hands were required to man the pumps to keep us dry, then none of them slept. "All hands, all hands on deck!" the shipmaster or first mate would call. "Tumble up, lads, lively now!"

The hours from four in the afternoon until eight at night were called the dogwatches, one watch split into two. Though no one could ever explain to me why they were called dogwatches, they served to make seven watches in twenty-four hours, instead of six, and thereby changed the pattern so that the men who took the midnight watch one night would go below and sleep those precious hours the following night.

At the end of each watch the men heaved the log, a routine I liked to witness, for it proved to me we were actually making progress through the endless ocean. The log was a weighted chip of wood attached to a hundred-fathom rope with knots tied along its length at measured distances. "Watch!" one man called as he dropped the chip over the stern. As the thick, slimy rope played out through his hands he counted the knots while another man watched the sand run through a thirty-second log-glass, calling "Stop!" when the last grain slid through. The ship's speed was calculated using basic arithmetic and noted in the record. *Canopus* was not a fast ship, but a steady one. Six knots was considered breakneck speed for her.

The quarterdeck was off-limits to the sailors, except as required to carry out their duties, and the officers and gentlemen knew their place as well; they never went forward of the waist unless it was absolutely necessary. A vessel's foredeck was Jack's domain, while the stern of the ship was reserved for the better sort, but I in my various disguises had access to both.

At four o'clock in the afternoon Mrs. Blake and I took our tea and had our chat. Afterward we set the wardroom table for the gentlemen and supper was called at six. The sailors' supper was usually the remains of their midday meal. Those of us in the wardroom often ate leftovers as well, although we had more variety to our fare than did the seamen. Theirs was a monotonous diet of salt beef, salt pork, and sea biscuit washed down with grog or beer. (I recalled the scraps of food Dalton had shared with me when I was hidden away in the bosun's locker.) But at the gentlemen's table we occasionally dined on fresh fowl and goat cheese, and always we had claret or good Madeira wine.

MacPherson nearly always piped the sun down and the men joined in singing some ballad or hymn, which made even the gruffest sailor dewy-eyed with nostalgia. At eight bells, which corresponded to eight p.m., the watch would be set; half the men would go below and sleep until midnight, and so it would continue through the night.

Every morning the sailors stowed their hammocks and scrubbed the decks, covered with salty rime and littered with goat droppings. Every morning at daybreak the doctor and I visited the lieutenant. And every morning after a breakfast of coffee and porridge we held sick call on the foredeck for the rest of the crew. A ship sails by routine as surely as by wind and water, I discovered.

On Saturdays MacPherson put me to work fumigating the lower decks, a horrid task that took hours and involved scrubbing everything in sight with strong vinegar water, then burning brimstone, which made a disagreeable odor but purified the air. Young Willie was put to work helping me, in spite of his loud complaints that he was being placed under petticoat rule. But I had no real authority. I was but a glorified scullery maid indentured for passage.

In honor of the Sabbath the sailors were allowed to leave their hammocks strung all day long. Although the ship still had to be sailed and a lookout maintained, on Mr. Blake's orders no unnecessary work was to be done. On Sundays, instead of the ringing of hammers, we were subject to the dissonant scraping of Earnshaw's fiddle and the occasional hoot that came from a surreptitious game of cards on the foredeck.

The gentlemen preferred backgammon to pass their leisure time. Mrs. Blake worked on her infant's clothing, hand-sewing the tiny rolled hems with a stitch finer than any I could hope to make. On Sunday afternoons Captain Blake would read aloud a few passages from the Bible, but although held on the quarterdeck in the shade of an old sail rigged as an awning, the readings were poorly attended. Our sailors weren't a pious lot, Mrs. Blake explained.

Once a week the ship's company practiced at arms. The marine sergeant drilled his red-jacketed men at musketry, while Lieutenant Molesworth gave his nephew a fencing lesson. I watched with envy, for it looked like great fun and I was certain I could parry and lunge as well as Willie.

Blake ordered the ship's four cannons fired and the two swivel guns mounted on the taffrail. Because *Canopus* was a merchantman there was no dedicated gunner. "A gunner who does nothing else is a luxury we can't afford," Mrs. Blake had explained.

It was Brian Dalton who took on the responsibility, in addition to his duties as bosun's mate. It was not without its dangers, as cannons were known to explode. But Dalton took pride in his work, giving the guns as much attention as he gave the ship's rigging.

And so the days and nights dissolved one into the next, as effortless and unstoppable as breathing. The ringing of the ship's bell became time itself, captured and lived in half-hour packets.

By day I took the part of doctor's assistant. Only MacPherson himself spoke directly to me and it was my duty to obey him. Loblolly, surgeon's mate, and nurse, I was. For an hour or two in the afternoon over a pot of hot tea I was a woman, enjoying Mrs. Blake's intimate, wise-woman talk. Then for a brief, sweet time each night I became a boy and sought the company of raw sailors who taught me to sail a ship.

NINE

We dawdled over our tea. The afternoon sun slanted through the ventilation hatch above us, illuminating the purser's face with amber light. She looked as if she carried a great secret.

"Mary, you're positively glowing," I said. "Do you feel as well as you look?"

She winked. "Must be the sea air, Patricia. It puts a bloom in the complexion."

We were now addressing each other by our first names. On board ship, associations develop quickly and are tightly woven. Indeed, she seemed like a kindly aunt or an elder cousin.

This would be Mary's third lying-in. Her first child, a daughter, was also born on the water. I couldn't imagine giving birth on a pitching ship.

"Sarah grew up on *Canopus* and a great help to me, she was. I tell you, Patricia, I miss her dearly. Not a day goes by I don't think of her. She married a landsman, a Whitby draper, and they have a babe of their own now. My grand-daughter, Ellie." Mary stirred her tea dreamily, the spoon tinkling against the china cup.

Their second child was a boy, born three years after Sarah. He died at eighteen months. Mary's usually expressive face became a mask when she told me this. "We called him Johnny. He took ill with the coughing fever," was all she said. I dared not press her for details, for I could tell the years had not buried the grief very deep.

My own mother had died of a fever, though what sort I never knew. MacPherson said there are different varieties. The slow nervous fevers, the putrid malignant fevers, the shipboard and jail fevers. Each manifests differently, requiring different interventions, but all can be deadly.

"After our Johnny died I decided not to have any more children." Mary set her cup down and sighed, gazing at something beyond me. Her face had a look of resolve.

I wanted to ask her how that was done. How a woman avoided having children. I knew how babies came about, of course, but I didn't know if there was a way to do the deed yet prevent the consequences. Perhaps it was all a matter of chance. So much of life seemed to be a matter of luck, often of the cruelest sort.

"This one," she said, coming back to the moment at hand and looking down at her rounded profile, "was a bit of a shock. This one is what you call a 'change of life baby.'" She leaned forward on her elbows, chin cupped in her hands, and smiled. "Life is full of surprises, Patricia. You'll see."

I hoped not. I felt I'd had enough surprises lately, and none of them pleasant.

"Might I ask," I said, reddening, yet unable to contain my curiosity, "how one goes about avoiding such circumstances?"

Her laughter was as welcoming as the tinkling bell above a baker's door. "First of all, I'd advise you to wait until you're safely married and under the protection of a good man. For your sake and the sake of the child. Because there is only one foolproof way to prevent conception and that, my dear, is sleeping in separate beds. But I don't advise abstinence, not if you want a happy marriage."

Warming to her subject, she rubbed her hands. "Now, then; marry an older man, that's my advice. Not an old grandpa, but a man who is settled and knows his mind. Not only will he be a better provider, but a man of experience knows things a young one does not."

"What sorts of things?"

Our tête-à-tête was interrupted when the cook brought in the evening's supper—a steaming kettle of stewed chicken and dumplings.

That night in my hammock I fantasized a different sort of life, one in which Mary was a kinswoman so that we might continue our relationship after landfall. I imagined her visiting me at my Barbados plantation, where we'd take our tea in my garden, the smell of rosemary and thyme all about us, and the sleepy hum of bees. Mary would bring me news from the larger world and I would send her off with baskets of fruits, flowers, and fresh-cut herbs.

Willie became my brother, only in my reverie he did as I bid and wasn't so annoying. In my dream I taught him

how to ride the windmill, a thrilling stunt I remembered
from my youth. We raced our horses and although mine
was faster, I would sometimes let him win.

Dalton kept popping his head into my fantasy as well.
He would never do as my husband, of course; only a gentleman with title or property could I consider. Still, I felt a
strong bond between us and kept trying to work him into
my imagined life, casting him as my footman, my butler,
my overseer. But I knew he was not suited for any of these
roles and he would never take orders from anyone but a
ship's officer. Brian Dalton was a sailor, not a servant.

Eight bells. It was just after midnight, the middle watch. I
got up, put on my sailor's garb, and crept up on deck. A
half-moon sank into the sea, leaving us in rich darkness. On
the foredeck the larboard watch was enjoying a smoke,
their voices blending with the swish of water against the
hull. Upon seeing me the men fell silent.

They knew me by day as the stowaway, the young lady
in reduced circumstances now indentured to the ship's surgeon to pay for her passage. They might have also caught a
glimpse of me late at night, clothed in trousers, exploring
the deck and climbing the rigging with the bosun's mate.
Yet except for Dalton, I had never acknowledged them nor
had they ever spoken to me. The sailors knew their place; it
was I who had stepped out of mine. Dressed as I was on
their foredeck, I had crossed an invisible boundary, con-
founded the game, and now none of us were sure of the
rules.

It was Dalton who first spoke. "This is Miss Patricia

Kelley, the surgeon's loblolly. She likes to climb to the tops for a breath of night air. Pretty sure-footed she is, for a lass."

"Good evening," I said, a bit too haughtily.

I don't believe the men knew what to say. Likely they were glad to have someone new to break the monotony of their night watch, and the fact that I was a female got their attention. But that I was such a tomboy, a big-boned Hippolyta in sailor's clothes who took an interest in ropes, spars, and the like—I don't think they knew what to make of it. Frankly, I didn't know what to make of it myself.

Dalton introduced his mates and I peered hard in the darkness to distinguish them. There was Doughal, a likeable lad with an easy smile, and Cunningham, a lanky man who walked with a limp but moved like a gazelle in the tops. There was the stout, straw-haired Hans, who spoke with a Danish accent, and back at the helm was the handsome Juan Fernando Pérez, whom the men dubbed "Quixote."

"Aren't you going to introduce me?" a bald man, toothless and bow-legged, piped up. "The name's Earnshaw and make no mistake, lassie, I'm the best foretopman there is. Why, I taught these boys everything they know." He punctuated his introduction by spitting a wad of tobacco onto the deck at my feet.

The voice sounded familiar. I remembered hearing it when I was hidden away below the foredeck. It was the chanteyman's voice, yes, but there was something unpleasant about it I could not put my finger on.

"Ah, you're full of it, you old sot," Doughal said good-naturedly. The others chuckled in agreement.

"Shut your traps, bullies," Earnshaw groused. "I know about you. A lady by day and a hoyden by night."

"And what of it?" I said, straddling the bowsprit and crossing my arms in what I thought was a self-assured fashion.

He shrugged. "I have nothing to say about what feathers you birds choose to wear. Breeches, petticoats, what do I care? You can fly up that rigging stark naked if you like."

The men laughed, but nervously.

"Hold your tongue, ye old cur," Dalton said, "or I'll teach ye some manners."

"Oh, I am shaking," Earnshaw taunted. "I am quivering."

Dalton gave him a threatening look and the little man backed down.

That voice! Now I remembered. Earnshaw was the man who'd grabbed me and torn my skirt that first night aboard! I shuddered at the thought of lying beneath the likes of him. But the old sailor never said whether he recognized me or not. Perhaps he hadn't gotten a good look at me in the dim light, or maybe he had been too drunk to remember the brief encounter.

"Well, Pat Kelley," Earnshaw continued, dipping into his pouch for another pinch of tobacco, which he poked under his shriveled lower lip. "Seeing as you like to climb, perhaps you wouldn't mind standing my watch in the tops whilst I take a little catnap."

"What do I watch for?" I realized I was being baited but played along just the same. Dressed as I was in sailor's garb, I felt as bold as an actor onstage.

"French warships, mostly. And pirates of any nation."

"What's in it for me?" I said.

He shrugged. "A plug of tobacco, maybe. Do you smoke?"

"No."

He scratched his head. "Chew? Take snuff?"

"Neither. But perhaps I could sell it back to you toward the end of the run when you're all out."

The others laughed and soon Earnshaw joined in.

"You know, Pat, I don't mind having you about. Boy or girl, you're better looking than all these ugly Jacks together." He held out his hand to me in a conciliatory fashion and I shook it. Gripped it warmly, confidently, the way I imagined a man would. I felt I had just won a hand of cards.

TEN

Friday, the twelfth day of December, MacPherson and I reported to the great cabin first thing in the morning to inquire about the lieutenant's health. Outside the door we could hear Molesworth talking. It sounded as if he was dictating a letter. I distinctly heard the words "Martinique" and "hostile vessels," but I had no idea what he was talking about.

MacPherson's big red knuckles rapped at the door and we were bid to enter.

The lieutenant was dressed but unshaven, his dark stubble startling against his pale and quivering cheeks. His clerk, Simmons, sat at the desk under the porthole, quill in hand, hunched over until his pink nose nearly touched the paper. He wore no spectacles but knitted his brows together and squinted to make the most of the cabin's dim light.

Tibbs and Young Willie were cleaning the lieutenant's sleeping quarters, just off the great cabin on the starboard side. The door was open and I could smell the vinegar and hear the sound of rags being wrung.

"You must shave me this morning," Molesworth commanded. "It seems Tibbs has scalded his hand on the tea-kettle and can't manage it. Simmons is too arthritic from gripping the quill and I would be a fool to trust Master Young with a razor."

MacPherson nodded. "I was a barber and a surgeon before I became a doctor. But I'll have a look at your man's hand first."

"Tibbs!" Molesworth called.

Tibbs appeared, dripping rag in one hand, the other hand shoved in his pocket.

"Show the doctor your injury."

He came before us and opened his trembling hand. A red splotch covered his palm. The center was ominously white.

"That will blister, surely," the doctor pronounced. "Miss Kelley, apply salve to this man's hand and bandage it, but not too tightly. Tomorrow we will prick it."

"William, fetch me my shaving kit," Molesworth called. "And lash my chair fast."

The seas had grown to considerable swells, causing the ship to roll. I stopped my bandaging to watch in wonder as MacPherson's hands, those great bear paws, grappled with the brush to apply lather to Molesworth's face. With two sausage-like fingers he held the twitching cheek firm, pulling the skin taut, and scraped with amazing speed.

On land surgeons were sometimes barbers too, as in the old days, as handy with a razor and strop as with a scalpel. But a ship surgeon's status was above that of a barber-surgeon and officers were expected to shave themselves or have a servant do it. Yet Dr. MacPherson seemed to take no offense at being ordered to perform this menial task, beneath his station. Instead he worked with a mindful purpose, as if shaving the lieutenant was as significant to the officer's health as a good bleeding or a dose of calomel.

I returned my attention to the task of wrapping Tibbs's hand, but I had not MacPherson's skills. It was a sorry bandage I made, a lumpy, unwieldy club that the servant looked at askance.

"How fare the men?" Molesworth asked when the doctor had finished.

"They are hale but for the odd complaint."

Molesworth's laugh was a raven's caw. "That'll change when we get to warmer waters. The isles are filled with fevers and fluxes to lay us low."

"I've been there and seen it," MacPherson agreed. "But I fear most for the foot soldiers arriving on our consort vessels. We seamen come and go quickly but the soldiers will likely spend the rest of their lives at some fever-ridden fort. Poor devils."

"Have you been bleeding and purging our sailors?"

"Nae, they refuse it. Tough men they are and fear nothing but the surgeon's knife."

Molesworth shook his head. "An uneducated and suspicious lot."

"By and large they are. But the strong will survive and God alone can save the weak." MacPherson wiped his hands on a handkerchief he carried in his vest pocket.

"If God can save anyone these days, I'm impressed," Molesworth said. "It seems to me he is resting on his laurels, all those Old Testament marvels and miracles. Just once I would like to see God save somebody." He flung his hand. "Anybody at all."

I saw the red creep up MacPherson's neck but he held his tongue. We gathered up the instruments and took our leave.

After breakfast we held sick call on the foredeck. One of the marines reported but was reluctant to speak of what ailed him. At last he blurted out that it pained him to make water. MacPherson had him drop his trousers and he examined his private parts right there on the foredeck. I averted my eyes, pretending to look at the sails.

"'Tis the venereal pox, I'm afraid," the doctor said. "Make a note of that, would ye, Miss Kelley? Aye, 'tis the mercury salts for ye, my lad. That's the price ye pay for your bit of pleasure."

"What's the matter, boy?" Earnshaw quipped, jumping down off the bowsprit. "Sprung your mainmast, did you?"

The young man hung his head, abashed.

After our noonday meal MacPherson had me read from his medical texts. I found it stuffy below in his cabin and hard to concentrate, especially on a stomach full of salt pork and sour cabbage. Like a schoolmaster, the doctor quizzed me.

"What's the first line of defense for putrid fevers and tropical agues?" he asked. With his spectacles on the end of his nose he resembled a very large owl.

"Cinchona, or Peruvian bark."

"Correct. And for the flux?"

"Clysters and bleeding," I said. "Add blistering and purging for the bloody flux."

"And prayer."

"And prayer," I repeated.

"'Twas said in irony, Miss Kelley. The bloody flux is a formidable disease and many die from it no matter what we do. But it never hurts to pray and may in fact do great good." He scratched his head and reached for his pen to make a note in a leather-bound book he kept in his breast pocket.

MacPherson lectured me continuously on the importance of keen observation.

"Open your eyes and look," he would say. "Then describe what ye see as best ye can. But don't neglect the information your other senses are gathering. For instance, what does the man's pulse feel like? Is it fast or slow? Does it bound or is it weak? Is the skin clammy? Is it hot and dry? What does a cough sound like? Dry and hacking or moist and rattling? Learn to be specific."

"Yes, sir," I said. "Be specific."

"Our observations can teach us more than books," he droned on. "The trouble is, ye never know if it was the treatment that cured, or the man's own constitution. Or what role Providence plays in our game. Still, observation is the key."

I nodded, doing my best to smother a yawn, and failing.

"Ye're not getting enough sleep, Miss Kelley. Perhaps ye're spending too much time on deck late at night," he said sternly.

I swallowed hard and looked down at my hands.

"There are few secrets aboard a ship," he added.

I nodded glumly, hoping he wouldn't confine me to the cabin at night. How to explain that I felt most alive up in the rigging, the wind in my face, hanging on for dear life? How to tell him I'd rather learn the names of the ship's sails, the names of the stars we steered by, than the names of the surgical tools and the correct doses of medicines?

"See that your nightly activities don't interfere with your daytime responsibilities." MacPherson's voice sounded gruff but I detected a softness, an understanding.

"Yes, sir," I said gratefully. "I'll try harder, I promise."

"Ye have a good mind and a bold spirit, lass. Ye might come to like this sort of work if ye give it a chance."

ELEVEN

I woke at eight bells, knowing the larboard watch had just come on deck. Four o'clock in the morning. I waited half an hour, until one bell was struck, before slipping into my pants and jacket. Stealthily opening the cabin door, I slipped past MacPherson, snoring in his hammock. Topside, the just-before-dawn air was delicious.

"What if the Old Man finds her up here?" Quixote said. "Dressed like that?"

Doughal shrugged and took a draw of his pipe. "What of it?"

"It would not be good for her to be seen mingling with the likes of us."

We sat on the foredeck, Quixote, Doughal, Earnshaw, Dalton, and I. Cunningham was aloft, Hans at the helm. The moon had already set. High overhead Orion ruled the sky. On the western horizon Cetus, the star whale, seemed to be slowly falling into the sea.

"She wouldn't be the first female to pull on tarred trousers and call herself Jack," Dalton said, which made me wonder what he meant and how many other women like me he had known.

"True," said Doughal. "One of the best sailors I ever worked with was a woman aboard His Majesty's frigate *Hoboken*. We sailors had our suspicions about her sex but mum was the word, as she did her share of the work and then some."

"How did you find out he was a she?" Quixote asked.

"It was only when she ran afoul of the first lieutenant that we had absolute proof. He accused her of stealing his private stash of beer and ordered her flogged. Twenty-four lashes."

I winced.

"As is required," Doughal went on, "the ship's company all turned out to witness the lashing, and she was ordered to strip to the waist to receive her due."

"And then what happened?" I said, all ears.

"There was a great sound, a whoosh like the wind from the chest of every man aboard as she bared her beautiful white dumplings for all of us to see. I'll never forget the sight of her, standing there defiantly, shoulders back, chin high. She was a woman and she was afraid, but by George she was ready to take her beating."

"Was she flogged?"

"No," he said. "You cannot flog a woman, not aboard a ship of the British Navy, you cannot. By hell, a woman is forbidden even to witness a flogging. She was put off the ship as soon as we made landfall, and we were mightily sorry, for we had lost a good mate. But the lieutenant, he was livid."

"Why?" I said.

"Because she went unpunished. His pride was hurt."

"But did she do it?" I persisted. "Was she guilty?"

Doughal laughed. "Damned if I know. She was no saint, to be sure."

"You are all too young, the lot of you," Earnshaw said, "to remember the female pirates Mary Read and Anne Bonny. Those colleens didn't try to pass themselves off as men, but they were the manliest of wenches that ever boarded a ship with cutlasses in their teeth. Dressed, robbed, and swore like men, they did. And would've hung like men when they were finally captured but they pleaded their bellies and were spared."

"Pleaded their bellies? You mean to say they were pregnant?" said Doughal.

"Stuffed as Christmas gooses, the pair. And it saved their ruddy necks, it did. Though one died in prison and the other, well, I don't remember what happened to her but she came to a bad end just the same. Women in breeches can never come to any good."

The men all laughed roundly at this but I didn't. I remembered the night I came aboard and how these very men fell on the prostitutes like drunken beasts. I remembered my fear and loathing of these men who were now my late-night companions. Having been accepted by the group, I now wanted to set myself apart a bit. I wasn't a rough-talking, dirk-brandishing pirate, nor was I an easy target. I decided to reestablish my status as an educated young lady.

"I'm no freebooter," I said. "And I have no interest in breeding with sea robbers or sailors of any sort. I'm going to Barbados, where I have a sugar estate waiting. In Bridgetown I'll be quitting this ship—and good riddance to all of you."

"Oh, well, la-di-da," Earnshaw quipped. "Don't you like our company?"

"I only come up here at night because I can't stand being cooped up in that coffin of a cabin with the doctor snoring outside my door like a great sleeping bear. I only come up here for the fresh air and exercise. As for dressing like a sailor, I can't very well wear my lace-trimmed gown aloft, I'd get tar all over it." An unexpected lurch of the ship sent me to my knees, but the clumsy stumble and the good-natured chuckles that followed broke the tension. I had to smile myself at how easily the sea had managed to humble me.

When it was Dalton's turn at the helm he gave me the wheel and showed me how to steer by the compass on the binnacle. He cautioned me not to overcorrect, to let the boat have her way a bit.

We spoke in low tones on the quarterdeck so as not to wake Molesworth or the other officers sleeping beneath us.

"Ye've a good hand for the helm," Dalton said.

"It's just like riding a horse."

He laughed softly. "Nae."

"'Tis," I insisted, determined to have the last word.

"I don't see it. Horses have four legs and walk on the ground and are not steered by a rudder as a ship is."

"It feels nearly the same to me."

He made a derisive snort through his nose, which maddened me.

"And what do you know of horsemanship, Dalton? Have you ever ridden to hounds?" I said it sarcastically, for of course a man of his sort would have never had the opportunity to learn to ride and hunt. A man like Dalton might be a footman or a groom, he might even learn to drive a carriage, but he would not in his wildest dreams ride for pleasure. The thought of a man like Dalton hunting fox was nearly as ludicrous as a girl sailing a ship.

"Nae, Princess, I've never ridden to hounds. But I have ridden ships halfway around the world and back again. A sailor's privilege, maybe his only one, is that he can blow with the wind. I have a master to answer to, but if I don't get on with him I can pick a new one. If I don't like the West Indies I can go to the East Indies; I can stay within sight of England or I can go around Cape Horn. But you're right, Princess, I've never ridden to hounds."

I hung my head, abashed. Through an accident of birth I had been born to a man of property, not through any effort of my own. Up until now I had led a sheltered life, educated secondhand from books and by spinsters and fussy old men who themselves had never been anywhere. If I had been born a boy and to poor parents as Dalton had, perhaps I too would have gone to sea to make my living.

"Watch your course now. You're falling off."

I looked up and turned the wheel sharply.

"Easy now, don't overcorrect."

Frustrated, I sighed.

"Are ye angry with me?" Dalton asked softly.

"Why should I be?"

"I don't know. But ye've been tetchy with me since Madeira. What's the matter?"

"Those girls I saw you with," I blurted out. But I couldn't finish my accusation. To accuse him of betraying me I would have to proclaim my feelings for him. And that could lead to no good, I was certain.

"Oh, so that's what's bothering ye. Why didn't ye say so?"

I shrugged, biting my lip.

"There's people in every port trying to take a sailor's hard-earned money," he said. "I'm sorry ye saw that. But those mollies didn't profit off me this trip, though they did their best to tempt me."

All I could do was nod, relieved.

"Watch your course now, watch your course," he cautioned, and I put my mind back to the task of steering the ship.

The sand ran through the half-hourglass, Dalton struck the bell, and Cunningham came down from his lookout perch aloft.

"May I take his place?" I asked, eager to climb.

"Aye. But take care, Princess."

The ratlines creaked under my bare feet; the rigging swayed as I climbed higher and higher, jamming my feet into the narrow toeholds, until I reached the upper crosstree. Here I secured myself and surveyed my domain. The rest of the convoy was a scattering of yellow lights to windward, a cheery constellation of ships' lanterns moving slowly across the dark sea. The stars themselves were reflected in the waters, and I marveled that so many people lived their lives without ever seeing such a sight as this, the sea at night from the top of the mast. *When I'm an old woman,* I vowed, *I'll remember how I went to sea and climbed aloft.*

Dalton rang the ship's bell three times. To the east the sky was beginning to lighten. Reluctantly I gave up my perch and climbed down.

The first mate's voice accosted me as I dropped down onto the deck.

"Who goes there?" Mr. Kent said. "Who is that?"

"Me, sir," I said.

"'Me'? Who the bleeding hell is 'me'?"

"Kelley," I said breezily.

"Kelley? *Miss Kelley?*" he said incredulously, stepping forward until his face nearly touched mine. I saw his jaw go slack.

"Couldn't sleep, sir. So hot below, you know. Went aloft for a bit of fresh air."

He touched my arm as if to see if I were real.

"Is it all right, sir? That I climb?" I adjusted my cap and stood tall. "I'm quite agile, you know."

He blinked several times, then happened to look down at my bare feet, which were of course covered with tar. "Do take care, Miss Kelley," he breathed.

"Thank you, sir."

Then, as quickly as I dared, I slid past him toward the companionway.

"Oh, Mr. Kent," I said, pausing on the top step. "You might ask the bosun to check the seizing on the maintop halyard block. It's beginning to fray."

TWELVE

Every morning I heard the doctor just outside the door as he cleared his throat and swung heavily to the floor, his feet making a resounding thump. Then came the knock to announce his entry, for he had to wash his face and shave. Afterward he waited outside while I made ready, and we were off to the great cabin to visit Molesworth, as was our routine.

After that we held sick call for the rest of the ship. The experienced seamen prided themselves on not getting sick, but one day Quixote reported with symptoms of the venereal pox and MacPherson prescribed the usual treatment of mercury. The Spaniard cursed the "fireship" he'd slept with in Madeira, predicted the others would get it as well (but none of them did). The same day Young Willie got sick to his stomach from eating too much plum pudding and cried for his mama, he was so miserable. As his mother wasn't available, he asked for me, and I gave him his medicine and stayed with him the rest of the evening until he was purged of the plums.

When they saw me by the light of day the seamen acted as though I were a completely different person, and perhaps I was, dressed properly and accompanying the doctor, or talking with Mary as we strolled the quarterdeck before taking our tea in the afternoon. The men averted their eyes and never once looked at my face. If they spoke to me at all it was a polite mumble, for I was no longer of their ilk.

It seemed the small world of the ship was actually two separate worlds that had in common only the elements that surrounded them. We were like corks dropped into the sea at the same time, bobbing and drifting on the same current. Yet somehow I was able to inhabit both spheres.

On the eve of December 16 we were just finishing supper when I saw Mary catch her husband's eye; a silent communication passed between them.

Her own plate scarcely touched, she excused herself from the table and went to her cabin. Captain Blake sent me to attend her.

"I'm no midwife, sir," I said.

"No, but you're a female. You'll be of comfort and use to her."

"But—"

"I'll hang a hammock here in the wardroom."

Surely I was not expected to take on this task! I looked to the doctor but he merely wiped his mouth and nodded.

"Let nature take her course and if there are any undue complications, then come for me at once," he said.

"But I am completely ignorant of such matters. How will I know?"

"She'll tell you, lass. She'll tell you."

I had once seen a foal born in the stables of the boarding school and it seemed at once a magical and yet a very earthy process; the great gush of warm fluid, the tiny hooves and slender wet fetlocks squeezed out first, the mare panting, blowing, waiting for some force within to deliver her. I remember the raw smell of blood mixed with the familiar stable smells of horse urine and manure on clean bedding straw. A miracle, yet ordinary. Vulgar, yet divine.

For the first few hours Mary seemed to require little of me. She had drawn within herself and was greatly occupied with her own thoughts, for which I was glad. Up on deck MacPherson piped the sun down and the men sung evensong. I wanted to sing too but my voice was too high; it would have ruined the deep, homogenous sound.

The pains came erratically. At first she would rise with each one and pace the tiny cabin, three steps one way, three steps back. I sat in the corner on the only chair and read by candlelight one of the doctor's medical books. Actually, I only pretended to read, for I could not concentrate—how could I? The ship's bell announced the half hours as they crept by.

I helped her undress and put on a shift. She seemed to shine in the dark, her belly hard and taut like something about to crack. I hoped the doctor would come in time to receive the baby, to slip the cord from around its neck, to wipe its face, or whatever needed to be done. The mare had foaled herself; I had just watched dumbstruck.

My fear wore thin, I grew tired, and ennui set in. I stood up, stretched, yawned. Mary lay on her side, panting like a sick cat. I was struck by how much she looked like an animal. Mary, the woman I knew, seemed to have retreated, usurped by some overriding power. A pain started and she moaned aloud for the first time.

Looking for an excuse to escape for a few minutes, I took her chamber pot to empty. The deck was alive with the ship's company, everyone taking advantage of the calms, each in his own territory—the sailors forward at the bowsprit, the soldiers in the ship's waist sitting on the hen coops, the officers all on the quarterdeck leaning against the taffrail. The smell of tobacco smoke and the rich sound of men's voices and laughter hung on the heavy air. I felt sorry for myself that I was missing such a fine time on deck, that I was stuck below doing women's work.

"How does my wife?" Captain Blake asked, his brow furrowed with concern. "Is her time nigh?"

"I don't know, sir," I said truthfully. "I must ask the doctor to come see her."

MacPherson and I found Mary on her knees on the floor. I had a sudden fear she was dead and was relieved to hear her groan.

"Shall ye deliver there on the floor?" the doctor asked.

"I cannot abide the hanging cot any longer. Oh, God, relieve me."

"Miss Kelley, light more candles. Fetch an oilcloth and a bucket of oakum to keep the floor clean. A stack of muslin squares, too. And the surgical kit, just in case."

"So hot," Mary panted. "So hot, so hot, so hot."

"Are your pains close, madam?" he asked.

"Nearly continuous," she gasped, her face contorted.

"Then it should not be long," he said cheerfully.

I left to fetch the supplies and when I returned Mary was alone. "What could be so urgent that he should leave you?" I cried.

"We don't need him, not yet. This is woman's work, it's what we're born for."

Mary's eyes were large and luminous in the candlelight, dark against the pallor of her skin. Her hair had come out of its normally tidy nest at the nape of her neck and hung in damp ringlets.

"What must I do?" I said meekly. *Give me some simple task,* I thought.

"A sip of water," she said, breathing heavily. "And a wet cloth for my face and neck. That's a dear."

As I held the cup to her lips she shuddered and then held her breath, her face turning purple. The sound she made was frightening and I ran to get MacPherson, whom I found up on the quarterdeck playing a game of backgammon with Mr. Kent.

"I cannot do this," I declared, stamping my foot. "I am no midwife, I am not cut out for such business. Please, sir, you must come at once."

To my great relief he did come.

A male child was born just before eight bells; four in the morning on December 17. The cocks crowed his arrival. As I was sweeping up the blood-soaked oakum, I could hear the men aloft as they untied the gaskets holding the sails, as they braced round the yards and worked together to pull the halyards and set the sails. The wind had come up fresh and we were under full sail.

But Mary was still bleeding, and bleeding heavily, it seemed to me. Dr. MacPherson said I was to massage her lower stomach, squeezing her flesh in my hands as if I were wringing out a rag, and induce her to drink quantities of an herbal concoction he instructed me to prepare. I did as he instructed, terrified she might die, yet I felt a longing to be up on deck, doing that sort of work, men's work, difficult, dangerous, yet straightforward. I wanted to feel sticky pitch in my hands, not Mary's flaccid white flesh, and I longed for the surge of fear when the boat rolls on the waves, not this complicated anxiety of attending a woman in childbed. I dreaded the day when I would have to go through what she had been through, caught in the grip of that terrible power I had witnessed last night.

The bleeding slowed and Mary slept. The babe slept too, in the crook of her arm. Up on the quarterdeck the gentlemen drank to Blake and the health of his new son, and the seamen were given an extra ration of grog to celebrate.

The babe suckled well and thrived. I thought he was a rather ugly tyke with his thatch of matted black hair, his angry red face, his piercing squall. But Mary looked at him through a mother's eyes, her face radiant with love. He was called Johnny.

"Did you have no good prospects back in England?" Mary asked me over our customary afternoon tea at the wardroom table. Johnny was asleep in her lap, lulled by the boat's vigorous but steady roll. A lazy tabby cat purred in my lap, kneading its claws in my dress.

"Prospects? You mean for marriage?"

"Why, yes. Marriage. There are few other ways for a woman to get by."

"Queen Elizabeth managed quite well," I quipped. In truth, there had been no proposals, no courtships at all.

"Might I remind you, you're not a queen," Mary said dryly.

"Father had hopes of me marrying well, but the suitors he had in mind were not to my liking."

"Can you afford to be so choosy?"

"Why must our fortunes always be tied to a man?" I said, cross.

"Their fortunes are tied up with ours as well, though not so obviously. Behind every successful man is a good woman, you can be assured of that. Either a wife, a mother, or both. Besides, what do you know of running a sugar plantation?"

I shrugged. "Very little." It was so easy to be honest with Mary, for she never passed judgment. "You're right, I suppose a husband might be of benefit to me."

"Now you're thinking practically."

I sipped the last of my tea. "Still, he must be clever yet not talk too much, for I can't stand a man who must always voice his opinion about every little thing."

Mary nodded. "I like the quiet ones myself."

"One thing he must have."

"What's that? A title? An allowance?"

"No. His teeth. His own teeth. Well, most of them, anyway."

We both laughed and I felt close to her in a way I had never felt toward my schoolmates and teachers. *Had my mother been as caring, as lively, as practical as Mary?* I wondered. Margaret Kelley had been an indentured servant, probably illiterate, much to my chagrin. But without my father, I too was a penniless servant.

After tea I minded little Johnny while Mary napped, carrying him about the quarterdeck, watching the men finish their afternoon's work. Dalton passed close by me on his way down the mizzenmast, having replaced a block. Recognizing his particular aroma of pitch, tobacco, and sweat, I felt my heart quicken in spite of myself.

He stopped, turned around. Our eyes did not quite meet. "How are ye, Princess?"

I was surprised that he spoke to me on the quarterdeck in broad daylight. Captain Blake was at the helm and Molesworth at the rail, peering through his spyglass.

"Well enough, but I'll be better when we reach dry land."

"Dry land is highly overrated. And then what will ye do, have a few wee ones of your own, I suppose?"

"That's no concern of yours," I shot, immediately sorry, for he touched his cap respectfully and turned to go.

"I'll be glad to get to Barbados," I said, not wanting him to leave just yet. "The sea is monotonous and much too big. I don't think I like it."

He stopped, turned slowly to face me. "Sometimes I feel that way myself."

"But you're a sailor. I should think you would love the sea."

He adjusted his cap as he inched toward me. "When

I'm on the water I sometimes long for land. But after a few weeks ashore I start missing the roll of the ship and the rattle of blocks. The smell of pitch and hempen rope. The way the world looks from the crosstrees on a fine, starry night." A quick gleam of light crossed his face. "I believe I am cursed that way."

Our eyes met briefly, then flew apart.

"Climbing terrifies me, yet I love it."

"'Tis not terror. Fear, aye."

"You know, then? You've felt it too?"

"Of course."

"What is it, then? Why do I like it so much?"

He shrugged. "I don't know. Feeling my heart knocking in my chest keeps me awake, that's sure. The prickling in my skin reminds me I'm alive and makes me want to stay that way. Maybe 'tis the same for ye."

"Alive, yes! And aware, like an owl. All ears, eyes, senses. Do you suppose an owl's stomach tingles too, when it's flying? Does it ever fear falling, I wonder?"

Our eyes met again and this time I recognized in his something vital, something we shared. But I had no word for it and it seemed hopeless to pursue.

THIRTEEN

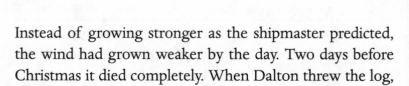

Instead of growing stronger as the shipmaster predicted, the wind had grown weaker by the day. Two days before Christmas it died completely. When Dalton threw the log, it splashed off the stern and just sat there, bobbing like a cork on a leash.

Captain Blake paced the quarterdeck, muttering, scowling. The sailors grew short-tempered. They talked little, sang not at all, and spent their off-hours sleeping on deck in the shade of the sails. Mary's baby squalled; the hens flapped and cackled in their pens. Even the cats came out of their lairs in broad daylight to voice their discontent. But to no avail. The air remained hot and still.

MacPherson had little for me to do except memorize the names of the bones of the human body, all two hundred and six of them. Phalanges, tarsals, metatarsals. Scapula, clavicle, tibia, fibula. I made a game of pairing them with the dozens of sails, the scores of lines that made up *Canopus*, and thus committed them to memory. I suppose he knew what he was doing, giving me mental work to do. Something to occupy my mind.

To be motionless was frustrating; I felt completely at the mercy of the elements. Our predicted four-week crossing from Madeira to Barbados had already become five weeks and threatened to lengthen into six if conditions stayed like this. It had already been more than three months since my father died. I worried that if I didn't show up soon to claim the estate, someone else might.

"If this keeps up, we'll have to go on rations," Mary warned.

"What the devil has happened to our winds?" Blake ranted. "And at this latitude, this time of year!"

Mr. Kent stood at the rail, staring out at the endless ocean. "The weather is not what it used to be," he mourned. "In the old days the easterlies were right as rain in these latitudes. The only question was how much sail to risk. To run out stuns'ls or not." He clicked his tongue prophetically. "I fear the world is changing."

Lieutenant Molesworth came on deck and held a moistened finger up to feel for a breeze. His usually immaculate shirt was damp with perspiration.

Christmas Eve I slept on the quarterdeck, under the stars. Or tried to sleep. The ship rolled violently, shaking me from side to side, but made no progress. I stumbled to the foredeck to join the sailors but they were sullen and queasy and in no mood for telling stories or singing fo'c'sle songs.

"How fare ye, Princess?" Dalton asked.

"Dreadful. Can nothing be done?"

"I could put out the sweeps and row ye to Barbados."

I snorted, ignoring his teasing.

By starlight reflecting on the water we could make out the shapes of three other ships, those of our convoy. Above us Sirius, the bright dog star, followed Orion as he prepared to plunge into the sea. The Earth still turned and the stars still moved, though we did not. *Canopus* and company seemed frozen in time.

Dalton reached for my hand and I let him take it. We laced our fingers together.

"What if we're stuck here forever?" I said. "What if the wind never comes back?"

"But it will, Princess." There was a resignation to his voice. "It always does."

"Let's go aloft," I said suddenly. "To the t'gallant yard."

"In this swell? The way those masts are swaying ye'll toss your dinner all over the deck."

I grinned, in spite of my misery. "So what? It can't be worse than this, can it?"

His laughter was a welcome sound. "Why not? We wash the deck every morning anyway."

"Aloft, then."

"After ye, Princess." He dropped my hand and followed me up the ratlines.

FOURTEEN

At first light on Christmas Day, the air began to stir.

"All hands on deck to make sail!" Captain Blake's voice boomed.

He hardly needed to give the command, for the men had leaped to the rigging and were scrambling up the lines and out on the yards, happy to be working. As they untied the gaskets, the sails fell free, blowing like bedsheets on wash day. They raced down the stays and hauled the halyards home, singing all the while.

Like some sleeping sea monster the ship groaned and sighed as she came to life and began to move, throwing her rounded shoulder into the sea.

"Aye, lads, she's dancing now," Blake called out from the quarterdeck. There was real joy in his voice, infecting us all.

*   *   *

MacPherson poured himself a second cup of bitter coffee. Mary and the officers had broken fast earlier; the doctor and I had taken to having our coffee and porridge after sick call.

"Miss Kelley, will there be someone to meet ye in Bridgetown?"

I shrugged. "I don't suppose."

"Do ye even know anyone in Bridgetown? In all of Barbados?"

"No. But I remember the house servants. Mamie and Napoleon and Cecil."

He scratched his head and frowned. His scalp was pink beneath his thinning hair.

It occurred to me that I had never seen the man wear a wig. Like most of the seamen, even the gentlemen, he wore his hair pulled back into a queue and tied with a ribbon.

"Do ye have counsel? An advocate?" he pressed.

"Not that I'm aware of. But I'm sure my father had. It's only a matter of inquiring."

His furry manbrow wrinkled with concern. "I have a connection in Bridgetown, a distant cousin. A merchant he is, but can perhaps recommend an attorney. And I'll take care of the fee, don't worry."

I forced a smile. "You are too kind, Dr. MacPherson. But I don't believe that'll be necessary."

Later that afternoon Mary poured the tea while I held Johnny over my shoulder, jiggling him to keep him from crying.

"What do you know of that man Dalton?" I asked.

"Who? Dalton? The bosun's mate?"

I nodded.

She pursed her lips, shook her head. "Not much. His people settled near Whitby, from the north of Ireland they came. Laborers, as I recall. He's a good seaman but we cannot promote him just yet, for Mr. Blake's nephew is our bosun. 'Tis a shame and I hope we don't lose him over it, for Dalton is a better man for the job than our Henry, I do believe. Why do you ask?"

"Just curious. I wish he were a gentleman, for I like his looks."

"Bah! Looks are impermanent. The best of them grow fat or gray or bald, just as we do."

"Still, I like to look," I admitted.

Her eyes danced. "As do I."

I raised my eyebrows.

"Oh, you're thinking what, a wrinkled old married woman? And I tell you yes. Yes, indeed."

She refilled our cups while I shifted baby Johnny to the other shoulder. He made a mewling sound, like a kitten.

"Of course," she continued, lifting her hand as if waving good-bye, "you can look all you want, but don't get involved with the likes of him, that's my advice. Now, then, what do you think of Dr. MacPherson?"

"I'm much indebted to him." I knew what she was hinting at, but wished to avoid the issue.

"Mmmmm." She sipped her tea, eyeing me across the rim of her cup. "Anything else?"

"He's very knowledgeable," I said. "An excellent teacher."

"As a man, I mean."

I shrugged. "Too old."

"He's not old! Why, he's younger than I am. He's barely five-and-thirty. And he has all his teeth, near as I can tell."

I smiled wryly. "Perhaps he does."

"What about Henry Blake?"

I wrinkled my nose. "Never."

Suddenly Mary's eyes became serious and penetrating. "Come down off your high horse, young lady, and tell me. What are your prospects? What is your plan?"

"Things will sort themselves out when I get there," I said lightly. The fact was, I had no plan. I was counting on my father to have come through for me. Surely there would be papers, documents, a will.

She was not amused. "They say a bird in the hand is worth two in the bush, Patricia." Her face, concerned and skeptical, was more than I could bear.

I rolled my eyes and sighed.

The baby began to cry and I was glad to hand him back to Mary, who put him to her breast in an easy manner. The way I might twirl a curl of my hair absently around my finger while thinking of something else.

Mary Blake, such a practical, make-do woman. She could provision a ship, balance a ledger, milk a goat, please a husband, nurse her own infant. I was in awe. Yet none of those responsibilities appealed to me. Though I cared for her, was indebted to her, and admired her, I didn't want to imitate her. Mary's life was not mine. My father had been the third son of a baron and I was destined for a different life.

Late that afternoon the ship's company, every one, turned out on deck to enjoy the last of a glorious day that had put us in motion again. We looked expectantly to the horizon, a complete circle of blue against blue. And I thought how vastly monotonous the ocean is. Water and sky. Water and sky.

Captain Blake was in fine spirits; the light danced in his eyes and he hummed a tune and ordered the stuns'ls bent.

We fairly flew, scudding along on a breeze. The sky was rimmed with puffy clouds, like sheep grazing on the edge of a deep blue plain, the Salisbury Plain of England. Where I had spent so many years just waiting, a caterpillar in a cocoon. Waiting for this crossing.

At sunset the bagpipes cried and it seemed to me I was hearing my own life put to music. The pain, the desire, the sweet ache pulled from my bones and made beautiful.

"Damned Jacobite music," Molesworth muttered to no one in particular from his accustomed station on the windward side of the quarterdeck. "What we need is a lively jig, a hornpipe, not this melancholy subversion. Where's that screeching fiddler? Have him strike up a tune."

FIFTEEN

Mr. Kent interrupted our noonday meal on the sixth day of January with news that foul weather was in the offing. I left my plate of salted beef and turnips and followed him up on deck to see for myself. The idea of a storm at sea was thrilling to me, for at least it would break the monotonous routine.

On deck the sun shone hot and bright. All I could see ahead were shades of blue—indigo, azure, aquamarine. I was vaguely disappointed. The color of the sea blended with that of the sky and it was hard to distinguish where one ended and the other began. Walking forward to the bow, I peered under the sprits'ls as the ship rose with the swell, but could see nothing in the way of a storm cloud ahead. If anything, the wind actually seemed to have lessened. Hans and Doughal walked out on the jibboom to hand the sprits'ls. High above me the sailors worked, taking the stuns'ls down.

Wondering what the stir was about, I leaned against the rail and closed my eyes against the sun's glare, listening as the men tidied the decks and dragged the poultry pens to the companionway to be sent below. Young Willie was sent to catch the unwilling goat and tie her up belowdecks as well. *All this activity over a drop in the air pressure,* I thought lazily. Maybe tonight we'd have some rain and I could at least rinse the salt out of my clothes.

Dalton dropped down from the rigging beside me, his bare feet black with tar.

"G'day, Princess. If ye're looking for the squall, it's behind ye," he said, bemused, jerking his thumb over his shoulder. "If ye're going to be a sailor, ye must learn to look to windward to determine the weather. Not in the direction the ship is pointing."

I turned to face the wind and saw a thin line of dark clouds far off the starboard beam. Even as we spoke the wind became fitful, shifting, dropping, then gusting to life from a new direction. The sails hissed and cracked their displeasure.

"Doesn't look like much of a storm," I said.

Dalton raised his eyebrows. "'Tis bad luck to taunt Neptune."

I smiled, for sailors were known to be greatly superstitious.

"The glass has fallen," he explained. "'Tis the wrong time of the year for a hurricane, but we could still be in for a deuce of a gale."

Mr. Kent stood on the quarterdeck and called out in his deep and sorrowful voice, "Hand t'gallants! Reef tops'ls! Lively, lads."

Bosun Blake took the order forward, barking down the hatches and companionway, "All hands on deck to shorten sail! You, Dalton, no time for chatting with the girl! Bear a hand there! Away, aloft!"

Dalton leaped up on the rail and flew up the ratlines, losing his cap in a gust of wind. I had been aboard long enough to know he resented being ordered about by Captain Blake's nephew, who was half the sailor Dalton was. But now was not the time for anger, for the line of clouds was fast approaching. Behind it, the sky was the color of a new bruise and the sea had turned to gunmetal gray. The listlessly tranquil afternoon had transformed itself before my eyes and I could now believe we were in for foul weather. I returned to the quarterdeck, where I could watch the action without getting in the way. Mr. Kent took over the helm, sending Cunningham aloft. Long-legged Cunningham bounded up the ratlines two at a time, sliding out on the footrope with the studied nonchalance of a circus performer.

Those men belowdecks ran up the companionway and jumped to the rigging like gibbons to trees. Other men scrambled across the deck to work the lines, unwrapping the coils of rope down to one turn on the pin, awaiting the command. Every man seemed to know exactly what to do even before the order was given; the calling out was only to orchestrate the maneuver.

"Ready on the mainmast!" Henry Blake called from the ship's waist. "Ease away!" Hempen ropes slid through the tough, tarred hide of the sailors' hands. Meanwhile, the sky darkened and the wind picked up, snapping the loose sails violently. I worried the topmen would be shaken off like crumbs from a tablecloth.

Out of the black sky the wind hit, slamming *Canopus* onto her side. I grabbed for something to save me—'twas the grating over the ventilation hatch that kept me from being flung to the larboard rail. Water flooded the decks, swept over me; I was sure I was drowning. But the boat groaned and righted herself, leaving me clinging to the grating like a clump of seaweed. I choked, snorted, and gasped for breath; my nose, my throat, my chest burned. Above me the flailing legs of sailors dangled from the yard and I wanted to scream "Hold on!" but could not form the words. Miraculously, the men did not fall. They held on, regained their footing on the rope, and continued to work. I felt a fierce admiration, nay, a love, for these rough, stouthearted men.

Once the t'gallants were furled the men began to reef tops'ls, grabbing fistfuls of wet canvas and hauling it in. I wished I could help them, they were so few, yet even had I been wearing my trousers instead of my dress I could not have gone aloft. Skylarking on a fine night was one thing, but this was beyond my capabilities. I was overcome with fear.

Another gust of wind hit, bullying the boat, holding her down as if to drown her. But this time the men on the yard were ready and kept their footing as they wrestled the stiff sail, rolling it, tying the gasket around it, subduing it at last. *Canopus* recovered, pressed doggedly on. One by one the sailors dropped to the deck, dripping wet, their fingers bleeding, faces ruddy. *Canopus* now scudded along on a scrap of sail. The wind howled with a vengeance, driving spume like fog across the deck.

The rain came. Not drops, but stinging pellets of rain. White, wind-driven sheets of rain. The sea had become hard, looking more like rock than water; we were caught in a violently changing landscape, a cataclysm. The waves were huge blocks of granite, solid plateaus that rose abruptly and left deep canyons that our little ship was in danger of falling into. I was shivering but could not bring myself to go below to my cabin. I had to look, to see this force with my own eyes.

The sailors moved around the deck, coiling lines, making fast lifts and braces, relashing the small boats stored amidships. There was an exuberance, an energy that drove them. It showed in their faces, alive, and in their movements, brisk and exact. And in their voices, sharp and clear as crows'. Earnshaw's voice carried over all. He worked with a will, shouting encouragement to the others. He seemed transformed into something better, something fine.

"Ho there, lass, you'd better get below before you find yourself swept out to sea," he said, his face lit up like the shining face of Christ in a medieval painting. I wished the storm would infuse me with the same sublime strength. I sat on the deck, wanting to be a part of the brotherhood of seamen, yet unable to move.

The captain bounded up from below. "Go below at once, Miss Kelley," Blake roared. "Report to Dr. MacPherson. There's been an injury."

I wanted to ask who was hurt and how badly but Blake was now at the pumps, working alongside his men to rid the vessel of the great quantities of water we had taken on. I found my legs and scrambled to the companionway as *Canopus* pitched and plunged.

Belowdecks it was dark as night. I found MacPherson in the cabin, gathering his kit.

"Lieutenant Molesworth has been injured," he said. "He's in his quarters."

With difficulty we groped our way aft. Two marines dutifully guarded the door to the great cabin and I thought it ludicrous—as if their bayonets could prevent a mutinous storm from taking the ship! On second glance they looked rather ill. One bent over and coughed up a string of yellow bile onto his shiny black boots. The air below was warm and foul and I fought my own urge to vomit.

The great cabin looked as though it had been looted, the floor littered with plates and silverware, books that had toppled from shelves. Sheaves of paper had fallen like ash and I nearly tripped over Simmons, crawling about on his hands and knees, trying to clean up. Now and again he paused to quell a retch. Above us a lantern swung wildly from its hook. From the shadows I could hear Willie crying softly for his mother and I felt a wave of compassion for him.

Lieutenant Molesworth had been thrown across the cabin and was sitting on the floor clutching his arm. His face was nearly translucent in the dancing yellow light. I had a madcap notion that if I peered at him intently I would see right through him.

"It's my right elbow," Molesworth said between clenched teeth.

Gingerly I helped him slip out of his coat sleeve, then his shirtsleeve. He flinched, biting his thin and twitching lips, lips that had gone white. His elbow was purple and as swollen as an overripe plum. His forearm hung like a broken stem; it made me queasy to see it. I focused my attention on his wrist. *Do not be sick,* I coached myself. *Do not faint, do not vomit.*

The doctor ran his hands up and down Molesworth's arm, squeezing and prodding it. "Does that hurt?"

The lieutenant sucked in his breath sharply; the muscles in his face writhed.

"'Tis dislocated," MacPherson pronounced. "We must reduce it immediately before any more swelling occurs. Ye will provide traction, Miss Kelley. Put your hand against his shoulder and lean with all your weight."

This I did while MacPherson grasped the lieutenant's thin wrist in his great strong hands and pulled.

"Resist me, Miss Kelley. Push harder!"

I leaned against Molesworth's quivering shoulder with all my might, felt MacPherson's powerful pull and pushed against it. I heard the dull click of bone sliding into the joint as Molesworth let out a yelp and collapsed.

"Better?" the Scotsman asked.

Molesworth nodded weakly. "Better."

"Good. Now we shall bind it."

The doctor took a long strip of cloth and wound it about the bent arm, tucking in the end. He fashioned a sling from a triangular piece of linen, tying it behind the lieutenant's neck.

"Do ye want something for the pain, sir? Laudanum?"

"Laudanum?" Molesworth was indignant. "What do you take me for, an opium hound?"

MacPherson shrugged. "Suit yourself. Time and rest will mend ye."

With Tibbs's help we got the lieutenant to his cabin and

into bed. Willie's sobs grew softer and when I peeked in on him, I found he had fallen asleep. MacPherson and I groped our way back to the surgeon's cabin, kicking fallen rubble out of our way.

"Try and sleep, Miss Kelley, for the gales may last some time and we shall need to be rested."

There would be no supper tonight; it was dangerous to light the stove and impossible to balance kettles and ladles in this violently unpredictable motion. I didn't care for any myself, for I doubted I could keep anything down if I could indeed get it to my mouth without it being flung from the spoon. But I hoped the sailors might have at least ship's biscuit to gnaw on, for they would need to keep up their strength.

MacPherson lashed the cabin door open at my request. I couldn't bear to be confined within and I had a great fear that the door might get jammed, as had happened to Mr. Kent's cabin. Beams and bulkheads groaned under the force of water and wind. I was sure I would not be able to sleep a wink, but I was glad to peel off my soggy gown, my salty petticoats, my dingy underpropers; wrap myself in a scratchy woolen blanket; and crawl into MacPherson's hanging bed.

I lay in the darkness, forbidden to light so much as a nib in these conditions because of the risk of fire. The night became a world of sound and sensation, much like it had been when I was hidden away in the bosun's locker. The screams of the wind in the rigging began to sound melodic in a mad sort of way, as if hell's angels were howling. I could hear the shouts of the men on deck and I could hear the creaking of the pumps being worked continuously to keep the seawater from overflowing the bilge and ruining the cargo, or worse yet, sinking us.

In spite of the noise I felt alone and abandoned in the darkness. I remembered Young Willie asleep in the great cabin and I wished he were here with me so that we might comfort each other. I prayed that we would endure. I prayed the men would not be washed overboard, that the powerful, unconscious sea would not swallow us up.

The next thing I knew it was four bells. Morning. The gales continued, though more doggedly now than furiously. We were able to fire up the stove and have hot porridge for breakfast, though it was quite a trick to get it from bowl to mouth. The gentlemen, even Dr. MacPherson and Lieutenant Molesworth, all took their turns at the pumps and at the helm so that the sailors could eat. The day continued, no longer terrifying, just miserable, wet, and tedious. It seemed we would survive.

By nightfall the winds were abating but we could see no lights from our consort vessels. We had been blown apart and off our course but there was nothing to be done until daylight except to keep sharp eyes out for ships or land. Before the gale hit we had been less than two hundred miles from Barbados.

By sunrise the following morning the winds had dropped and the sun was doing its best to burn through the tattered gray sky. I went up to empty my bucket and see for myself what daylight would bring. Except for a circling seabird, our plucky little vessel was alone on the ocean; not one ship in our convoy could be seen. Master Blake stood at the taffrail and took a sun sight; he guessed we had been driven as much as fifty miles off our track. There was nothing to do but regain our northing and rendezvous with the rest of the ships in Carlisle Bay.

Due to the sailors' quick actions we had not lost so much as a cockerel to the sea. I wondered if my prayers had been answered or if I had just been fortunate. If the universe was indifferent to us, then luck was as good a god as any, I decided, kneeling down to kiss the deck, sparkling with rime.

To my embarrassment Earnshaw came up behind me, a worn-down holystone in his hand.

"*Psssst,* sailor lass," he hissed. "Don't waste a kiss on that plank o' wood. I got a timber you can kiss, if you've got a mind." He winked lewdly.

I stood up, haughtily brushed my skirt, and gave him the most withering stare I could muster. "You disgust me, you lascivious old goat. I was merely expressing my gratitude to Providence for seeing us through the storm."

"What, that little blow? That was nothing," he scoffed, fishing a wad of tobacco out of his pocket and sticking it in his cheek. "Hardly more than a breeze." He laughed and returned to his scrubbing, bursting into an off-color work chantey. The others joined in lustily. Even Blake picked up the tune; I heard him humming it as he went below.

Apparently things were back to normal. The weather had passed, taking with it the magic that had transformed us. Earnshaw was no longer a shining hero who risked his life to save the ship; he had been changed back into the ugly little troll he had always been, and I could scarcely wait to quit this lumbering vessel.

SIXTEEN

It took six days of sailing close-hauled to regain what we had lost during the two days of gales. For me it was a maddening week. Everyone else seemed to take the delay in stride, but it seemed to me that the closer we got to our destination, the farther away it became. MacPherson laughed and called that "Zeno's paradox," in reference to the Greek sage. He said I must learn patience, but there was not a shred of it in my nature.

At last we regained our northing and fell off until the wind was well aft of the beam. There was no sign yet of any of our consort vessels but landfall was thought to be close at hand.

Sunday. Everyone turned out on deck to watch for land and to rest in the shade of the awnings. We were sailing lazily under tops'ls, stays'ls, and forecourse alone, the maincourse and t'gallants hanging loosely from their yards, ready to be set at a moment's notice. Mary stripped baby Johnny to his bare skin; he had developed a rash on his bum. But for modesty's sake, none of us would've needed a thread of clothing, so warm was the sun.

MacPherson worked on his notes under the quarter-deck awning, but thankfully did not require my assistance. Molesworth remained below, dictating letters to Simmons. Two perspiring marines were forced to remain on guard outside the great cabin door and I felt sorry for them, down there in the ungodly heat.

I longed to wash my dress but Mary forbade it, as we had not enough freshwater to spare. It would have to wait until we were at anchor off Bridgetown, which would hopefully be this time tomorrow. I had tried washing it in seawater but it never really dried and felt sticky ever after, because of the salt. Everyone's clothes were as bad or worse than mine were, so I supposed I could wait one more day.

After the midday meal we returned to the deck to loaf in the shade of the awning while the wind drew us ever closer to landfall. I was nearly asleep when I heard the man in the tops call down to the officer of the watch.

"On deck, ship ho!"

"Top, where away?"

"Hull-down, off the quarter to windward!"

"At last our consorts are catching up," I said drowsily to Mary, lifting a damp, salt-sticky coil of hair and enjoying the fleeting coolness on my neck.

But Mary had stood up and was looking intently to windward, squinting fiercely against the water's glare. She hugged her sleeping babe close against her and said nothing.

All around me the ship came instantly to life; gone was the lassitude, the after-dinner indolence. Molesworth clattered up on deck and Captain Blake scrambled up the ratlines, spyglass in one hand, moving with the speed and agility of a young topman. I roused myself and went to the rail for a look, but could see nothing. The fierce white sun made my head hurt.

"Hull-up," Blake called down to the deck. He took another look through the glass. "She's a frigate. French."

"A French frigate to windward," Molesworth repeated, his words dropping like stones onto the deck.

"Bloody hell, we're doomed," Earnshaw muttered from the helm.

"He's right," said the bosun, young Henry Blake. "We cannot outrun her. A merchantman is no match for a frigate."

Now Molesworth swore, and to hear foul words from his mouth was alarming. My mouth went dry.

"Perhaps it's one of ours, taken a prize. Can you make out her colors?" Kent called up to Blake.

He could not.

It was common for ships to change hands. Built in one country, captured by another, sometimes won back again or taken by a third party. His Majesty's Navy had captured nearly a hundred French merchant ships already this year, I had heard Molesworth say. No one knew for certain how many British vessels had fallen to the French, but one thing was for certain—*Canopus* would make a fine prize, loaded as she was with gunpowder and cannon.

If the frigate was under French command, she had possibly come across some of the other merchant vessels in our convoy and captured them. In any case, she had the advantage of wind and firepower, and she was built for speed.

Looking at the other grim faces, I could see I was two steps behind in my thinking.

A slow, thick fear oozed into my brain, bubbling like tar melting in the sun. I hurried over to Mary, standing at the rail. She gave me a pinched smile but her eyes betrayed her.

Blake slid down from the crosstrees along the backstay and dropped to the deck.

"It seems she has spotted us. She has adjusted her course." He paused for breath and wiped his brow with the back of his billowy sleeve. "Curious that she's not under full sail in this air. No courses. No main topmast. Perhaps she has suffered some damage to her rigging."

"We are no match for a frigate to windward, damage or no," Blake's nephew said. "Might as well strike our colors now and be done with it. Run up the white flag."

"Hell's fire, I will," the elder Blake shot. "I'll be damned if I'll give up my ship that easily. Are you certain your name is Blake, lad?"

Molesworth rolled the barrel of his spyglass between his white hands. "Captain Blake, do you think your paltry four-pounders and a handful of raggle-taggle sailors brandishing kitchen knives are any match for a well-disciplined French crew with four times our firepower?"

"I don't give a damn how many guns they have, we'll give them a fight they'll not soon forget," the gray-haired captain growled.

"Your vessel is insured, is she not?" Molesworth took another look through his spyglass. The sunlight on the water was dazzling.

"Bah," scoffed Blake. "Lloyd's is the biggest pirate on the seas. My four-pounders are better than any paper policy."

"Ye gods," Blake's nephew muttered. "One well-placed cannonball and we'll be blown to the very stars. Uncle John, please reconsider."

Blake gave the bosun a baleful look.

"Let us assume her rigging *is* damaged," Molesworth continued, still rolling his instrument between his hands. "Damaged from the storm, perhaps. Perhaps she has already taken other vessels and her crew is stretched thin. Will your men fight, Captain Blake?" His eyes were hidden under the shade of his hat, but I could see the tremors of his jaw.

"They'll fight, all right," Blake said, nodding vigorously. "These boys are scrappers, afeared of nothing. But what about you, Lieutenant? Are you willing to take such a risk?"

"I won't make post captain moldering away in a French prison, waiting for an exchange." Molesworth telescoped his glass and pocketed it. "Now, then, if we are going to resist them, we must be clever about it. We must do something altogether unexpected." He looked from man to man.

"Unexpected, aye." Blake's eyes darted around the ship, as if he might find a useful idea lying about on the crowded deck. "They'll expect us to drop down like a bitch in heat for them."

"Then that is what we must do," Molesworth said. "We must play the part they are expecting, right down to the wagging tail."

"Sir, I protest," Henry Blake said. "It would be madness for this undermanned tub of a merchant ship to take on a French frigate."

"Precisely, Mr. Bosun." Molesworth's lips curled into a canny smile. "Captain Blake, call the ship's company—the cook, my staff, every living soul. Lively now, let's rehearse our parts; the curtain is about to rise. Mr. Bosun, you are either with us or against us."

"It's madness, I tell you. This is a merchant ship, Lieutenant. You cannot make me fight, I refuse to."

"I can't make any man fight. But you'll be confined to your quarters until further notice. Captain Blake, see to it, or my marines shall take him in hand."

Henry roared indignantly as his mates led him down to his cabin and bolted him in.

"And stuff a stocking in his mouth," Molesworth added. "We can't have him giving us away."

SEVENTEEN

"Captain Blake, set the main course and stays'ls and have your gunners ready the starboard cannons for firing," Molesworth said. "Send the rest below, except for the women, the boy, and the helmsman. Keep the old fellow at the wheel." He paused to look at us, to make certain we understood.

We all stared at him, hushed, drinking in every word. Even the animals were quiet.

"When the frigate is close enough to get a good look through their glasses, which will be any moment now, I want them to see a slovenly, undermanned bucket plodding along under badly trimmed sails. Loosen the sheets and lifts until the sails luff like petticoats. I want them to see the women lounging on deck, I want them to see laundry hanging out to dry. I want them to think *Canopus* is a floating hen coop. Do we understand?"

I nodded solemnly along with the rest. My throat was thick with a lump I could not swallow. The white sails were visible from the deck now. No need for a spyglass to see we were being hunted down.

Dalton and Doughal loaded and primed the two starboard cannons, then found a scrap of shade on the foredeck where they splashed a bottle of rum over themselves and sprawled out, pretending to be stuporous.

Mentally, I rehearsed my role. Had I been worthy of my upbringing I never could have done what Lieutenant Molesworth asked of me. But Molesworth knew what everyone aboard knew: Late at night I put on tarred trousers, took off my shoes, and climbed the rigging. No one spoke of it, but they knew. As the doctor once told me, there are few secrets on board a ship.

Now I was to climb in broad daylight, in front of Mary and the gentlemen—and the French Navy! Yet it would be worth what remained of my dignity if Molesworth's plan worked. Barbados was just a short sail away. The plantation, so close. Truth be told, it gave me a thrill, frightened as I was.

The frigate closed the gap. Willie, Mary, and I had positioned ourselves on the weather quarterdeck where we could be easily seen. Mary nursed her baby and Willie and I pretended to play a game of backgammon. I rolled the dice, my hands trembling. Willie sat on his to keep them from shaking. For once he did not chatter obnoxiously, but was quiet, his eyes round with fear. I took my own breaths in shallow gulps.

The ship was now very near. I could hear voices, the sound of orders shouted. On the stern ensign post the French colors whipped smartly in the wind.

I heard the rumbling as one of their guns was run out; seconds later a shot whistled across our bows. I jumped, nearly fainting at the blast that followed.

"Heave to!" The command was in English, bellowed through a speaking horn.

"Ladies, wave to them," Molesworth called up through the ventilation hatch. "Helmsman, heave to. Willie, strike the colors."

Mary and I waved our handkerchiefs. Young Willie lowered St. George's Cross, then helped Earnshaw and Cunningham back the mizzen tops'l and loosen the sheets on the main. It was a poor job of heaving to, but it slowed our way enough to satisfy the Frenchmen, while keeping us ready to sail off quickly, should our plan work.

Mary and I continued to wave furiously while the men moved with feigned clumsiness, like drunken bears.

The others were below, waiting with dirks. Molesworth's marines too were armed and ready in the shadows of the wardroom.

Meanwhile, the French sailors lowered their pinnace. They sang out in unison as they hauled on the davit tackle. So close was the frigate, I could hear the rattling of the wooden blocks and the rasp of rope pulled through the sheaves.

"Mary, count the guns, if you can," Captain Blake called up through the grating.

"Most of the gunports are closed," she reported. "And I'm counting, let's see . . . six guns run out. There seems to be quite a lot of activity aloft. I can't tell for certain from this angle, but they seem to be replacing the main topmast."

"That would explain why they're not under full sail in a fine breeze as this," Earnshaw commented.

"Saucy bastards think they can take us with one hand behind their back, do they?" Blake said. "We'll give them something to fix."

The fact that the frigate was in the process of being repaired gave us a whisper of a chance. That—and our proximity to Barbados.

My role was to distract the officers. I was to enchant them, beguile them, seduce them. Yet I was no beauty, and certainly no coquette. Father once said I had as much charm as a wildcat. But I knew how to be outrageous, yes. I could hold their attention. I must.

"Toss that mane of yours," Lieutenant Molesworth instructed me through the grating. "That red hair of yours in the sun, that ought to get their attention. Don't lose your nerve, Miss Kelley. Don't become a lady on us now."

I was too frightened to be angry or abashed.

Willie and I stood at the rail, watching as their pinnace approached, the coxs'n calling the cadence in clipped French. Hardly any need to row, as the breeze and the swell pushed them in our direction. Eight burly men and a coxs'n rowing two officers, one barely more than a boy. Both dressed smartly in royal blue jackets, tricorn hats, gleaming swords. They laid the boat expertly alongside.

I leaned over the rail, intentionally displaying as much of my shallow cleavage as I could. I caught the coxs'n's eye. He was a pimply-faced youth with a big blade of a nose. He commanded the men to raise their oars, looking at me all the while. That was all the encouragement I needed.

"Are you taking our ship, messieurs?" I called out. "Do

be kind, gentlemen; we have a baby on board and my father is not well."

As if on cue the baby began to wail.

"Madame, mademoiselle." The elder lieutenant nodded to us, touching the brim of his hat. "Ladies, we are coming aboard. If you will drop us a line we won't be forced to use our grappling hooks." His English was flawless.

"Please don't harm us, monsieur," Mary pleaded, patting the bawling babe vigorously on the back, which made him cry all the louder.

The lieutenant climbed up the shipside ladder and stepped onto the deck with great familiarity. "Where is your captain?"

"Below, in his cabin," Mary said.

"Why does he cower below, leaving his quarterdeck to women? Come, give up your ship like a man," the lieutenant called loudly. He stamped his heel twice on the deck, as if he were knocking on a door.

"My husband is quite ill, monsieur."

Timing the roll of the ship, the other men scrambled up the side. I watched the coxs'n tie his boat's painter around our fife rail. He glanced scornfully about our quarterdeck, where we had recently strewn empty buckets, dirty laundry, and goat droppings for effect.

"Papa!" I called down the companionway. "Papa, come up at once! The Frenchmen are on board. They mean to take our ship! Willie, go down and get our father and help him up!"

Willie clattered down the companionway, pretending to fetch the captain.

"Well, I certainly hope you are gentlemen," I said, looking first to the lieutenants, then to the coxs'n.

"You English don't know the meaning of the word," he answered contemptuously.

Wigless and hatless, Blake stumbled up on deck looking slovenly and unkempt. His gray hair hung in greasy strings to his shoulders. He leaned on Young Willie for support.

"And who have we here?" the lieutenant said.

"I am Captain Blake," the shipmaster said irascibly. "Are we at war?"

"Are we at war? Are you mad? Has the sun addled your brain, Captain? Of course we are at war, for years we've been at war, and I am taking your vessel for the King of France."

Now the younger officer spoke up. "What is the nature of your illness? Is it putrid fever?"

"How should I know?" Blake groused. "Do I look like a bloody physician?" He hacked convincingly and spit into the scuppers. "A fever of some sort, I should think. My wife is not long out of childbed and she too is weak. Since you are taking us, perhaps your surgeon can see to us."

The French lieutenant turned to the others. "I will not have their foul contagion on my ship; we'll leave them on board under guard and send over a crew to sail this barge to Martinique." He then turned back to Blake. "What are you carrying?"

He did not know, then, what we had in our hold. He must not have come across any of the others in our convoy, carrying soldiers and armament too. "Manufactured items," Blake lied coolly. "Linens and woolens. And salted herring, sixty-eight barrels."

"What weapons have you?"

Blake lifted his shoulders in a dispassionate shrug. "What you see on deck. The usual armament a merchant-man carries to fend off pirates and Frenchmen."

"Bah. We are only evening the score. What is wrong with your sailors?" He nodded toward Dalton and Doughal, sprawled on the foredeck.

"Sick. We have all been sick," Blake said with a shrug.

The French officer snorted. "Sick with English grog, no doubt. Take me below to see the cargo. And fetch your manifest. The genuine one, not your customs invoice."

Blake shuffled toward the companionway, dropping to his knees once in a convincing fit of coughing. The officers reached into their breast pockets for handkerchiefs, which they held across their noses and mouths against the imag-ined effluvia.

At the top of the companionway the French lieutenant turned to his coxs'n and gave orders in French. "Stay here and guard them. Make certain those sots on the foredeck don't decide to be heroes. If they do, shoot them." Then the two officers and two armed sailors followed John Blake below to the wardroom.

Willie and I exchanged glances. It was time for me to distract the remaining men.

"Might I climb up to the maintop and retrieve some-thing I left up there?" I smiled coyly and pointed aloft.

"No," said the pimply-faced coxs'n, who seemed to be in charge. "You are to remain as you are."

Looking first at the coxs'n, then at the other mariners, I

tilted my head, feeling more like a marionette than a coquette. Untying my bonnet, I pulled it off and shook out my tangled hair, letting the wind catch it.

"Please, sir. My undergarments are up there. It will only take a few minutes."

The coxs'n's mouth opened and closed like a fish. I saw his Adam's apple bob as he swallowed. "Pardon?"

"You see, I left my underpropers up on the maintop. I washed them and left them up there to dry. We wouldn't want them to blow away, now would we?" I babbled. "You won't allow your men to shoot me if I climb up there and fetch them, will you?"

"*Non.*" He cleared his throat as if to gain control of the situation. "But be quick about it."

"Of course, monsieur. *Vite, alors. Tout de suite.*"

I handed the coxs'n my bonnet and he held it in both hands, like an egg. All eyes followed me as I kicked off my shoes and gathered my skirts up, exposing my white legs from the knees down.

"Don't look," I admonished, stepping up on the rail beside the lieutenant.

"I'm telling Mama," Willie piped, picking up his cue. "Mama, Patricia is climbing again!" He jumped up and down on the deck, laughing and shrieking. "Ha, ha, ha! You're going to get a whipping, you little hussy!"

"Patricia!" Mary shouted, adding to Willie's uproar. "Come down this instant! You shameful girl! What will these men think?"

I forced a giddy laugh and started up the ratlines, my skirts tangling about my legs, making it difficult to climb. Willie and Mary continued their racket below, and the baby howled. I prayed this would be enough noise to cover up any scuffling belowdecks.

At the futtock shrouds I looked down and caught sight of Dalton looking up at me, and it gave me courage. Pretending to miss a step, I screamed loudly, dangling from the shrouds, thrashing my legs.

Two French sailors dropped their weapons and leaped onto the rail, scrambling up the ratlines to help me. The others simply stared. Meanwhile, Dalton and Doughal lit the fuses to the starboard cannons and I hung on tight, feeling the cannon blasts even before I heard the roar. Feeling the vibration in my hands.

Dalton's shout told me his shot must have made good. I looked over my shoulder to see the frigate's fore stays'ls shredded, torn sheets and halyards dangling, dancing like kite strings on the wind. The men on their way up to rescue me now paused, shouted to one another, then dropped to the deck, rushing for their weapons. But Doughal and Dalton kicked aside the muskets and fell upon the Frenchmen, pummeling them with their fists.

I regained my footing and wrapped my arms through the rigging. I was afraid to watch, yet I could not tear my eyes away. Our men and Molesworth's marines came up from below; dirks flashed in the sun and the grunts and bellows of men struggling were like those of wounded animals. I clung to the rigging, a hare in a net.

"Make sail! Sheet home!" Blake's voice boomed. "We have only to cross their bows, lads!"

The damage to the frigate's stays'l was just what we needed, for the moment. The warship fell off, unable to hold course, while *Canopus* stood on, braced hard up.

Earnshaw scurried to the helm and took control. Blake and Kent leaped to the main sheet with Cunningham and Quixote. Slowly *Canopus* began to make way, but she had not enough wind in her sails to drive her out of firing range. Like a bad dream, we inched along, as if sailing through mud.

"Princess!" Dalton shouted. I looked down to see him tying the hands of a bludgeoned mariner with a length of twine from his pocket. "Make sail! Unfurl the t'gallant!"

"What?" I screamed. "What do I do?"

"Untie the gaskets!" He dodged as another French sailor slashed at him with his sword.

Jolted out of my paralysis, I climbed as quickly as I could, but my skirts made it difficult, wrapping around my legs, my bare toes catching in the hem.

I heard the great booms of the French cannons firing, felt the reverberation in my bones. *They're firing at us,* I realized. It did not seem quite real. A loud crack like lightning and I turned my head just in time to see the mizzen cro'jack yard explode. Splinters of wood rained down on the deck.

Canopus desperately needed the extra push the main t'gallant would give her. I reached the crosstrees, but with my voluminous skirts there was scarcely room for me to stand. If I could have taken them off I swear I would have, but I could not manage the buttons with one hand.

Reaching for the yard and kicking my leg free of its feminine trap, I climbed out onto the footrope, not daring to look down. Focusing on each gasket's knot as I fumbled to untie the salt-stiff twine, leaning into the yard for balance. Hearing the fracas below. Not daring to think where the next shot would hit. What it would feel like to be cut in half by a cannonball.

The footrope bowed under my weight, my bare feet feeling their way along as I stepped cautiously back to the crosstrees and climbed out to the windward yard. As I untied the last gasket, the t'gallant sail fell free and the wind filled it. Far below me Willie, Mary, and Tibbs sheeted it home.

Just then another cannonball smashed our spanker gaff, blowing it out to sea in a tangle of spar and line. But *Canopus* had picked up speed and before the frigate could get off another shot, we were at right angles to her bow and out of the range of the cannons. Without her stays'ls the frigate could not make our course. The French sailors fired their bow-mounted swivel guns at us, but none found their mark. Just a little farther, a little more sea room, and we might make it. Put up all sail and run like hell. By the time the frigate repaired her rigging, we would be at anchor in Carlisle Bay.

As soon as we were well out of firing range and the sails properly set, we mustered amidships. All present and accounted for; all of us alive. There were injuries, to be sure. Dalton's forearm had been deeply lacerated while fending off a saber, and though he had bound it tightly with a strip of canvas, MacPherson insisted on probing the wound and redressing it. I myself was unscathed.

Molesworth kept the two officers prisoners, to be relinquished in Bridgetown, but we released the sailors to their pinnace, as we had not enough men to guard them. Stripped of their arms, we cast them loose, their wounded frigate still in sight.

Relief flooded me, made me jelly-legged and giddy. We had beaten the odds, we were almost home. It seemed too good to be true.

The trade winds were most favorable now, driving us directly for our landfall. Blake ordered all possible sail and the men worked with a will, putting up the stunts'ls. We were fortunate to have lost only our cro'jack yard and spanker gaff.

Rum was passed out to all the men and Captain Blake opened a bottle of his best brandy for the officers and ladies. Henry, our bosun, was released and magnanimously forgiven. Though he insisted we had merely suffered a fool's luck, he was quick to empty his glass.

Molesworth retired to his cabin to log the day's events. We all gave him three cheers and my hoorah was as loud as any. Were it not for his courage and his daring plan I would be on my way to a French prison, or worse, at this very moment.

The rest of us spent the evening on deck, celebrating our escape and recounting over and over our individual roles, what we did to save the ship from capture. If anyone thought less of me for playing the part of the hussy, no one said so. I heard only praise for my bravado. Although the crew remained in their customary stations on the foredeck and in the waist, and the officers stayed aft in their customary station, something connected us and made us one. We were a strange but close-knit family, this company of souls, and *Canopus* was more than a home, she was our fortress. And I thought that perhaps here at sea on a ship, a woman could be what she wanted to be.

Land was close by, though we could not yet see it. Terns circled, screaming, diving. Flying fish broke the water, skimmed over the surface, dropped back into the deep. A school of porpoises came to ride our bow wake, swimming with jubilant speed, as if they too were possessed with the same fire we were. As they leaped out of the water, I caught glimpses of their gleaming, smooth bellies, the rare color of dawn.

The sailors did not pay much attention to the birds and fishes, for they were quite drunk. Even Young Willie fell down puking into the scuppers. I declared to Mary that it was the best day I ever lived.

Sunrise. The excited buzz of voices on deck told me Barbados was in sight. I rushed up on deck to see the island looming green and shimmering in the morning light. The ship's company was undaunted by hangovers. I heard Captain Blake humming a tune as he shaved. Mr. Kent walked with a bounce in his step and a light in his ever-sorrowful eyes. Even Molesworth seemed less miserable and did not insist on a bleeding or purging that day.

The clouds above us were billowy white and finer, I thought, than any clouds that ever obscured the skies over England. The men braced the yards and trimmed the sails, and as we rounded the north end of the island I could smell it—tantalizing whiffs of earth, weed, flower, and cane. The smell of a home I had dreamed into existence.

PART TWO

ONE

We dropped anchor in Carlisle Bay, the first of our convoy to arrive.

But now that I was here I was in no great hurry to go ashore. I found a dozen tasks to be done, even after the men had lowered away the longboat for Molesworth and were readying the cutter for the rest of us. It took no time at all to gather my possessions: the cloak I had come aboard with, my sailor clothes, the hat and the journal MacPherson had given me, and of course the letter from my father, to prove my claim. Yet still I lingered. The hanging bed needed freshening. I straightened the doctor's desk, dusted his books, and polished all the surgical instruments, though they gleamed already. I think I was afraid to leave the ship.

MacPherson returned to the ship after dark with

unpleasant news. An acquaintance of his in Bridgetown, a fellow Scot, knew of the Hatterby plantation up in St. Lucy's Parish and had heard about my father's death.

The doctor's face was stern and I wondered if he was about to scold me. "Mr. Russell tells me the Hatterby plantation has been sold," he said.

"Sold?" I shook my head. "No. That can't be true."

"Circumstances may have forced your father to—"

"It can't be," I interrupted, refusing to hear him out. "I'm certain once I get there I can make sense of it all. Someone has no doubt taken advantage of the situation, hazarding that I would never show up. Perhaps some of my father's servants are still about and will remember me." I heard the desperation in my own voice.

"Ye must not get your hopes up."

I bristled. "Really, sir, I am sure this can be worked out and I am not about to let the matter go on hearsay alone. I've come all this way and I've nothing left. Will you accompany me?" I demanded.

When he looked up his eyes were as moist and soft as I have ever seen them.

"Aye, lass, I'll go with ye," he said. "Tomorrow morning."

We rode horseback, for no carriages were to be had that morning, all of them rented out or in the shop for repair. To me that was no setback, for I much preferred a saddle to a gig. I loved nothing more than feeling the saddle beneath me, the reins in hand, the smell of a sweat-lathered horse and linseed-oiled leather.

My happiest memories of growing up were of riding to hounds across the hills and glens of Wiltshire, jumping an occasional log, stone wall, or hedgerow. When I was a schoolgirl, my favorite daydream was returning to Barbados, where I could keep an entire stable of horses instead of just one. Where I could stay out for days, ride around the whole island if I chose.

We took the road inland, north toward St. Lucy's Parish. Just outside of Bridgetown the sea of cane fields began, vivid green and whispering. The steady clop-clop of our horses' hooves was soothing and as the land rose, so did my hopes. *I have returned to the land of my birth. It shall be mine, it shall. On a day as lovely as this, nothing can go wrong.*

I turned to look at MacPherson. Sitting straight and square-shouldered in his saddle, he looked ahead, not seeing the beauty around us. His face was set like an old stump. Perhaps he was sorry to be losing my services, for when I left he would have to replace me. Or do all the work himself, even the lowly tasks of cleaning and polishing instruments, washing the dressings and hanging them like stockings to dry in the sun. I felt no pity for him; he would replace me soon enough.

Early memories sprung to mind as if they had been stored here, in the fertile ground. Vivid images, lush, dense. The memories had no language, just a sense of familiarity, of knowing. *This place was home.*

"This is it, just ahead." My heart seemed to float as I recognized the mahogany trees that lined the lane. But they didn't look the same; they were bigger and fuller than I remembered, and the lane itself so much shorter.

The great house came into view, shabby and over-grown, yet still elegant somehow. The outmoded parapets like white waves against the red shingled roof, the azure sky. Hounds bayed; I heard a peacock scream and felt a sweet deep hurt in my breast. A hurt I did not want to let go of. I fully expected to see my father come out of the house with a glass of sangaree in his hand.

"I'm afraid I don't know what to say, Miss Kelley."

The men were red-faced, the both of them. Mr. Smith swirled the wine in his glass and appeared to study it.

We sat in the dim parlor, the shutters closed to keep out the sun. The maid brought tea on a silver tray. She was of high color, with skin like cinnamon. A girl my own age, not the ebony-skinned, white-haired woman whose image flashed suddenly in my mind.

My eyes flew around the room, found the stairway and followed it as far as I could see. Mahogany paneling, the tall clock still on the landing. My father's clock.

"Ah, well," his wife said, her accent giving her away as an unrefined woman of the North Country. "I am sorry that ye have come all this way, Miss Kelley. All this way for nothing."

"Won't you look at my letter? Just look at my letter, won't you?" With fumbling fingers I took it out of the envelope.

Smith cleared his throat and smiled with cold conde-scension.

"You have your letters indeed, miss. Letters from your father, as no doubt any young schoolgirl has. But I have something more valid and indisputable than letters, Miss Kelley, for I have the deed. A legal document recorded in Bridgetown. I purchased the plantation, all two hundred acres, lock, stock, and barrel from Mr. Hatterby shortly before . . . he . . . ah . . ." He cleared his throat. "That is, before . . ." He stopped abruptly, looking to MacPherson for assistance.

But MacPherson was at a loss for words. It was I who spoke. "Before he died? *Before?*" I said incredulously. "But that can't be!" I sorted frantically through the letter, looking for the one passage in particular that would clear up this terrible mistake.

Smith turned to MacPherson, speaking out of the corner of his mouth, but loud enough for me to hear.

"The chap was in a bit of a spot, he was. Didn't know the first thing about farming and hired a drunken Irishman for a manager. Had a soft spot for the blackamoors, squandered his money on women of all colors, and gambled the rest on the horses, so they say."

"What sort of charade is this?" I demanded, my voice piercing as a piccolo. "Common merchants squatting in my father's house, living like grandees, dragging his name through the dirt!"

"Miss Kelley!" MacPherson thundered, glowering at me. "I must apologize for the young lady's impetuous accusations but she is quite distraught by the course of events."

"I can see that," Smith said coldly.

"Perhaps if we could see the actual deed," MacPherson pressed.

"You want to see the deed?"

"Please understand the young lady's distress. She grew up believing to be given the estate in dowry. She has a letter—"

"Yes, yes, of course she has a letter." Smith snorted with contempt. "Fathers write letters and promise many things to their wheedling young daughters."

"Daughters, sons." Mrs. Smith shrugged. "If every one of his issue surfaced and came straggling in, why, we might as well run a parish orphanage!"

"The point is," I blurted out, ignoring her insult, "my father loved this place. He never would have sold it, not while he had breath in his body."

"He may have indeed loved it," Smith said, his voice clipped. "The man apparently suffered no lack of love and no lack of restraint. In the end it cost him a lot of money, much more than he had. His debt was called and he had to sell his plantation. I am sorry to be the one to tell you, and so brutally, but those are the facts and I am a straight-forward man."

I could no longer hear him. I saw his mouth move, saw his red-jowled face wiggle like a cock's comb or a turkey's wattle, but my head was filled with a roar, the roar of a wave crashing. I could not bear to hear any more and I certainly did not care to see a legal document that had their name on it. Whatever had happened, this was all a mistake.

MacPherson was rising now, quite red in the face. And I felt a deep pain inside, a deep and burning shame as we walked out of the cool, dark house back into the white light of midday. Sparks shot inside my head, behind my eyes. MacPherson took my arm tenderly, yet I was not faint, I was in no danger of collapse. Outside the gate I broke away and walked toward the barn; then, impulsively, I began to run. MacPherson did not try to stop me. He stood by the horses, watching.

I ran to the cool sweetness of the barn where I had played as a child. Where the sound of snorting horses was a constant comfort, and the stable boys sang as they went about their work. Where the smells of grain and dried grasses and the odors of the animals themselves all mixed together and made me feel at home.

I made my way through the barn, empty but for one mare dozing, her head foreward and outstretched, her weight shifted onto three feet, the hindquarter resting. Through the barn and out to the mill beyond. Where the windmill turned the great wheel that pressed the cane until the juices ran. The windmill was rigged like a sail, and we used to dare each other to grab hold of the moving arm and ride it up and around.

Down the hill I ran, my skirts lifted like those of a six-year-old tomboy. Down to the boiling house, where I had not been allowed to go during harvest for fear of getting scalded. Inside it was dark and I smelled the bagasse, cane trash, rotting and fermented.

A man stood in the shadows with a great puncheon across his shoulders, which caused his head to thrust forward, like a mule. He stood looking at me, a bemused expression on his coffee-and-cream face.

"Are you looking for someone?"

"Who are you?" I said dully.

"The cooper's apprentice. Are you lost?"

"No. Not lost. Undone."

I felt his eyes examining me. His hair was brown and

curly, though not the tight dark curls of a Negro. A mulatto, he was. It was hard to tell his age, yet he said he was an apprentice, so I guessed him to be about my own age.

He set down the barrel and continued to stare at me.

"Do I know you?" I asked.

A flicker of a smile crossed his face. "Your father was Sheldon Hatterby," he said. His voice was well modulated and somehow familiar.

"Yes," I said, feeling validated. "How did you know that?"

"I see him in you. Something about your chin and the way you hold it. And your high manner of speaking—they are his."

Apparently the mulatto was educated to some degree. He looked as though he had a great deal of English blood in his veins.

"So you knew Mr. Hatterby?"

The mulatto laughed, but without mirth or pleasure. "Yes, I knew him."

"You worked for him?"

He wiped his hands on his sweat-stained shirt. "I was born here, in the slaves' quarters. Hatterby apprenticed me to a cooper when I was ten." He paused and dared to look me straight in the eye. "He was my father too, you know," he said, with an air of bitter spite. "We have that in common, you and I."

I felt as if the wind had been knocked out of me. My head reeled.

"No," I breathed.

The mulatto nodded. "Indeed. Sheldon Hatterby, lord of the manor, fathered me on one of his field hands."

Father had never mentioned other children, certainly not mulattos. But of course he would not mention them, if indeed they existed. I too was illegitimate. But my mother was Irish, not African. Red-gold hair and milky skin. That was another thing entirely.

"Look at me, past the color of my skin and the broad bridge of my nose. Look into my gray eyes, look at my Englishman's lips, and tell me you don't see your father," he challenged.

Though in the barn's dim light I could not clearly see his features, I felt the truth of his words pelting me like stones. From the rafters a pigeon chortled.

"My name is Rupert and I am a free man. Mr. Hatterby gave me my freedom. I suppose I should be grateful." He dug at the dirt with the toe of his shoe. "My mother died when I was two. Twenty-four years old, she was, and worn out. Field hands don't live long, you see. That's why the owners have to keep on buying more, breeding more."

I didn't want to hear about his mother's sorrow or his burdens; I was overwhelmed with my own. "But did he give you his name?" I blurted out. "Tell me, are you Hatterby?"

Rupert's laugh was dry. "I am Hatterby, yes. Rupert Hatterby."

My face stung as if I had been slapped.

"Don't look so shocked. Slaves are usually given their owner's name. So much more convenient, you know, than those mumbo-jumbo names they come over here with."

I could not bear to hear any more, yet I had to know the truth. "Are there more?"

"More? You mean bastards like us?"

I nodded, hating the word.

"Mulattos or white?"

"How many children of any sort?" I said, tight-lipped.

Rupert just shrugged. "How should I know? And why should I care whom a rich white man beds? But I do remember you. He used to talk about you, how he sent you to England to be educated. His little redhead. His favorite. You are his little Patra."

"I am."

"The Irish maid's daughter."

"My mother was Irish." I could not bring myself to admit to the mulatto what he well knew. That she was but a servant.

"Is it true he sold the plantation?"

"It is true. A week before he hung himself."

A new shock—was there no end? "Hung himself? Father hung himself?" I shook my head. "No, you are lying! All of this, lies!"

Rupert shrugged, a quick and flippant movement. "Believe what you want."

"Mr. Hatterby died of an infection," I said numbly. "An infection, I was told."

"I'm sure he was infected with something," Rupert said with a sardonic smile. "But a rope around his neck is what did him in."

"What?" I gasped as the blood seemed to empty from my head. "How dare you!"

"I ought to know. 'Twas me who found him. You would have thought he might have been man enough to use a pistol. Only criminals hang by their necks."

I wanted very much to slap his smirking face, to feel the sting in my palm. "Look here, you upstart. My father, whatever his faults, was a good man. He loved me, he promised me the plantation." I struggled to keep my voice reasonable, and failed. It came out broken and squeaky. "That's why I'm here, why I've come all this way. This is all I have in the world."

"Well, then, Patra." He pursed his Englishman's lips and sighed in mock sympathy. "It seems you've come a long way for nothing. The plantation now belongs to Mr. Smith."

"Then why are you still here?"

He shrugged. "The new owner pays the same as the old. Don't be envious; it's not as if I were a true son, a real Hatterby. I make barrels for a living. I reside in a shed, not the great house."

"But he promised it to me."

"You're a woman," he said, as if I were a fool. "Women have no property rights."

"It was to be my dowry."

He made a flippant sound through his nose. A laugh of sorts. "If it's a plantation you want, why don't you do the obvious? Marry a man who owns one. That's how white women get along in this world." He stooped to pick up his empty puncheon.

"Why didn't he tell me?"

"Who knows? Maybe he was ashamed. Or maybe it just slipped his mind." Rupert Hatterby adjusted the weight on his shoulders and walked away.

Back in the sunshine MacPherson waited. He took me in his arms as if I were a child; I think he expected me to weep. And although I buried my head in his shoulder and felt his arms gently hug me, no tears fell. It was not grief I felt but rage, and the sound that came out of me was not the sound of a young woman crying.

The road to Bridgetown seemed forever and the heat was unbearable. I found no pleasure or consolation in the ride. The trade winds had died and the coconut palms and the sugarcane no longer whispered to me.

Aboard ship I ran straightaway to the doctor's cabin and shut the door. I felt bright with shame, as if the entire world could see I was the illegitimate daughter of a ruined man. I was sure everyone could see my humiliation, a glowing beacon. Toward my dead father I felt only anger.

There was a hesitant knock at the door. "Patricia, it's me," Young Willie said.

"Go away."

"I'm sorry about your farm."

"Does the whole ship know my business?" I couldn't face Willie, couldn't face anyone right then. After a moment I heard his little footsteps as he left.

Now what was I to do? Go into service? Even if I ignored my pride, I knew nothing of housekeeping, not the first thing. Neither could I sew, except for the fancy needlework they taught us in school, at which I had proved to be all thumbs. Perhaps I could tutor young ladies, but I had no connections. I knew no one who would employ me.

I could ask the Blakes to take me back to England, but then what? Return to the country school where I grew up and grovel for a position? Go back to the backstreets of Portsmouth and sell my favors? No, I could not bear it.

I thought of taking my own life. Doing what my father had done when life got out of control and he could no longer face his creditors. Suicide. There were so many ways to end it all. I could hang myself from a timber, Papa's little girl. Or steal a firearm and blow my brains out. I could plunge a dirk into my heart, just to the left of the sternum, fifth intercostal space. Thanks to Dr. MacPherson, I knew the correct anatomical landmarks. Then again, I could poison myself from the medicine chest, or I could simply step off the ship and into the cold blue arms of the sea. It was far easier to think of ways to end my life than the means by which to continue it.

I could hear them above me in the wardroom: the Blakes, Mr. Kent, Dr. MacPherson. Their voices amplified by the wooden hull, the humid air. They were talking about me.

"Poor thing." Mary's voice.

Mr. Kent's mournful tone. "Poor, yes. But foolish."

"No," Mary insisted, "just young and naive. She believed her father."

"But to think an illegitimate child, a daughter at that, had any claim to land."

"Well, I think she acted quite bravely under the circumstances." Mary's voice again. "She's very resourceful."

"She is." Captain Blake's voice. "But look where her bravery and resourcefulness have got her. It might have been easier had she not been educated and raised as a gentlewoman."

"Perhaps she could find a place as a lady's companion." Mr. Kent's voice. "Or a governess."

"She hasn't the temperament nor the connections," Blake answered. "I daresay her profligate father has ruined her chances."

I heard the familiar sound of MacPherson clearing his throat. "She's welcome to stay on as my assistant. In fact, I hope she does."

"The girl is indebted to you," said Blake. "She must work for you according to the terms of your agreement."

"I cannot force her to work for me if she doesn't wish to," the doctor said. "She is free to go or stay as she pleases."

Blake laughed. "By God, I've never known such a generous Scot!"

"Then ye have not met but reivers and rogues, for most of us are soft at heart, though we be tight of fist."

The sound of their laughter carried along the timbers and their talk turned to other topics.

At four in the afternoon the heat belowdecks was unbearable and I could stand it no longer. I sought relief under an awning on the quarterdeck, where I watched the men unloading cargo, as they had been doing since sunup this morning.

Everyone on board seemed in high spirits but me. I felt alone, and a stranger among them.

At sunset the doctor played his pipes and I looked forward to the doleful sound, yet as I gazed toward the lights of Bridgetown, I could not admit my defeat. I realized what I wanted most was not so much the real estate as an asset, but what it stood for in my mind. Had it not been worth a farthing, I still would have wanted it.

The plantation was my earliest memory, my best and

most vivid dream. It represented my father, and my mother too, for only on the plantation could she exist with any sort of dignity. I was born on that land, I had roots like the mahogany trees that lined the drive, I was part of the enduring soil. The plantation was my past and my future, my reason for being. I couldn't just forget it.

I waited in vain for a sign.

TWO

Five days after we arrived in Barbados, the last of our convoy came straggling in and their cargoes destined for this colony were unloaded. We prepared to make way for our next stop, the island of Antigua, a two-day passage to leeward, where the remainder of the military supplies were to be delivered.

MacPherson and I had just finished sick call and were taking inventory of our supply of medicaments when the big Scotsman put down the brown bottle of laudanum in his hand.

"Will ye walk the quarterdeck with me, Miss Kelley?"

I had nothing else to do. The present moment kept opening up, a yawning gap, impossible to leap over. I couldn't dream of a future, I couldn't reliably remember my past.

MacPherson offered me his arm and I took it. His thinning hair had been brushed and freshly powdered. We stood at the stern looking west, away from land. The water was dazzling and it hurt my eyes to look upon it.

The doctor cleared his throat. "Miss Kelley. Patricia."

"Sir?"

"How old are ye, lass?"

I thought for a moment, counting back. My birthday had come and gone, unnoticed. I had not thought of it myself.

"Seventeen."

He blinked with surprise. "I would have thought ye were a bit older. Still." He cleared his throat again. "Patricia, would ye consider marrying me?"

His somber voice tolled, reverberating through my bones, and I was held in the grip of his awful gaze.

"My hair has turned from red to gray and I am nearly old enough to be your father, yet I've not forgotten how to love. I'll be good to you. Will you have me, lass?" he thundered.

I couldn't speak. I didn't want to marry him, but I was in no position to refuse.

"Ye have suffered a terrible blow, ye have. And I own neither plantation nor title, yet I am not a poor man. I have saved a considerable sum over the years. Enough to buy a cottage on a bit of land. On Barbados, if ye would like. Surely there is room for one more physician in Bimshire. We could have a garden, raise some animals. And I would buy ye a riding horse and a fine saddle. I would treat ye well, I swear it."

I felt like I was falling from a great height. My stomach

rose into my gorge, my heart seized. All I could see was the doctor's outstretched hand.

"Your offer is most kind, Dr. MacPherson," I managed to say.

"Kindness has nothing to do with it. Damnation, I care for ye, lass. Do ye think ye could come to love me, even a wee bit?"

He gripped my shoulders. His eyes startled me, for they were more brilliant than I remembered, and deeper. I was looking at a man who had dropped all his guard, all his pretenses. Still I did not answer him.

Dr. MacPherson was an educated man. He wasn't wealthy, but he had a dependable income, a savings. Perhaps through MacPherson I could even regain the plantation someday.

On the other hand I felt no desire for the doctor. And worse, I had feelings for another man, a man I could never marry.

Clearly, I would have to marry someone, or be reduced to other sorts of servitude. If I chose the latter, all my education and upbringing would have been for naught. To continue in the life I was used to, I needed a husband who could support me.

Yet it was hard to give up my imagined freedom. Frightening to think of handing over my future to this stodgy man—a stranger, really, although I had come to recognize his step on the deck, the way he cleared his throat, his crisp lime and laurel smell, his lobster-red hands.

When I was growing up, the only choices I'd ever made were which frock to wear to what occasion, which bridle path to ride. I did not choose my studies, the books I read, the hour I retired. Even my friends were chosen for me, though truth be told, I held no classmate dear to my heart. Had my father lived, he would have chosen my husband and I would have complied, though I wasn't much interested in marriage, children, any of that. Marriage was but a distasteful requirement to my inheritance, the plantation. Now it seemed but a distasteful requirement to my survival.

Yet not to choose, to passively wait for fate to deal the cards, was intolerable. Better to blunder, to make a great mistake than to sit like a stump and let someone else arrange the details of my life.

After dark I climbed to the foretop to be alone with my thoughts. Sat on the fighting deck and surveyed the harbor. So still was the air I could hear voices ashore, laughter and drunken oaths turned loose on the warm night air. Lantern lights from dozens of ships reflected on the calm bay. I had a flagon of rum I had stolen from the storeroom, which I drank now in burning gulps. The liquor softened me, loosening my joints and flattening my eyes against the back of my head. The view lost its depth, and my shame its sting.

"Drunk on duty, it appears."

His voice vibrated my bones, made me hum like the string of a viola.

"G'd evening, Dalton," I said, feeling giddy. "Care for some punch?"

He shook his bare head. The wind blew his dark hair, unbound. "Who are ye tonight? Sailor or surgeon's mate? Laddie or lassie?"

"I hardly know. Perhaps if you would kiss me, I might decide," I said recklessly.

"The liquor makes ye bold."

"No, the sound of your voice does." I tilted my head back and he gave me a brotherly brush against my cheek. I felt the stubble of his chin and smelled him: the tar, tobacco, and sweat smell of the bosun's mate.

"I'm surprised to find ye still here, Princess, and not on your plantation. Are ye having trouble saying farewell to a sailor's life?"

"There is no plantation. Not for me." My voice broke and my eyes brimmed, spilling over. I didn't care.

"I am sorry to hear that." He touched my shoulder with his blackened hand. Squeezed it. "What will ye do?"

"Throw myself from the t'gallant yard," I slurred.

"Nae," he said, smiling. "Ye won't."

"Then I suppose I shall marry the doctor."

He said nothing but stroked my hair. The space between us closed and softened.

"There's no other choice," I said.

The idea had never completely formed in my mind that I might throw all convention to the wind and take up with Dalton. Marriage was out of the question. Any relationship with the bosun's mate existed only as a fantasy for a few vivid minutes at night when we found ourselves high above the deck, breathing in the fresh wet air, aware of ourselves as never before. During those moments I had no future to consider and no past to protect. That I might have chosen this way of life did not seem possible to me. "There's always a choice," Dalton said, breaking into my thoughts.

"For you, perhaps."

"For ye too," he insisted.

"What would you do if you were me?" I took another swallow of rum.

He shrugged. "I never had a plantation to lose and I don't know which end of a plough to stick in the ground." He scratched his chin. "I'd sign on a ship, that's what I'd do. Where ye work so bleeding hard ye don't have time to grieve for what ye've lost or to wish for what ye cannot have."

"If you were me, you'd sign on a ship?" I laughed. "As if I could. And who would have me?"

"I would. We could run away and join the pirates." The ends of his mouth turned up in an ironic smile and I had an intuition he was at once serious, yet not.

"A pirate, now why didn't I think of that?" I brushed back a strand of hair from his eyes.

"'Tis a grand life, I hear. Prizes are divided equally; it's share and share alike."

"Oh, a grand life you'll say when you find yourself at the gallows with a black sack over your head."

"No one lives forever." He cupped my face in his hands.

"No, Dalton, but—"

He put his tar-stained finger on my lips to still them. "Brian," he said.

"Brian," I repeated. The sound of his given name, the way it felt in my mouth, was thrilling.

"I shall miss ye, Princess."

"Patricia. My name is Patricia."

He nodded, his eyes black and impenetrable.

"Say it," I whispered. "I want to hear you say my name."

But his mouth covered mine and the sounds of our names were lost. I pressed myself into him, forgetting the world and its rules, forgetting who I was, forgetting everything but my hunger for that nameless, intangible thing.

Aeneas MacPherson and I were married at sea on Sunday, the eighteenth day of January, 1761. It was a clear day, stunningly bright. The sky, a blue bowl turned over our heads; the horizon, a perfectly drawn circle. The winds, fresh out of the northeast. We expected to sight Antigua before nightfall.

Captain Blake performed the ceremony on the quarter-deck, before the ship's entire company. We had no wedding bands to exchange, but the doctor gave me a gold locket that had belonged to his mother. With quivering hands he clasped the chain around my neck and I felt its cool, unfamiliar weight against my breast.

"Till death do us part," I heard myself say.

Young Willie stood next to his uncle Molesworth, looking like a tiny replica of the man, right down to the dirk at his side. I had never noticed that before, their resemblance. Except that Willie's young face was round and rosy while the face of Molesworth was gaunt, white, and twitched so fiercely I thought his flesh would rip.

"Under the eyes of God and this ship's company, I pronounce you man and wife." Blake looked at us both and smiled.

I gave Aeneas MacPherson my hands. Watched them disappear inside his. Formidable appendages—strong enough to crush a walnut, skillful enough to incise, ligate, suture the tiniest vessel—yet tender now and trembling. We pledged ourselves to one another, and like a wren with a broken wing cupped in a child's palm, I felt both saved and doomed.

The sailors mumbled their congratulations, all of them, including Dalton. Earnshaw struck up a lively jig on his fiddle, while a cask of grog was tapped for the seamen and a cask of wine for the ladies and gentlemen. Tibbs had made a raisin pudding with rum sauce, enough for everyone to have seconds. I danced with the gentlemen in turn and with MacPherson, my husband. *My husband.* I shuddered at the thought. This was someone else's life I had fallen into.

Willie climbed to the main t'gallant so that he could be the first to see Antigua. Such a proud little peacock, preening and squawking for praise. He spotted it of course, precisely at six bells, and made such a fuss one would have thought he was Christopher Columbus. I had half a mind to hike my skirts and go up after him just to shut him up.

It happened without any warning at all and I don't know why, for he was an agile lad, a regular mountain goat. Perhaps it was his shoes—stiff, new, and shiny. Or his tight breeches and waistcoat, not meant for climbing. Perhaps he had drunk too much grog.

It seemed he fell in slow motion like a leaf, and just as silent. For a moment everything stood still—the ship, the wind, the waves—and we were all suspended in the terrible moment. Most of all I dreaded the sound he would make, the inevitable, final sound. I wanted to shut my ears as well as my eyes but could not.

Time released us, the world moved again. Young Willie kicked and grasped as he fell as if he were swimming through the air. Somehow he caught hold of the main tops'l brace, or perhaps it was the backstay, I don't remember, but he could not hold on and he fell to the deck, landing on the ventilation hatch with a sickening thud.

MacPherson rushed to his side and the sailors crowded around but I stood frozen, unable to move.

"Miss Kelley, I need ye! Come at once!"

Filled with dread, I obeyed.

THREE

I reached out to touch the doctor's shoulder to let him know I was there, for I could not yet speak. Willie lay limp as a frock dropped from a clothesline; I feared a sudden gust of wind might pick him up and carry him away.

One of the men cursed, shattering the silence.

"Oh, God," I heard myself say.

Willie's cheek rested upon the deck; his eyes, half open, seemed to stare at MacPherson's shoe. Bloody spittle dripped from his mouth and I had an urge to wipe it clean, but did not. I simply stared, unable to comprehend it. Willie was dead. Yet how could this be? Only a second ago he was quite alive.

If I could reverse the world's turning just a few minutes, I would scramble up the ratlines after him, I would call out a warning. I shouldn't have been so mean to him—why was

I? I cared for Willie, I had come to love him, I realized with a stab of guilt. Yet I seldom had a kind word for him, or a sisterly embrace. And now it was too late. It would always be too late.

My eyes played tricks on me, for I saw him move, a slight twitch. Perhaps it was but a death spasm. Though I had never watched anyone die, MacPherson had told me that sometimes when a man dies from his wounds he does such a thing before he finally succumbs. Then slowly the body cools and the blood settles to the lowest places, causing a purple color known as lividity. Later rigor mortis sets in, the body becomes rigid. Eventually that too passes, as the body begins the natural process of decay. *But this can't be happening to Willie,* I prayed.

He moved again, his small fist clenched. I watched, unable to tear my eyes away, saw his chest rise and fall. Heard him struggle and gasp for breath. Held my own breath as he gasped again. Willie was not dead!

"He breathes," the doctor whispered.

Gratitude filled me like sunlight; I was bursting with it. The others sighed, murmured, moved closer for a better look.

"Don't touch him," MacPherson warned. "We must move him carefully, for he may have broken his back. Hans—go fetch a board wide enough to carry him." MacPherson continued to give directions to all of us and I took comfort in the decisiveness of his voice.

Hans and Doughal soon came clattering up the companionway, carrying a lid they had pried off a sea chest. We lifted Willie onto it and lowered him through the grate to the officer's wardroom, for we had no sick berth, it being filled with cannons and kegs of gunpowder. The cook had already set the table for supper, and we bid him to clear it so that Willie might be examined on top of it. The doctor prodded and pressed with his thick fingers, mumbling to himself as he moved from the boy's head to his toes.

"Bleed him," he said to me when he was finished. "Take a full cup."

With trembling hands I rolled up Young Willie's white sleeve and wrapped the tourniquet snugly above his elbow. Felt his smooth arm for an engorged vessel. Poked his skin with the scalpel, felt the blade pierce the resilient vein. Watched the blood trickle into the brass pan.

Willie's eyelids fluttered. He opened his eyes, looked at me curiously. "Where am I?"

I laughed with nervous relief.

"Hold still, you little dickens!"

"Where am I?" he repeated.

"Don't you remember? You're aboard the ship *Canopus*. You fell from the upper yard."

He sat up and looked at the blood running into the pan, then looked at me, his eyes wild and uncomprehending.

"Where am I? I don't understand. Where is my sister? What have you done with my mother?"

"Be still, lad," MacPherson commanded. "Ye're being bled. Call Lieutenant Molesworth," he said to the marine at his post outside the great cabin. "Perhaps the boy will recognize his own uncle."

Yet he did not.

"You're not my father," he said suspiciously when the lieutenant appeared by his side. "Who are you, sir?"

Molesworth's face collapsed in a torrent of twitches

and he returned to his cabin. Mary looked at me, eyes wide. We both looked to MacPherson, who was making a note in his pocket book.

"He's been knocked senseless," the doctor said, as if that should reassure us.

One of the ship's cats poked its head into the room, curious to see what was going on.

Willie spied it and a flash of recognition crossed his face. "Here, kitty, pretty kitty," he called, holding out his hand and wiggling his fingers. But the cat fled, no doubt remembering Willie's teasing and tail pulling, even if Willie himself did not.

"Ye must be part cat yourself," MacPherson said, "for a cat has nine lives and always lands on its feet. 'Tis a miracle ye've broken no bones."

The doctor turned to me. "He shall sleep here tonight, not in his cabin. We must keep a close eye on him."

Willie had already fallen asleep. I finished bleeding him and bandaged his arm with a strip of linen.

"I'll sit with him," I said. I could not bring myself to leave his side. Each breath he took seemed a wonder, and I vowed to be more indulgent of his annoying ways. I touched his hand, plump and pink. Ragged, little-boy fingernails embedded with dirt. To think he'd nearly died this very day! Yet he had not.

Mary appeared out of the shadows, candle in hand.

"Go to bed, Patricia. I'll stay with him."

I did not move.

"Go on now, your husband waits."

Her words made my stomach tingle uncomfortably. That I was married seemed as improbable as Willie's fall.

"Go, Mrs. MacPherson," Mary said with mock sternness. "Go enjoy your wedding night."

I could feel her smile in the dim light. The flickering candle cast her shadow large on the bulkhead.

"Enjoy it?" I said, wrinkling my nose. "That's impossible."

"Don't be such a goose, Patricia." Mary placed the candle in the lantern hanging from the beam. The feeble light shone now on Willie's face, which twitched slightly like the face of a dreaming dog.

"Give the man half a chance," she said. "If you make up your mind you're not going to love him, then you haven't got a prayer."

"A prayer for what?" I said petulantly. Knowing what she meant but resisting.

"For happiness, Patricia. Allow yourself to have a few moments of pleasure each day. Words of advice from an old married woman."

But I am not old, I thought. *And I don't like being married.*

"For you, perhaps. But for me it is not that simple," I said.

"Oh, but it is." Mary sat on a sea chest and drew her legs up under her like a girl. "Dear child, contentment is not something you are born into like title or wealth. And it cannot be stripped away or squandered. It is there for the taking, for all of us."

But it had been a long day and suddenly I was weary of her aphorisms, her relentless optimism. For someone who toiled her life away on a trading ship without a proper house to call home, what did she know of happiness? I crossed my arms perversely and for a time neither of us spoke. We simply watched Willie sleep as the ship swayed and groaned. Water slapped the hull relentlessly and the ship's bell clanged seven times.

Then without a word Mary went back to her cabin, and I was glad to be alone with my brooding thoughts. But she soon returned, carrying a package wrapped in brown paper, which she placed in my lap.

"What's this?"

"A gift for you, Patricia. From me. On your wedding night."

"Oh. I—"

"Yes?" Mary's smile could cheer anyone.

"Thank you. You are the kindest person I have ever met."

My hands trembled as I untied the string and unfolded a fine linen nightdress, exquisitely embroidered. It was much finer than anything I had ever seen Mary herself wear.

I didn't trust myself to speak. I felt fragile, some rare piece of porcelain perched too close to the edge of a shelf.

"Do you like it?" Her voice was gay and girlish and I was envious of her easy, wholehearted delight. "I hope it fits. Stand up and put it on, let's have a look."

"But when?" I blurted out. "I mean, how did you . . ."

She smiled that famous Mary smile, her face breaking into fine lines, reminding me of so many little rivers. A watershed, her face.

"I had it made for you in Madeira," she said. "For your wedding trousseau."

"Madeira!" I was amazed. "How did you know back in

Madeira that I would marry the doctor? You took a great risk, for I was not at all inclined, you know."

"I know," she said, beaming. "I remember well, yet I don't think you'll be sorry. Let me know in ten years or so if I am right."

I felt a rush of warmth that replaced all my peevishness. "I hope we will still be visiting one another in ten years," I said. "I hope you will always call on me, wherever I am living. I am very grateful to you, Mary."

I stood to embrace her.

"Be happy, Patricia," she said, as if bestowing a blessing.

From the adjoining cabin the baby cried, and I felt her tense momentarily. "Shhhh," she whispered, and I don't know which one of us she was comforting. Two warm, wet circles of milk leaked through her bodice onto my own and I felt a sudden longing for the mother I never knew. I squeezed Mary Blake tight against me, missing her though she was not yet gone. Then I left her to attend her baby Johnny, while I went to attend my husband's needs.

Do what you have to do, I counseled myself. *To get the plantation back.* For I considered my marriage to MacPherson a step down that long road.

"How is our patient?" he asked when I entered our cabin.

I looked with dismay on our tiny bedchamber, crowded with MacPherson's sea trunk, his desk, medical kits, and stacks of books. The lantern hanging from the beam cast a wan glow on the tiny space. The seas were too rough to open the porthole and I felt insufferably hot. Closed in, unable to breathe properly. How could I possibly survive this night?

"Willie sleeps easily," I said, remaining in the doorway.

"Good. He will likely regain his senses in the morning." The doctor scratched his thinning hair. "I have been remiss," he said. "Our sleeping arrangements are not suitable."

"What do you mean?"

"I am a large man and ye are a big-boned lass. We shall not the two of us fit in this hammock." He smiled sheepishly.

I looked directly at him, saw the black holes of his pupils enlarge, nearly consuming the blue rings around them. He desired me. A knot rose up from my chest, nearly choking me.

"I meant to have us a larger bed made, but . . . I thought we might . . ." He cleared his throat nervously. "Just for tonight. You may have the hammock, of course. But I . . ." He foundered completely. The only time I had ever seen him at a loss for words.

"We can make a bed on the floor," I said evenly. If I had to consummate my marriage, I would as soon be on the cool floor than be stuffed into some narrow box hanging by ropes from the beam.

MacPherson sighed, a great gush of air. In the candle-light I could see him, his eyes now bright with expectancy.

"Just for tonight. I shall have the carpenter make us a proper bed first thing in the morning."

I busied myself shaking out blankets and linens while he undressed.

"I've noticed ye have an eye for the bosun's mate," he said, quite matter-of-factly. I heard the rustle of linen as he pulled his arms from his sleeves.

"The bosun's mate?" I said with as much disdain as I could muster. "He's but a common sailor."

"Nae, he's an uncommonly good sailor. A better seaman than the bosun himself."

"I know nothing of that," I said curtly, placing the bedding on the floor and smoothing the wrinkles. "Why, I've hardly noticed him. Hardly at all."

"Ye fancy him to be beneath ye, yet ye fancy him still," MacPherson persisted. He leaned against the bulkhead, pulled off his shoes one by one, and let them drop to the floor.

"Dr. MacPherson! Really, sir, I don't know what to say." Yet I could not in truth deny it. Could the man see through me so easily?

"Aeneas," he said, unbuttoning his breeches. "I hope ye will learn to call me Aeneas."

"Aeneas," I repeated. The name felt strange in my mouth.

He blew out the candle; darkness dropped over us like a net.

"Come to me." His voice was thick.

I stood up, my knees trembling. Overwhelmed with his presence, I saw there was no escape. Aeneas MacPherson then tipped my chin up and kissed my lips long. I closed my eyes and tried to imagine the forbidden man, but the smell of bay leaf and lime would not let me.

"Ye need not say anything, I won't question ye further," he whispered, his hands unfastening the buttons of my dress. "I suspect a young lady has many desires. Same as a young man."

How his big fingers could be so fast I do not know. He

slid the bodice down over my shoulders, down over my hips, and bade me step out of it. Untied my petticoat, lifted the chemise over my head as easily as if I were a child.

"Now, let me show ye," he said, clasping my hands. "Let me show ye what an old man knows about love."

FOUR

At that very moment there came a knock at the cabin door.

"Go away," MacPherson growled.

"Doctor! You must come quickly!" I recognized Henry Blake's voice.

"What the devil! Damnation, man, can it not wait?"

"I am mortified to disturb you, sir, but it's Young Willie. He is having fits."

MacPherson cracked the door open. I wrapped myself in a sheet.

"Fits, ye say?" he bellowed. "A seizure?"

"Dr. MacPherson!" Mary cried from the wardroom, where Willie lay. "I cannot wake him! What must I do?"

"I'll be there at once. Miss Kelley, bring the surgical kit," he ordered, calling me by my former name. "We've no time to waste."

The twitching had subsided when less than two minutes later I burst into the wardroom, kit in hand. Willie lay motionless, as if in a deep sleep. But his breath came in strange, noisy grunts.

"He's hemorrhaging," MacPherson said. "Bleeding into his brain. We must open the skull and release the pressure. Someone inform Lieutenant Molesworth."

The wind had come up fresh on the starboard quarter and although it was a following sea, we pitched on the swell. How on earth MacPherson planned to open Willie's skull, especially in these conditions, I knew not. And what he would expect me to do to assist him, I dared not imagine.

"Cut his hair off here and here." He pointed behind the boy's ears, at the base of his skull. "It doesn't need to be pretty, just cut it off."

I snipped off two fistfuls of silky brown locks.

"Scalpel and trepan, Miss Kelley. Muslin gauze. Mrs. Blake, would ye fetch us a pail of freshwater? With haste, please."

I fumbled in the box, the instruments rattling like silverware. Handed him the scalpel, which gleamed in the flickering candlelight. Picked up the trepan, heavy as a hammer, it seemed.

"I need more light," MacPherson said. "Bring me candles, lanterns, whatever ye have. And mirrors—bring the gentlemen's shaving mirrors and set them up to reflect the light. Quickly now. We might lose him if we don't release the pressure. Miss Kelley, hold his head steady. Nae matter what, don't let it move."

I felt my knees go weak; my head reeled. Had MacPherson not grabbed my arm, I might have fainted or fled to the uppermost yard of the rigging.

"Look at me," he commanded.

His eyes glittered like crushed glass in the eerie yellow candlelight, magnified by the mirrors. He squeezed my arm until I flinched. "Breathe slowly. Don't fail me. I need ye."

The doctor needed me? That Willie's life might in part depend on me was the most sobering realization I'd ever had. I was glad now for my intensive training. Glad MacPherson had made me memorize the instruments by touch. Glad I was familiar with the anatomy of Young Willie's skull.

"I'll do my best, sir," I said earnestly.

Satisfied that I would neither faint nor flee, the doctor rolled up his sleeves. "Now, then, we must be exact. We must move and act precisely. Do ye understand?"

"Yes, sir," I said, though I did not understand any of this. I directed my attention to the gravelly sound of the doctor's voice. Remembered that the doctor was my husband and this was our wedding night. A bad dream, all of this.

MacPherson's fingers searched for a landmark. He made an incision with the scalpel and dark blood oozed forth. Stuck his finger into the hole and probed. I looked up to see Molesworth in his nightshirt and cap in the doorway, mouth agape.

"Trepan," MacPherson barked, and I handed it to him, watched him screw it into Willie's head with all his might, grunting as he did so. Like he was a carpenter, a common laborer, not a physician. I heard a dull crack and a thin stream of blood shot out, spattering my face. I thought how warm it was, Willie's blood. Like goat's milk. Another hole, and another. At last MacPherson was satisfied, but I was certain we had killed the boy.

Willie now lay still and pale, his head wrapped in a turban of muslin. He remained in a profound sleep, but his breathing seemed less labored. Molesworth went back to his quarters and the marines resumed their positions. The doctor and I began to clean up the mess. We wiped the blood from our hands and put the instruments back in the box.

"In fifteen years of practice I have never had to do this before. Not on a living being," MacPherson admitted.

"Never?" I was incredulous. He had seemed so sure of himself.

He thought a moment, scratching his forehead. "Only once. For practice. On a cadaver."

"Then how could you do it?"

He shrugged. "The procedure itself is fairly straightforward. I knew the landmarks. Where to drill the holes." He dropped a bloody rag into the bucket at our feet.

I shook my head. "But what if . . ." I could not finish the question.

The doctor closed the instrument box with a snap. "Someone had to do it, and there was nae one else aboard this ship more qualified," he said, looking at me sternly. "'Twas the lad's only chance."

I looked at Willie, pale and unmoving. "Then he will recover? You have saved him?"

"I know not," the man who was now my husband admitted, wiping his brow with his sleeve. Suddenly he looked haggard. His big shoulders sagged. I might have embraced him then, or told him how courageous he had been, yet I did neither.

At eight bells—midnight—we bled the patient and changed his dressings, which were by now thoroughly saturated with blood. Captain Blake paced the quarterdeck above us; we could hear his footsteps and his nervous humming. Mr. Kent passed through the wardroom on his way up to take over the watch. He bent over the boy and whispered something.

MacPherson and I took turns watching Willie through the night. The ship's bell rang every thirty minutes, yet he slumbered on. When the doctor could no longer stay awake, he woke me up to sit beside the wardroom table where Willie lay. I sat in one of the dining chairs, my arms folded on the table beside his head, where I could hear the sound of his breathing and feel the roll of the ship. And I thought how one is never safe in this world, not for an instant. Though I might survive the moment, those around me whom I had come to care for could fall at any time.

I was at his side at first light. After the watch change I heard Dalton coming down the companionway. How odd I should recognize the sound of his footstep.

He appeared in the doorway of the wardroom. "How is he?"

"I don't know," I said. "Alive, at least." I touched the boy's forehead as I spoke, as if to convince myself.

"And ye? How are ye?"

"The same."

His eyes were dark and I could not read the look on his face. Perhaps I was too exhausted. Perhaps there was nothing to be read.

Young Willie woke shortly after sunrise, and though he had his wits about him, he could remember nothing of the preceding day, or indeed of the entire voyage. If he remembered anything of the crossing he could not recount it, but spoke only of his mother, his sister, and his father, who had died when he was five. Overnight he seemed to have aged; he was no longer a little boy, no longer the Young Willie we knew. MacPherson said he might suffer from fits the rest of his life; it was too early to know for sure. His uncle Molesworth decided Willie should return to his family in England under the care of Mrs. Blake rather than continue with him aboard His Majesty's frigate *Eos*.

"I'll not be responsible for any further mishaps," he declared. "If he wants his sea time, he'll have to gain it under someone else's command."

As MacPherson's wife, I too would be following Molesworth to his new command. Leaving Willie and the sailors I had come to think of as brothers. Leaving Mary. Leaving the bosun's mate.

After breakfast MacPherson and I both napped on the floor of our cabin. He was too exhausted for lovemaking, for which I was relieved. But the inevitable event hung like a ripe plum over my head.

We awoke a few hours later to the sounds of the men on the foredeck flaking the anchor cable, Blake's voice shouting instructions. I hurried up on deck to have a look. We had arrived at English Harbour on the island of Antigua, a dry, hilly scrap of an island. There were forts on either side of the entrance to the harbor and on nearby hilltops, the intended receivers of the remainder of our cargo.

The men lowered the boat and rowed Molesworth to shore; he was in a great hurry to see the frigate he was to command. They soon returned with the news that the ship *Eos* was hove down in the careenage for repairs, but the vessel was in much worse shape than he had been told. The hull and the rigging had been damaged in a skirmish with a French ship off the coast of Martinique. Molesworth was in a rage about the delay, but I welcomed it, for I had no desire to trade one floating prison for another. Confining and uncomfortable as she was, *Canopus* was my home.

Mary would not take her baby ashore because of the dangers of tropical fevers. The air was better out in the bay, MacPherson advised. It was the foul miasma emanating from the shallow waters and marshes, aggravated by the tropical heat, that caused disease. Out at the edge of the anchorage where we were, the air was cleaner and cooler. Then too someone had to keep an eye on Willie, for although he was much improved, he was not yet himself.

I was happy to do Mary's shopping for her so that I might have a look about town. After the noon meal MacPherson arranged for two of the sailors from the starboard watch to row us ashore. The sun was a dazzling white and the water a glassy aquamarine. I reached my hand over the gunwale and scooped up a palmful; it was warm as a baby's bath.

Just ahead of us a slaver's tender was unloading its human cargo; a dozen emaciated blacks stumbled out of the launch onto the sand, their ankles shackled as if they were wild animals. One woman among them cried out and was silenced by the harsh snap of a leather whip. I looked away in revulsion. Perhaps to divert my attention, MacPherson pointed out the naval dockyard under construction. Great pillars were being laid, above which he said a sail loft would be built, but I could not imagine it. All I saw were the black men stripped to their waists, lifting rocks from a great pile on the land and passing them along to three men standing knee-deep in water.

The waterfront was a clutter of warehouses, workshops, chandlers, forges, and taverns. Sailors and soldiers sauntered along the rutted street, loitering for a smoke wherever a scrap of shade could be found. Slaves rolled hogsheads of sugar along the dock to be hoisted into waiting tenders. Laundresses walked slowly in the heat, baskets slung on their hips or balanced on their turbaned heads. They smelled of sweat and spice; their imperturbable faces glistened. So many shades of dark skin, from blue-black to coffee and cream. The image of the cooper's apprentice on Barbados leaped to mind and I squirmed uncomfortably. Rupert Hatterby, my half brother!

We purchased the fruits and vegetables Mary wanted and arranged for them to be sent to the ship, then made our way back down to the shore. Across the bay in the careenage the frigate *Eos* lay on her side in the shallow, marshy water.

So this would be my new home, I thought, dismayed. But not for long, MacPherson had promised. I must keep after him to buy a house on Barbados. Likely he could only afford a cottage but someday we would find a way to buy back the estate. The afternoon sun was blinding and I had a headache from squinting. I swatted at an invisible insect humming near my left ear.

"My dear," MacPherson said, "I've booked us a room at the Commanders' Inn. So that we might have a proper honeymoon." He sounded quite pleased with himself.

I made no response but looked off across the bay.

"'Tis a good room," he added, as if to win me over. "The best in town."

"My head aches," I whined.

"I have a remedy for that," he said, almost gruffly, taking my hand in his own and leading me up the path toward the main street. I could see the rooftop of the inn, the clay tiles radiating heat in shimmering waves.

Might as well get it over with, I thought. *At least we can get out of this wicked sun.* MacPherson hummed a tune, which grated on my nerves.

Up the stairs, down the hall to the room at the end. He groped in his pocket for the key and fumbled with the lock, breathing hard. It was the first time I'd ever seen his hands shake. Last night, drilling into Willie's skull, they had been far steadier.

Once inside the dark room, shades and shutters drawn to keep out the sun, he slowly undressed me and carried me to the bed. I closed my eyes as he undressed, squeezed them tight. I would remain aloof and cold to his touch; I was determined not to like it.

But the man slowly wore away at me with his touches, his kisses, his whispered endearments. Wore away at my aversion and embarrassment until I began to feel pleasure at his touch, and I gasped his name. *Aeneas!* I opened my eyes and saw him shaking with emotion, his blue eyes moist with gratitude. And I hugged the big man to me, felt his solid weight press me down into the mattress.

He kissed my ear and murmured, "I love ye, lass."

"Aeneas, you're a good man," I whispered back.

"I hope ye'll come to love me someday."

"Someday, yes."

"And our babies, I hope they'll have your green eyes," he said playfully.

What he didn't know was that Mary had given me a sponge soaked in vinegar water, and I had used it so that I would not conceive.

I shrugged. "We'll see. Though I hope it's a while before any children come along. I'm not quite ready for all of that."

He was quiet for a moment. "Then I shall take precautions," he said, touching the tip of my nose. "Ye must forgive me for being in a hurry. I forget how young ye are, my lovely bride."

His breathing slowed, then deepened. I realized he was falling asleep.

I grew up with the luxury of sleeping alone. In boarding school, although we shared rooms each girl had her very own bed. This sleeping together would take some getting used to. Not so much the sex act as the tossing and turning afterward. For though Aeneas had been a leisurely and most considerate lover, he fell to slumber immediately, throwing his great hairy arm across me like a tree limb. His body produced so much heat I didn't know how I should ever sleep. I shoved him over and claimed my territory, but on his back he snored.

★ ★ ★

In the morning he brought me coffee from the kitchen and a bouquet of fresh flowers. "I hope your headache is much improved," he said with perfect seriousness, though his blue eyes danced mischievously.

That night I offered to stay aboard ship with the baby while the Blakes attended a dinner party at one of the plantations. Young Willie required supervision as well. He had survived his trepanning and seemed much improved, yet his memory had not returned and he could not be trusted to look after himself. Molesworth invited Aeneas to dine with a visiting admiral, which Aeneas was keen to do.

Except for a skeleton crew, most of the sailors were ashore spending their money in the taverns and brothels. They had spent the last two days unloading gunpowder and loading barrels of raw sugar and would be weighing anchor in the morning, weather permitting. Having fulfilled the contract with the navy, *Canopus* would soon be England bound. I was glad to have the ship nearly to myself.

When the babe and the boy were both asleep, I dressed in my trousers and climbed to the fighting top to enjoy the view. As I half hoped, the bosun's mate saw me and followed, taking the ratlines two at a time and pulling himself up and over the futtocks in an easy, elegant way. I wanted to say good-bye to Dalton in private, but I was unprepared for the emotion I felt upon being on the fighting top with him once again.

"Good evening, Mrs. MacPherson." His voice was reserved.

"Hello, Dalton."

I sat on the platform and he towered over me, his black-streaked arms folded across his chest. "I thought your sky-larking days would be up," he said.

I felt a flash of annoyance. "And why should that be?"

He shrugged. "None of my business. But had I a wife, I would keep her better occupied at night."

I flushed. "You are right—it is none of your business. And how you boast! You sailors think highly of yourselves, don't you?"

His laugh was conciliatory. "Come on up," he said, reaching for the shrouds, climbing up, and stepping out on the main tops'l yard above my head. He then sat down on the spar, straddling it with his long legs. "The weather's fine up here."

I hurried to follow him.

"Just because I am married doesn't mean I've become a bird in a cage," I panted, hoisting myself onto the tops'l yard and swinging one leg on either side, facing Dalton. The furled sail made a wide and comfortable cushion, yet I squeezed my thighs and clutched a gasket, for heights still made me giddy.

"Ye look like ye're riding to hounds," he taunted, his own legs dangling loosely. The smell of tobacco drifted toward me as he pulled out his pouch and filled his pipe.

I ignored the jest. "A woman has a right to a bit of freedom, don't you think?" I demanded.

He said nothing, sucking thoughtfully on the stem of his pipe.

"And you, Dalton. Are you certain you don't keep a wife somewhere?"

"Nae, Princess, not I." In the starlight I could see a flicker of a wistful smile cross his face. "A wife is but a worry. I too like my freedom."

Suddenly the bantering ground to a halt. He finished his pipe in silence and knocked the embers out, and we watched them take off on the breeze. Those dark eyes of his were as unreadable as ever.

"I am quitting the ship," he said.

I clenched the gasket as if I were falling. "What will you do?" A pebble formed in my throat; I tried to swallow it.

"Join the navy."

"Why?"

"The war. Why else?"

"And what do you care about a stupid, senseless war?"

"I care not a damn. But here on this ship I can never rise higher than bosun's mate, not with the shipmaster's nephew as my boss. And then there are the prizes. On a naval ship every seaman gets his share of a captured vessel."

It seemed he was justifying himself to me. "If I don't join up," he said, "I'll be pressed into service. Grabbed out of some tavern or off this ship, even, for the Royal Navy has that right. But if I volunteer I can have some choice of vessels. I'll be paid a sign-on bonus."

I felt a wave of hope. "Then why don't you sign on with Molesworth's frigate?"

He turned to look at me, his face suddenly open, as I had never before seen it. "Would ye like that, Princess?"

I could not look into that window, his face. Easier to look down to the deck so far below. "I have gotten rather used to having you around," I said lamely.

We fell silent and the sound of a slapping halyard diverted Dalton's attention.

"I must go see to that." And he was gone.

By daybreak the wind was up and *Canopus* pulled on her anchor as if anxious to go. On deck the men were readying the windlass that would lift the anchor free of the sands that held it. Molesworth and his company had quit the ship last night, leaving only Aeneas and me to say our goodbyes. Those remaining had finished their business in Antigua and were thinking only of the blue road home.

After so many weeks of longing to be free of the ship, I now found it hard to leave her. I had not planned on missing these people, these rough sailors, this confining old boat. I had not anticipated this ache I now felt. My few belongings were bundled up and sitting on deck. My husband was impatient to leave, yet I lingered below, walking through the vessel one last time as if I might have forgotten something.

The great cabin that Molesworth and his retinue had occupied was once again Mary's dining room; she had already set the table for the midday meal. Behind the table I saw Young Willie staring out the open stern port.

"I've come to say good-bye, Willie."

"William," he said, still staring out the window. "My name is William Young."

"Yes. Well. I shall miss you, William." I walked closer, squeezed his shoulder. Only then did he turn and face me, and I was torn by the empty look I saw.

"Thank you," he said solemnly.

"Do you remember me?" I asked. "Do you know my name?"

He thought for a moment, shut his eyes, then opened them again. "Your name is Patricia," he said flatly.

I wanted to say, *Don't you remember us romping in the rigging? The way you used to drop oakum on me? Don't you remember finding me in the bosun's locker, and the storm, and the French frigate we outsmarted?*

Yet I said none of that. "Have a good voyage back to England, William Young." It was hard to speak past the knot in my throat. "Don't give Mrs. Blake any trouble. Take care of the cats and the goat for me."

He cocked his head and a light flickered in his eyes as if he were just now seeing me. "You remind me of my sister," he said. "My sister wants to marry Mr. Longley."

I had to turn my head to hide the tears that blurred my eyes. The little boy called Young Willie was gone and I mourned him, yet there was nothing to do. The world kept pushing us on.

I started to go, stopped, and bent down to kiss the top of his head. Smelled his little-boy smell for the last time. He touched the spot where I had kissed him curiously, as if he might find something there, stuck to his hair.

Up on deck the others were waiting to bid us farewell. Mr. Kent tipped his hat, his face as grave as ever, and bade us adieu. Henry Blake clapped MacPherson's hand, then took mine with a slight bow, as if he meant to kiss it, but didn't. The sailors stood by, hands shoved in their pockets, not knowing how to say good-bye to me now that I was no longer one of them. Captain Blake and MacPherson shook hands, clapped one another on the back. Mary held her little Johnny and I leaned to kiss the top of his bonnet.

"I shall miss you, Patricia," Mary said, wiping my tear-streaked face with a corner of her apron.

"You have saved me from ruin." I tried to smile, a crooked contortion. "I shall be forever indebted to you and Mr. Blake."

I realized only then that this part of my life was over. Our afternoon tea talks, her motherly advice, the comfort of her hands brushing my hair were never to be experienced again. I touched her cheek with my lips; how soft it was.

FIVE

Aeneas and I kept our room at the Commanders' Inn; the frigate *Eos*, our new assignment, was still on her side in the careenage. All work had come to a halt for lack of wood. A shipment of timber from the northern colonies was over-due and Molesworth feared the French had captured it. He spent his afternoons at the waterfront, pacing, fuming, speculating, and questioning every passing officer. Mean-while, the shipwright and his mates, more accustomed to the inevitable delays of island living, waited patiently in the dark taverns of English Harbour.

I did not like it there, although our rented room seemed spacious compared to the cramped cabin we would un-doubtedly have on board ship. We took our meals in the dining room downstairs with the other lodgers, mostly seafarers, factors, and disreputable women. I missed Mary Blake sorely.

Every morning we reported to Lieutenant Molesworth, who had taken lodging in the officers' quarters not far from the inn. Although it was only a short walk to Molesworth's lodging, not half a mile, every step seemed a brutal punishment in the bright heat of an Antiguan morning. Aeneas did not want to spend the money on sedan chairs for us; neither would Molesworth or the navy pay for them.

"Walking is good for the constitution," he insisted, his face red and perspiring. "But someday when we're settled ye shall have your riding horse and the best saddle money can buy, I promise ye."

After seeing to Molesworth's needs we would breakfast at the inn and seek shelter in the shade during the heat of the day.

"I will be glad when this tour of duty is finished," my husband confided one morning over coffee and muffins. He unbuttoned his collar, as if to better breathe. "Lieutenant Molesworth is by far the most difficult patient I have ever attended, and yet I am not at liberty to drop him. At least when we are back aboard ship I shall have the sailors to treat. They respect my opinion and generally follow my advice."

I shrugged. "Why argue with him? Give him what he wants. Wasn't it you who told me what a man believes is often the best medicine?"

"Only to a point," Aeneas said, drizzling molasses on his muffin. He had developed a fondness for the sweet black syrup. "Some animals don't know when to stop eating and will eat until they burst. Sometimes men are the same way.

With food, with drink, with opium. With women." He chewed his muffin thoughtfully, his brows knitted in concern. "I believe our lieutenant has an unnatural dependence on medical treatments."

Yet I cared not a whit what troubled Molesworth; I had worries of my own. Here I was on a strange island where I had no chance of recovering what was rightly mine. Although Antigua was less than two hundred miles from Barbados, it was downwind. To go directly to Barbados from Antigua was difficult and time-consuming, for ships can't sail into the wind. To get back to my plantation I might have to return to England by the customary sailing route, following the prevailing winds and currents. Here on Antigua I was about as far away from Barbados as I could be. Yet there was nothing to do but wait.

I spent the afternoons sitting under the palm in the courtyard, reading medical books. This pleased my husband, and he "promoted" me to surgeon's mate. Of course it was just between husband and wife, for the navy would never acknowledge a female, much less pay her—though there were always stories told about girls disguised as men and serving aboard ships. Most of these tales involved a love-struck lass who went to sea to find her long-lost sweetheart, but I did not believe them for a moment. Or rather, I believed the stories themselves but not the motivation. More likely women dressed as men and went to sea not for love but for want of a regular meal and a place to sleep. Or perhaps they were tired of living a life confined by skirts and society's demands.

Aeneas seemed unperturbed by the waiting. He spent the better part of each day compiling his copious notes into a book. He believed physicians placed too much emphasis on convention rather than results. He believed in keeping accurate records; he believed in sharp observation. Molesworth chastised him for his unorthodox practices.

"The trouble with you, MacPherson," the lieutenant said, "is you think too much. Just bleed me, purge me, and give me Peruvian bark."

"I think," Aeneas retorted, "because God gave me a brain for it. And eyes to see."

Yet in the end Molesworth usually had his way, though it became harder and harder to find a willing vein. Even when I did, the blood dripped rather than flowed. It looked to me like rose-colored water.

At the end of the day when the sun hung low in the sky we would walk out to Berkeley's fort on the hillock at the mouth of the harbor. Here we had a fine view of the other hilltop forts surrounding the settlement, the whole harbor, and the sea where the sun seemed to sink, coloring both sky and water exquisite shades of pink and orange. The doctor took to bringing his pipes along on these sunset walks. After the bugler played the evening tattoo, Aeneas answered with an old Highland tune so mournful I always had to wipe away the tears, for it reminded me of our days aboard *Canopus* when he piped the sun down.

In the evening we played backgammon but I was a poor opponent, for I did not care if I won or lost. Sometimes Aeneas went to the tavern for a pint of ale after dinner, but he never stayed away long. Truth be told, I was glad for his company; indeed, I had no other.

★   ★   ★

One evening, a fortnight after *Canopus* had left, we were dining alfresco at a table in the inn's courtyard. The air was thick with humidity from an afternoon shower, and although there was a slight breeze, it did little to cool us. The cayenne in the pepper pot stew brought beads of perspiration to our foreheads.

"I saw your friend Dalton this afternoon," Aeneas said, pulling out his handkerchief and wiping his brow.

I ignored the remark and kept on eating, yet the bit of meat in my mouth refused to be swallowed.

Aeneas looked at me until I was forced to meet his eyes. "He told me to tell ye farewell."

"Farewell?" I repeated.

"He is leaving at daybreak, if the winds hold."

I reached for my wine, hoping Aeneas would not notice my shaking hand. "That's curious. I thought he had signed on to Molesworth's frigate."

The look of victory on my husband's face was unmistakable.

"It appears your bosun's mate signed on to the brig called *Riegel*, anchored out at the harbor mouth. I promised to pass along his fare-thee-well."

I set my glass down, splashing a few drops onto the white damask tablecloth. "Why?" I said as nonchalantly as I could manage. "I thought . . ." The words stuck in my gorge.

"Perhaps he was offered a sign-on bonus or a bosun's ticket." Aeneas tore a piece of bread and dipped it in his stew. "In any case, the young man saw an opportunity and seized it. The *Riegel* is a fast ship; she'll likely see some action somewhere and he'll make the best of it. He'll rise as far as a man of his station can, I'll wager."

"Then I wish him well," I said as evenly as I could. Indeed, why should I care? I wondered. The bosun's mate could not help me regain what was mine. He was nothing but a foolish indiscretion, a shipboard dalliance best forgotten. But although I put Dalton straight out of my mind, I no longer had an appetite. I blamed it on the heat.

SIX

The rains came early that year. Storm after storm passed through, followed always by intense heat. Walking to the officers' quarters one morning, we were caught in a squall and drenched to the bone.

Molesworth bid us to enter his sparsely furnished room. He was in full dress, pacing the floor, some missive in hand. Tibbs gathered up his breakfast tray and whisked past us on his way downstairs to the dining room.

"Don't just stand there dripping like a pair of drowned rats. Let's get to work, MacPherson; I wish to be bled of half a pint. And then I want you to see if there is another doctor on this godforsaken rock who can advise you as to a more effective prophylactic against the tropical diseases. I've read about an herbal concoction of some sort that prevents the ague."

"'Tis only three days since we last bled you," Aeneas said. "And ye are taking the Peruvian bark daily."

"Remove half a pint. I'll be the better for it." Molesworth sat down on his neatly made bed and rolled up his left sleeve.

"By God, sir, I will not be dictated to as if I were a cabin boy," Aeneas said. "Ye've been bled and purged and taken the bark until ye scarce have humors left in your body. If sickness befalls ye, God forbid, there's nothing left to be done, our ammunition has been spent. We've depleted the magazine trying to scare off the enemy, do ye understand?"

"My good doctor," Molesworth said, folding his hands in his lap and wiggling his long white fingers impatiently. His nail beds were dusky. "Might I remind you of your duty? We're taking these precautions to keep my humors in perfect balance so that I won't succumb to this dreadful heat."

"Look at yourself, man!" Aeneas boomed. "Ye have nae meat on your bones, your tic has worsened, and your gums are nearly as white as your skin. My observations have shown—"

"You would do well," Molesworth interrupted, "to stick to the teachings of the renowned physicians than to go off willy-nilly on your own. Really now, MacPherson, of what possible value are your simple observations?"

I waited for Aeneas to explode, but he did not. "My simple observations might keep ye healthy if ye would listen to a little common sense," he said evenly. "Ye need to build up your strength and fortify your constitution, for that's the best defense against disease."

Molesworth laughed. "And who do you think you are, a

simple Scotsman from the hills, to go against the wisdom of Hippocrates and his ilk? As to my strength, I'm certain to regain it when I am at last standing on the quarterdeck of the ship I've been assigned to command."

There was an uneasy pause while both men seemed to search for a resolution to their confrontation. The clock on his secretary ticked loudly and much too slowly, it seemed to me, and my wet clothing clung to me most uncomfortably.

"As you wish," Molesworth said at last, standing up and holding his arm out for me to button his sleeve. As if I were his manservant! Yet I did so, for Tibbs had left the room.

Molesworth walked to the window, opened the shutters, and looked out to sea, squinting against the bright morning light. "I will forgo your services for a week."

Aeneas cleared his throat in a conciliatory fashion. "In my opinion, Lieutenant, ye should only be bled again if symptoms of disease arise. But a week is a start and I think ye will see your color and strength improve. Shall I continue to call on ye every morning?"

"That won't be necessary." Seeing no ships on the horizon, Molesworth turned back to face us. "If I require you before we set sail, I shall call for you. Go." He waved his hand as if we were mosquitoes. "Go on. Enjoy your holiday. Tour the countryside." His voice rose, trembling precariously like a child climbing a wobbly ladder. I wondered about his sanity. Was he losing his mind in this heat?

"See the Negroes sweating and toiling in the glorious green cane fields," he continued in a grandiose fashion. "See the sailors and soldiers drinking themselves stupid in the rum shops. See the gentlemen wasting their money at the brothels and game tables." He stopped, panting for breath, his fine nostrils flaring. "Meanwhile"—I sensed he had climbed to the top rung and was ready to topple—"I am trapped here waiting—waiting—waiting for my ship to be ready! Can't you understand? It is this infernal waiting that is killing me!"

"I understand." Though Aeneas's voice was steady, the veins in his neck were purple and bulging. "My regards, sir." He reached for the doorknob just as Tibbs returned.

"Tibbs, see that Lieutenant Molesworth eats properly. At least two servings of meat and three servings of vegetables every day. And a glass of wine every evening. Come for me if he requests my services."

With that we took our leave, and I was glad to be putting the disagreeable Molesworth out of sight and mind for an entire week.

Yet the week stretched long, for there was nothing for me to do but read medical books and gather the dirty clothes for the laundress. My husband was absorbed with his writing. I wished I were at sea again, for at sea everything was just beyond the horizon and anything seemed possible. Setting foot on land seemed to have solidified my fate into a small, hard stone.

I seized every opportunity to go on an errand, anything to keep from sitting too long in one place. I perused the shops, looking for necessaries. What I really wanted was a new pair of trousers, though I had not had occasion to wear pants since *Canopus* had taken her leave. Yet I kept the outfit Dalton had given me, as he had never asked for it back.

One night after a slow game of backgammon (I lost again), Aeneas went out for a pint, and perhaps to challenge a worthier opponent than I. As soon as he was gone, I became restless and irritable. I paced the plank floor and threw myself dramatically onto the bed. From the open window I could hear drunken voices and laughter below in the street. What fun everyone else seemed to be having! I was curious to go out myself and see what all the merriment was about, but for a woman to go out alone at night was unthinkable. What did Aeneas expect me to do, darn his stockings? Read the pharmacopoeia?

Impulsively, I opened the top dresser drawer, pulled out the bundle tucked way in the back, and changed my clothes. I braided my hair into a fat queue at the nape of my neck and pulled my cap on, adjusting it rakishly. When I looked in the mirror, a gawky freckled lad looked back.

Though I had no shoes such as a sailor might wear ashore, I put on my brocade slippers and hoped no one would notice in the dark. Dug my pin money out of my purse and down the back stairs I bounded with no intent but to glide through the street, unnoticed, at night. To see who was abroad, to stretch my legs and walk away the time.

I started down the rutted street, dodging piles of horse manure and muddy puddles. The night was filled with disembodied voices ricocheting like billiard balls in the darkness. There were no street lamps here, only the flickering tallows from public houses. Damp clouds obscured the moon.

Over at the careenage the men were still working on the frigate, far into the night, the ring of their hammers carrying across the water. Aeneas had said she would be ready to sail in a few days, yet I had noticed that when it came to ships all estimates were too optimistic.

I headed for the nearest public house. A group of soldiers stumbled past me; one of them nearly knocked me over.

"Look out there, you scurvy little sea dog! Are you looking for a fight?"

His companions pulled him away. "Don't pay him any mind, lad, he's had a bit much to drink." They lurched on, the three of them, laughing and singing a ribald song.

I was thrilled and frightened at once, for my disguise had worked; those soldiers had mistaken me for a sailor! Why, this was almost as much fun as a masquerade ball! With aplomb, I continued toward the Spouting Whale Tavern, fingering the single coin in my pocket, my housekeeping money for the week. Meant for the laundress and the water boy, but a drink of beer sounded so much better.

In the dim tavern light a preponderance of red coats and tricorn hats caught my eye; military men, mostly. The room was humming with talk. No one looked twice at me, except the keeper of the bar.

"Are you waiting for your master?" the burly Portuguese said to me, placing two glasses of brandy on the bar for the gentlemen beside me.

I nodded, afraid to speak lest I reveal myself.

"Then deliver your message and don't take up space at my bar," he growled.

I sidled away through the crowded room, wedging my way between tables where men dealt cards and puffed on their pipes, slipping past groups of officers who stood—

glass in one hand, the other free for gesticulating—talking promotions and prizes.

Just then I saw my husband sitting at a table in the corner playing backgammon. He glanced up, looked right at me; my breath stuck in my chest. Heart pounding, I slouched toward the door, where I paused to look back. Aeneas was once again studying the board in front of him, lost in that fierce concentration of his. I returned to the street, relieved he hadn't recognized me.

The next tavern was the Pelican's Roost. I entered, inching my way through the crowd. On my right a group of merchants discussed the price of molasses. On my left a sawyer and a shipwright complained about the scarcity of lumber. My eyes scanned the room and I spied Simmons, Molesworth's clerk, at the far end of the bar, drinking alone. Fearful he'd recognize me, I ducked out.

I was about to return to our room but heard the jagged squawks of a poorly played fiddle and thought of Earnshaw, that cantankerous old goat. I found myself following the sound to its source—a lively grog shop at the far edge of the waterfront. Here there were no liveries, cabs, or chairmen loitering outside, waiting to drive some gentleman home. Just two sleeping mongrels that I nearly tripped over just outside the door.

The fiddler was a scrawny man with an ill-fitting wig askew on his head. He sat on a chair just inside the doorway, cheerfully sawing away.

"Ahoy, Jack! Come in, don't be a stranger," he said in the loose, loud voice of a drinking man.

I slipped past him into the candlelit room. The floor beneath my feet was packed dirt; the chairs were empty barrels, all occupied. The place reeked of rum and sweat. I joined the men leaning against the bar and casually ordered a beer from the tall, dark-skinned bartender wearing a striped turban.

"Just off the boat?" she asked, placing a pint-sized pewter mug in front of me. High cheekbones, full lips. Her voice was a cat's purr. "Merchantman?"

I nodded, lifting the mug to my mouth and sipping the froth.

"You got fever on your ship?"

I shook my head.

She leaned closer and I saw her eyes were dark brown and shining. "You clean?"

"Clean?" I said indignantly. "Of course I'm clean. Clean as the rest of these ruffians."

She smiled, fingering a gold earring that protruded from beneath the edge of the turban. "You like a woman tonight?"

I nearly choked. Wiped my mouth with my sleeve. "No."

"Miss your mama, sonny? Older woman can comfort you. Can hug and kiss you. Teach you about love."

"No!" I looked wildly around for a way out.

"Then maybe you want a young girl? One your own age?"

I squirmed, shook my head, my face bright red. "No girls at all."

"Why?" She looked at me intently. "No money?"

"That's right," I said, grasping on to the excuse. "No money."

"I could give you credit," she said in her soft, throaty

way. Leaning so close I thought she was going to kiss me, she lowered her eyelids and licked her full lips. "If you like."

"Watch out for her, boy; she's a crimp," a scruffy man behind me said with a laugh. "She'll get you in debt, then she'll sell you to the next press gang that comes looking for sailors to man His Majesty's warships." He squeezed up to the bar next to me and put a copper on the counter. "Say, Aggie, give me another tot of rum and leave this poor lad alone. He's big for his age but he's years away from shaving, can't you see? Now me, I'm full grown and have a pocketful of coin. Come on over here and wag your sweet tongue at me, Aggie lamb."

I left my half-finished beer on the bar and bolted, squeezing past the fiddler, jumping over the sleeping dogs, and running through the rutted street toward home.

I had no sooner returned to our room, rolled my seaman's clothes into a bundle, and stuffed them in the drawer when I heard Aeneas mounting the creaky wooden staircase; I knew his heavy, deliberate step. Quickly I pulled my nightshift over my head, jumped into bed, pulled the covers up to my chin, and turned my face to the wall. I feigned sleep. But the more I tried to slow my breathing the faster it came and my eyelids fluttered like moths.

Aeneas undressed in the dark and eased himself into bed beside me. The mattress sagged under his weight and the ropes squeaked. He must have misread my heavy breathing as desire, for he was aroused and reached for me, and I returned his embrace. In the darkness I could not see his wrinkled face, his faded, thinning hair. In the darkness we were both young.

*　　*　　*

I awoke to a pounding at the door. Though no light came through the shutters I could hear carts rolling in the street below. Nearly dawn. I turned over and buried my head in the pillow.

"Who is there?" Aeneas bellowed.

"Tibbs, sir."

"Bloody hell, man, do ye know what time it is?"

"Lieutenant Molesworth is ill, sir."

"Ill? How so?"

"I don't know but he's terribly ill. A raging fever. He's quite out of his head."

Aeneas rolled over, stumbled out of bed, and threw open the door, though he had not a stitch on. "Return to him, stay with him, I'll be there straightaway."

"Are ye awake, Mrs. MacPherson?" he said to me. "Rise and dress, for we have our work cut out for us."

SEVEN

Molesworth was stretched across the bed in his nightshirt, his sheets tangled in a knot at the foot. The left side of his face was engaged in a fusillade of rapid winking and erratic twitching. His eyes were yellow.

Aeneas, undaunted, rolled up his sleeves and went to work. "Pulse is rapid and thready," he said, picking up the lieutenant's wrist. "Skin: hot, dry, jaundiced. Please make a note of that, Mrs. MacPherson."

I nodded, though I had brought nothing to write on.

"Dose him with calomel," the doctor continued, "and bleed him half a pint. Cover him so that he might sweat it out."

Aeneas walked toward the door, motioning me to follow.

"I am off to the fort to see if this has befallen the soldiers as well," he said. "I must speak with the garrison surgeon; we may need to improvise a hospital."

"But what is it?" I whispered. "What is wrong with him?"

Aeneas was not one to mince words. His face was brutally honest. "Yellow fever," he said.

I winced. "Are you certain?"

"Aye, lass. I have seen it before."

I was seized with panic. Of all the tropical diseases, the one called yellow fever was the most feared. It came on swiftly, caused horrible suffering. It was said that more than half of those who came down with a bad case of yellow fever didn't survive and that once a victim began to vomit the black bile, he might as well call the undertaker.

"What shall we do, sir?" I said.

"Ye have your instructions. Bleed him, dose him, diaphorese him. Keep the window wide open and wash everything in sight with vinegar water." He reached for the doorknob. "Meanwhile, I must go to the fort."

"Don't go!" I grabbed his arm. "Please don't leave me alone with him."

"Ye're not alone; ye have Tibbs." He nodded toward the servant who cowered in the corner of the room.

"But what if he—" I could not say the word.

Aeneas said it for me. "What if he dies?" His eyes hardened. "Then we'll see that he has a proper Englishman's burial."

"No!" I clutched his sleeve in both hands. "I cannot stay here!"

The doctor's face was imperturbable. "Ye can," he said calmly. "I won't be gone but a few hours. Send Tibbs to fetch me if his condition changes." He kissed my forehead, pried my fingers off his arm, and calmly left the room. I ran to the window and watched him lumber along toward Fort Barclay.

"Aeneas!"

He heard me, paused, and looked up to see what it was I wanted.

"I am not cut out for this," I cried.

"Ye must rise to the occasion, lass," he said, continuing on.

"Damn you," I swore, stamping my foot. "I won't stay here," I called out after him. "I am going back to the inn this very minute. How can you expect me to do this?" But Aeneas did not hear me and continued on his way.

Yet I did stay. Angry and afraid, still I could not bring myself to leave Molesworth in his condition. With shaking hands I bled his vein as Aeneas had instructed, then I measured out the calomel and fed it to him from a spoon. He could not hold a cup in his hands; he could not even sit up. Flat on his back, the lieutenant choked on nearly every spoonful, turning red in the face. I rolled him over and pounded on his back until he gasped a great clean breath and tried to tell me something, but could not form the words.

As I leaned over the sick man, it occurred to me that I was breathing the tainted air that surrounded him. I imagined I could smell the poisonous effluvia, began to believe I was ill. Was I not perspiring and nauseated?

"Tibbs, feel my forehead," I commanded, but he shrunk away, hands clasped behind his back.

In a flurry of fear I doused everything with vinegar

until the acrid scent filled my head. Then, having nothing else to do, I paced the room.

The sun climbed in the sky. Simmons showed up to work, but seeing his employer in bed and gravely ill, he backed out the door and fled down the stairs in spite of my pleading.

I still had Tibbs but he was more an annoyance than a comfort to me, for he was terrified and would not come close to the sick man. Instead he remained at the far side of the room, busying himself with mindless tasks and humming nervously all the while, a repetitive little ditty. Exasperated, I sent him to fetch the laundress to wash the soiled bedding.

A squall approached the island, bringing gusts of cool wind with it. The air was greatly refreshing but played havoc with the papers on Molesworth's secretary, and not wanting to close the window, I shuffled through sheaves of correspondence and newspapers in search of a paperweight.

A recent copy of the *Barbados Gazette* caught my eye; I glanced down the list of shipping arrivals, scanned the death notices. The man's name seemed to reach out off the page and shout at me: *William Smith of the former Hatterby Plantation, St. Lucy's Parish* . . . Eagerly I snatched the paper and read the brief article. It was he, the man who bought my father's estate! Smith was dead of an apoplectic fit, just last week; he had left no heirs but his wife.

Even before I came to the end of the notice a great wave of hope rose up from within me. This was the opportunity I needed. My thoughts raced ahead to the land that was rightfully mine.

The sound of Molesworth retching brought me back to the unpleasant moment at hand. He rolled over and heaved onto the floor a great quantity of stinking black vomit, after which he collapsed, his head hanging over the side of the bed, his greasy pigtail dangling limply alongside his ear.

"Help me," he moaned. "Please."

I rolled him over and wiped his mouth with my kerchief. His eyes fluttered open and I gasped, for they were not just yellow, but shot with red. Blood began to drip from his nose and I made a dab at that with my kerchief. Then I saw the blood seeping through the bandage on his arm where I had bled him, nearly an hour ago. Fresh blood, it was, and seeping through rapidly. I bound his arm with a fresh strip of muslin, washed his face, and wondered how best to clean up the puddle of black vomit congealing on the floorboards.

At last Aeneas returned, but with alarming news. Nearly half the soldiers stationed at Fort Barclay had the yellow fever, or "yellow jack," as they called it; seven men and a child had died overnight.

"God help them," he said, removing his hat and wiping his face with his kerchief. "The army surgeon is a drunken, craven crackpot who does nothing for his men, but hides in the taverns drinking himself to oblivion. I must enlist nurses and gravediggers. I must go find a slave contractor and hire as many Negroes as I can. With crop time approaching there may not be many. . . ." He shook his head, overwhelmed.

"Can you get a nurse for Lieutenant Molesworth too?" I pleaded.

He looked at me as if I were daft. "I don't believe ye

understand the situation, my dear. Any nurses I can obtain will be needed at the fort. Besides," he whispered, leaning close to my ear, "our lieutenant may not survive the night."

A feeling of doom pressed down upon me. Was there nothing to be done?

When Tibbs finally returned, he was without a laundress; he had found no one willing to wash the sick man's bedding for fear of contagion. And so it was I who carried it down to the shore and washed it myself, rinsed it in a bucket of rainwater from the cistern, and hung it to dry in the midday sun. Meanwhile, Aeneas went to procure his nurses and gravediggers. Afterward, we took our dinner back at the inn: steaming calabashes of callaloo soup and johnnycake.

"Eat hearty, lass; we will both need our strength in the days to come," Aeneas warned.

He did not have to tell me to eat heartily, for I was famished. But I didn't want to think of the sick men and the hard work ahead. Instead my thoughts raced to Barbados. I told Aeneas of William Smith's death notice in the *Barbados Gazette*.

Though he appeared to look at me, my husband's eyes were far off and I knew his mind was busy with other matters. "Aye, and many more will surely die before this fever burns itself out," he said absently.

"I'm not talking about the fever," I said, stirring my soup impatiently. "It's that squatter Smith I'm speaking of—the man who claimed to have bought my father's plantation. He died just last week, of apoplexy, and left no heirs but his wife." I brought a spoonful of soup to my mouth and blew on it. "And so I thought I might pursue the matter. Perhaps challenge the will, file a claim—"

I paused midsentence, for Aeneas was glowering at me.

"What in God's name are ye talking about?" He smacked the table with the palm of his hand and I felt as if he had slapped my face. "England is at war, lass! Men are dying in the North Atlantic, in the Mediterranean, in Calcutta. Right here among us, men, women, and children are dying of fever—why, our very own lives are at risk. And ye talk of a childhood promise. Dear wife, ye have nae claim to that property, we have been through all that. The plantation is but a vagary, a childhood chimera, and ye would do well to forget it!"

I bowed my head but I was not abashed, I was seething with resentment.

"Now, then, ye must stay with the lieutenant this evening, for no one should die alone. Keep him comfortable, whatever it takes. I must organize a military field hospital, for there are nae facilities here and we have only seen the beginning of this outbreak. I have to see the governor; I have to write the admiral in Jamaica." He pulled his notebook and pencil out of his pocket and scribbled something. "We'll need surgeons, apothecaries, nurses, laundresses. We'll need medicines, linens . . ." His scowl disappeared as he organized the details of his mission.

I kept a most unwilling deathwatch. Sitting at Young Willie's bedside had been the closest I had ever been to the great mystery, and I wanted no part of it. Every breath Molesworth took I feared would be his last—the suspense was intolerable. I did not like Lieutenant Molesworth, but I did not wish him dead and I most certainly did not want to watch him die. With each labored breath I hoped more fervently for his life.

The hours passed slowly and I was beside myself for want of something to do. I took a leaf of paper from the desk and wrote a letter to the registrar of wills in Bridgetown, stating my claim to the Hatterby estate. I signed my name as Patricia MacPherson, wife of Dr. Aeneas MacPherson of the frigate *Eos,* English Harbour, Antigua. Though I knew my husband would be furious, I felt I had nothing to lose. Then I sent Tibbs off to post it, for there was a packet leaving in the morning.

"Happy to, Mrs. MacPherson," he said, pocketing the letter. "Then, if you don't mind, I'll be returning to my own lodging, seeing as you're here to stay with the lieutenant." His eyes darted from the sickbed to the door.

"But I do mind, Tibbs," I protested.

"Sorry, missus, but I am worn to the bone," the man said, not meeting my eyes. "I stayed with him last night and didn't get a wink o' sleep."

"So you are abandoning me?"

Tibbs hung his head and walked to the door. "I'll return at first light tomorrow," he said.

"Wait! Where can I find you, should I need you?"

"I have a bed in the attic above the pitch and tar store." With that he closed the door behind him and bolted down the stairs.

Now I was alone with the dying man. I lit as many candles as I could find, yet still it was not enough. I longed for daylight. Was it true most people drew their last breath in the wee hours? Was it true the heart sometimes continued to quiver and thump erratically even after the last expiration?

I don't believe the lieutenant even knew I was there, yet I spoke to him as if he did, more for my benefit than his; it calmed me to hear my own voice. I chattered on, mostly about the plantation and how someday I would be mistress and hold parties and masquerades. I would own a stable of fine horses—racehorses. My father used to dabble in racing; it was quite fashionable in Bridgetown.

But before long I had talked myself out, my fantasies spent. I looked out the window to see what stars had risen, but no stars could be seen. Only the lanterns on the ships at anchor and their reflections, sparkling trails on the black water.

Molesworth moaned, startling me. I turned from the window.

"Sir? What is it?"

He looked at me most lucidly, though his eyes were yellow and streaked with blood.

"A drink of water?" I asked.

He shook his head and opened his mouth but only a groan came forth.

"The chamber pot?" I desperately wished Tibbs would return.

Molesworth licked his thin, parched lips. "Too late," he panted, closing his eyes from exhaustion.

And then I smelled it, worse than the vomit, a great pond of liquid black stool. Since Tibbs was gone I would have to clean it myself, for the stench was unbearable—yet I was not certain how to go about cleaning up such a mess.

What I would have given for one servant, one chamber-maid, one capable nurse!

I considered going out to find Tibbs—he was either at his lodging or, more likely, at the Pelican's Roost—but I did not want to leave Molesworth unattended. And so I summoned all my willpower and cleaned him myself.

When I was done I scrubbed everything in sight with vinegar water and dabbed clove oil from the medicine chest under my nose. Then, just for something to do to take my mind off of death, I tidied his desk, stacking his papers into orderly piles. His gold pocket watch had fallen to the floor and I bent to pick it up. The piece was smooth as a pebble and had a nice heft to it; it felt solid in my palm. The face was exquisite but the hands had stopped at ten minutes past twelve and when I held it to my ear, it was silent. I was afraid to wind it for fear I would break the mechanism. Turning it over I saw the inscription: *To H.M. with love, from T.M. June 3, 1755.* I marveled at this bit of mystery. I knew nothing of the lieutenant's personal life, and to think that someone cared so much for this disagreeable man—it made me wonder. Was it a present from his mother or sister? His betrothed? His mistress? I could only fancy.

I fingered the locket that hung around my own neck, the gift Aeneas had given me on our wedding day. As if it were a talisman and by rubbing it I could derive some of his wisdom and fortitude.

Molesworth's eyes were upon me and he seemed quite lucid.

"Your watch, sir," I said, opening my hand that held his timepiece. "It fell."

With his nervous tic, it was hard to read the man's face. Was he scowling?

"I was just admiring your pocket clock. It's lovely. But the hands have stopped and I don't know how to set it."

He reached out his thin yellow hand and I thought perhaps he was going to set and wind it himself. But instead he clutched it tightly to his chest and closed his eyes as if to shut out the world. I pulled the desk chair close to the bed and sat down.

I was keenly aware of the invisible barrier separating us. He believed me to be a common girl made good by my marriage to Dr. MacPherson, yet I had lost even this distinction the instant I pulled his soiled nightshirt over his head, saw him naked, and wiped his arse. I was now a nursemaid for a man on the edge of his life, helpless and alone.

Gingerly I put my hand on his arm and stroked it, as if he were a house cat. He flinched at my touch, shuddered, and then the tears spilled down his twitching yellow face. At first he cried without making a sound. Not knowing what to do, I stopped and pulled my hand away, but he grabbed it and pressed his feverish lips against my fingers. I dared not move.

After a long moment he released me and turned his head away, eyes closed.

"Do you want something for the pain?" My voice quivered. "Some laudanum, sir?"

He shook his head. Then he opened his eyes and looked at me intently, and it was as if the door between us had been flung wide open. There was no longer anything separating us—nothing in the way. I felt I could see Hugh Molesworth quite clearly and that he could see my true and innermost self. For that brief instant we might have been the best of friends, we might have been twins, we might have been lovers.

"That won't be necessary," he said at last, closing his eyes from the effort and breaking the spell.

He slept a deep and restful sleep. I sat in the chair beside him, reading the old newspapers on his desk until my eyes too became heavy. One of the candles had burned out and I blew out two more so as not to waste them, and I sat in the chair just listening to the sounds of the night. Muffled voices out in the hall, the sound of a key in a lock, a door opening, a door closing. Outside, the clop-clop of a single horse walking. The rasping sound of Molesworth breathing, the sough of my own breath. My mind drifted.

My mother died of fever and I survived the very same fever, my father once said. Was it the yellow fever or some other sort? I wondered. I remembered almost nothing of my mother or of being sick myself.

I sat down on the floor and leaned my weary head against the wall; the straight-back chair was unforgiving and there was no other furniture in the room but for a wardrobe and Molesworth's trunk. I found it cooler on the bare floor. Molesworth continued to sleep peacefully; his breathing, though noisy, was as regular as the sound of surf on a pebbly shore. I thought of the doctor with a pang of longing, wishing he were here to tell me what to do. To comfort me in his strong but gentle way.

My head dropped. *I'll just lie down and shut my eyes for a minute,* I thought. The wood planks smelled of vinegar. . . .

★ ★ ★

I woke suddenly, bathed in a patch of moonlight, my neck stiff, my arm numb. Remembering where I was, I listened for the sound of Molesworth breathing but heard only a cricket. Wide awake now, my heart in my throat, I was afraid to look at him. I was afraid to see death. I held my breath and listened intently, yet I could not hear him breathing. The cricket stopped its chirping and a deep silence hung over the room.

I sat up, heart palpitating. Forced myself to look at him. His body was illuminated in the wan light of a crescent moon. His face, usually tormented with twitching, was at rest. His mouth, agape.

I told myself to stand. To move my legs. I approached the bedside as if it were an altar. With dread I touched his hand. It was still warm.

Then I saw his chest rise and fall, almost imperceptibly. And again, soft as a whisper. Again. Hugh Molesworth was still alive. Still another breath—the extravagance of life!

I sat next to him on the chair, where I could watch the miracle of each inspiration. I allowed my own breathing to fall in step with his, a sort of duet. Outside the birds stirred and sang their first notes, yet the man slept on.

The sky lightened to rosy gray. Downstairs I could hear the cook and the scullery maid, just coming to work. I went outside in the hall to the top of the stairs and called down ebulliently to them.

"Could you bring a tray of tea for Lieutenant Molesworth and me?"

"Tea?" the old cook said, wiping her hands on her apron. "Then he has made it through the night? His man Tibbs said he would surely die."

"He lives," I said triumphantly. "As do I. And we would like some refreshment, the both of us."

Molesworth woke and sipped some tea from the spoon. He looked at me gratefully. His eyes, still yellow, were no longer bloodshot.

Aeneas came shortly after sunrise, stoop-shouldered and red-eyed.

"We lost three," he said wearily. He did not seem surprised that Lieutenant Hugh Molesworth had survived the night. Perhaps he was too exhausted to show it.

Molesworth continued to improve, growing stronger each day. And Aeneas's field hospital grew into a tent city where a crew of contract slaves cared for the sick. Though many died of the fever that week, many more might have died had it not been for Aeneas and his nurses.

As he regained his strength, Molesworth regained his old personality as well, which was perhaps the surest sign of his recovery. The first thing he did was to dismiss me as his nurse. In a week's time he was quarreling with the doctor again, dictating his own treatments and correcting us when we addressed him as "Lieutenant," for he was now captain of the frigate *Eos*. And though he was barely strong enough to walk, he insisted on boarding his ship.

"There is a war on," he said haughtily, as if we had not heard. "And we are already ten days behind schedule. We shall set sail at first light."

Aeneas and I had packed up our few belongings and were on the dock when the news came. A letter from Captain Molesworth's own hand and signed by Admiral Harding, dismissing Dr. MacPherson from the *Eos* and reassigning him to the hospital ship *Virgo*. Mr. Farrington, the surgeon already warranted to the *Eos*, was to remain the medical officer in charge of the frigate.

"I've been sacked," the doctor said in disbelief.

I was astounded. "Can he do that?"

"Aye, lass, he can." The creases in my husband's face looked suddenly deeper. Deep as canyons. "'Tis still a captain's prerogative to choose his surgeon. No doubt Hugh Molesworth wants a pushover. One who will do his bidding, not give him advice."

I reached over and took his big red hand in mine. "That's his loss. He'll not find a better doctor in the whole navy."

He squeezed my hand warmly. "You're too kind, my love. But a hospital ship will be quite a different thing entirely than a merchantman or a frigate. 'Twill be a hard lot for ye to bear, I fear. A hard lot for the both of us."

I swallowed hard. "No matter," I said, summoning my resolve.

EIGHT

"Look! There she is." Aeneas pointed to the ship just visible on the horizon.

We stood on the ridge of Barclay Point, having walked out here to pipe the sun down, as had become our custom, just as it had been aboard *Canopus*. Nearby at the fort the soldiers were preparing for their evening review and vespers.

"That's her, I'll wager. Aye, that's *Virgo*." He put down his bagpipes and pulled a small spyglass from his pocket.

"This will be hard work, my lass," he warned, peering into the wooden tube, his face screwed tight as he squinted. "The hardest work imaginable."

I said nothing, thinking that if Aeneas thought it would be hard work, it would really be difficult. He was indefatigable.

"Perhaps ye would prefer to remain here, on land," he offered. "We can keep the room at the inn. Or look for more suitable lodgings, if ye fancy."

"That would be money foolishly spent," I said. Truth be told, I didn't want to squander my husband's wages on temporary quarters; I preferred to save it. Besides, I was dissatisfied with waterfront life. There was nothing here for me.

"May I have a look?"

"She's a bit run-down at the heels," he warned, handing me the glass. "Needs a coat of fresh paint."

I held the instrument to my eye and saw a three-masted ship, poorly sailed and poorly trimmed, lumbering along, dowdy as a peasant. Even her ensign was tattered.

I sighed as I handed him back his glass. "How soon can we go to Barbados?"

He looked at me intently. "Are ye so certain that Barbados is where ye want to live, lass? The climate is intolerable, the threat of fevers constant. Not to mention what a young woman would do for pleasure. Do ye know that high society in Barbados is nothing more than a day at the races?"

"What do I care about society?" I said. "It has never cared about me. I would be quite content to ride my horses and spend time in my gardens."

"Horses and gardens are not unknown in other parts of the world," he said dryly. "Are ye not afraid of the tropical diseases?"

"Not as long as we breathe fresh air. Didn't you say it was foul air and effluvia that cause the fevers?"

Aeneas looked out to the placid sea. "Immortal youth," he sighed.

I kept looking at him, waiting for his answer, fearful he might change his mind about Barbados. My life was now knitted up with his and I felt completely at his mercy. What if he chose never to quit the navy? What if I was forced to follow him from ship to ship for the rest of our days?

He seemed a thousand leagues away, his eyes soft and watery. At last he spoke. "When the war is over and I collect my pay, we shall go wherever ye wish."

"Then I live for that day," I said with determination. "Until then I will stay by your side, be it on ship or on shore."

He put his bagpipes down, placed his big hands on my shoulders, and turned me toward him. "It will not be the life ye are accustomed to." His eyes blazed. "Do ye understand? It will make our crossing on *Canopus* seem like a promenade in Ranelagh Gardens."

"No matter," I said, feeling my chin quiver. "I am not above hard work."

"God, ye are a plucky lass with a true heart and I love ye for it," he said, gathering me in his arms and pressing his face in my hair. "My dear Patricia." He tipped my chin up and kissed my mouth, holding my face in his hands as if it were an egg.

I closed my eyes and kissed him back, feeling as though I had deceived the old man. Though I cared for him, I did not feel true. I did not feel plucky. I felt desperate.

The following morning Captain Charles West met us on *Virgo*'s quarterdeck. West was a bitter man and made no attempt to hide it. His career had recently taken a bad turn. Other men of his rank were awarded more lucrative commissions aboard battleships destined for engagements in the North Atlantic, the Mediterranean, the Indian Ocean. But *Virgo* had been disrated from a fifth-rate battleship to a floating hospital, and Charles West left aboard to command the sickly crew.

West had big eyes that bulged and threatened to pop out of his head if he coughed or sneezed. When he spoke, he spat out his words.

"Follow me, I will show you to your quarters," he said, lurching for the aft companionway with the jerking movements of a dour marionette. "Boys! You there! Bear a hand and bring the doctor's trunk. Step lively, now!" Two pock-marked servants no older than Young Willie carried our sea chest between them.

Virgo was much larger than the merchantman *Canopus;* it took half again as many steps to cross the deck. Yet below-decks she was even more cramped and crowded than the smaller ship had been. Once down the first companionway we had to stoop, for there was only four feet of headroom in that part of the vessel. Down another companionway to the orlop deck, deep in the ship's belly. Here we crouched for a moment while our eyes adjusted to the darkness, before groping our way aft past the operating theater and a locked cabin that was the purser's storeroom.

"And here is the dispensary." West reached into his pocket for a set of keys and unlocked the door to a narrow cabin containing built-in medicine cabinets and a single chair.

"I must warn you, we are low on medicaments."

The surgeon's cabin, our quarters, was adjacent to the dispensary and was just as small. There was no furniture but for a bunk along the bulkhead with drawers underneath.

I noticed with a sudden anxiety that there were no ports at all to let in fresh air. But of course not—we were on the orlop deck, which was above the hold and just below the surface of the water!

Aeneas's eyes took in the dark space in one shrewd glance. "I will require a desk for my writing," he said.

Desk? I was stunned. We have no opening for fresh air and he is worried about a desk? Why, there is not enough room for a desk in this cubbyhole of a cabin; it will have to go in the dispensary. But I held my tongue in front of the captain.

"I'll see what I can find, but don't get your hopes up," West grumbled. "The ship has been stripped of most of her furnishings, armament, and best men. All transferred to a first-rate man-o'-war and sent to see action somewhere. Somewhere other than here."

The smell reached me just then and I put up my hand to cover my nose. I looked to Aeneas and he gave me a sympathetic glance. The odor was that of two hundred and twenty-one ill-cared-for sick men.

West's Adam's apple bulged as he cleared his throat. He said nothing of the stench. "Well, then, MacPherson, you'll want to see your charges, I'm sure. You know your way around a ship, I trust?"

"Of course," Aeneas said.

"Because I don't go forward on this ship, Dr. MacPherson. Not if I don't have to. My first lieutenant is dead of the fever and my second is ill in his cabin. God willing, you'll be sending me some mended men up from below so that we may run this ship as she needs to be run, eh?"

The captain made his way aft, toward the companion-way, and I was happy to follow, toward fresh air.

"I will do my best," Aeneas said, stooping so as not to hit his head on the low deckhead. "But I am no miracle worker and these salty, reef-studded waters are not Lourdes."

"They are the devil's own waters," West said over his shoulder. "They don't call these isles the white man's grave-yard for nothing. Why, if it weren't for the blackamoors, we'd still be in Bridgetown, for I had not enough hale men to set sail."

"I hope the Negroes I've contracted will work out as well belowdecks," Aeneas said.

We hurried upstairs and stood once again on the sun-drenched quarterdeck, breathing deep the clean air. Above us two sailors were at work tarring the lines and I eyed them with envy. The pungent scent of pitch drifted down, a welcome relief from the stench below.

The captain and the doctor continued to converse and I stood by, wishing I too were aloft. Or somewhere else entirely. I looked for a bit of shade that we might stand in, but the sun was directly overhead and shadows were scarce.

The captain was frowning. "I must say, I don't generally condone women aboard my ship. I'm not speaking of well-bred women like yourself, Mrs. MacPherson." He nodded his head toward me. "The wives of officers are always welcome. A fine lady makes pleasant company at the dinner table, to be sure. But the females who sneak aboard and inhabit the lower decks are a discredit to their sex." He shook his head vigorously. "No discipline. Why, they refuse to follow orders, they waste freshwater on washing their garments, they distract the men from their work, and in general are nothing but a nuisance."

"I respectfully disagree," Aeneas said. "The lasses are spunky, they lend a hand, and they comfort the men. But she is your vessel to command as ye see fit."

West shrugged his shoulders, a jerking movement. "If I could command her as I see fit, I would have no women of the common sort aboard."

"We do need help below," Aeneas pressed. "Surgeon's mates, nurses, loblollies, and laundresses."

The captain nodded begrudgingly. "Perhaps the blacks will be better workers than the white-skinned molls that take up residence in the fo'c'sle. Rooks and rantipoling tarts, the lot of them—why, they guzzle and gamble like sailors!" He sighed, resigned. "When do you expect them?"

"This very afternoon," Aeneas said. "Have ye informed the purser and cook of their arrival?"

The captain's laugh was a short bark. "The cook jumped ship in Barbados and the purser lies ill in his cabin, just next to yours."

"Good God," Aeneas groaned. "Things are worse than I feared."

"We'll make the best of it," West said, blinking rapidly. "Join us for dinner tonight. My wife would like to meet you both; she pines for civilized company in these backwaters."

"Honored, Captain," Aeneas answered, touching the corner of his hat. *It would have been unheard of to refuse—not that I had anything else in mind. Dinner at the captain's table sounded like a welcome relief.*

"Just after sunset, then. In my private dining cabin." With

that he left us, heading aft to the poop deck, where two sailors were rigging a canvas awning.

"Now I must go to work," Aeneas said to me. "Ye may go to our cabin if ye are not up to it."

"But I cannot breathe down there," I protested.

"The smell will be worse forward where the sick are housed."

"It's not just the smell, sir. I cannot stand to be enclosed in such a small space."

His broad shoulders seemed to crumple and his face fell. "I should never have brought ye here," he said. "Ye were raised to be a gentlewoman, not a surgeon's mate. Forgive me. I was thinking only of myself—of having ye by my side day and night. Your lively spirit, your bold ways enliven me. The way your eyes snap. Having ye next to me, I—" He looked at me as if he were drowning.

I touched his sleeve. "I will be fine," I said with false bravado, for I could not bear to see the doctor break down. He was my strength. "I don't mind a little hard work. Besides, I am still in debt to you for paying my passage."

"Oh, my dear girl," Aeneas whispered, hugging me close. "That is all in the past. Whatever ye do now must come from the heart and be given freely." He released his grip and held me at arm's length, tilting his head as if I were a portrait he was admiring. "Why don't ye go into town and see if ye can find yourself a ready-made gown to wear tonight?"

"I have no need for new clothes," I said with far more confidence than I felt. "Come, Dr. MacPherson, let's go see to your patients."

NINE

We discovered the worst cases on the lower deck, amidships, separated from the rest by ragged curtains cut from old sails. Hammocks bulged like tumescent cocoons, hanging side by side, nearly touching one another.

"Nae proper cots," Aeneas muttered, taking note of the situation. The floor was cluttered with buckets spilling over with black vomit, bloody feces, and rust-colored urine. I squelched a gag and would have escaped topside for fresh air, but the sound of a man crying kept me down in the abyss. I followed Aeneas to a dirty hammock where a young man lay naked but for a rag between his legs.

"Please, sir," the wretch panted. "Please shoot me, run me through with your blade, throw me into the cool water so the sharks may chew my bones."

"He's raving," Aeneas said to me, raising one of his eyebrows. "Dose him with laudanum. Later, when the Negroes come aboard, we'll clean and fumigate this place. Good God, I've seen barnyards cleaner than this."

We moved systematically through the rows of hammocks, writing names and observations in the medical log, followed by the treatments they were to receive. Near the end of the row a boy no more than ten years old seemed to be near death. His hand was limp as a glove; he said nothing when I picked it up and squeezed it. His breath smelled like rotting fruit. I looked at Aeneas but he just shook his head.

We found an old man who had just died but was still warm. His eyes were fixed like a doll's. Eyes without shine. He looked not quite real, an alabaster man with stubble on his chin. I thought we should cover his face with a sheet but Aeneas said no, it would draw the others' attention to the fact he was dead. He simply reached over with his thick fingers and closed the eyelids. We walked on.

Beyond the curtain, forward into the vast lower deck, more men lay in hammocks, on sea chests, on wooden tables that hung from ropes. Some sprawled on the floor amid heaps of clothing and grimy, reeking linens.

"Where in God's name are the surgeon's mates and loblolly boys?" Aeneas thundered. "Is there not one soul on board this ship to care for these wretches?"

"They've gone ashore, and who can blame them?"

It was a girl who spoke. She straddled a hammock near the forward companionway, her bare legs dangling one on each side. A shaft of light from a porthole fell on her as she combed her tangled black hair.

"Say," she said, looking at us hopefully as we approached. I thought she would have been quite pretty but for the pox scars on her face. "You folk wouldn't have any rum, now would you? The fever sure makes a girl thirsty."

Aeneas was momentarily disarmed. "I don't think it's rum ye're needing, lassie. Dr. Aeneas MacPherson, I am, and this is my wife."

"How do," she said, flashing us a crooked-toothed smile. "My name is Liza."

"Liza? And what is your family name?"

"'Tis of no importance, sir," she said with a shrug of her slight shoulders. "I never had much of a family, at least not a family one would be proud to claim. I'd prefer it if you would just call me Liza."

"As ye wish. But who are ye with? Who keeps ye?"

"Well, sir, I used to be Billy's girl. Billy Bowles, captain of the foretop. But we had to drop him in the sea, less than a fortnight ago."

"I am sorry to hear that," Aeneas said. "The fever, was it?"

Liza tugged at a stubborn knot in her hair until it tore loose in her comb. "Aye. And I was laid up with it too, but I seem to have gotten better. Seems I am going to live, don't you think?"

"I would say ye have cheated the reaper this time," Aeneas said with a smile.

"How old are you, Liza?" I asked.

She squinted and stared at a fistful of hair, as if trying to read her age somewhere in the thick dark locks. "I don't exactly know, ma'am. I believe I am eighteen, though I might only be seventeen. I was raised in the parish orphanage and they had no records of my birth. A foundling, I was."

"What will you do? What are your plans?" I persisted, curious as to the future of this vagabond.

"The captain wants to pass me off to the next ship bound for England, but I won't go. There's nothing for me in England, nothing but trouble. I plan to stay aboard this vessel."

"I've been in a similar situation," I said. "But how will you accomplish it?"

"Oh, I've got a new sponsor, one of the ordinary seamen. He goes by the name of Buck. I aim to marry him proper so that I can collect the widow's fund if he dies. And if he happens to live, I plan to be there when this ship pays off, standing right behind him."

Aeneas scratched his head, bemused. "Well, Liza, in the meanwhile, how are ye at doing laundry? Taking care of the sick?"

She narrowed her eyes. "Depends, sir. What's in it for me?"

Now Aeneas laughed aloud. "What's in it for ye? I'll put ye on the muster books as a laundress, that's what. Ye'll get a share of rations and draw your own pay."

"My own pay? I'm in."

"Ye'll be answering to Mrs. MacPherson here, so don't give her any grief."

One of the seamen came clattering down the forward companionway, whistling a tune.

"Oh, Buck! Did you hear that? I am to be entered in the muster book," Liza said, swinging out of the hammock and approaching the barefoot sailor. She too was barefoot, the soles of her feet black. Her muslin gown was worn to a sheen. Its hem was ragged, the left sleeve nearly torn from its seam, and her apron was stained beyond hope.

Buck laughed and grabbed her by the waist to kiss her, but as his eyes adjusted to the dark he saw Aeneas and me and composed himself.

"This is Buck," Liza said. "The man I was just telling you about. Buck, this is Dr. MacPherson, the new ship surgeon. And his missus."

"Pleased to meet you." Liza's friend gave us both a wide grin.

"Buck. Is that your Christian name or your surname?" Aeneas asked.

The man laughed puckishly. "Both. I am Buck McBuck, son of a Buck."

Aeneas wasn't amused by his flippancy. "How long have ye been with the ship?"

"Since London. A press gang caught me in a tavern, but I gave them a deuce of a fight."

"And what sort of work did ye do in London?"

"I was a linkboy. I took gentlemen like yourself down dark and dangerous streets at night. Lit their way with a torch and kept the cutpurses at bay. Occasionally I obtained things for them."

"I am well aware what linkboys do," Aeneas said dryly.

"Well now, if you'll excuse me, the bosun's mate has sent me on an errand." Buck touched his tarred cap, blew Liza a kiss, and disappeared forward, into one of the storage lockers.

★   ★   ★

The Africans arrived later that afternoon: ten young field hands, wide-eyed and silent. Most of them didn't know a thing about household duties—all they knew was how to cut and stack cane. Aeneas put them in my charge. I immediately made Liza chief laundress, in command of a barrel of water and a washboard on the foredeck, and gave her half the girls. The others I took below to help me fumigate the sick berth.

One of my girls had seen house duty and could speak the King's English nearly as well as I. Her name was Penelope and she had the features of a mulatto: rich brown skin, full lips, a slender nose. She said she was thirteen years old, and already she was taller than I. Her shins poked out from beneath the hem of her calico dress like two saplings, and her feet reminded me of those of a young pup, feet to be grown into.

I showed Penelope what needed to be done: buckets emptied, floors scrubbed, vinegar sprinkled, brimstone burned. The bedridden bathed and fed. She learned quickly and worked with a will.

"I'd rather tend sick folk than cut cane," Penelope said with a shrug when I praised her efforts.

While the nurses and laundresses were carrying out their respective duties, Aeneas and I dosed the sick with Peruvian bark and prepared the dead for burial. There were two that day. Hastily we sewed the bodies up in their own hammocks, added some shot for weight, and with the help of a sailor slid them out the gunports and into the bay. It was gruesome, exhausting work that continued well past sunset.

That evening Aeneas and I washed up in our cabin. We had been invited to sup with Captain West and his wife.

"This is much worse than I imagined," my husband confided, splashing his face with water from the pitcher. "There are not nearly enough well men to properly attend the ship, much less attend the sick." He looked at me and shook his head sadly, water dripping from his nose. "The morale here is grievously low."

I handed him a towel. "Then we must do our best to infuse the men with courage." But it was I who was in need of courage. I clung to the hope that the ship would be sent back to Barbados, or England, or that the war would end and Aeneas would be relieved of his duties. Surely something would happen so that we would not have to stay aboard this miserable ship.

TEN

Captain West greeted us in his private dining cabin, a well-furnished room quite in contrast with the rest of the ship. In spite of the heat he was in full dress, complete with powdered wig and waistcoat. His eyes bulged so, I feared they might burst out of his head and roll across the floor.

Mrs. West was a fair, fat woman whose eyes seemed to counterbalance her husband's; they were deep and close-set, like finger marks in a lump of dough. She was dressed in silk of the latest fashion and waved herself languidly with an exquisite ivory fan.

We sat at a grand mahogany table where the captain's servants served us plates of stewed goat with fresh vegetables. The other three ate with gusto, but I could not get the smells out of my head, nor the emptiness of the dead boy's face. I picked and poked and moved the pieces of meat around but could not bring myself to take a bite.

"The menace I fear most is neither France nor Spain, but these unhealthy climes," Aeneas said. "We lose more men to fevers than we do to cannonballs and musket fire."

"Indeed. And the seamen know it, they do." West drained his glass and motioned to the cabin boy, who stood with his hands folded, gazing out the open port. "They would run, given half a chance," the captain continued. "Sign aboard the next merchant ship sailing north with a hold full of molasses. Therefore, I have forbidden them to go ashore. Only the officers may leave the ship."

"Captain West," I said, "how long do you intend to remain here?"

"Until I receive orders otherwise, madam. In the meanwhile we will make repairs and hope enough of the men regain their health so that we may sail when the word comes."

This was not what I wanted to hear. Was this a hospital ship or a prison ship?

"Mrs. MacPherson," Mrs. West remarked, dabbing her chin with her linen serviette, "you've scarcely eaten a bite of your dinner. Is it not to your liking?"

"It's delicious, I'm sure," I hastened to explain, feeling all eyes upon me. "I've just had such a day. I cannot—" I stopped, for the day's grim work could not be brought up at the dinner table.

"Have some more wine," the captain urged, reaching for the newly opened bottle the boy had just delivered. "That will boost your appetite."

"My wife was raised for a different sort of life than I have been able to give her," Aeneas said. "She is not accustomed to the . . . indelicacies . . . my work often entails."

"Yet she chooses to be by your side. Very commendable," West said, raising his glass. "To England's steadfast wives."

"I was not raised to live this life either," Mrs. West complained to me after the men had taken their brandy up on the quarterdeck. The captain's wife and I remained in the dining room drinking claret, attended by the yawning servant boy. Mrs. West had perhaps been sipping claret all afternoon; she was becoming maudlin.

"I should have stayed home," she lamented, dabbing at the corners of her eyes with her table napkin. "I fear I may not live to see my home again. It seems Captain West is out of favor with the Admiralty or he would have been given a better command." She looked in my direction, her eyes red and out of focus. "That is the trouble with this world, Mrs. MacPherson; your fate and your fortune depend on your connections. Nothing to be done about it, I suppose."

She squelched a hiccup. "Many years ago my uncle offered Captain West a place in his counting house, but did he take it? Oh, no. He wanted the prestige the navy offered. The chance for advancement. Well, now look at us." Her words were beginning to slur together. "I will rue your decision to my grave, Charles. My life would have been so much better if only . . ." She seemed to lose her thread of thought and stared into the dregs of her wine, forgetting I was there.

*   *   *

Many died that first week we were aboard the *Virgo*. Yet many recovered and resumed their shipboard duties or were traded to other ships in exchange for more sick men.

The days, the weeks, passed slowly, each one much the same as the last. One afternoon I was taking Tarkinton, a recovering fever victim, for a walk on deck. A few sailors worked listlessly on the foredeck, painting the cannons and swivel guns.

"Well, if it ain't Charles Tarkinton! I see you are still among the living."

I turned my head to see Buck at the rail, paintbrush in hand.

"Buck, is that you?" my patient said. "Haven't they hung you yet?"

Buck grinned, dropped his brush over the side, and wiped his hands on his trousers. "Good to see you up and walking," he said, clapping the other man on the back.

"Say, Buck, now that I am on the mend, you know what I would like?"

Buck scratched his ear. "Seems to me you still owe me for some goods I procured for you in Tenerife."

"And you know I'm good for it, once the ship pays off," Tarkinton insisted.

"You want rum and tobacco, you go see the purser. He's recovered now, I hear." Buck's eyes sparkled mischievously.

"Bah!" Tarkinton scoffed. "The purser is a brigand. Your terms are more favorable. As for sweethearts, they won't come near a hospital ship. And the purser, though a thief, is no pimp. But I know you can get them."

"Why, Tarkinton, I don't know what you mean," Buck

said with a wink. "You'll have our surgeon's mate here quite flustered. She has her loyalties, you know. Don't put her in a position."

"I don't know what either of you are talking about," I said. "And I don't think I want to know. Come now, Tarkinton, you've had enough of this hot sun for one day." I tugged on his arm and took him below.

Sailors were a rough lot, I knew. Some of them had even been taken from prisons to serve aboard His Majesty's ships. But I did not want to believe that Buck was an unscrupulous man. Self-serving, perhaps, and deviously resourceful, but not without conscience.

ELEVEN

We received orders to sail for St. Christopher—or St. Kitts, as it was called—to deliver our recuperated sailors to a waiting warship and take on more sick men. We would weigh anchor that night, if the wind held. I was keen to leave, ready to trade the few tired charms of this plundered isle for whatever the next one had to offer. Since my life was not as I wanted it to be, I longed for change of any sort.

My husband was to spend the day ashore seeing to the fledgling hospital he had organized. Although still little more than a collection of tents on Barclay Point, the governor had approved the building of a permanent structure. Aeneas wanted to visit Monk's Hill, the site of a battery overlooking English Harbour, for he was convinced the air was more conducive to health at that altitude.

I was entrusted to visit the apothecary to obtain more

medicines, as both the ship's stores and Aeneas's own kit were severely depleted. Captain West allowed me to take Liza with me, though it was against his better judgment.

"Do not let her leave your side," he warned as I prepared to climb into the jolly boat. "A woman of her sort can get into all kinds of mischief."

Down in the boat Liza's bright laughter could be heard as she flirted with the coxs'n's mate.

"See that she brings nothing on board this ship other than medical supplies," Captain West said. "No tobacco, no liquor, no girls of her sort. I am allowing her to go to assist you in carrying your purchases. Don't let her out of your sight, Mrs. MacPherson."

I gave him my word.

The waterfront was bustling that Saturday morning as we got out of the boat and made our way toward the apothecary. Liza paused to trifle with some men loitering in the shade of a manchineel tree, drinking from a bottle passed from one to the next.

"Come on, Liza." I didn't like the way the men were looking at us.

"But these are my friends, Missus Mac. Why don't you go on about your business with the apothecary. I'll just wait here in the shade. With my friends."

"Liza," I said sternly, remembering what Captain West had said.

The men stared, brazen as rooks.

She dismissed me with a giggle and a wave of her hand. "Go on without me."

"I'll just be a few minutes," I said. "Don't go anywhere. Promise me."

"Why, Missus Mac, where on earth would I go?"

The apothecary's shop was less than a furlong away; I could see the sign from where I stood. "Stay right here, Liza. I mean it."

"I'll be right here waiting for you."

I went.

The bell above the door rang as I entered. Inside, the shop was dark and smelled of pungent herbs. The soft sound of snores came from a monkey sleeping on the counter, head cradled in the crook of his hairy arm.

"May I help you, miss?" The apothecary appeared out of the shadows. He was a grizzled, gnome-like man with hair like cobwebs around the rim of his head.

"I'm Dr. MacPherson's wife." Aeneas was well known on the waterfront for his efforts at organizing the hospital.

"Ah, Mrs. MacPherson!" The apothecary bowed in the old-fashioned manner. "A pleasure indeed to make your acquaintance. Your husband is well, is he not?"

"Well enough, but sorely overworked." I pulled the list of needed medicines and the promissory note from my pocket.

"Yes, yes, yes," the old man said, wagging his head sympathetically. "A gruesome task, and a thankless one, he has taken on. Now, then, what is it the good doctor requests?" Pulling spectacles from his pocket, he adjusted them on his nose and peered at the list.

"Do have a seat, madam, whilst I attempt to fill your husband's order. I may not have all that he requires, for I'm running low on supplies myself. Sit down and rest yourself and I'll have my boy bring you a glass of cool sangaree."

Twenty minutes later I was back out in the bright sunshine, carrying a package the size of a hatbox. Not near what we needed, but better than nothing. Enough to get us to St. Kitts.

Liza was right where I had left her, sitting in the shade of the manchineel. Her companions were gone and she was alone, cooling herself with a tattered rattan fan. We hailed a boat and returned to the ship.

Aeneas returned after sunset and the two of us ate a late supper of cold leftovers in the wardroom. Meanwhile, on deck, a short-handed crew hauled up the anchor cable. Soon we would be under sail.

For an instant I longed to be up on the footrope myself, leaning over the yard, fingers flying to untie the gaskets, watching the great pleats of sail fall out of their folds and take wind. I thought about telling Aeneas how I felt, but he was explaining to me his observations of the effects of altitude on the incidence of fever cases, spewing numbers passionately. I dared not interrupt.

After our supper we walked the quarterdeck before retiring. Good for the digestion, Aeneas insisted. It had become our routine. But it occurred to me that he had not played his bagpipes for many nights now. That too was once a routine.

"Have you forgotten your pipes altogether?" I asked.

"My dear, aren't ye tired of hearing those same old tunes?"

"I miss hearing you play." I was surprised to hear myself admit that. For indeed, his repertoire was small. A few old Scottish airs and ballads were all he knew.

He smiled. "Well, then, tomorrow night I shall get them out of the trunk and serenade ye."

* * *

For the first time in a very long time, I fell asleep as soon as my head hit the pillow. It seemed like only moments later first light appeared, along with a loud pounding on our cabin door.

"Dr. MacPherson!" The second lieutenant's insistent voice. "Come quickly, sir. Ten men of my watch are down. Ten of my best sailors near death!"

The men were unconscious on the foredeck, facedown in their own puke. One of them twitched with violent convulsions, the way Young Willie had on my wedding night.

"Alcohol poisoning," Aeneas muttered, stooping down and sniffing. "Can ye smell it?"

The men reeked.

"A batch of bad rum, I'll wager," he said. "Let's turn them on their sides so they might better breathe and not choke to death on their own vomit."

"Bad rum?" I bent down to help him.

"It must have been smuggled aboard, for the captain forbids it. Only their daily allotment of grog from the ship's stores are the men allowed. Ah, the poor sorry sots."

"What must we do?"

"Not much to be done, I'm afraid. We'll bleed and purge and blister them, but I don't know what good it does. 'Tis a powerful poison, improperly distilled rum. Now where do ye suppose they got hold of the rot?"

And I felt sick myself because I had a feeling that Liza knew.

St. Christopher Island. Sugar plantations covered the lower slopes of the mountain like a lush green quilt. From the deck we had a fine view of Brimstone Hill, a magnificent hilltop fortress, and to the northwest the Dutch island of St. Eustatius rose out of the sea.

But I had no time to delight in our new landfall. Just as the starboard anchor splashed down off the cathead one of the drunken sailors passed away in a convulsive fit. His name was Timmy and he had been one of the topmen, a lad of sixteen who had never been sick a day in his life.

"What do you know of this?" I said to Liza as the two of us sewed him up in his dirty hammock.

She shook her head, her dark hair falling across her face. "Nothing."

"Did Buck sell him poisoned rum?"

"Now where would Buck get rum?" Liza said with feigned innocence. "Captain West doesn't allow it."

"You got it, didn't you?"

"How would I get rum? And where?" Though she looked at me, she did not meet my eyes.

"On land. From your friends."

Liza's voice had an edge to it. "Oh, come now, Missus Mac, your imagination runs away with you."

After Timmy was dropped into the deep his few belongings were auctioned off on the foredeck, according to custom. The proceeds were to go to his widowed mother and five sisters back in Portsmouth. The others had recovered from the effects of the rum, yet none would talk. Not one would say where he got the liquor that did Timmy in.

"Bosun, have them flogged immediately," Captain West said. "Thirty lashes a man until someone tells me who brought the damnable poison aboard."

I squirmed as if I were to be flogged. I felt certain Liza was lying, yet I had no proof. It was Penelope who found me belowdecks in sick berth. She pulled me aside and said in a low voice, "I don't like to talk, but I don't want to see anybody whipped. I've been whipped myself."

I gripped her bony shoulders and peered into her luminous brown eyes. "What? What do you know?"

On deck the men gathered to witness the punishment, which was to be delivered in customary fashion by the bosun and his mate. Just above us the gratings were removed from the hatches.

"Bosun, strip them to the waist," West barked. "Hurry now; I want this business finished so that I can enjoy my supper."

"Penelope! Tell me!" I said, shaking her as if to jar loose the information.

"Last night I was up in the fo'c'sle with some of the other girls. I saw Mr. Buck and Miss Liza filling the men's cups and taking money for it. I saw the men was drinking and gambling and such."

"Do you know how they got it on board?"

She straightened her shoulders and nodded with the dignity and majesty of a queen. "Under Miss Liza's petticoat," she said.

My eyes widened. "Beneath her skirts?"

"I saw the contraption," the girl continued. "It was a piece of rope tied around her waist. From the rope was hung pig bladders filled with rum. I saw her take it off. She saw me looking and threatened to beat me if I said a word."

"Where is she now? Do you have any idea?"

"Yes, ma'am. She and Mr. Buck are up in the fo'c'sle counting their money."

I ran forward, flung open the fo'c'sle door, and burst inside. There they were, just as Penelope had said. Sitting on a sea chest counting a stack of coins.

"Why, Missus Mac, what are you doing up here?" Liza said smoothly, but the startled look on her face gave her away. "This is hardly your part of town."

"Captain West has ordered nine innocent men flogged," I announced.

"I wouldn't call those boys innocent," Buck quipped, a wad of tobacco pocketed in his cheek.

"But they're to receive thirty lashes each. How can the two of you just sit there?"

Buck shrugged. "I'm not worried. It's not my hide."

"What are you doing? Counting your profits?"

"And what of it?" Liza tossed her head. "I went to plenty of trouble to get the goods and those lads were plenty glad to pay us for it. No one forced it down their gullets. How was I to know it was a bad batch?"

I felt sick with disgust. "You must tell the captain."

"Why?" Her eyes flashed. "So they can flog Buck instead?"

"Oh, they wouldn't flog me, darling," Buck said. "No, they'd hang me. And they'd throw you in jail to rot, my pretty raven-haired nightingale." He spit tobacco juice into a silver cup. "That is, if Missus Mac sneaks on us."

"Oh, she wouldn't do that. Would you, Missus Mac?"

Through the open hatch we heard the grunt of the bosun's mate as he swung the cat-o'-nine-tails, the deep cut

of leather knots against a man's back. I flinched as if I had
been struck, yet the sailor made no sound.

"One!" the bosun called out.

"You must say something," I insisted.

Liza shook her head. "You don't understand. We're just
trying to survive, me and Buck. But then, what would you
know about that? You were born lucky. You don't know
what it's like, not knowing where your next meal is coming
from."

Another grunt from the bosun's mate as he swung the
cat, followed by the smack of leather against skin.

"Two!"

"Harder, bosun," the captain barked. "Your mate swings
the cat like a girl. Perhaps he needs to be flogged himself."

"Aye, captain."

"Liza," I pleaded. "If you don't talk, I must."

"Oh, I see how it is," she said. "You're going to betray
me to soothe your own conscience. Well, go on. I wouldn't
want you to lose any sleep over the matter. But it won't
change a thing, I want you to know. The men will still be
beaten and Timmy is still forever dead."

The next lash made the man groan.

"Three!" came the bosun's voice.

"I must tell what I know," I said. "Not to ruin you, but
to make things right."

Then, before she could stop me, I hurried on deck to
find Aeneas. Aeneas would know what to do.

Captain West saw me and shrieked, "Avast!"

The bosun's mate stood with his arm raised, ready to
strike the bare, bloody back in front of him. All heads
turned my way.

"Good God, MacPherson—your wife—send her below immediately! This is no sight for a lady."

But I stood my ground and blurted out what I knew about Buck and Liza, begging the captain's forgiveness for my own lack of judgment. Yet when I was finished he sent me below and ordered the floggings to be delivered as ordered. Just as Liza had predicted, every man received his thirty lashes.

I spent most of the night tending to the men's injuries. They flinched beneath my fingertips as I dabbed grease on their torn flesh.

The next morning we discovered that Liza and Buck had jumped ship, taking with them articles of clothing and keepsakes they had stolen from the seamen's trunks. My husband was greatly relieved that she had not gotten to his savings, hidden in the false bottom of his trunk, locked up in our cabin.

Though glad they were gone, I was left with a lingering sense of guilt. I felt shame and remorse for what had happened, for my lack of judgment, my gullibility, my misplaced trust in Liza.

That evening Aeneas and I stood at the rail, watching the sun set. The doctor had taken the rum poisoning incident hard, much harder than the other deaths. So many other deaths, yet this one stuck with him; he couldn't seem to get over it.

"That poor lad resembled my nephew Patrick," Aeneas confided, gazing out across the bay toward Brimstone Hill, which towered above us resplendent and green. "About the same age, the same build. The same freckled, impish face."

"Your nephew?"

"A surgeon's mate on the *Dublin,* he was. Gone now. So young."

"You loved him."

"Aye. As long as he lived, Patrick MacPherson was a good lad, a brave heart. As was his father, my dear brother." Aeneas made a choking sound and said no more.

I held out my arms to him, for he seemed at that moment like a boy, lost and in need of comfort. And as we hugged one another, I too was comforted for all the losses that had befallen me.

"Ah, my wife, my good friend," he whispered, pressing his tear-streaked face against my neck.

On land the palm trees and cane fields shimmered in a rare golden light. The sound of a bagpiper playing vespers drifted across the water.

"Do ye hear that, lass? 'Tis coming from Brimstone Hill," Aeneas said, wiping his eyes with his sleeve. He pointed to the fortress high on the bluff. We stood in silence, listening to the faint strain of a tune, drinking in the melancholy notes until they died away.

"You were going to play your pipes tonight," I reminded him.

"Aye. But I'm afraid I haven't the strength," he admitted. "Five and thirty years—I am getting too old for all of this, my dear. But what I wouldn't give to hear 'Wild Mountain Thyme.'" He hummed a bit of the old tune in his gravelly voice.

"What a fine view they must have up there," he mused. "'Tis an impractical place for a fort—the cannon fire cannot reach the ships—but what a bonny spot for a man's home. How cool the air must be. Oh, lass, wouldn't I love to be a shepherd up in the mountains on an evening such as this." His red eyes brightened and he seemed at once content, yet inconsolably sad.

The sun dropped quickly, taking with it the rare golden light. A land breeze came up, carrying with it the smell of burnt cane.

Later, lying together in our bunk, I knew something was wrong. Every night Aeneas stroked my hair and kissed me before turning toward the bulkhead and falling asleep. But that night he didn't. Instead, he tossed and rolled, his legs twitched and jerked, and he scratched his bug bites until they bled. When I reached out to hold him, to calm him so that we both might sleep, I found his skin not warm and damp with the familiar smell of bay leaf and lime but burning hot and sour-smelling. It was the yellow fever.

TWELVE

"Dr. MacPherson, you must drink something," I said as sternly as I could manage.

He looked at me, his eyes yellow and glassy. Unfamiliar. "Please, sir?"

With difficulty, he sat up in bed, reached for the cup of water, and gulped it down. A bead of liquid ran down his grizzled chin.

"Bah!" he said, grimacing. His tongue was coated with something black. "Salty," he complained. "Is there nae freshwater to be had?"

"This is rainwater," I said. "Collected on deck just last night."

"Everything on a boat is contaminated with salt," he croaked. "But I thank ye for your efforts, lass." With that he lay down again and began to shiver, his eyes rolling back in his head.

I looked about our new quarters, as if a cure might be found in the fine dark-mahogany paneling. At my pleading Captain West had given us one of the empty officer's cabins. Though it had to be fumigated, we now had the luxury of a window—a gun port, that is. Which was what Aeneas needed most, I firmly believed. Fresh air and light.

But perhaps it was only what I wanted most.

The captain had yet to stop by to wish his physician well and I believed he was afraid to come near us. West and his wife remained aft, the most privileged part of the vessel, under the shade of their awning, sending instead a servant with a tray of fruit, biscuits, and wine. As if Aeneas were a guest at a hunting lodge instead of an officer aboard his rotting ship, too ill to report to duty.

"Shall I bleed you, sir?" I said. "Dose you again? Tell me what you need. A poultice, perhaps?" I was desperate for his direction.

"I wish I could have finished my life's work," he said, his voice unnaturally hoarse. "If only I had completed the manuscript and presented my findings. Oh, the time we waste, the hours we fritter away."

"No more of this talk, I won't hear it. You'll have plenty of time when you are well." Like a frantic hen scratching in the dirt, I busied myself with straightening his bed linens beneath him.

But Aeneas would not be silenced. "I used to dream of becoming a member of the Royal Society. Ha," he laughed weakly. "This rough old Highlander, can ye imagine? Of course, I had nae one to favor me, but that doesn't make it impossible. Improbable, perhaps, but not impossible. Other men of modest background have made their mark in the world, and some have even made it into that esteemed society." His eyes became wet and unfocused as he rambled. His breath, hot and rank.

"Rest, sir. You need your rest," I said, not able to acknowledge the lost desires he was unearthing and laying before me. Instead, I brought his bowl and razor to the bed, preparing to shave him. Any activity was safer than talking. I feared his words, those shovels of truth. *Aeneas so hates a whiskered chin,* I told myself in justification.

As I lathered the brush he grabbed my hand.

"I might have taken a different direction," he murmured. I didn't know if he was speaking to me or to himself. "Instead of medicine I could have studied the heavens and charted the stars. The very stars, can ye imagine? Astronomy, now *that* is lasting work. Not guesswork. Not this dabbling in medicinals, this bleeding, purging, and butchering in the name of Hippocrates. We are nae better than witch doctors in the wild jungles of Africa—why, the heathens might obtain better results than we do, we eighteenth-century charlatans pretending to know how to save people. Save them from what? And to think I might have discovered a star."

"We have a bit of Spanish fly remaining." I lathered his face briskly. "Perhaps I should blister you?"

He shook his head, causing me to smear lather across his lips. "All a waste of time," he said, licking at the soapy spume before I could wipe it away.

Quickly, deftly, I shaved his cheeks, pulling the skin

tight the way he had taught me. "Well, then, what would you have me do?" I asked. Surely there was a course of action to be followed, some knowledge he had kept from me; I could not accept the idea that nothing was to be done.

"Climb up here in bed," he said. "Let me feel your cool body beside me. I want to smell your hair."

I laughed, a nervous titter. "What, now? Let me finish shaving you."

"That can wait," he said gruffly. "Put the razor down, will ye? Take off your dress. Ah, lass, life is lived in the wink of an eye."

Fearful, I did as he bid, fumbling to unbutton my gown and pulling it down over my hips. Taking my undergarments off, clammy with sweat, dropping them to the floor. Shaking, I climbed naked into the bed with him. Stroked his arms, the hair on them dense, blond, and curly. I kissed his hot red hands, his freckled forehead, his feverish lips. I unloosed my hair and tumbled it in his face and was startled to hear him sob.

"Rest, sir," I said, hugging him tightly. "I am certain you will be better come morning." I dared not think of the alternative.

"Call me Aeneas. Call me your dear Aeneas," he whispered.

"Aeneas, my dear Aeneas," I murmured into his fuzzy ear. He ran his hands through my hair, squeezing it, stroking it, tangling it in his thick fingers. I kissed his face, his creased neck. I told him I loved him, again and again, as if to make up for lost time.

At last he fell into a restless sleep, but I remained wide awake. That Aeneas could possibly die from this was unimaginable. He was such a strong man, a good man. Indomitable. A better father to me than my own had been, and a better husband than I deserved. I must help him regain his will to live.

After midnight he awoke suddenly, puking the black vomit, and I was wild with fear. Then he had to go to stool and insisted on getting out of bed to use the chamber pot, refusing my help.

"Go out of the cabin and give an old man some privacy," he sputtered. I stood outside the door and listened as the fetid black liquid squirted from his bowels and the stench of it found its way beneath the door.

At last he called me and I went back in to find him sitting on the floor by the sea chest, its contents piled up on the floor. Breeches, waistcoat, handkerchiefs, stockings, a set of silver knives and spoons wrapped in cloth.

"Here is our small fortune," he gasped, holding up a long, narrow sack filled with gold and silver coins. "Enough for ye to live on for quite some time." He paused for breath.

I knelt by his side, not knowing what to do or say. The money meant nothing to me, not now. I couldn't bear to look at it.

"By God, ye're a plucky lass," he said. "Ye'll survive. I want ye to buy yourself a fine horse and a good saddle. Promise me that. And marry a man with a good heart."

"Don't talk that way, please don't, sir." His talk alarmed me; I would hear none of it.

Aeneas crawled back to the bed and somehow heaved himself up into it. I called for Penelope to help me empty the chamber pot. Between us we lugged the pot to the officers' roundhouse. The door was ajar; the seat, empty. We dumped the bloody excrement down the hole and rinsed the pot with salt water. Still the horrid smell lingered, but I was now so accustomed to this filthy work, it no longer gagged me as it once had. The sight of blood, the smell of stool, the sound of vomiting; one grows accustomed to it. Even to the suffering, the moans of pain. One tries to build a wall.

But this was my rescuer, my teacher, my husband. Aeneas MacPherson, my one true friend.

"He needs a nurse," Penelope said, interrupting my thoughts. "A colored nurse would be best."

"Why?" I asked. "What do the Negroes know?"

She shrugged. "The old ways."

"The mumbo jumbo? African sorcery?"

She blinked, her face unreadable in the dim light belowdecks. "What wisdom they have I don't know, but the British army officers use them, and the planters too. They say they have the healing touch."

We returned to the cabin to find the doctor unconscious. I shook him but he only flinched and murmured something I could not understand. He would not open his eyes, and when I pulled the lids up and looked into them, I saw they were not focused on me but on something invisible to me.

Wildly, I turned to Penelope. "We must do something. Do any of the girls on board have this knowledge? This healing touch?"

She shook her head. "No, ma'am. They're just field hands. And I am too young to have learned the secrets."

"Then where do we find one of these nurses?"

She shrugged. "I don't know. The forts, maybe. The

army officers employ them. They take them home and live with them."

"Dr. MacPherson needs a healer, not a concubine," I said sharply.

Penelope dropped her eyes. "Beg pardon, ma'am. I know the doctor don't need another woman in his bed. But the colored nurses know something, they do."

The Africans suffered far less from the yellow fever than did Europeans; maybe they *did* know something. Something our doctors did not. In any case, I was desperate and willing to try almost anything.

"Then I shall find him one," I said. "I'll go to shore and you'll look after Dr. MacPherson and tend to him as best you can. Keep him alive until I return."

I said nothing to Captain West, for he would almost certainly deny me permission. I would dress like a boy to attract less attention and to enable me to move faster. Without wasting any more precious time I put on my old sailor clothes and borrowed a pair of shoes from one of the bedridden patients. Penelope braided my hair and tarred it, sailor fashion, and I smudged my face with soot. I grabbed a few coins from the money belt and shoved them into my pocket before slipping over the side into the boat with the watering party, casting off for shore. None of the men gave me a second glance, for *Virgo*'s crew was constantly changing; those who recovered were put back to work and soon transferred to other ships. I gave the coxs'n's mate a shilling and asked him to wait for me.

A rainsquall passed, whipping the water into a chop that splashed over the gunwales and pelted us with rain so that we were soaked by the time we reached shore. As the sailors worked to beach the launch, I slipped away, running to the sally port of the small coastal battery, glad that I did not have wet skirts to slow me down.

A few militiamen of lower rank manned the fort. They sat around the west cannon, drinking rum and playing a game of dice on the hard-packed dirt. Against the wall two black men chipped rust off cannonballs.

The scruffy corporal looked up with annoyance. "State your business, boy." He was well into his cups.

"Patrick MacPherson, surgeon's mate from the hospital ship *Virgo*," I said, remembering Aeneas's dead nephew. "I'm looking for a nurse. A Negro, preferably. A good nurse who knows her business."

"We don't have such luxuries here," the corporal said with a wave of his hand. "We're not esteemed officers of the King's Army, we're militiamen protecting our home against the bloody French. And don't come too close with your filthy, fever-ridden clothes."

"The English officers have bought up all the good women for themselves," a gunner grumbled, rolling the dice. "Snake eyes! Damnation!"

The old man facing him laughed as he swept up a little pile of pennies from the dirt.

"So where would I find such a nurse?" I persisted. "Do any of you know?"

The corporal looked at me as if I were a bothersome fly. "You might find a few up on the hill."

"The hill?" I repeated stupidly.

"Bleeding Brimstone Hill, lad! Has the fever robbed you of what little sense God gave you?" He squinted as if to keep me in focus.

"Might I borrow a horse, sir?" I asked brazenly.

He stood up, stumbled, and nearly fell to the ground. Took two weaving steps toward me as if to get a better look. "What do we look like, a livery stable? Sailors requesting horses, what next? Get on with you, boy. Use the hooves God gave you."

He laughed and the others joined in, the sound of drunken men barking and baying at nothing.

I found the road, rutted and tortuous. Brimstone Hill seemed far away and impossible to reach, yet I ran toward it, for there was nothing else to do. My legs felt heavy and reluctant. High in the air above the hill a frigate bird soared with ease, as if mocking me. I soon had a stitch in my side. My feet burned and I paused long enough to stuff handfuls of grass into the toes of the too-large shoes, then pressed on. Coming to a fork, I instinctively took the left road, a rough path through dense thickets that seemed to climb toward the fort.

By now I was drenched in sweat. Gnats swarmed in front of my face, mosquitoes whined in my ears and bit my neck. Huffing and straining, I slogged on, hoping each switchback in the road would be the last, yet it continued to unfold, a never-ending path, a zigzagging labyrinth. I slowed to a walk to catch my breath, but the thought of Aeneas struggling for his life started me like the sting of a cat-o'-nine-tails. *He must not die,* I thought over and over until it became a chant, an incantation, a prayer.

A rock slipped beneath my foot, I stumbled, felt a hot stab in my left ankle as I fell. Fear drove me to my feet again. I shambled on, stepping gingerly on the left foot, hopping on the right. Another bend in the steep path. Now I could hear voices above me, wafting on the air like smoke, yet my destination remained elusive.

"Who goes there?" a sentry called from the undergrowth. "Quickly now, or I shall open your chest with a lead ball."

I saw a flash of red in the yellow gorse above me. "Don't shoot," I panted. "I am Patrick MacPherson, from the hospital ship *Virgo*. I've come for a woman. One skilled in herbs. For my physician."

"For your physician?" the sentry sneered. There was a thrashing in the underbrush and the fellow appeared before me; he was scarcely more than a boy. He approached me, brandishing his musket like a schoolyard bully. "Why doesn't your physician heal himself?"

"Please, soldier," I huffed. "Allow me to pass. I mean no harm."

The sentry put his pimply face close to mine. He was shorter than I, and reeked of perspiration and stale liquor.

"I don't know," he taunted. "What's it worth to you, Jack?"

I dug into my pocket and pulled out the first coin I touched, a Spanish gold piece.

The sentry whistled softly, snatching it out of my hand. "I won't ask who you stole that from. Now be on your way, sailor, and be quick about your business." He bunted my arse with the stock of his musket. "Before I change my mind."

I limped past him toward the next bend. Suddenly the

road ended, and I was inside the fort at last. Before me, a maze of walls, stone buildings, gardens, and stables. But now what was I to do? Who was I to see? I stopped to catch my breath.

Nearby, a company of Africans was at work laying rocks, constructing the base of a building, or perhaps a wall. Heaving stone upon stone, they sang as they passed the rocks, sang as they laid them into place. Their songs reminded me of the sailors' chanteys and I took heart.

Beyond them the earth dropped away and I could see the sloping patchwork of cane fields and gardens leading to the sea. And the great expanse of sea and sky encircling this tiny island. I could see *Virgo*, at anchor in the turquoise bay. I imagined Aeneas inside, grappling for his life. It was as if I had climbed Jacob's ladder into heaven and was now looking down on the world as the angels do. Now, more than ever, I needed an angel.

A group of children ran past, chasing one another in a game of tag. Feral, unkempt urchins, they were. I grabbed one by his arm and asked him where I might find a nurse, but he just looked at me balefully and refused to speak. The others stared at their toes, complicit as thieves in their silence.

"Oh, go on with you then, you little scamp," I said, turning him loose.

Looking around the hilltop, I heard female voices and smelled a cooking fire. Upslope I saw a rude encampment where a ragged group of women worked at preparing their suppers, and I inched my way toward them, favoring my lame foot.

Black, white, and mulatto women together, talking as

they chopped and stirred, working on a makeshift table, planks nailed to barrels. Several pots hung over a great pit of coals.

"Good evening," I said, touching my cap. They looked up from their cutting boards and kettles, their faces flat and hard as though nothing could penetrate them. Not unkind, just wary.

"I am in need of a good nurse," I said. "For the ship *Virgo* anchored down off Sandy Point. Please, can you recommend a woman skilled in the healing arts? My master pays well," I added.

"Sit down and catch your breath," the one closest to me said. She held an infant to her breast, crooked in one arm. With her free hand she brushed a lock of fair hair back from her burnt, weathered face. A face streaked with black from the charred and greasy kettle. Her eyes were green. My own eyes, it seemed.

"What's your name, sailor?"

"MacPherson. Patrick MacPherson," I said, becoming more comfortable with the name. "And you, ma'am?"

"Brigit. My man is a private in this regiment. Weaver's his name, and this here is his bairn," she said, nodding toward the nursing babe. "What's wrong with your foot?"

"It's nothing. I twisted my ankle."

"Let me have a look. Pull up your pant leg."

The flesh above the top of the shoe was swollen and purple and I winced when she touched it with her dirty fingers.

"I have no time for this," I said, still panting. "Our surgeon is close to death. I must get help."

"Rest yourself, MacPherson. Here, this will fortify

you." With her free arm she poured me a cup of rum from a monkey jar, the babe still at her breast.

So thirsty was I that I drank it down, and it filled my stomach with fire and spun my brains. Yet it dulled the throb in my ankle.

"No time to rest," I said. "My—the doctor—he is very ill."

"What ails him?" Brigit asked, refilling my cup.

"Fever," I said.

"Most of the nurses here have all the work they want," she said, pulling the baby from her breast and laying it in the grass as if it were a rag doll. Absently she buttoned her bodice, eyeing her cooking fire.

"I just want one for a few days."

She narrowed her eyes. "I don't know. The officers are jealous of their nurses. They don't generally lend them out to other men."

"But my doctor is dying," I blurted out, my voice breaking. "And no one can help him." I choked back a sob and pressed my thumb and finger into my eyes to keep from crying. The women stared mutely.

I was tired. Heart weary. Wishing I could sit down on this cool hilltop with these wretched women and sup with them. Watch the sun set and hear the pipes play. Put the children to bed.

"Old Darcy might go with you," Brigit said.

"Who is old Darcy and where do I find her?"

"She's a slave, or was one until she got arthritis so bad her owner set her free so he wouldn't have to feed and house her. Old slaves can be more trouble than they're worth."

"But that's against the law, is it not?" I said. "To abandon a slave."

The women all looked at me incredulously.

Brigit laughed, a sound like a brittle stick snapping. "Just because something is written in the books doesn't mean it's the law. The law is what men do, not what they say or write." She picked up a wooden spoon and stirred one of the kettles.

"Old Darcy has a way with herbs and roots, to be sure," Brigit went on.

"Is she a witch?" I asked.

"You mean an obeah. An African sorcerer. They don't call them witches." She shrugged and stirred more vigorously, scraping the bottom. "I don't know. 'Tis said she has the healing touch. Some sort of knowledge or African wisdom. Though most of the white men don't care about the sorcery. Most men would rather have a voluptuous young mulatto for a nurse, not a wrinkled old black prune of a woman."

"Where is this Darcy? Where can I find her?"

"In the deadhouse."

"The deadhouse?" I felt a chill at the back of my neck.

She brushed a limp strand of hair that had fallen across her eyes. "That's where they keep the bodies until a grave can be dug. One of our women died this afternoon. Childbed fever."

My eyes swam. The rum had loosened me, weakened my legs and my resolve. I regretted having drunk it. The sound of drums reverberated off the mountains as the evening review began.

"The dead require so much work, nearly as much as

the living." Brigit drank again from the monkey jar. "There's the body to be washed and rubbed with herbs and wrapped for burial. The hole to be dug." She rambled now, her tongue freed by the spirits. "Most of the Africans and coloreds, they won't go near the deadhouse. But Darcy will. For a small price, that is. She'll do everything but dig the hole. The soldiers do that."

"Where is the deadhouse?" I asked.

Brigit jerked her thumb. "Just over there, to the north. That long, low building beside the graveyard."

"I must go," I said, rising unsteadily. Dragging my tender foot, I made my way over to the stone building.

Inside it was cool and dark. There was a faintly sweet odor of decay in the damp air. I walked down a row of corpses toward the obeah woman, the only other living being inside the deadhouse. I could not see her face, just the bones of it, a shadowy skull wrapped in a turban. She was bent over a body, dressing it. Her own body was as skinny and twisted as a hawthorn branch.

I introduced myself as Patrick MacPherson, the name rolling right off my tongue. I told her why I had come. "Please help me," I said. "Please." I had never begged anything of anyone.

Darcy's eyes moved up and down my body. "Why do you dress like a boy?" Her voice was a raven's croak.

"Because it suits me," I said, taken aback. She was the first person to see through my masquerade, or at least the first to confront me about it. "It's easier to get around in breeches," I added.

She laughed softly. "I 'spect it is."

Darcy agreed to see Aeneas, though she made no promises. Her fee: one shilling. And that only if he survived.

"First we must see to the leg," she said, pointing to my lame ankle. "Go back with the womens and have some supper. I make a poultice to draw out the swelling."

"There's no time."

"No other way. I'm not strong enough to carry you. Be quicker in the end."

I did as she said.

It was dark when we started down the hill, old Darcy with her basket of herbs under her arm and I limping, my ankle bound up in rags. I kept hoping someone would come along in a cart or a buggy, someone I could beg or buy a ride from, but no one did. We shuffled in silence, each of us absorbed with our own thoughts.

What if I arrived too late? I could not bear it. Only now did I realize a better man than Aeneas MacPherson I would never find.

Venus was a beacon on the western horizon, but by the time we reached the waterfront where the coxs'n's mate lay asleep in the skiff, it had long disappeared into the sea. There was yet no moon but Orion was rising over the mountains to the east, his shield a perfect arc, his belt glittering like sapphires against the profound darkness.

THIRTEEN

Penelope met me at the rail and I knew then, the moment I saw her face.

"How is he?" I demanded, ignoring the dreadful prescience that filled me. I had a strange sensation of falling, as if I had stepped across the edge of an abyss.

"I am sorry, missus," Penelope said. Her young face seemed to be carved of wood. "I begged him to hold on until you came back. Forgive me, but I could not save him."

"No!" I grabbed her by her thin, square shoulders. "It can't be!"

She looked at me, expecting to be struck, and I wanted to strike her in my rage. Instead, I grabbed Darcy's crooked arm, pulling her across the deck and down the dark companionway. I no longer felt the pain in my ankle; I felt nothing but dread as I flung open the cabin door.

"Aeneas!" I said loudly, as if to wake him.

He was covered neatly with a clean sheet of linen, his arms at his sides. The flickering candlelight cast a wan yellow glow on his face. Yet it was not his face, not quite. It was a mask, a remarkable resemblance, yet it was not he. I inched toward the bedside, my breath stuck in my throat. I watched his chest closely, for I had been fooled before. I had seen Young Willie and Molesworth come back from the edge of death. I knew it could happen. I had seen miracles with my own eyes.

"Breathe, Dr. MacPherson," I commanded. "Breathe for me. You must rally, sir. I've brought help, I've found a nurse who can do remarkable things. Please, Aeneas?"

Yet when I dared to look at his eyes, half open and staring at eternity, I knew he would not. His hands, those huge, competent bear paws that could suture the tiniest ligament, were as cool and heavy as blue-veined marble. It seemed impossible that these dusky fingers had ever moved so deftly. He was no longer Aeneas but a cast in his likeness. Aeneas was gone, yet I could feel him here in this cabin. I could feel his warmth, his vigor, his intelligence in the air around me, or perhaps it was just a powerful memory. Stricken with grief, I bent to kiss his face for the last time. A trace of a familiar odor, that of bay leaf and lime, lingered like a ghost, reluctant to depart.

We laid him to rest on Brimstone Hill in the soldiers' cemetery. The view from the prominence was exhilarating. I know Aeneas would have approved, even though it was a foot soldier's boneyard and perhaps not fitting for an educated man such as he. The Aeneas I knew was a man whose allegiance was to science, God, and country rather than any military organization, and though he was a physician, he kept a bond with the common man and with his own humble roots.

Down at the anchorage Captain West ordered *Virgo*'s cannons fired in salute. At the fort a soldier beat a solemn tattoo and I paid the army piper to play a Scottish air. And I wept for Aeneas MacPherson, who was an honorable man and loved me true. I did not realize what a gift I had been given until it was too late, forever too late. Must life always be that way?

FOURTEEN

Having buried my husband, I was now at a loss. I did not know how to begin anew, only how to continue. I did not know who I was, apart from a dead man's wife and a dead man's daughter. But for a while it didn't matter who I was.

Three weeks after Aeneas died there was still no replacement for his position, yet the sick continued to need care and there were so few of us to do the caring. With no ship surgeon it fell to me to give guidance to the rag-tag collection of laundresses and loblollies. I made Penelope chief nurse, a promotion of my own invention that carried no monetary reward, yet she was proud to assume the responsibility. When I asked the captain if he could enter me on the books as ship surgeon so that I might receive pay for my work, his eyes nearly popped out onto the deck.

"But women cannot serve as surgeons aboard His Majesty's vessels," he sputtered, taken aback that I had dared to ask. "Only as laundresses. And that is unquestionably far beneath your station. Though I am grateful, Mrs. MacPherson, for your kind services. You'll be pleased to know there is a qualified naval surgeon awaiting us in Charlestown on Nevis. So your laudable though demeaning work will soon be finished." He flashed me an empty smile. "We shall sail as soon as the wind comes up."

We stood on the quarterdeck under the shade of the awning. Mrs. West sat in a plantation chair, a glass of sangaree in hand; one of the cabin boys diligently fanned her. She appeared to have fallen asleep and I wondered that the drink did not spill.

"What is to become of me, Captain West?" I said.

"Not to worry, my dear. You have your husband's savings, do you not? As soon as we make landfall you can find passage back to England."

I stared at him. He didn't understand. There was nothing in England for me.

"Now, then, chin up. You must sup with Mrs. West and me, the way we did when Dr. MacPherson, God rest his soul, was with us. My wife misses your company and implores you to leave the emptying of bedpans to the Negroes, who are far more suited to the work."

I swallowed the curse on my tongue, for I could not alienate the Wests, not yet. I was dependent on them. "Perhaps another evening, Captain West," I said evenly. "I must get below and finish counting our supplies and medicaments. Your new surgeon will want to know what he has to work with, will he not?"

"Quite right. Oh, I almost forgot. Here's a letter addressed to you, posted from Bridgetown back in April. It just arrived with today's post; must've been misrouted. Says here, care of HMS *Eos*. Have you family in Barbados?"

"Once upon a time," I said, reaching for the letter.

He looked at me curiously but I slipped the letter into my skirt pocket and bid him good evening. Went belowdecks to my cabin and lit a candle. Tore open the seal and unfolded the single sheet of water-stained paper.

The handwriting was cold, black, and unequivocal. I read it in one glance. The former Hatterby estate had lawfully passed to Mr. Smith's nephews; my claim to the property was unsubstantiated and invalidated. Any further inquiries would be refused and returned, unread. Regretfully, Mr. Charles W. Johnson, Esq.

I took it to the washbasin and touched the candle to the corner. The paper turned to ash and smoke in a matter of seconds and I was left with a bad smell in the cabin.

A fresh breeze stirred from the east.

Captain West gave the order and the second lieutenant called out in a brittle voice, "Weigh starboard anchor!"

The bosun, still recovering from the fever, piped the message listlessly on his whistle and the dispirited sailors began hauling without a song. The only sounds that broke the morning's stillness were their grunts and sighs and the thump of cable, thick as a man's arm, being faked down upon the deck.

"Anchor a-weigh!"

"Sail due west," the master said to the sailor at the helm, "until we can clear the point. We must stay well off the reef."

But the wind lightened soon after we weighed anchor and by noon there was scarcely enough air to fill the worn tops'ls. The wretched ship ghosted along. For hours the Dutch island of St. Eustatius taunted us off the starboard beam while Brimstone Hill remained in sight off our larboard quarter. I stood at the rail looking at the mighty green promontory where the body of Aeneas MacPherson lay.

At last we cleared the point and headed for Nevis, a small island to the southeast that looked like a green China-man's hat floating on the sea. But shifting winds soon beleaguered us; the sails backed and the master cursed his luck. A late-afternoon squall sent our few sailors scurrying aloft to shorten sail, and the rest of us hurried below, out of the pelting rain. I managed to rig my square of canvas and bucket to collect some of the rain, for there never seemed to be enough freshwater on board. The men had taken to soaking their soiled clothing in barrels of urine, for the want of freshwater!

Meanwhile, the cook's mate—a feeble-minded, bandy-legged Welsh boy—had been injured when a cask of salt pork fell on him. The poor fellow had remained down in the hold for some time trapped beneath the barrel, peeping for help like a baby bird. It was Penelope who had discovered him, rolled the barrel off, and brought him to me to be examined. The flesh under his armpit was the color of a bruised grape; moving my fingers down his bony rib cage, I felt a lump and an unnatural hollow. The boy shrieked with pain. The ribs, fourth and fifth, were likely broken, but I was not certain what should be done. I felt a flash of anger at Aeneas for deserting me. "Broken bones knit themselves, given a chance," he once said. Relying on that, and not knowing what else to do, I wrapped a wide strip of cloth around the lad's rib cage, dosed him with laudanum, and put him to bed.

The squalls continued into the evening, one after another, each one more furious than the one before, without a break in sight. We had not enough able seamen to reef the sails and the ship heeled over, groaning under its weight of canvas.

"Man the pumps!" Captain West bellowed. "We're taking on water!"

Hearing the urgency in his voice, my throat tightened.

The *Virgo* was a leaky vessel, and she was losing her caulking, rotting away. Yet who was available to work the pumps, with all able hands desperately working to shorten sail and steer the ship? Unable to leave the sick berth myself, I sent some of the African girls up to lend their strong arms to the pumps.

I was down below in the cabin reviewing the structure of the rib cage in Aeneas's anatomy book when I heard a thud and felt a sickening jolt. Above my head the lantern swung wildly, throwing shadows against the bulkhead. Terror, like a mortar, exploded in my chest. I dropped the book and ran up to a confusion of sailors stumbling about in the darkness, the captain and the bosun shouting orders in desperation.

"Faster on the pumps, faster! Bloody hell, we're sinking!"

"Ease sheets at once! Ease clews, bunts, reefs!"

The ship fell sharply to larboard and I scrambled for a handhold to keep from sliding into the scuppers.

"Find the hole! We must find the hole and fother it!"

"It's too late! We're going down!"

"You there, lower the boats! Lower any bloody thing that floats!"

My mouth grew suddenly dry, my worst fears come true. The ship was sinking. And though the shore was less than a mile away, it might have been a thousand miles, for I could not swim.

Wild with panic, I ran below, tore off my gown, fumbled into my old sailor clothes, moldy with disuse. If the ship was going down, I didn't want my legs encumbered by voluminous skirts. I yanked the money belt out of the bottom of the sea chest and with fumbling fingers tied it about my waist. Aeneas's savings—it was all I had left in the world.

On deck the shouts of the men grew more desperate, and with a groan and a snap of timbers, the ship fell further on her side. Terrified of being trapped below, I snatched up the box of surgical instruments and fled toward the aft companionway. The ship lurched, throwing me to the floor, and I crawled toward the stairs as water swept the lower decks. Struggling up the steps, I ran to the rail, where some of the sick men were making their way into the ship's boats, to safety. A group of laundresses huddled near the shrouds, awaiting their turn.

"Penelope!" I screamed, but she was not among them; she was nowhere to be seen.

I heard a loud crack that I thought was a cannon blast before I realized it was the sound of the vessel breaking up.

"She's afire!" someone shouted. "Fire astern!"

Somewhere below a lantern had fallen; smoke billowed out the stern gun ports.

"Abandon ship! Every man for himself!" Captain West's voice called out above the confusion. I saw Mrs. West in a bosun's chair being hoisted over the rail with a block and tackle, as if she were a hogshead of molasses.

I must find Penelope. I ran down the forward companionway, away from the fire, but the water was knee-deep in the lower deck. Made my way through the rows of empty hammocks, calling her name, clutching the surgical kit, the coins and gold pieces swinging heavily from my waist.

I heard an eerie howling from amidships as I slogged my way to sick berth—it was the feebleminded cook's mate being dragged by Penelope from his hanging cot. Sleepy with laudanum, he must not have known his life was in peril.

"We must get off the ship," I panted, breathless. "There's fire astern and we're going down!"

She looked at me patiently. "Yes'm, I know. Can you help me with the boy? He don't have the sense of a rat."

What a capable nurse she was. I envied her clear head, her implacable calm. Yes, of course, the boy must be helped to safety.

I snatched one of his arms and she held the other and between us we pulled him, stumbling and sobbing, up on deck and over to the rail, where someone helped him over the side. Men stood huddled in the channels, holding on to the shrouds, waiting for the next boat that would take them to shore. Flames from below cast a flickering light on the dark sea and the smell of burning pitch filled the air.

The ship moved again and someone fell against me, pushing me to the deck; a foot stepped on the back of my head, grinding my face into the plank. I bit my tongue, tasted blood. Mad to escape, I jumped up and grabbed for the boarding rope, swung my leg over the rail, and felt for the footholds. Below me, the crowded jolly boat tossed on the waves. But someone snatched the rope from my hands and knocked me off balance. I realized I was falling. It seemed a long way down and I clung to the box of instruments with both hands, as if it could save me.

The water was a hard slap that knocked the surgical kit from my grasp. Cold and heavy, the ocean closed over me and I sank, kicking and thrashing, into the darkness. Deeper and deeper, the water squeezing my head, ears hurting, lungs burning. Something seemed to burst in my chest and fill me with a madness that spread throughout my body and mind. I wanted to breathe, had to breathe, must breathe!

The money belt pulled me down like an anchor, and I knew I must drop it to live. I grabbed wildly for the belt, tried to tear it off, could not. Panic filled me like a fire. I groped and grabbed to no avail.

As I began to lose my hold on consciousness, panic subsided, burning out. Still, I could not rise. My feet brushed the bottom; I realized I was going to die. It all happened so quickly. Though I still longed for air, it was more of a wistful memory of desire.

Open your eyes, a voice said. A clear, calm voice inside my head. *Find the belt, then pull it down over your hips. Slowly and deliberately. As if you had all the time in the world.*

I opened my eyes. The water was dark and murky, yet I

could see shapes and shadows. I looked down and saw it, the belt hanging low on my hips, much lower than where I expected it to be. I grasped it firmly in both hands and pulled it down. So easy.

Drop it, the inner voice said, and I obeyed.

The belt fell to my ankles and I stepped out of it, kicking my feet clear. Looking up, reaching for the surface, I began to rise. Fought to stay conscious as the fuzzy blackness filled my head. Broke the surface, gasping, thrashing. One moment of relief as I gulped fresh air, then panic reignited—I could not swim. Instinctively I kicked and flailed, then felt a wave wash over my head, the salt water stinging my nose and burning my throat.

"Help me! Help!" I called, swallowing more water, choking, gagging. Yet there was no one to save me. No one to hear me.

Virgo lay on her side, engulfed in flames. The smaller boats were nowhere in sight. Underwater again, and up, choking, my heart about to burst. I looked for something to save me, and saw a dark shape in the water—a wine cask! I lunged for it, but my flailing only pushed it farther away. Like a wild thing I thrashed, but to no avail. Again the water swept over my head.

Be still, don't fight. You will rise to the surface and the cask will come to you.

I looked up through the water, saw the barrel over my head. Reached up with my arms and encircled it. The cask buoyed me, lifted my head above the water, just high enough to breathe. And there, just below the surface and slowly sinking, was the box of surgical tools I had in my hands when I fell. I reached for it, clung to it with one arm and the life-saving wine barrel with the other. Too weary to do anything but hold on, I abandoned myself to the waves.

Out of the darkness a woman's voice spoke to me. A very worried voice, quite real, near my left ear.

"Are you alive?" Her hand was warm upon my forehead.

I opened my eyes and found myself lying on the beach, clutching the gold locket that Aeneas had given me, still around my neck. At my side, his surgical kit. When I tried to speak, I vomited seawater.

She wiped my face with the hem of her skirt.

I tried to stand but fell to my knees.

"You're shivering, you can't stay here." She took off her wrap and placed it around my shoulders. "Let me take you to my home."

The Good Samaritan gave me her arm and together we shuffled through the sand toward the glow of a lantern in the window of a nearby house. Inside, she toweled my hair dry, dressed me in one of her nightgowns, and put me to bed. I slept for two days.

PART THREE

ONE

I opened my eyes to an unfamiliar sight: a plastered ceiling above me, not the planks of an upper deck. Looking around the room, I marveled at the safety of its four sturdy walls and the simple, comfortable furnishings. A press cupboard, nicked and scratched but covered with a fine piece of lacework. A stack of books and a vase of orange blossoms on the nightstand. And at the foot of the bed where I lay, Aeneas's surgical kit, water-stained but intact.

How astonishing to be here, to be alive! I fingered the coverlet draped over me. The smooth feel of cotton was luxurious; the mattress of feathers beneath me, miraculous. How easy this new place seemed, with nothing for me to do but breathe. Wafts of baking bread and orange blossom soothed me. From outside, the cooing of doves, the rustle of leaves.

I couldn't bring myself to think of the disaster. Pushed the screams and the smell of burning pitch from my mind.

There was a knock at the door and my benefactress appeared. She was a dark-haired woman whose delicate face had a determined set to it. A furrow between her brows seemed permanently etched.

"I am Rachel," she said. "And you, my poor survivor, are awake at last." A rufous child hid shyly behind her skirts, examining me with one curious, critical eye.

"This is Alexander." She reached behind and took his hand, pulling him out to be introduced. "My youngest. He's six."

I was confused by her easy familiarity, her first-name intimacy. Had we met before?

"Rachel?" I said tentatively.

"I know we've only just met, but I detest the name Mrs. Lavien, I am no longer Miss Faucette, and I cannot yet be properly called Mrs. Hamilton," she said frankly.

I struggled to sit up and the woman gave me a hand, plumping the pillow behind my back.

"Who needs surnames?" I said, still muddle-headed. "They're never our own anyway."

Rachel's smile was rueful. "How true. First we're given our father's name, then we take our husband's. Only our given name remains the same. But what shall I call you?"

"Patricia. And I'm indebted to you, Rachel, for taking me in."

"*Mon Dieu,* I was afraid you would never wake up," she said, leaning over the bed and hugging me with her slender arms.

"But what of the others? Were there many survivors?" I was almost afraid to ask.

Her face fell. "Only a few, from what I've heard."

The breath rushed out of me and my head spun. Though I suspected as much, the news was hard to bear.

"Did you have family aboard?" she asked gently.

I shook my head. "But there was a young mulatto girl. Penelope." My throat was tight. "I don't suppose . . ."

Rachel lifted her slight shoulders. "I'm sorry, I don't know."

"She might be alive, she might have made it to shore. Somehow. It's possible, you know. Penelope is a strong girl, with a level head."

Rachel lowered her eyes. "*Peut-être.* One can hope."

I couldn't consider the alternative. Not just then.

"Is there someone I should notify?"

"There is no one."

Her dark eyes glistened. She touched my shoulder. "Patricia, are you hungry?"

"I am," I admitted.

She brought me up a tray and I supped in bed on a bowl of conch stew and a slab of country bread. Rachel hovered over me in a motherly fashion as I ate.

"Where is this place? Where am I?" I asked between spoonfuls of the creamy, flavorful soup.

"Why, you're in Charlestown, on Nevis."

I nodded slowly, looking around the room again, wondering at its simple perfection.

"And this house you're in belonged to my father, God rest his soul. It's my last tie to this ruined, decadent isle," she said, a touch of bitterness to her voice.

"Were you born here?"

She nodded. "My father came here from France, a Huguenot refugee. He was a physician and made a good life for us here. But now he's dead and gone, and Nevis too has seen better times."

"I was born on Barbados," I declared. "And raised in England. But for the past ten months a ship has been my home."

Having somewhat regained my strength, I was eager to get out of bed and explore my surroundings. Rachel called for Flora, a young African girl, to take away my tray while she herself helped me to dress. Rachel was a slight woman and her gowns were too small for me, so I asked for the sailor clothes I had been wearing when she found me on the beach. Rachel gave me a quick, curious glance as she retrieved them from the press cupboard, freshly laundered and cleaner than I had ever seen them.

"When I knew the ship was going down, I put these on so as not to be encumbered by my skirts," I explained. "Actually, they are much more practical than long gowns, petticoats, and corsets, don't you think?"

She smiled. "Perhaps."

I wanted to go out of doors, and the others accompanied me, Alexander running straight to the water's edge, looking for sand crabs. Flora ran after him, scolding him for getting his breeches wet. I saw two men scavenging something from the surf. One of *Virgo*'s broken spars, it appeared.

I could see the tops of the wrecked ship's fore- and mainmast out on the water, shimmering gold with light from the setting sun. We could hear the men's voices floating on the thick air. The squalls that had done in the *Virgo* were long gone. The air was still. Palm fronds hung motionless, as if exhausted from their rattling and waving.

"I suppose I must go somewhere," I said, feeling lost. "I can't continue to impose on your kindness."

"With Mr. Hamilton away, I could use the company," Rachel offered. "If you'd like to stay on for a while. I occasionally take in boarders," she added.

"But I have nothing to offer for my keep. My husband's savings are gone. I lost all I had out there." The reality of my situation became suddenly clear.

She reached for my hand. "*De rien.* Don't worry about that, Patricia. We'll find a way."

Tears of gratitude stung the corners of my eyes.

"Well, then. It's settled. Let's go back and put Alexander to bed. Then we can have a glass of claret, you and I."

"Alexander!" She called to her son, who had wandered quite far down the beach. "Alexander Hamilton, *viens ici maintenant!*"

The child took a few more defiant steps in the opposite direction, away from Flora's grip, just to prove his independence. Then he shrieked with laughter and came running back to his mother's side as the poor servant hurried to catch up.

That night I slept restlessly, worrying about Penelope, hoping she had survived. And the cook's mate with the broken ribs for whom Penelope had risked her life—had he survived? I also worried about myself. Having survived, how would I now continue?

I wondered if Aeneas's money might somehow be

found. These Caribbean waters were transparent and not so terribly deep. If I were fortunate enough to spy the canvas belt lying on the sea bottom, then perhaps with a good length of rope, a hook, a pole, or a net, it might be recovered.

Early the next morning I revealed my intentions. Rachel looked at me askance, likely realizing the folly of this endeavor. But she didn't try to dissuade me.

"It just so happens I have a little boat," she said. "'Tisn't much of a vessel, and she's in need of a coat of paint. But she floats and she sails. And so do I. I'll help you look, if you like. Though it seems highly unlikely we shall spot your treasure, much less recover it."

After breakfast Flora and Alexander helped us drag the boat from its mooring on the sand down to the water's edge. It was a lazy blue morning, the water and sky a blur of azure, aqua, and turquoise. It seemed impossible that tragedy could happen in the midst of such tranquil beauty as this Caribbean sea.

Once the boat was launched and the mast raised, Rachel picked up her skirts and climbed into the stern. She would steer the boat while I worked the sheets, peering over the gunwales for my money belt.

I was disheartened to see beachcombers searching through the flotsam and jetsam last night's high tide had brought ashore. Planks, casks, wooden bowls, odd shoes. By law, when a ship is abandoned it becomes any man's property. Out on the water a school of shallops and jolly boats circled the wreck like hungry sharks, looking for valuables to recover.

Our little boat skimmed over the reef, the same wall of

coral that had wrecked the *Virgo,* a large ship with a deep draft. Here the warm, shallow waters were alive with colorful fish. Shimmering yellow tangs, blue and yellow parrot fish, and exotic Moorish idols with their graceful, whiplike dorsal fins darted over the rugged landscape of coral. In the crevices sea anemones waved their seductive, poisonous tentacles. Eels leered, waiting for an unsuspecting meal.

Then abruptly the reef dropped off into deeper, darker water where the *Virgo's* charred topmasts reached up like the wrists of a drowning woman. A wave of nausea came over me as I recalled the cries of panic, the smell of smoke, the cracking sound the vessel made as she broke up on the submerged reef.

Looking into the deeper waters, I could recognize parts of the deck and the rigging lying askew on the bottom, surrounded by heaps of debris from the bowels of the ship. It would be next to impossible to spy an object as small as a money belt, which might have slipped beneath the coral or some other object. Still, we tacked the little boat back and forth, back and forth, all the while staring into the water, hoping beyond hope to see a scrap of white canvas. Though it occurred to me the pouch would now be gray, having been underwater for several days.

Hours passed and the sun triumphantly climbed to its zenith, blazing down on us and burning our faces and hands and parching our throats. I was just about to give up when I saw a round gray object on the sea floor.

"Look there!" I called excitedly, loosening the sheet. Rachel put the tiller up into the wind and the sail flapped as the little boat came to a halt.

We both peered over the gunwale and there, perhaps

only fifteen feet away on the sea bottom, a face stared back at us, openmouthed. The hair, like delicate seaweed, waved softly on the surge. Though I didn't recognize the features, I had probably known the victim, for a surgeon and his mate are acquainted with nearly everyone aboard ship. I found myself transfixed, unable to look away. Rachel too stared into the watery grave, until a brightly colored angel-fish appeared and began to nibble at the corpse's bottom lip. We gasped, horrified, and set the boat in motion again. Toward shore, as fast as we could go.

As soon as I was certain I wouldn't retch, I turned to look at Rachel, who was gripping the tiller. Her sun-browned face had blanched white and when she met my eyes we both nodded grimly. Death was always so close at hand.

But I had escaped with my life, and I thanked God for sparing me. The burning sun now felt like a blessing and I realized the riches I had been given were still safe, within. They could never weigh me down.

The wind was behind us now, a favorable direction. I eased the sheets and Rachel pointed the bow of the boat directly at her house, now less than a hundred yards away.

On shore Flora was calling out, waving at us furiously.

"Something's wrong," Rachel said, her voice tightening. "Where's Alexander?"

TWO

"Now, then, Alexander, let me have a look," I said, cradling the bleeding appendage in my hands.

The laceration was on the fleshy part of his instep; he had stepped on a shard of glass from a fishing float, buried in the sand. I probed the wound quickly. A small artery had been severed, but direct pressure would stop that. An irrigation to clean it, a few stitches, a thick dressing, and he would be good as new.

The boy looked at me gravely. "Can it be fixed?"

"Quite easily," I assured him.

"Will it pain me?"

"Only briefly. You may cry if you like, but you may not need to. Squeeze your mother's hand if it stings."

"You have a real talent for doctoring," Rachel said when

I was finished and Alexander's pink foot was neatly bound with strips of her petticoat.

"I learned everything from my late husband, who was both a physician and a surgeon."

"My father was a doctor and I know good work and a good bedside manner when I see it. Why, if you were a man you could make a good living at it, I would think."

"I didn't take to it at first," I admitted. "But it's a useful set of skills to have, though I don't believe in many of the more extreme remedies. My late husband used to say that the body heals itself, given the proper conditions." And I fell silent, remembering Aeneas and his wisdom. His caring. His strength.

Rachel read to Alexander, as was her custom, every evening after supper. They were in the middle of Defoe's *Robinson Crusoe,* a book I had heard much about but had never read, as novels were forbidden to us at school. Flora and I fell under the story's spell too until the boy fell asleep in his mother's lap and she closed the book, marking her place with a scrap of paper.

"I'm parched," she declared.

Flora brought us a carafe of claret and two glasses.

We stayed up late drinking wine on the porch. The night was thick and dark with little hint of a breeze. Next to me Rachel smelled like warm milk with a drop of vanilla.

"Patricia, though I want you to stay with me, you must know that your reputation might be at risk if you associate with me for any length of time."

I simply looked at her. What could she possibly mean?

Rachel gave me a sad twist of a smile. "I have lost society's approval; I have ruined my name. Yet I can't say I'm sorry for what I've done."

"Nonsense. You're a kind and generous person for finding me on the beach and taking me into your home. And helping me search for what I've lost." The words felt like a psalm in my mouth.

"Listen. Let me start at the beginning, so you will understand," she said, lifting her wineglass to her lips.

"I was born here on Nevis. As I told you, my father was French, my mother English. They lived together a number of years before they married. Those sorts of arrangements are not uncommon here, especially on this island, which the French and English have fought over for so long. The navies and armies fight, but the men and women marry and have babies. Black, white, Jew, Catholic—these isles are one big pepper pot."

I felt she was telling me something she hadn't told many people. Something close to her heart.

"My parents separated, you see. They divorced. Then my father died and left me his estate." She sighed, looked up into the trees. "It wasn't all that much and I thought my prospects limited here in Charlestown. So I followed my sister to St. Croix, for she was to marry a well-to-do planter there. I was still young and so impatient. Easily swayed. I took my first opportunity, married a man named Lavien, and bore him a son. But he was a tyrant, impossible to live with. I could tell you many ugly stories about him." She arched her expressive brows and gave me a look as if to make certain I had understood her implications.

Yet I could not quite imagine. Had he threatened her? Beaten her?

"Yes, go on." I was drawn into her plight.

"I wanted to leave Lavien, but he wouldn't allow it. He did everything he could to control me. I escaped, but I had to leave the boy with him. Lavien kept custody, for he had the money and the means while I had none. He hunted me down and had me thrown in gaol."

"Gaol? For what?"

"For not living with him. By the law of St. Croix, he could do that. He denounced me as a whore, yet for years he refused to grant me a divorce, purely out of spite."

"But you got away," I said, admiring her for her hardihood.

She nodded. "I did. But it was James Hamilton who helped me get away. I took up with the Scotsman. My mother approved, for his family had a coat of arms. Yet he had no money, and little luck." Her mouth twisted wryly into a semblance of a smile.

"So he's good to you, this Scotsman?"

"Well, he took me away from Lavien. For that I'm grateful."

"But is he good to you?"

She shrugged. "I'm not afraid of him. He was born a gentleman, though he hasn't much to his name. His father has both property and title, but James is the fourth-born, so his portion was slim."

"But you get by?"

She studied a seam in the sleeve of her gown and picked at a loose thread. "We manage. James is in . . . shipping. Well, at the moment he is. And my inheritance is gone, but I've learned to economize."

"And where is Mr. Hamilton?" I asked.

There was a pause.

"The last I heard he was in St. Croix, drumming up investors. I expect to hear from him soon."

"Oh." *Another absent father,* I thought.

"Things could be worse," she said. "He's not a bad man. He means well; it's just that most of his schemes don't come to fruition. He's a dreamer."

"We're all dreamers," I said, remembering my own conceits of being mistress of my father's plantation.

The darkness deepened like velvet. All around us tree frogs squeaked like rusty hinges.

"I no longer care what the world thinks of me," I announced.

"Those are brash words, but empty," Rachel said. "I know, for I have said them many times myself. Yet the truth of it is, I do care.

"My first son, Peter, has been lost to me," she continued, her voice even and cold. "He is Lavien's son and by law a child belongs to his father, not his mother. And even after I moved back to Charlestown the gossip followed me. Here on Nevis I have no friends, no social connections. Because of my status, Alexander and I are outcasts."

"Your status?"

"I'm not married to Mr. Hamilton. Indeed, I cannot marry him, can never marry anyone else. So Alexander is a bastard and I am living in sin."

"But that's unfair," I said indignantly. "Especially to Alexander."

"*C'est la vie, ma chère.* And that's the law. Lavien had me jailed for adultery; he thought it would break me. It didn't. I refused to come back to him. Eventually he divorced me and married again, but he made certain I was forbidden to."

She looked off into the darkness.

"The one dream remaining in my life is for my children to be properly educated so that they might make their mark in the world instead of being slandered by it." She ran her hand lovingly through Alexander's ginger curls. "With any luck Alexander will someday escape these ravaged isles and go somewhere he can hold his head up and be respected. Perhaps even make a name for himself. A good name, that is."

We sat in silence, her story seeming to hang in the air around us.

I gulped some wine for courage. "Now you must know something about me," I said.

"*In vino veritas.*" She raised her glass in an encouraging salute.

The wine had warmed me and opened my throat.

"I was born in Barbados, a bastard child," I began. "My mother was my father's servant and he was wed to a better sort back in England. Poor Mother . . . I can't even picture her face, I must have banished her from my memory. I am ashamed of her, the woman who gave birth to me." To confess this to Rachel brought a deep sense of remorse, yet relief as well. There was no place to go but onward. I took a deep breath and let the words tumble out.

"I worshiped my father but he did little to earn it, other than to provide for my upbringing and education. Which is more than some fathers do, to be sure, and I am grateful. He wasn't a bad man, but he fell short of the mark. What I really wanted was his name and his presence in my life, but that he would not, could not give me."

Tears filled my eyes and spilled down my cheeks and I was glad it was dark, for I never liked anyone to see me weep. Rachel said nothing but her small sigh, the sympathetic note that came out like a tune, conveyed all.

I felt compelled to finish my story. "My father died when I was sixteen," I said, "leaving me nothing to live on. It seems he made quite a muddle of his affairs, so much so that he—" I had to pause and fortify myself with another swallow of wine.

"He took his own life. The plantation I hoped for was lost to me. Actually, it was never mine; I only fancied it to be." I was startled to hear my own words. The truth, out of my own mouth.

Rachel reached over and touched my knee sympathetically.

"I'm sorry. But you're young, you're strong, you have that in your favor. Find yourself a good man and go on living."

"No. I refuse to accept that. Why must our fate be tied to the whims and fortunes of a man?"

"What's the alternative, Patricia? I'd like to know."

THREE

While Alexander's foot healed I became his horse, carrying him on my back around the house, out through the garden, and down to the beach, tossing my head and neighing, to the boy's great delight. He named me "Friday" after the character in *Robinson Crusoe*, which he declared was the best story he had ever heard.

With some planks and rope that had washed up on the shore we fashioned a rude tree house. Actually, it was more like the fighting top of a ship, a platform nested where the main trunk divided, about twelve feet above the ground. We lashed together a rope ladder that could be hauled up to keep out pirates, French boarders, and other intruders.

I was glad the only clothes I had were my baggy trousers and my rugged sailor shirt, for I never could have had such fun wearing a proper dress. Though I claimed to be minding my young patient and keeping him off his foot, I lived those few weeks in a second childhood, safe in Rachel's house. I was beginning again.

When Alexander could once again bear weight, our days of leisure came to an end. Determined to enroll him in school, his mother dressed him up in a new pair of breeches and took him to Charlestown's Anglican School, where the planters' sons were educated. Though he was not yet seven, Alexander was a very precocious child. Rachel had taught him to speak French as well as English. He could read from a primer and write the letters of the alphabet. He was so very eager to learn.

"Wish me luck, Friday," he called as he walked proudly down the crushed-coral street, a slate under his arm. Though he limped a little, his face was flushed with anticipation.

A few hours later they returned home, the disappointment clear on their faces. Alexander went straight to his bedroom, refusing the lunch Flora had prepared.

Rachel broke down and wept.

"The Anglican School won't accept him. Nor will the French school on the other side of town."

"But why? He's brighter than many a ten-year-old."

She pulled a kerchief from her sleeve and wiped her eyes fiercely. "Because I'm not married to his father. Because Alexander was born out of wedlock."

"But you said yourself Nevis is one big pepper pot. That it's not uncommon for people here to live together outside of marriage."

"It depends on who you are, I suppose." Her voice was bitter.

"But I'm a—a natural child too. And I was educated in one of England's finest country schools," I said indignantly. "The best money could buy."

"That's just it. Money can buy respectability, if one has enough of it. Yet I haven't any money left. Except for this house and my father's books, my inheritance is gone. I have no friends here, no connections."

I reached for her hand. "How can I help?"

She shook her head, her eyes red but determined. "There's no future here for Alexander and me. When an opportunity comes along, I must take it, Patricia. And you must look for your opportunity too."

The following days were like ripe plums hanging from a hardening stem. Perfect, but growing heavier and soon to fall. Rachel insisted Alexander spend less time at play and more time studying.

We converted the fighting top to an arboreal schoolhouse and I became his science tutor. I taught him what I knew of how the human body works—the heart and lungs, the bones, the muscles—drawing out diagrams on the slate. Together, we became amateur ornithologists. With the instruments from my surgical kit we dissected a dead tern found at the water's edge and adopted a baby warbler that had fallen from its nest. We fed it with grubs, worms, and mashed-up fruit. (Amazingly, it lived, and eventually took off on its own.)

We were sorry to be finished with *Robinson Crusoe*, but

quickly became absorbed in *Gulliver's Travels*. The night deepened. Alexander fell asleep and was carried to bed.

"What will you do when I leave?" Rachel asked, for the tenth time, it seemed. "Go back to England? I daresay you could find a position as a tutor or a lady's companion. Really, Patricia, we must take one of my gowns to the seamstress and have it remade for you. You simply can't go around forever in your sailor's clothes."

I refused to consider it. "England holds nothing for me. I have no references, no connections, no influence any-where."

"Do you mean to stay in the islands? How will you get by?"

"I have a surgeon's skills," I said, feeling a warm glow of pride. "My husband made me his assistant. I worked by his side and when he died I took over his duties. I was the act-ing ship surgeon. That is, until the ship wrecked on its way to Nevis to pick up my replacement."

Rachel's eyes sparked curiously. "A female surgeon! And the navy permitted this?"

"Not officially. I wasn't paid. But I did the job as well as any man and the captain was glad enough for my services."

"I'm sure. What was it like?"

"Unspeakable. Horrific. Yellow fever and dysentery were far deadlier enemies than the French or the Spanish."

She nodded, wincing.

"Perhaps you could practice your skills on land. Be-come a barber-surgeon."

A sudden movement fluttered in my chest. Like bird wings. "Yes. I could do that. But would people be willing to let a woman bleed them, or shave their whiskers, or pull their rotten teeth?"

She shook her head. "Likely not. Not as long as there are men barber-surgeons to do the job."

"Then I shall dress in breeches and present myself as a man," I said, the idea seeming to come out of the blue. Its boldness was a fresh wind blowing.

We looked at each other, and the excitement of the plan seemed to shimmer in the air.

"You certainly have the height for it," she said with a nervous titter. "But do you have the audacity?"

"I shall be Patrick MacPherson," I announced, remembering Aeneas's dead nephew, and the night I had gone to Brimstone Hill in disguise, using his name. "I shall be Patrick MacPherson, surgeon's mate."

"Yes," she laughed, then quickly sobered. "'Tis a grand plan, Patricia. But I really think it would be wiser for you to return to England. Surely your home parish will take care of you."

I shook my head. "England is not my home. There's nothing for me there but debts at the boarding school. Debts my father couldn't pay." Everything was clear to me now. "I have been given the skills, the essential tools. I can earn my living by scalpel, bowl, and razor. If I must present myself as a man to be accepted, then I will." My heart thumped like a drum, giving me courage.

We looked at each other, eyes wide.

The next few weeks I rehearsed my new identity, much to the amusement of Alexander and Flora. I wore Mr.

Hamilton's clothes around the house, and while they weren't as comfortable as a sailor's, they were infinitely more practical than a woman's costume. Most importantly, they did not reveal my feminine features. My breasts were easily hid under a shirt and waistcoat and my hips are not well padded by nature. There was, of course, the most intimate physical detail to keep hidden: my menses. But my bleeding was scant and never affected my strength.

I practiced sitting, standing, and walking in a confident, masculine manner. Which, frankly, came easily to me. I practiced speaking from my chest, not my throat. Speaking directly. In statements, not tentative questions the way women so often do.

"You could pass for a lad of eighteen or even twenty, I should think," Rachel said, scrutinizing me.

What she was kind enough not to say was that my face and arms had become a mass of freckles that disguised the fact that I had no whiskers. The spots gave my face a rough and weathered look. I had always loathed my freckles but perhaps now they would be to my advantage.

After a week of practicing at home I was ready to make my debut in Charlestown as Patrick MacPherson. Late one afternoon I dressed in my attire and left the house alone, striding down Market Street to Dame Maggie's Tavern, the few pence Rachel had given me jingling in my waistcoat pocket. As it was early, there were only a few men—laborers and sharecroppers, it appeared—taking their suppers. No one gave me a second glance when I came through the door.

"Hello, stranger," a squawking voice said. I looked up to see a green parrot speaking to me from its perch above the bar.

"Hello yourself," I snapped.

I leaned against the bar, too jittery to have a seat.

"I'm Dame Maggie," a buxom Irishwoman said, turning from the tub of water where she was washing up dishes. She wiped her hands on her dirty apron. "What's your pleasure, lad?"

"A pint of ale, if you please."

"New in town, ain't ye?" She drew a foaming tankard from the tap and placed it in front of me.

I nodded, wondering if I was expected to pay now or if I could keep an account.

I decided to wait until she asked for the money.

"Patrick MacPherson's the name," I said with as much confidence as I could muster. "I was surgeon's mate on the *Virgo*."

"The ship that went down? Well, well, ain't ye a lucky one. A good many of them died and the ones that didn't have already shipped. The captain and his wife left for England a fortnight ago. Now I wonder, isn't a captain supposed to go down with his ship?" She didn't wait for an answer, but continued to feed me the news.

"Some Africans apparently survived, but they've given the authorities the slip, and rumor is they've headed inland, up the mountain, to hide out."

"Is that so?" I fervently hoped Penelope was one of them. As for Captain West and his wife, I wasn't surprised to hear they were alive.

"Where the devil have ye been hiding out these past weeks?" Maggie asked, wagging her finger at me.

"I wasn't hiding, I was quite sick. In fact, I nearly drowned."

She grinned at me, her eyes twinkling. "Nearly drowned, did ye? Well, then, that first pint is on the house. Drink to your health and rejoice in your luck, Paddy MacPherson."

"Thank you." I raised the tankard to my lips and took a long draw of the yeasty brown brew. "As to my luck, I hope it holds."

"Ye wouldn't be ilk to Gordon MacPherson, carpenter on the merchantman *Draco,* now would ye?" She leaned across the bar and inspected me with narrowed eyes.

"No, ma'am, not to my knowledge."

"Ye resemble him a bit."

"Why do you ask?"

She slapped her big-knuckled hand on the bar. "Why, the bloody reiver sailed off owing me a week's worth of ales, he did. And that ain't all." She jerked her thumb upward toward the second story, where I could hear a baby crying. "Ask my daughter Violet what else he ran out on. Left her with a squalling brat, he did."

"I am sorry to hear that," I said, my face growing warm. "But I'm no kin of that man and I'm sorry he shares my name."

"Reiver," the parrot squawked. "Son of a whore."

"Mind your tongue," Dame Maggie scolded the mouthy green bird as she reached in her pocket for a biscuit.

I took another swallow of the bitter brew to keep

up my courage. "Would you happen to know if the services of a good barber-surgeon are needed here in Charlestown?"

Her laugh sounded remarkably like the parrot's squawk. "So ye have given up on the navy, then? A deserter, are ye? Can't say as I blame ye, 'tis a hard life at sea."

I watched as she plunged two empty mugs into the tub of greasy dishwater, swished them around, and set them upside-down on the drain board.

"As to your prospects here," she continued, over her shoulder, "they ain't much good. Barber-surgeons we have aplenty. Too many surgeons and doctors, if you ask me. All of 'em charlatans in my book."

She seemed to remember something. Turned around, wiping her red hands on her apron. Leaned over the bar and lowered her voice confidentially, though only the parrot was within earshot. Her face, while plump, was careworn. Her cheeks sagged like empty pouches.

"Deserters generally come to a bad end, from what I've seen. I'm sure there'll be a battleship passing through soon enough. One that needs a good surgeon's mate. Or go over to St. Kitts—there's battleships aplenty in the Basseterre roadstead. But don't stay on Nevis; there's nothin' here for ye, lad. Go back to sea, that's my advice."

Sign on to a ship? A battleship? My breath quickened at the thought. A surgeon's mate's wages were modest and always in arrears, but room and board were guaranteed. There were dangers at sea, but there were dangers on dry land as well.

Gulping the rest of my drink, I thanked Dame Maggie and left, anxious to tell Rachel of my plan. I fairly sprinted down the road toward the warm glow of lights I had just begun to call home.

On the kitchen table I saw the remains of supper and an open letter. My heart slowed and skipped a beat. Upstairs I found Rachel, Flora, and Alexander packing books into crates by candlelight.

"Mr. Hamilton has sent for us," Rachel explained, her dark eyes shining. "He's arranged for our passage this Tuesday."

"What? So soon?" I felt a great weight of loneliness knowing my new friends were already leaving.

"Somehow he's arranged for us to be married," she said, fairly bursting. "On the Dutch isle of St. Eustatius. Once we're married we can go to St. Croix and Alexander can be enrolled in school."

"I'm happy for you," I managed to say. "And for you, Alexander." The boy's eyes were bright with hope.

"Oh, and Mr. Hamilton has found a tenant to rent this house, which should provide us some income until his business takes off. But don't worry, it will be a fortnight, surely, until the man and his family arrive."

So I would no longer have a place to stay here in Charlestown. I swallowed hard.

"And you, did you find a position, Mr. Patrick MacPherson?" she pressed.

"I believe I have," I said with as much enthusiasm as I could muster. Which wasn't quite true, but now I knew where I was headed.

I saw Rachel and her family off at Charlestown's pier. A tearful fare-thee-well it was, with promises to write. And I myself left the very next day. Serendipity seems to play such a great part in life. For as I was walking the beach the next morning, wondering what was to become of me, I came across an old fisherman sitting on his beached shallop, struggling to remove a fishhook embedded in his hand. I told him I was a surgeon and would be happy to extract it.

"But I have no money, sir. Will you take some fish? Freshly caught, they are."

"What I really want is to get over to St. Kitts. To Basseterre," I said. "Any chance of that?"

His toothless mouth dropped in astonishment. "That's where I'm headed this very day. To sell my catch to the navy. There's a fleet of warships gathering in the Basseterre roads. Looks like there's a battle afoot."

"That's where I'm bound," I said.

"A young man with your skills should be pretty useful on a ship of war."

I gulped. Though I felt no patriotic zeal and had no desire to take up arms, as a surgeon I could be of use to my countrymen. "I expect so," I said.

And so I crossed the channel on a fishing shallop, leaving Nevis behind, along with a silent prayer for Penelope. Though I had no home and no dreams yet to guide me, I was buoyed by the sparkling water and felt rich in the abundance of blue.

FOUR

In Basseterre I found lodging in a quadroon's boarding-house on the poorer side of town. As I was a surgeon looking for a ship to sign on to, she extended me credit and assured me the taverns would too. Though I had not a penny to my name, my prospects were good, for out in the anchorage sixty-eight naval ships waited impatiently at anchor, their ensigns and pennants whipping in the wind. Every day more sails appeared on the horizon, heading for Basseterre.

The war with France had been going on for six years, and now Spain had entered the conflict against Britain. Stories of victories and defeats arrived with every ship and I learned to speculate over my pint in the taverns. Soon I too could recount the alliances of governments and the maneuvers of armies and navies, but the motives disturbed me. From what I could see, this was a war of conquest, the nations fighting for control of far-flung colonies, control of the seas. Perhaps that's the basis of all wars. In any case, people would be wounded, people would become sick. My help would be needed.

It was a brand-new year: January 1762. I had just turned eighteen. Dressed in my new attire and steeped in my new identity, I frequented the taverns, hungry for the news and in need of a job.

The waterfront was buzzing with speculation. The most prevalent rumor was that Admiral Rodney was on his way aboard the *Marlborough* to lead the fleet and sweep the Spanish Main. Another rumor was that Admiral Pocock and the Earl of Albemarle commanded ten thousand troops that were preparing to storm either Panama City or Havana. Though the orders were secret, everyone had their guess.

In the taverns I felt in good company. The boasting, the jesting, the arguing, the unspoken friendship. Sometimes there were brawls, sometimes one hot-blooded gentleman called another out for a duel, yet I felt that if the enemy had burst in, we would have fought to the death. The beardless lads and the grizzled grandpas, all of us brothers in arms.

At the Noddie's Nest Inn I met two midshipmen off the *Culloden*. They in turn introduced me to their ship's surgeon, a ruddy-faced Scotsman well into his drink, but he had his quota of assistants and could take on no more.

At the Red Bullock, a lively waterfront tavern catering to warrant and petty officers, I found myself in conversation with a gregarious purser and a master's mate from the *Rose*. Although their own ship was complete, they assured me that many of the transports were in need of surgeon's assistants. I ordered another ale to bolster my hopes and another after that to keep them padded.

My new companions soon left with a prostitute, leaving me alone and feeling a bit sorry for myself as I stared at the flicker of candlelight against my pewter tankard. A new group of men walked through the door, pulling out chairs at the table next to the oaken cask that served as mine. By their dress, their powder horns, and their swagger, I knew they were gunners; I soon learned they were from the newly arrived *Richmond,* a fifth-rate frigate. I was half listening to their talk of langrage and grapeshot when I felt a tingle of recognition, a remembered dream. That voice!

His back was to me, his dark hair braided into a queue like so many of us wore. Broad shouldered in his jacket, it might have been any well-built seaman. *No, it must be the ale has befuddled my head,* I told myself. *The man you remember was a bosun's mate, not a gunner.* Yet the voice, the accent, the low laugh; Brian Dalton, it had to be! My breath quickened as a wave of longing for my old friend surged through me.

I strained to hear him apart from the others, but the noise in the tavern made it impossible. To make matters worse, the flute player and fiddler chose that moment to strike up their lively jig. The tapping of feet, the dull roar of voices, and the thrumming of blood in my ears all competed with the low vibration of his voice, yet I caught words here and there and the syllables struck a chord I could never mistake. I could smell in faint whiffs the alchemy of scents that was his alone.

All too soon the gunners drained their tankards and stood to leave, chair legs scraping the plank floor. He was so close I might have reached out and touched the hem of his jacket, yet I still could not see his face. I signed for my bill and followed them down the street toward the beach, Dalton's voice like a silver thread in the darkness. I watched them get on a jolly boat and sail it to the outermost frigate. Tomorrow, I vowed, I would seek a position on that very ship.

The cry of pelicans woke me at daybreak and I was too excited to eat breakfast. I dressed carefully, powdered my hair, and convinced a waterman to take me out to the *Richmond*.

The ship's surgeon sat at his desk, logbook open and quill in hand. Without looking up from his writing he bade me enter his gloomy cabin, which smelled of camphor. Only after he had finished his entry did he deign to look at me, squinting and wrinkling his furry eyebrows.

"Charles Brantigan, I am," he said by way of introduction. "State your business, young fellow."

"Patrick MacPherson," I said, removing my hat. "I'd like to sign on with you."

Brantigan removed his spectacles and rubbed his eyes. He seemed suddenly very tired. "I could use another mate. But what makes you think you're the man I'm looking for?"

"I am experienced and reliable, sir. Very reliable. And frankly, I need the work."

Brantigan scowled. "I would certainly hope that you are experienced and reliable if you are a surgeon. The fact that you need the work is hardly a qualification."

I stood my ground and said nothing.

"What did you say your name was?"

"MacPherson, sir. Patrick MacPherson."

"Well, Mr. MacPherson, have you any actual battle experience? What are you doing here on this godforsaken island?"

"I served aboard the hospital ship *Virgo*," I said. "For nearly a year." That was an exaggeration. "It went down, sir. Few of us survived."

He shrugged, unimpressed. "So you have seen fevers. Fluxes. Inguinal hernias. Lice and venereal pox."

"Yes." I felt my face reddening. My neck was hot and I desperately wanted to remove my stock and take off my waistcoat.

Brantigan drummed his fingers on his desk, a sharp tattoo. I struggled to keep my hopes up.

"A hospital ship is not a battleship, MacPherson. Have you ever tended a marine whose leg has just been ripped off by a cannonball or dug splinters of mast out of a sailor's face?"

"No, sir. But I am willing to learn," I shot back.

"But the question is, are you capable of learning?" The surgeon's eyes bored deeper. "Tell me, MacPherson, what is the appropriate treatment for a traumatic amputation?"

"Prevent exsanguination and shock," I said. "Wrap a tourniquet about the stump to control bleeding. Dress it and medicate for pain."

He nodded, unimpressed, and wiped his spectacles with his handkerchief. "A textbook response. But quite often an amputated limb scarcely bleeds at all, at least initially. The vessels clamp down of their own accord. Sometimes the victim feels no pain for hours, and then it is his missing limb that pains him. Often the poor fellow dies three weeks later of blood poisoning or gangrene, in spite of all your efforts. Are you ready for that, young man? Are you prepared to see a man beheaded by a cannonball, eviscerated by a saber, blown to bits by langrel?"

"I am prepared to do what I must," I said, swallowing hard. "When the time comes."

A look of extreme irritation crossed his face and he tapped his quill impatiently. "Young man, I am not talking about the operating theater of a hospital ship where everything is under the surgeon's control. I am talking about the cockpit of a battleship in action. Slipping in warm blood and entrails, the wounded stacked up three deep in the companionway. I am talking about hearing men cry like babies for their mothers, begging for you to relieve their pain or end their miserable life. Have you had that experience, MacPherson?"

I shook my head. "No, sir. I have not."

"Well, God forbid you do," he said, his eyes afire. "But that is what we must be prepared for. And no man knows how he will react until he finds himself in the situation. The strongest of men I have seen run, hide, or drop to their knees puking and gagging like a cat with a hairball."

Brantigan now leaned forward, his gaze nearly unbearable. "Look here, MacPherson. Do you really think you're good enough to be one of my mates?"

"I do," I said as surely as I could, though my stomach fluttered and my fingertips tingled.

Several unendurable seconds passed. I dared not swallow or even blink.

"Then you're the man," he said with a faint curl to his lips. "I will speak to Captain Elphinstone and he'll have you sign articles. Surgeon's second mate. You'll lash your hammock beside Dudley Freeman, surgeon's first mate. Your training begins tomorrow morning, bright and early at seven bells. Sign here." He opened a logbook, handed me his quill, and with shaking hands I signed my new name. Then with the small advance I was given, I settled my bills on land and purchased a pair of shoes that fit me better than Mr. Hamilton's.

The *Richmond* was but five years old, a fast frigate, well kept and efficiently sailed. The two hundred and twenty officers and men she carried were a proud crew and I was honored to be among them. Our captain was John Elphinstone, a calm and self-possessed man who proved to be a most brave yet prudent seaman. He soon won our respect and loyalty, to a man.

We quickly learned it was not Admiral Rodney's but Sir George Pocock's flag we sailed under. Our orders were still secret, yet we knew from the sheer size of the fleet that this would be a momentous encounter.

The bosun's whistle piped shrilly and the men began to work the windlass. Anchors aweigh, we left Basseterre roadstead on a fresh easterly under a press of sail, heading south until we were past sight of St. Eustatius so that the Dutch might not handily observe our leaving. For several days I was too busy to even look for the gunner who had reminded me of the bosun's mate I once knew.

Brantigan met with the other surgeon's mate and myself every morning after breakfast for sick call. At first no one was sick, for spirits were high; so we spent the morning rehearsing what we would do during battle and how we were to treat various injuries such as avulsed wounds, head trauma, severed limbs, and powder burns. I practiced using bone saws on old pieces of timber, and I practiced suturing, reusing the same piece of catgut until Brantigan was satisfied with my speed and finesse.

During the long afternoons I was put to work tearing sheets of muslin for bandages and picking oakum to be used for packing wounds. Some of the women aboard helped me with these chores and I was grateful for their company as much as their assistance. As was customary, the women were not entered on the muster books or officially recognized or provided for, but they were counted on nonetheless in time of battle. The wives were expected to help the boys carry cartridges up from the powder room to the guns, and if casualties were high, they were to assist the surgeon and his mates in the care of the wounded. The women of the ship were invisible, and though history would likely forget them entirely, I would not.

Surgeons and their mates were among the fortunate few who stood no watch on a ship but had the luxury of sleeping all night unless all hands were called to battle stations or to respond to some other emergency. For me it was more a curse than a blessing, for I had trouble falling asleep, as I always had, belowdecks. Now it was even worse, for I had not only my sense of confinement to quell, but my fears as well.

Brantigan slept in the surgeon's cabin, a tiny, airless cubicle, but private. Freeman and I, as surgeon's mates, had no cabin but hung our hammocks like sailors on the lower deck, just aft of the sick berth. We were separated from our patients by a mere curtain of canvas.

Freeman was Brantigan's second cousin and had been apprenticed to him when he was thirteen. He was older than I, nearly twenty he was, and he had seen action in the Gulf of St. Lawrence aboard this very ship. He had far more experience than I did, and he knew it. He tried to cow me with stories of gore, death, and dismemberment.

"You'll see plenty of blood soon enough, and you'll know then why the decks of a battleship are painted red," he said, tying the foot of his hammock up with two half hitches around the crossbeam.

"Yes, I suppose so," I said as calmly as I could manage. Wishing he would change the subject.

Freeman kicked off his shoes and hoisted himself into his hammock while I was still fumbling to lash mine. "I hope you are not going to freeze at the first round of artillery fire," he prodded. His big white feet dangled over the sides of his hammock.

"Your feet stink, Freeman," I said, at last securing my hammock with an unseaman-like knot and flinging myself into bed.

He just laughed. "Have you ever smelled a gangrenous wound, MacPherson? Next to a rotten leg, my feet smell like jasmine." He wiggled his long toes for emphasis, then curled himself into the sling of canvas. "Brantigan says you've no battle experience. I hope you don't water your pants when the first man falls."

"Are you calling me a coward?" I shot back.

Freeman snorted. "Don't be so defensive, my friend.

I'm just trying to prepare you. Toughen you up, you know? A man never knows how he will do in battle until he is fired upon and hears the screams of his compatriots as they fall all around him."

"Thanks, mate," I said dryly, extinguishing the hanging lantern and turning my back to face the canvas wall.

"Say, MacPherson, do you play whist?" Freeman said, his voice disembodied in the utter blackness.

"What?" I said, still facing the wall.

"You know, whist? Or any sort of cards?"

"Never."

"What are you, a Quaker or something?"

"Not that I know of," I quipped. "I'm just not very good at cards."

"A pity. Thought you might like to be my partner. The officers play in the wardroom most afternoons," he said, flaunting his association with the ship's gentility. "Never know what connections you might make. Besides, it helps pass the hours."

"I don't think you'd want me for your card partner," I said.

"Don't worry, I'll teach you."

"I detest gaming."

"We'll fix that. Sweet dreams, MacPherson." Freeman yawned with great abandon and soon began to snore.

Meanwhile, I lay wide awake in my cocoon of a hammock, listening to the muffled sounds on deck and the whispers of the ship as she slid through the water.

FIVE

The gunner was bent over the stern starboard swivel gun, his back toward me. It appeared he was cleaning it or inspecting it in preparation for the gun drill that afternoon. I approached him, my heart banging. The closer I got, the more certain I was.

"Brian Dalton," I said, removing my hat so that my unpowdered hair, though braided up in a queue, would shine red in the sun.

He glanced over his shoulder, his face showing annoyance at being interrupted.

"So," I said breathlessly, my throat tight around my words, "I see you are no longer a bosun's mate."

He raised his hand to shield his eyes from the bright sun. His nose was smudged with black powder, his sable eyes as unfathomable as ever. I watched his pupils widen into the dark rings surrounding them. His jaw slackened and a whoosh of air escaped his mouth, as if he had been punched in the stomach.

"Patrick MacPherson; do you remember me?" I said, extending my hand. My smile, though wide, quivered.

His mouth dropped open. He was visibly shaken as he clasped my outstretched hand. I felt I was struck by lightning. The breath knocked out of me.

Dalton's face had drained of all color but for the black smudges that now stood out in relief.

"Princess?" he said, his voice barely audible.

When I heard his old pet name for me, my eyes stung and I was overcome by wordless memory. His smell, the saltiness of his lips.

"I cannot believe my eyes," he said at last, looking me up and down, still holding my hand. "How fare ye?"

"Well," I said. "And you?"

He nodded slowly, his eyes wide.

"I suppose I have changed somewhat since we last saw one another," I admitted, looking down at my gentleman's attire.

"The name 'Princess' no longer fits, that's for certain. But why? What has become of ye?"

"It's a long story," I said, rolling the corner of my hat and wondering how to begin. "I became who I am to survive. Because my pride could not allow me to face a life of poverty or charity. I am a surgeon's mate," I added with a measure of esteem.

Behind us we heard voices approaching. One is never alone for long on a ship. The master and first lieutenant had come up the aft companionway discussing matters of navigation. Octants in hand, they approached the rail where we were standing.

"Meet me tonight." Dalton turned his attention back on the swivel gun. His hand trembled as his blackened finger rubbed the touchhole.

"Where?"

"Aloft on the fighting deck," he said, blowing into the hole. "Half past midnight; one bell."

I watched as he moved on to the next gun and began to inspect it. Four midshipmen joined the officers on the quarterdeck to take noon sights; meanwhile, Mr. Stevens, the bosun's mate, appeared in the ship's waist and piped the first call to the midday meal.

Dalton took his meals with the other warrant officers, and I, a mate of a warrant officer, took mine with others of my station. Our table was a wooden top suspended on ropes between two twelve-pound cannons. What a turnabout from the days aboard *Canopus* when I fancied myself a lady and sat at a table with Mary Blake and the gentlemen in the officers' wardroom, sipping good wine instead of grog! I didn't think I could ever go back to being Patricia Kelley, bastard daughter of a ruined gentleman. Well educated but without influence or property. Nor could I go back to being the widow MacPherson, late husband's savings lost at sea, now dependent on charity. My disguise had given me the freedom to move from world to world. To cross invisible boundaries and to experience life from different perspectives.

My messmates were five: Dudley Freeman; Goodwillie,

gunner's mate; Hicks, the sail maker; Wickham, carpenter's mate; and Iris, his young wife. The Wickhams had been with the ship since it was first launched five years ago and had seen action in both the St. Lawrence campaigns and the Channel blockade. Iris was plain as a sparrow, her teeth were falling out, but she never hesitated to smile and show what was left of them. We all enjoyed her cheerful company. Her laughter, her sisterly attentions. Freeman told me she had birthed twins last year, but both were stillborn. Two years before, she had delivered a baby who lived only a week. Of course Iris herself never spoke of this. Nor did her husband. Shipmates never speak of tragedy. They say it's because sailors are a superstitious lot and think it's bad luck to do so. But maybe it's selfish to speak of sorrow, for who hasn't had his share?

Across the table there was Goodwillie, a bandy-legged boy with a clubfoot and an easy laugh. Goodwillie could find the best in any situation, no matter how grim. When the tension got thick, he would always say something unexpected and funny, causing us to break out in yelps of laughter. I suppose he was thirteen or fourteen years of age, though I never heard him say. He was loyal to Dalton, the chief gunner; in fact, I believed he worshiped him.

"What do you say to that, MacPherson?" the carpenter's mate prodded.

"Pardon?" I had been lost in thought, stirring my bowl of salt beef and boiled peas.

"Don't mind MacPherson; he's a nervous Nellie," Freeman said to the others. Though I was irked by his comment I decided to play into his hand.

"I suppose I am a bit jittery," I said. "Having trouble

sleeping as well. So don't be surprised if I get up in the night and go on deck for a bit of air."

"You'll feel better," Goodwillie said, tearing a bite of biscuit with the side of his mouth, "as soon as we have something to do. The waiting is the hardest part."

The men all nodded and grunted in agreement. But Iris, like many women, had a way of disarming a person. Of knocking a hole in one's bastion with a seemingly innocent but penetrating question.

"Have you a wife, MacPherson?" she asked, innocently enough.

"No," I muttered, stirring my stew more vigorously.

"A special girl?" she persisted.

My hand holding the spoon trembled and I had to put it to work, stirring, stirring, stirring. No one else spoke to relieve me. I knew she was waiting for me to elaborate. I lifted a spoonful of broth to my lips and forced myself to swallow it.

"I was once married," I said. "But my—he—she—died," I sputtered.

The sound of spoons scraping bowls seemed to me to be making an incredible din.

"I am sorry for your loss," Iris said. "You are so young." I could feel her eyes upon me, filled with womanly empathy. I willed myself to stay strong and remain silent.

I was now off the hook. Iris turned to Goodwillie and asked him if he had a girl he fancied.

"I fancy them all, Mrs. Wickham," he said earnestly.

We all laughed, glad for the opportunity. And lifted our mugs to wives, to sweethearts, and to England.

★　★　★

That afternoon we were piped to battle stations. I still did not recognize the various toots and tweets on the bosun's whistle and had to rely on Freeman to interpret these for me. Of course my mate was all too glad to exhibit his greater knowledge. After reporting to the cockpit we were allowed to watch the men practice at arms, a fine display of skill, I thought.

The sergeant drilled the marines at their muskets and the master-at-arms rehearsed the sailors and landsmen in the use of small weapons, while the junior officers parried their swords on the quarterdeck. But most impressive of all was the firing of the ships' cannons.

Dalton had appointed a captain for each gun and a crew of sailors to operate it. There was much good-natured rivalry between them to see which team could fire their piece the fastest and farthest. The cannons themselves seemed to be part of the ships' company and the men referred to them with pride and affection, calling them by such names as Smoking Annie, Hot Lips, Maggie May, and the like.

The gun crews moved quickly and efficiently, like the inner works of a clock. Worming, swabbing, loading, ramming. The running out of cannons with heaves and grunts, a touch of the linstock to the powder, and the cry of "Fire in the hole!" A flash and then the cannon leaped back like a beast in chains. The boom was deafening; I could feel it like a fist against my chest. Then the cloud of smoke and the smell of black powder. I remembered watching Dalton fire the few small cannons on the merchantman *Canopus*—now here he was the warranted gunner of a thirty-two-gun frigate. My old friend had done well for himself.

After the gun drill we all settled back into our afternoon routines. Then came the dogwatches and a sudden, spectacular nightfall. Here in the tropics the days are never long. Supper was a quiet affair, each of us deep in our own thoughts or worries. Little was said. The bell clanged, the watch changed, the evening wore on. I stretched out in my hanging bed, pretending to sleep.

Midnight. The next half hour passed so slowly I was certain the sands in the ship's glass had clotted. At last, the bell rang and I slipped out of my hammock and made my way in the darkness through the rows of bulging hammocks and up the companionway onto the deck. The night was a fine one. A steady wind, the sails casting moon shadows on the shimmering water.

It felt good to climb the rigging after so long. The sticky tarred rope in my hands again, the give of the ratlines underfoot. This time I climbed in shoes, for I was a gentleman now and gentlemen don't skylark barefooted, though skin gives a better grip than leather. I recalled with a flash how the rough ratlines used to cut into the soles of my bare feet, producing a strangely agreeable discomfort. Agreeable, I suppose, because it meant security, especially when the rigging was wet.

Reaching the futtock shrouds below the fighting top, I could already smell his pipe. I negotiated this awkward section of rigging as best I could, for the futtocks require a bit of nerve and upper body strength, and I was sorely out of practice. Pulling myself up, out, and around the alarming angle of the ratlines, I flopped onto the relative safety of the fighting top, where Dalton stood, leaning against the mast and smoking his pipe.

"I see ye have not lost your grace aloft," he said wryly.

"You might have given me a hand," I panted, struggling to my feet and brushing my breeches, now streaked with tar.

"Ye don't need my help," he said with a sad smile. "Besides, how would it look, one man helping another over the futtock shrouds? We aren't on an undermanned merchant vessel anymore. The watch on a navy frigate never sleeps." He puffed his pipe and I inhaled the smell as if to store it in my head forever. "Unless ye are ready to give up your manly disguise."

"It is no longer entirely a disguise," I said with an edge of irritation. "It has become my way of life. If I were to reveal my other self, what would become of me? I have no means of support, Mr. Dalton."

"Ye could always marry the ship's doctor."

His words cut me to the quick. I looked away, out to sea. "And what would you have done in my shoes? You had options."

"Not the one option I wanted at the time," he said. I could feel his eyes still on me.

"I don't make the rules in this world," I snapped.

"Nor do I." His voice had softened and was conciliatory.

"Tell me." I composed myself and turned back to face him. Wanting to reconnect with that closeness we once shared. "Where have you gone and what have you done these many months? And when did you give up ropes and rigging for gunpowder?"

Dalton shrugged in his laconic manner. That simple gesture nearly made me crumble with an unnamable emotion. A mixture of regret and desire.

"I've been back to England, but I didn't stay long," he

said. "Nothing much has changed there. Then I signed on to the *Richmond* as a gunner because they needed one and I had some experience. I knew the guns. And I could read and write, which the Ordnance Board requires."

I must have shown my surprise, for he said, "I'll wager ye didn't know that about me. Ye probably thought I signed my name with an X."

True, I had thought him illiterate. But not ignorant. "I no longer judge people by the same standards I once did," I said simply. "So you became a gunner. What then?"

"We took part in a Channel blockade and we saw action off the coast of France," he continued, not elaborating. Eyes averted, remembering.

"Action? You mean a battle?" I pressed.

He nodded, sucking on the stem of his pipe. "We took a French frigate."

"What was it like? Were there many casualties?"

"Aye," he said, his face clouding. "More than enough. War is every bit as bloody as they say, Princess. I fear ye have chosen the wrong line of work."

"I did not choose my trade, just as I did not choose my sex," I quipped.

He looked at me with opaque, unfathomable eyes. "What happened to the Scottish physician ye married?"

"He died of fever." Instinctively I touched the locket that I wore hidden beneath my shirt.

"I am sorry for your loss." He did not lower his eyes but held mine fast in his gaze.

"Aeneas MacPherson was a good man." A painful knot formed in my chest as I spoke of him. "He shared his life with me, he taught me a surgeon's skills. He loved me, and

I grew to love him." I wanted Dalton to know this. That I had loved my husband.

"And I loved his wife," Dalton said, his voice hoarse. "Though being only a sailor, I was in no position to have her myself."

My head reeled. Dalton had loved me? I had loved him too, and desired him. I desired him now; a burst of warmth was flowing through my veins, my heart quickening upon hearing his voice. Love and lust—can they exist together? Could two people be so fortunate to have so much in common? Can life be so magnanimous?

"I am no longer the girl you knew aboard *Canopus*," I said, my eyes still searching his.

A hint of a smile sparked in his eyes. "Then who are ye?"

"I don't know," I admitted, allowing a smile to break through. "I'm still finding out."

"Fair enough," he said. "So tell me how ye came to be a surgeon's mate."

I told Dalton all that had befallen me since I last saw him on Antigua, and he listened without comment until I had run out of words.

"I too have changed. I've become a gunner, I've seen battle. Men killed and ships destroyed." He paused and shook his head as if to rid himself of memories. "And through it all I have thought about ye. More often than ye know." Dalton's eyes were shining with such intensity as I had never before seen. His voice broke when he spoke again. "I never dreamed I would see ye again."

We stood entranced, our eyes swimming, until I broke the spell.

"Do you have a wife?" I blurted out, twisting the button of my jacket and dreading to hear his answer.

He laughed and slapped his thigh. "By God, ye may dress like a man, Patrick MacPherson, but ye ask a female's questions! Do I have a wife? Well, I have not been a monk all this time, that's certain. But nae, Princess; I have not married."

I longed for him to touch me; I wanted to feel his strong arms around me once more, to press my mouth against his, but it was impossible. With more than two hundred souls aboard, there was no privacy. If we were seen embracing, I would have to reveal myself as a woman to keep us from being executed for sodomy. Dalton and I must not embrace, we must not touch. We would have to be careful even what we said to one another. There are few secrets aboard a ship, but this one must be kept.

SIX

At the end of May a staging of British vessels took place off Hispaniola. Frigates, battleships, victuallers, munitions ships, bomb vessels, and transports—two hundred ships under Sir George Pocock's blue flag and fourteen thousand soldiers commanded by George Keppel, the Earl of Albemarle—all gathered in Cape St. Nicolas. By now the plan was no longer a secret from the crew; the entire fleet was to sail up the Straits of Bahama to take Havana, Spain's port city on the northwest coast of Cuba. To take it by surprise, as no one in their wildest dreams would expect an attack from that direction. The Straits was a passage that hadn't been used for over a century, studded as it was with cays and unmarked reefs and rife with treacherous currents. It was an audacious plan.

On the twenty-seventh we entered the Straits. The *Richmond* led the way, her small boats going ahead, taking soundings and marking the channel with buoys. Captain Elphinstone had an old Spanish chart, booty from one of the galleons Admiral Anson captured years ago. But the soundings were old and he was wise not to depend on it.

The captain posted a dozen lookouts aloft on all three masts, as well as on the bowsprit. We sailed slowly, cautiously, dispatching our boats with messages, hastily drawn charts, and navigational information back to the flagship. Admiral Pocock developed a set of signals using flags by day and torches by night, so that the entire fleet might safely negotiate the channel. It was a harrowing sail and there was never a moment when we could let down our guard and relax. Everyone aboard felt the strain yet no one spoke of it, for that is the way of seamen. To do so would show weakness and might bring bad luck. Sailors are a proud and superstitious lot.

Every man aboard was strung tight and it was the implacable routine of shipboard life that kept us from breaking. Every man had his dull but necessary duties that gave him something to do with the burden of time. The livestock needed to be fed and the mangers mucked out. The rust accumulated on the ironworks and begged for chipping. Rigging continually needed mending, decks needed scouring, and the anchors strung up on the catheads needed to be coated with fish oil. The officers studied Anson's old chart, wrote in their logs, and sent dispatches to Pocock; meanwhile, eager young servants polished their masters' shoes and swords, made their beds, and climbed in the rigging to look for coral heads that could sink us.

Though there was plenty of work, there were still long hours to be endured. Many officers and men played cards, dice, or backgammon. Though gambling was forbidden, it was generally overlooked if the stakes weren't high and drunkenness did not get out of hand.

Many a man slept whenever he could, grabbing an opportunistic nap in the shade of a sail. For them sleep was a refuge. But I could not nap; I could scarcely sleep even at night. I lay in my swaying hammock until the wee hours listening to the sounds of the ship, my mind racing. Even more than dying, I feared failing in my duties, letting my shipmates down. I feared witnessing the death of others and being powerless to save them. I feared panic and mayhem. And most of all I feared losing Brian Dalton.

Every morning upon arising after a fitful sleep I was immediately aware of the turmoil that began in the pit of my stomach and found its way to all parts of my body. The tingling stayed with me all day, yet there was nothing to do but endure it.

We entered waters that were studded with low-lying cays. Dangerous waters on all sides. The officers paced the decks like cats, twisting their spyglasses anxiously in their hands. All eyes were on the alert for the ruffled appearance of shoal water and the lighter turquoise color of shallows; all ears were listening for the warning cries from the lookouts posted in the tops of every mast.

On the afternoon of June 3, a line of squalls formed to windward and we cursed our luck as they swept closer, as if we were magnets. Soon the wind pelted us with stinging rain and pushed the sea into mounds. We held our course and the watch stood by, ready to leap into the rigging to shorten sail.

Yet I knew we needed every bit of power from full sail to keep us from being swept leeward, onto the shoals. Captain Elphinstone stood by the binnacle, ever watchful, while the master conning the ship shouted instructions to the two men placed at the helm. Ours was a situation that called for quick, sound judgment and steady nerves.

But my nerves were far from steady. Driven by nausea, I staggered to the leeward rail and spewed the remains of my dinner into the frothy sea. Memories of the *Virgo* going down in flames overcame me; I dropped to my knees, trembling.

"Oh, Christ, the wind is veering," the master shouted to the first lieutenant. "Tighten the sheets, haul on clews, bunts, and reefs. Full and by, helmsmen! Sail 'er like hell, lads!"

I vomited again, retching and gagging.

The shoal water was just off our larboard beam and every man could see it. It looked like boiling green water. The ship seemed not to make any headway, and I prayed the wind and the seas would not push us to leeward.

"Two to starboard!" the master barked to the helmsmen.

"Two on, sir," came the affirmation.

I felt a firm hand on my shoulder. Dalton's hand.

"Take heart, MacPherson. We're going to make it," he said cheerfully. "Look, there's blue sky to windward."

Through my fear and nausea, his reassurance comforted

me. I closed my eyes and breathed in deep gulps of air. Cupped some water running in the scuppers and washed a spindle of yellow bile from my chin.

The squall passed quickly, leaving behind clear skies and calm seas. The *Richmond* sailed on, unscathed.

Evening was drawing near and I was one of the ones assigned to go to the cays. Here we were to light bonfires and keep them burning all night until the entire fleet had passed through the maze of islands into safer waters beyond.

I arranged to go in Dalton's boat with Goodwillie and three sailors. Dalton nodded at me as I climbed into the launch but neither of us spoke. I took my seat and picked up an oar. Rowing toward the low-lying island, we passed through a break in the reef. The strong outgoing current tried to sweep us away and we had to paddle fiercely to keep our small boat from broaching. Once inside the lagoon it was easy going to the pink sandy beach. Laughing with relief, we waded ashore, dragging the boat behind us and tying it to a mangrove root.

The island was hardly bigger than the deck of a warship and was inhabited only by terns and coconut crabs. Yet the ragged reef encircling the sliver of land could have sunk our entire fleet. We gathered palm fronds and coconut husks to use for kindling and set to work cutting mangrove branches to supplement the wood we had brought from the ship. Our orders were to maintain a fire on each end of the cay throughout the night.

I had hoped for time alone with Dalton but there was

much work to be done. Although the sun was low on the horizon I was soon dripping with sweat, as were the others. We talked and joked as we gathered fuel and swatted at the mosquitoes and the sand fleas that clung to us. When at last we had two fires burning and had divided ourselves into two groups of three to attend them, some of the men decided to refresh themselves in the lagoon. They stripped off their clothes, left them hanging on mangrove branches, and ran naked into the turquoise water, eager as dogs fetching sticks. They called to Dalton and me to join them.

"Ye mates enjoy yourselves," Dalton called. "MacPherson and I will keep a lookout for any sand sharks that might be lurking in the lagoon. They are known to feed at twilight." He looked at me and winked.

The frolicking came to a quick halt and the men soon slogged out of the water, their bodies glistening. I envied them for how cool and clean they must feel after their short bath.

We cooked our supper of salt pork and dried peas, a bland and colorless stew that was our fare three nights a week aboard ship. Somehow it tasted heartier tonight, cooked over a fire in the sand. I scraped my bowl clean, then took my finger and wiped up what was left, licking it so as not to waste a drop.

Like schoolboys on a holiday, we were. Laughing, joking, telling stories. Talking of how we would survive if the fleet took off and left us stranded here. How we would sharpen mangrove sticks to spear fish and weave palm frond fibers into nets to catch birds. Drink coconut milk and collect rainwater. Roast crabs.

"I wouldn't eat a crab," Goodwillie said with disgust. "Scuttling scavengers, they are. Like eating a spider with a shell."

"Ye'd eat one if you were hungry enough," Dalton said.

"I'll be damned if I would," his mate maintained, stretching out on the sand and making himself comfortable.

"Ye'll eat a fish, won't ye?"

"I'll only eat fish if there's no meat to be had."

Dalton added another branch to the fire, poking it restlessly.

"How about a game of dice?" Goodwillie suggested, patting his pocket.

Dalton shook his head. "Ye already owe me a king's ransom."

"Come on, sir, be a sport."

The gunner shook his head and laughed. "All right, mate, ye're on. We'll play for coconuts."

The sun sank into a golden sea. We sat entranced, watching the last trace of sunlight replaced by light from the swelling moon high overhead.

Goodwillie drank his portion of grog and settled into the sand to sleep. Like any sailor he could fall asleep at will. Within minutes his breathing was deep and regular. We could see the fire at the other end of the cay, saw it leap and sparkle as more logs were added. We could hear the low voices and occasional bursts of laughter from the three men attending it.

"'Tis good to be with ye again," Dalton said earnestly. "Yet I wish ye had not come. I fear for your safety. And for what ye will see and hear in the days ahead."

"I've seen and heard much already," I said. "Death is not new to me."

"Ye have not yet seen battle," he reminded me. The scent from his pipe drifted my way.

I wrote my name in the sand with my forefinger.

"What will ye do afterward?" Dalton asked.

"I don't know," I admitted, writing Brian's name next to mine. "What will you do?"

He shrugged. "When the ship pays off, I might take my wages and go have a look at the northern colonies."

"America?" I picked up a handful of the coarse sand and let it run through my fingers, obliterating both names.

"Aye. America. I have a mind to see that country."

"I've heard it's a rugged land," I said. "Indians and wild beasts on the edge of every town."

He laughed. "Sounds like my sort of place. Why don't ye come with me?" His tone was playful, but his eyes asked something more. By the light from the bonfire, they shone expectantly. At that moment I would have gone anywhere on earth with him. Anywhere at all.

"I'm in no position to take a wife, yet I must ask ye just the same. Could ye be happy with the likes of me?" His voice cracked. Gone was the playfulness. He leaned forward earnestly and I could hear him breathing.

I didn't know how to answer him. I wasn't sure what happiness was or even who I was. But I desired him, that much was sure. I wanted to lose myself in that blind hunger we both felt. To do away with words, customs, manners, clothes. To forget war and disavow death.

"Could you be content with a woman like me, Mr. Dalton? That's the real question. For I cannot go back to the girl I once was, the stowaway you taught to climb the rigging. Nor could I ever be a sailor's wife, keeping a man's cottage and minding his mewling brats while he was off at sea for months on end. I am ruined for all of that, you know. Look at me," I said, pressing my freckled, sunburned cheeks between my ragged hands. "Is this what you want?"

The questions hung in the air like smoke and we said no more but stared into the fire, the glowing red embers and leaping yellow tongues of flame entrancing us. Dalton kicked at a log and a shower of sparks shot skyward. Out at sea we could see the silhouettes of ships making their way through the marked channel, the moon and our fires to guide them. In the sand beside us, Goodwillie slumbered. Dalton stood and pulled me to my feet.

"Let's take a swim," he said.

"But I cannot," I protested. "I don't know how to swim."

His laugh was low and teasing. "Ye won't have to. Come on, don't be afraid. The water is warm and I was jesting about the sand sharks."

He nibbled my earlobe, his breath hot. He murmured something as his stubbled cheek brushed against my neck. I was afire, but nervous about Goodwillie, sleeping so close by. Dalton stood up, pulled me to my feet, and motioned me to follow him to the water's edge, where we stripped off our clothes, leaving them where they fell in a heap on the sand.

Brian pulled me out to dark waters. Touching now, bodies pressed together, kissing deeply. I remember the taste of salt, the coolness of the water against my hot skin. The force of our love obliterated all need for words.

SEVEN

On the fifth day of June we were clear of the treacherous straits, the entire fleet having come through the passage without damage. It was an incredible feat of seamanship and bravado, but we had no time to celebrate, for we were less than forty miles to windward of Havana, our intended prize.

The troops disembarked some distance east and began marching; meanwhile, the warships made for Havana's harbor. The Morro Castle soon came into our view, an immense, seemingly impenetrable stone fortress rising from the east heights as if it had been hewn out of the cliff.

Across the bay to the west was the governor's fort. Inside the walls, a cluster of elegant mansions, tiles gleaming in the sun. Above the roofs rose the spire of a massive cathedral, nearly as formidable as the castle on the opposite shore. Beyond the fort's protective wall, a sprawl of wooden buildings and rutted roads disappeared into the dense tropical brush. This was Havana, the richest city in the New World, and our intended prize.

Cannons blazing, *Richmond* led the frigates and warships to the harbor mouth. There were only twelve battleships in the spacious anchorage—apparently our arrival had been a complete surprise. The men cheered as they fired the guns, the women and children came on deck to watch, and our officers stood on the quarterdeck in full dress in spite of the heat.

The frigates immediately set up a harbor blockade. We assumed the army was preparing to take the castle from the unfortified eastern ridge, the fortress's only weak spot. But the news soon came that instead of assaulting while the soldiers were fresh, General Keppel had ordered a siege.

"A siege? Is he brainsick?" Captain Elphinstone said to the ship's master as they stood on the quarterdeck. "We win him the advantage of complete surprise and he throws it away on a siege! It'll take months to win and we'll lose many men in the process."

"I expect that is all he knows of warfare, sir," the master said. "The earl's a parade-ground officer. Never has seen a real battle, especially not one in these deadly climes."

"Damnation!" Elphinstone cursed. "The price in men's lives will be higher with a siege than it would be with an all-out attack. Soldiers are already dropping from the heat."

The news quickly spread through the ship.

"Let's storm the fort," the sailors shouted. "We'll show those bloody landsmen how to fight."

The men would soon have their chance.

The next few days the word from shore was even more discouraging, as the lay of the land was making it difficult to cut off the castle from the city. Colonel Howe and eighteen hundred troops were sent to the west side of Havana to attempt to sever communications and divert the city's water supply. Meanwhile, on the east side, engineers were laying saps and building batteries from which to fire upon the castle. But the soldiers weren't accustomed to such heat, and their progress was slow.

Sailors were sent ashore to assist, taking the best gunners with them. They soon proved their worth, for seamen could fire their cannons twice as fast and much more accurately than the army artillerymen. It was apparent that if we were to win this prize for Britain, it would take every one of us working together.

Dalton, Goodwillie, and one of our gun crews were among the first to go, taking with them two twelve-pounders and a wagon of shot and powder. Dalton came to find me just minutes before he left; I was counting drugs in the dispensary.

"I am going to shore to follow the sappers," he said, wide-eyed, his face flushed. "Goodwillie and I, we've just received our orders."

I clung to a vial of guaiacum, nearly crushing it in my fist.

He pulled me to him, kissing me swiftly. A hard kiss it was, and I felt his teeth against mine.

"Dalton!" the first lieutenant's voice called from above.

"Aye, sir. I come!" he called, then dropped his voice. "Don't worry, Princess," he whispered, looking at me intently. "Ye are still my Princess, aren't ye?" His eyes were deep black wells with points of light on the surface. "Luck has been with me so far."

"You're going to need more than luck," I said, gripping his arms.

"Nae, lass; in battle good luck is the best friend a man can have."

He turned and left. I stood as if paralyzed, listening to the sound of his footsteps bounding up the companionway. I could do nothing to stop the tears that welled up in my eyes and the fear that gripped my heart. The thought of losing Dalton again was unbearable.

We received word that General Elliot had taken possession of the outlying town, though skirmishes with peasants continued. There was as yet no artillery fire, but the men were constructing breastworks and requested more sandbags. Glad for something to do, I helped to cut old sails and biscuit bags that would be filled with sand from the landing beach.

Our people aboard the *Richmond* remained healthy, though reports from the land were not encouraging. A number of the foot soldiers, ill clothed and unaccustomed to the heat, had already fallen. Other ships were landing cannon and stores to assist the army in their siege. If Albemarle had attacked at once we might have been on our way home by now, victorious. Instead we continued our blockade of the harbor, while on shore the able were burying the first victims of heat and tropical disease.

On the fifteenth of June the rains came. No short-lived squalls, these, but days of gray skies and downpours. A mixed blessing, for the water was needed, and aboard ship we collected as much as we could.

Three days later the rains had ceased and the sun rose, hotter than ever. Brantigan sent word for Freeman and me to report to the dispensary. We found him preparing a kit of medicinals.

"You two are going ashore," he said, "to help the army set up field hospitals." He handed Freeman the box. "I'm giving you all the laudanum and Peruvian bark I can spare. Gather up as much linen and oakum as you can carry—and of course your surgical kits."

My stomach hardened into a stone. I nodded, mute with dread. But at least ashore I would have some chance of seeing Dalton.

But Freeman broke out in a smile. "Aye, sir." He beamed, undoubtedly glad for the chance to see some action.

"Be diligent with your logs," Brantigan continued. "Make certain to identify each man you treat and record what regiment he is with, or if it is a seaman, his ship. God be with you," he said, and dismissed us. His face was pinched with doubt.

EIGHT

Freeman and I were rowed ashore, accompanied by two boys to serve as loblollies and messengers. Sailors from one of the ordnance vessels were unloading mortar and cannon at the beach, cursing the ungodly heat.

The four of us trudged up the steep and slippery path, following a party of soldiers carrying stores to the siege camps. A captain dressed in full battle regalia greeted us. I wondered how he could tolerate his heavy red coat, his oppressively hot hat. The army's uniforms were designed for colder climes than this. I was glad the navy was more practical about matters of dress. I had left behind my gentleman's tight woolen breeches for a sailor's loose-fitting canvas pants and cropped jacket, placing comfort over rank, yet still I reeked of sweat.

The captain had orders for us to organize and operate a field hospital directly behind the north battery. There had already been numerous deaths, he said, from heatstroke.

Soldiers carted cots, canvas tents, and barrels of food from the supply ships, leaving them in a heap for us to set up. The soldiers paid us no mind; we were petty officers of the navy and had no jurisdiction over them. Luckily we had our own boys from the *Richmond* to help us.

The first thing we did was to set up a canvas awning for shelter. In spite of the recent rains our supply of fresh-water was frightfully scant and the riverbed was little more than a muddy wallow. Barrels of water had to be hauled up from ships that had little enough for their own use.

Just before sunset the battalion surgeon stopped by, had a look around, and judged that we had things well in hand. We asked for a cook and some nurses and he said he would see what he could do. He then returned to the main field hospital and the four of us, Freeman and I and our loblolly boys, ate our supper of hard cheese and ship's biscuit. Water was too dear to waste boiling meat.

The sun disappeared behind the hills and darkness followed like a blanket. Out came the crabs, large as serving plates, rustling in the shadows at the edges of our camp. The loblollies amused themselves by catching two and roasting them over the coals of our campfire.

That night I washed my face with a scrap of linen I kept in my pocket and cleaned my teeth with a green stick cut from a nearby branch. All this with my allotment of one tin cup of freshwater. I soon learned to drink my ration and not waste it on the luxury of toilet.

We set up our cots and collapsed. Though the mosquitoes attacked without mercy, I fell immediately asleep and did not wake until first light and birdsong.

After a breakfast of more cheese and biscuit Freeman and I walked through the woods to the west battery for news of the siege. The officers were not anxious to fraternize with us, perhaps because we were seamen or because we were not of sufficient rank. When would the artillery begin to fire? we wanted to know. Had the city been cut off? They had no answers and no word of Dalton and Goodwillie. All I knew for certain was that they were not part of the west battery, yet there were many batteries and camps all over the countryside. Our gunner and his mate could be anywhere.

That afternoon we sent one of our boys to General Elliot's camp to see what news he might learn from the foot soldiers and servants. He returned with word that firing on the fortress would commence tomorrow, as all the batteries were ready and mines in place.

"I hope we start blowing things up soon," Freeman lamented. "This monotony is tedious. I wish we had women. Fat, ripe, lusty tarts. Where are they? The army is hoarding them, I'll wager. How about I teach you to play cards, MacPherson?"

I agreed. I too felt a desire for action. Horrible as it sounds, I found myself wanting the bombardment to start. The waiting was the hardest part.

At daylight on the first day of July our batteries began to fire on the fortress; the enemy returned fire vigorously. Foolishly, Freeman and I went to the battery for a better view, as if this were a celebration of fireworks. At the mouth of the harbor our bombships and battleships let loose their artillery and the sounds were deafening. We watched the spectacle in awe until stray cannonballs and pieces of iron started whistling through the trees around us.

By nightfall I was weary of the roar and thunder of artillery. I prayed Dalton was safe, but try as I might I could not bring the memory of his face clearly into mind. He was becoming, once again, a dream.

With the beginning of the bombardment came our first cases of tropical disease. Not just diarrhea and heat prostration, but fever—the dreaded yellow fever. Soon the fever victims greatly outnumbered the war wounded and we ran out of cots. We gave up our own and slept on the ground, shoulder to shoulder. Our new cook fell sick; his eyes turned yellow and his urine black. He became delirious, calling out for his mother until he finally fell into a coma and died just forty-eight hours after taking to bed. We had him dragged off into the trees until the burial party had time to dig his grave. I could not bring myself to think of the rats and the coconut crabs that would chew at his body.

More seamen were dispatched to assist in the siege and they brought with them cannons, gunpowder, and spools of old cordage to serve as mantlets for the sappers and gunners. What they did not bring enough of was water. There simply was not enough clean water to be had.

On the morning of July twentieth the battery nearest us was attacked by a rag-and-bone band of enemy soldiers and peasants armed with muskets, shovels, and axes. The skirmish was hot but brief; as soon as the firing ceased,

Freeman began running through the trees toward the carnage. Our boys were on his heels and I forced myself to follow, my heart stuck in my throat. I nearly tripped over my first patient.

The engineer's face was gray. He had a ragged hole in his chest and his wound was making a sucking sound as he struggled to breathe. Freeman said not to waste my time on him, but I could see no other victim and I could hear no other cries for help. I dragged the engineer back to our hospital, my hands under his armpits. He never once cried out in pain.

More wounded were brought to us, some on litters, some on the backs of their comrades. Before I could tend to the dying engineer, I was given a second man, whose leg had been ripped away by a grenade.

"Take care of this one first," Freeman ordered. "He has half a chance."

I moved as an automaton, doing without feeling. Cutting off the ragged flesh, the splintered shard of femur remaining, and the stringy white tendons so that the amputation was clean, then swabbing on hot pitch to seal the artery before binding the stump. All the while the man screamed and begged for relief, in spite of the rum I had given him. But I put his cries out of my mind; I refused to hear them, for I feared sympathy would cripple me.

"Keep still," I barked. "Keep still, by God, if you want to live!"

When I had completed the gruesome task, I held the flask of rum to his lips until he had taken his fill and his head slumped back against the crook of my arm.

I turned back to the engineer, lying on the ground behind me. He was still alive and I gave him another sip of rum but he choked on it. As he choked, pink bubbles formed at the corners of his mouth and he began to rattle loudly with each breath. Yet he looked at me, his gray eyes bright and pleading.

Behind me the amputee cried out, "My leg! My leg! What have you done with my leg?"

I turned to him and saw that the bandage had soaked through, a vivid cherry color. I knew this one would die if I did not stop the flow of blood spurting out of his femoral artery with each beat of his heart. Not knowing what else to do, I sat on him to hold him still and pressed on his groin with all my might, ducking to avoid his other knee, for he was kicking his good leg wildly. All the while I kept glancing at the engineer, who was looking at me, gasping and gurgling. Freeman and our boys grappled with their own patients; no one could assist the fever patients who called helplessly for water like baby birds in the nest.

From my position astride the writhing amputee I watched the light go out of the engineer's eyes.

"Does anyone know the dead man's name?" I asked as our boys dragged him out of camp into the bush. "The engineer, who was he?"

No one answered me. Within the hour I no longer thought of it myself, for we had more victims brought to us.

The days and nights wore on. We did the best we could but there were not enough of us, and not enough supplies.

When men got well enough to walk, we sent them back to their camps and batteries. Some we returned to the transports to convalesce. Those who died we had carried off into the woods to be buried. I had succeeded in hardening myself, far exceeding my own expectations. I began to resent the endless stream of patients and I silently chided them for being so foolish as to get themselves shot or to fall prey to illness.

Yet callused as I was, I never grew accustomed to the first glimpse of a fresh mutilation. Gaping red gashes, raw and ragged muscles, white cords of tendon, the sheen of fasciae! Just when I thought I had seen it all a new definition of agony arrived and I had to remain nonchalant, as if I were pulling a splinter, so as not to unduly upset the victim or the other patients. The surgeon must never cringe nor show his revulsion.

The wounded sometimes survived their initial injuries, but within days or weeks they sickened with blood poisoning and there was nothing we could do to save them. The worst of it was that the wounded men knew well what the future held for them. The few who did survive terrible wounds did so, I believe, because they refused to acknowledge what seemed certain. Once a man accepted his fate the light in his eyes went out and he died.

On the twenty-second of July we heard the popping of musket fire close at hand. Minutes later some of the wounded were brought to our hospital. The first was a seaman, unconscious. Though his hair was matted with blood and his face shaggy with beard, I felt a shock of recognition. It was Goodwillie.

His scalp wound bled profusely; I probed it with my shaking finger and found that the shot had not penetrated his skull. Thank God.

"You're a lucky man," I said to him when he regained his senses.

"MacPherson," he whispered. A smile lightened his grimy face.

"Aye. You are in good hands. But where is Dalton? Is he alive, do you know? Was he in the skirmish with you?"

Dalton's mate appeared dazed. He shook his head slowly as if to clear it.

"The last time I recall seeing him was—some time ago. Yesterday or the day before. I cannot say for sure."

"Try to remember," I urged, wiping his laceration with a bloody scrap of muslin wrapped around the tips of my fingers. Being very low on muslin, I could not afford a bandage, but I stuffed some oakum into the wound to stanch the capillary flow.

Goodwillie winced, trying his best to bear up. "Mr. Dalton left camp to find water, that much I know. But I don't remember if he ever came back." A look of consternation crossed his face. "I cannot recall," he said sadly.

I could not help but think the worst.

"He'll be all right," I said with false certainty. "Don't you worry about Mr. Dalton."

"Aye," Goodwillie agreed. "He's safe as a fox in a hole, I'll wager." But his words sounded hollow and we both knew the truth.

Just then soldiers dragged two more casualties through the brush for us to salvage. Freeman took charge of a badly wounded grenadier and gave the other, a Spanish officer, to me. A musket ball had penetrated his upper left arm, fortunately missing both bone and brachial artery. I cleaned and dressed the ragged wound with strips of precious muslin as his guard stood by.

The Spaniard was uncomplaining and thanked me for my care. His English, though heavily accented, was exceptional; far better than the few words of Spanish I knew.

"I'm afraid we're quite low on laudanum," I said. "How about a tot of rum for the pain?"

"Better to save it," he said. "There are those who need it more than I."

I was moved. "What is your name, sir?"

"Emilio Medina Fernández."

"You are an officer?"

He nodded. "Captain."

"Captain Fernández, you are a compassionate man. But if you change your mind, let me know, for rum is the one supply we have no shortage of."

Freeman, who was working just next to me, his arms bloody to the elbows, laughed loudly. "You don't say!" he exclaimed, his face flushed as he worked to save the grenadier. "Men may die from their wounds, men may die of fever and for want of clean water, but by George, no man need die sober!" He laughed again, as if giddy with excitement, and the master-at-arms guarding the Spanish prisoner laughed too.

Freeman's patient grunted, whether in agreement or pain I knew not. But the grenadier's color had improved considerably. Perhaps he would live after all.

My mate was one of those men who seemed to thrive on situations such as this. Freeman was emboldened by the nearness of death, and though I held no natural fondness for my bunkmate, I had to admit he was a good surgeon. For all his bragging, he knew exactly what he was doing and he enjoyed doing it. He entertained no doubts, never questioned the efficacy of the techniques we used, and believed wholeheartedly in the purposefulness of his work.

That night, after the bombarding had ceased and the smell of burned powder had faded, we boiled some of our precious water for coffee to celebrate a good day's work. Tonight no one in our camp was at death's door. Our bedridden were sleeping. The sounds of men's voices from other camps drifted through the woods along with the smells of their suppers. The night seemed tranquil, almost cheerful, and I felt like we were on a goose hunt, camping in the North York moors. I imagined Dalton, alive and well, sitting around one of those other fire rings, enjoying his pipe.

Freeman meted out our dwindling coffee, dividing it between the two of us and our walking wounded: Goodwillie, the Spanish captain, and the guard. We stretched it with rum, so that each man had a full cup.

"I am honored," Captain Fernández said, graciously accepting a trickle of spirits.

"How is your arm, sir?" I asked. A circle of pink the size of a penny had soaked through his dressing.

"Let us just say I am well aware of its presence," he said with a forced smile.

"Say, Captain," Freeman said. "Do you play whist?"

The Spaniard continued to smile. "Doesn't everyone?"

Freeman snapped his fingers, greatly pleased. "Goodwillie? You in?"

Goodwillie grinned. "Aye. Though I've no specie to wager. Only a bit of tobacco."

We gathered around our makeshift table, an empty ammunition crate. Freeman shuffled his greasy, dog-eared cards and dealt them out.

"Clubs are trump," he announced, turning over the last one.

And I thought, *How strange, this war. Men shooting at one another by day, gaming together by firelight at night.*

"Captain Fernández," I said, fanning out the cards in my hand. "Have you encountered a British naval gunner by the name of Dalton? Warranted to the *Richmond*. Dark hair, dark eyes."

The Spaniard shook his head. "No. He is your friend?"

"Yes," I answered. Goodwillie and I exchanged glances in the firelight.

"Then I hope you are reunited," Fernández said, studying his cards. "I know what it is to lose a friend in battle."

"What are we fighting for, anyway?" I asked, the rum loosening my tongue. "Can anyone tell me?"

"Don't be so maudlin, MacPherson," Freeman said. "We're fighting for the bloody harbor and all the ships in it. What else? Certainly not for the rest of this godforsaken rock."

Goodwillie led with a jack of diamonds. I followed with an eight of diamonds.

"Of course, it will simply be traded back at the peace talks," Freeman continued with a shrug.

"All a game." The Spaniard winced as he tossed in his card, a six of diamonds.

"Then what is the point?" I demanded.

"You ponder too much," Freeman chastised. "What you need is to roll a randy wench. What I wouldn't give for a bit of pudding right now!"

The others grunted in agreement.

"The point is," my partner continued, trumping with a deuce of clubs and gathering up the cards with a smile, "to win the hand. To stay alive. To collect your pay at the end of the game." With a stick, he made a tally mark in the dirt.

"Hear, hear," said Goodwillie, lifting his cup in a mock salute.

"I respectfully disagree," Fernández said. "The primary object of battle is not to keep your life."

"Maybe where you come from," said the master-at-arms, sitting in the shadows behind him.

"Then what is the object of war, *mon capitaine*?" Freeman quipped. "To get yourself shot and killed?"

The Spaniard looked at Freeman with his shining black eyes. "When a man goes to war, he must keep his honor clean at all costs. Though he may kill or be killed, he must keep his soul untarnished."

"And how do I keep my soul untarnished in this ungodly fetid wilderness?" My partner sniffed his deeply stained armpits for emphasis.

"He's right, you know," Goodwillie said, defending Fernández. "War is a terrible thing. The things a man sees in battle he carries with him the rest of his life. Unspeakable sights."

"It is not the things a man sees in war that are unspeakable, but the things a man does," the Spanish officer said. "Actions are what tarnish the soul."

"Elegantly put, *amigo*," Freeman said, slurping his coffee. "But I want to come out alive, no matter what."

"There are fates worse than death," Fernández said with conviction.

I supposed there was truth in that, but it sounded like a riddle and I had no desire to work it out. I hadn't had but a tot of rum to drink, yet I felt muddle-headed. I continued to play the game, but I had the oddest sensation that I was watching myself play, watching the four of us from some distance. Looking down at our little camp from a tree branch, the crescent moon, the faint, hazy pinpoint of light in the constellation Hercules. I smiled to myself at the thought of Hercules swinging his brute club against the universe.

I woke much later that night, long after Hercules had set, aware of an aching in my breastbone and behind my eyes. I groped for my blanket, pulled it up to my neck. By sunrise I knew I was sick, for I could not rise. My body ached, my joints were burning, I longed for water. I tried to speak but all that came out of my parched mouth was a whisper.

The next thing I knew Freeman was bleeding me. But my vision was blurred; I was watching him through a fog.

"I'm cold, Freeman. Where's my blanket?"

"You're burning up, MacPherson."

I shook my head, shivering. "Not a fever, can't be."

"It's a fever, all right," he said tersely, squeezing my reluctant arm, milking the vein. "Now don't you go bloody dying on me, you hear?"

"Why do we call it fever when it feels so cold?" My teeth chattered and my shoulders shook uncontrollably.

As if through a mist, I could see his face peering down at me.

The Spaniard came to bid me farewell; he was being escorted to a prison ship. He thanked me for attending his wound. His face seemed vague, the features blurred. I knew him more by the sound of his voice.

I had no idea of days or nights, only one long ache. Shaking with rigors, then on fire. The world closed in on me until the world was inside me. Nothing outside my skin mattered. My eyes burned, the roots of my hair hurt. Every breath felt like a rake in the back of my throat.

"You must drink," Freeman ordered. "I won't have you shriveling up and dying on me, MacPherson, you hear me?"

I closed my eyes and shook my head. To drink seemed an impossible task.

"Come on, man; drink up, get well. Damnation, I need you!" He spoke harshly but I could hear the concern behind his words. I hadn't liked him much at first but Freeman was a good man. I wanted to tell him that.

At last, I took the cup to shut him up. His voice hurt my ears, clanging inside my head like a cowbell. Yet I was glad for his presence. Didn't want him to leave me, not now.

Sometime later he made me drink some broth from the stew. Though I only had a few mouthfuls, it exhausted me, and I fell into a sound sleep.

When I came to my senses, it was dark and quiet but for

the snores and mutterings of sleeping men and the monotonous chirping of a tree frog. I had a great urgency to make
water and struggled to get up, my head spinning.

"What is it, MacPherson? What do you need?" Freeman
mumbled from his cot.

"Full bladder," I said.

"Don't be such a girl. Hang it over the side and piss on
the ground."

I waited until the sound of his breathing fell in step with
the other slumberers. Gathering my strength, sucking it in
with each breath. Slowly, I slid off my cot onto all fours, not
trusting myself to stand. Crawled out of the camp like a
tortoise, toward the latrines.

I squatted over the trench, my pants around my knees.
It was too dark to see if my urine was black but it hurt like
fire to make water. Suddenly my stomach rumbled and
cramped, my bowels broke loose, and I could smell the
foulness as it poured out of me. The unmistakable smell of
blood and feces.

I collapsed on the ground beside the latrine, gathering
strength to crawl back to my cot. I dozed off, then woke to
the sound of his voice, as clear and as certain as any sound
I've ever heard.

"Come to me, lass," Aeneas MacPherson said. I am certain it was he.

I saw a figure in the bush, perhaps ten yards away. A
large frame with big hands hanging. I fumbled with my
trousers and lurched toward the shape as it receded into the
wood.

"Aeneas," I croaked. "Can it be?"

The figure paused and I struggled toward it, thrashing

through the underbrush, thinking I must be mistaken. I had to find out. Yet for every step I took the man remained at a distance, tantalizing as a rainbow. I pressed on, stumbling and weak in the knees, yet determined. I had to get closer; I had to see his face.

My surroundings seemed unfamiliar. No clearings or paths. Yet surely I could find my way back. Just a few more steps. I moved slowly, as if in a dream, my feet catching in the tangled undergrowth. I stopped, panting for breath. The shadow man paused too, as if waiting for me. A movement of air, the slightest of breezes, rustled the leaves and caused me to shiver.

"Aeneas," I called again. "Wait!"

I don't know how long I stumbled through the trees. At times I lost sight of the figure, but when I did, the sound of Aeneas's voice urged me on. Or was it a voice inside my head? A part of my mind told me this was but a hallucination brought on by the fever. I would have gone back to camp but I was lost and the moon was gone.

I tripped over something, thick and soft as a body, and tumbled headlong into a ditch. Lying there, my face against the mucky clay, the stench was strong. A latrine, this hole. Or an open grave. I managed to turn over but I could not get up; I had no strength left. The rigors returned and I gave myself up to them. I no longer heard Aeneas's voice, only my own fevered moans. Looking up, I saw the stars through the slats of the palm fronds but I did not recognize them. A crab crawled across my face, obliterating the sky.

NINE

"*Éste muerto?*"

"*No. Mira; él respira.*"

I came to my senses. Looked up out of my muddy hole. Six Spanish soldiers armed with muskets, pistols, and sabers looked down at me.

"Who are you?" The officer spoke to me in English.

"Patrick MacPherson, surgeon's mate. British Navy," I whispered.

They talked among themselves. It sounded as though they did not know what to make of me. Perhaps they thought I was a deserter.

"Are you wounded?" the officer asked, prodding me gently with the barrel of his musket.

I shook my head, unable to say anything more. My tongue was swollen in my parched mouth. The bright light of day felt like a firebrand against my eyes and the pain in my joints was unbearable.

"We are taking you prisoner," the officer said. "In the name of King Charles of Spain."

They lifted me up out of my grave and I heard myself cry out just before I lost consciousness.

Here was a world of shadows and muffled sounds. No thoughts, just sensations. Fleeting images. As if I were floating through time, clinging to a raft of driftwood, washing toward shore. My feet already lost to me, the numbness rising up my legs. Heart pulling, pulling like an exhausted oarsman. The sound of waves against pebbles made a rasping noise I could hear, a sound like breath in the back of my throat. Parched. Scorching sunlight, the inevitability of reaching the shore. Closer now, the land. Searing hot air above, cool dark water below, the contrast was unbearable. A desire, a thirst. A longing for comfort, for oblivion.

When I awoke, I was in a bed; an old man with a wizened face was bleeding me. He said something in Spanish, I did not understand. I tried to sit up, but could not.

The old man shook his head. "Be still. Rest."

I lay back and watched the red stream trickling from my arm. The ground beneath shook with the tremors of mortar and bomb blasts. I was aware of the sour smell of sickness, heavy in the air. The smell of warm blood—was it mine?

"Where am I?" I mouthed, but the surgeon paid me no mind.

"Where am I?" I tried to shout but it came out a squeak. What was the word in Spanish? *"Donde?"*

"El Morro," he said, an edge to his voice. His face was furrowed in concentration.

I nodded, closing my eyes. The Morro fortress, object of our destruction. Around us the stone walls were falling, the artillery of my own people destroying them bit by bit. And I had not the strength to move.

The surgeon talked to his assistant, their voices hushed but urgent. *"Mujer,"* I heard him say.

Woman. I looked down. My clothing had been loosened, my jacket removed. So they knew my secret, but what did it matter now? I was too weak to escape, too weak to protect myself from my captors should they want to take advantage of me. I yearned only for water and a long, uninterrupted sleep. *May my death come quickly and mercifully,* I prayed. Far beyond feeling terror, I felt only regret. Regret for what? Try as I might I could not remember what it was.

His smell now replaced the odors of sickness—the air was suddenly infused with it—and I knew what it was I longed for, yet could not recall the word for it. Neither could I picture his face nor bring to mind his name, but I knew his smell, and I knew the sound of his voice. He was talking to me now; what was he saying? I strained to hear but could not make out the words, just the cadence of them. The sound of waves lapping.

"Dalton," he said, clearly this time. "Brian Dalton." Like a bell ringing.

The sound of his name took shape and I held on to it. It

had weight and gleamed in my hand like silver. His name. Then someone blew the candle out, or maybe it was the wind, and I felt myself falling. I dropped his name, forgot all words. Fell into that cool sea of darkness where I knew not my own name, where nothing even had a name.

TEN

In my dream it was Dalton who saved me but he had a shaved head and was gaunter than in real life. I wondered if I had died and he was an angel, though he had no wings.

He carried me over his shoulder as the flames spread and the walls crumbled around us. Muskets firing, swords and bayonets clashing, cannonballs slamming into rock. Somehow we moved through the scene of destruction while those around us fell. I could feel Dalton's shoulder pressing into my stomach, his arm squeezing the back of my thighs. I was being carried over his shoulder, my head dangling down, the blood rushing to it, pounding. Such a lucid dream.

Then I came to my senses and found it was not a dream at all. I was indeed flung over Dalton's shoulder, my head splitting with pain. And a great burden I must have been, for I was not a dainty sprite of a woman, but nearly Dalton's own height.

Struggling to free myself, I caused us both to fall to the ground.

"Princess!" Dalton's eyes were wide, his voice a hoarse croak in my ear. "Come!" He leaped to his feet and pulled me to mine. "We'll be killed here."

My head spun, I could barely stand. Taking a deep breath, I bit my lip to keep from fainting.

We were in the middle of the fortress courtyard. Officers shouting orders, men running blindly in every direction. Dogs barking, chickens scrambling for cover. A woman with a child tucked under her arm scurried past us, her skirt trailing in the dust. From the stables horses screamed, and between explosions I heard the tolling of the church bell.

Along the east wall a few bedraggled infantrymen were loading their weapons, their faces blank as corpses.

"Away!" Dalton barked, jerking my arm nearly out of its socket. I heard the crack of musket fire from behind, and the whistle of a ball as it passed my left ear filled me with terror—a sense of panic that felt like cold seawater closing over my head.

They mean to kill me, I realized. The back of my neck tingled, the hairs on my arms stood up. Though the fever had brought me near to death, this was a new and violent threat. Sickness might be fought with a strong will to live, but will is powerless against a lead ball smashing through one's skull.

This fear filled me with unaccountable strength. I bolted, running toward the nearest structure before I realized it was on fire. I saw people streaming out of it, hobbling on crutches, carried on litters. It was the hospital where I had been kept—I recognized the old surgeon who had bled me; I saw him drop to his knees, gasping and choking.

"This way," Dalton shouted, pulling me toward the west wall, the only outer wall of the fortress not being pummeled by British artillery. We crouched behind some empty barrels and paused to catch our breath.

"Are ye well?" Dalton asked, peering at me intently. His face, lean from want of food and water, was dark with soot and stubble. His shaven head, a stark white moon marred by razor nicks and glistening with sweat. Beneath the surface of his right temple, a blood vessel pulsed.

"Well enough," I gasped.

He nodded, touching my face with his blackened fingers, as if to reassure himself. I took his hand in my own and squeezed it, pressing it to my lips.

"How did you get here, Dalton? How did you find me?"

"They took me prisoner, along with some sappers. We heard a rumor from the guards that one of the Englishmen in the hospital was really a woman in disguise." A smile flickered across his face. "Thought it might be ye. When our men breached the fortress walls and fires broke out, I made good use of the melee and broke free," he explained in his laconic, unadorned way. "Found ye in the hospital, nearly dead ye looked to be. And ye are very pale still. Shall I carry ye?"

I shook my head. "I think I can make it. But how do we get out of here?" The smoke and dust was thickening, making it hard to see or breathe.

"We must move along this wall to that hole in the north wall. The seawall."

He pointed but my eyes stung and I could not make it out. I was seized by a fit of coughing.

Dalton took off the dirty rag that was his neck scarf and tied it around my face, covering my nose. "Princess, ye must follow me. We have a short sprint to freedom. Do ye hear me?"

I nodded, breathing in through his bandanna, gathering my waning strength.

"Keep hold of my hand, love. Trust me."

Just then there was a deafening explosion that knocked us both flat. I felt the shock through my body and thought for a moment I had been shot. The ground beneath us shook and debris rained down like hailstones.

"The magazine!" Dalton yelled, pulling me to my feet. "Let's go!"

I ran, following him. My legs moved, I know not how. Already my burst of strength was fading and I wanted nothing more than to lie down. Ahead I saw the light coming from the hole in the wall, just as he said. Closer now, a triangle of blue, the shining sea beyond. Just a few steps more.

A figure in ragged homespun appeared out of the smoke, stepping in front of the door to our freedom. His eyes were hard, his mouth set. He held a saber, drawn and ready to slash. Dalton stopped in front of me, dropping my hand. I froze.

The peasant inched forward, widened his stance. Muttered something in Spanish I didn't understand. My voice was lost to me. I watched as the stranger's eyes widened, and I knew he was ready to strike. Knew the steel blade was at the level of Dalton's throat. Then Dalton was gone.

Quick as a cat he dove for the man's knees, knocking him to the ground.

"Go to the beach!" Dalton shouted, throwing himself on top of the soldier, grappling for the sword. A thin stream of blood sprayed my sleeve as the two men tumbled in the dirt at my feet, struggling for control of the weapon.

My head whirled and I fought to steady it. Should I pick up a rock and smash the Spaniard's head? What if I hit Dalton instead? I could not think clearly and feared I had not the strength.

"Go! Now!" Dalton's voice was a hoarse grunt as he fought to wrest the hilt from the man's hands. "Do as I say!"

I obeyed, ducking through the hole in the wall, leaving him there alone with the enemy, fighting for his life. Then I sucked in my breath, for I stood on the very edge of the cliff overlooking the rocky beach.

Out in the water, far below, three ships of our fleet were lined up broadside, firing upon the castle. I heard the whisper of a cannonball and felt the shock as it hit its mark somewhere behind me. I swayed, about to topple, vertigo muddling my senses. No choice but to make my way down the steep cliff. No choice if I was to save myself.

I lay on the ground, facedown. Reached over the cliff's edge with my foot to find a pocket in the rock. Holding on to a root with one hand and a crevice in the rock with the other, I took the first step down. Felt for another toehold with my other foot. Lower.

Staring at a wall of granite, I let go of the root and slid the fingers of my hand into a deep crack at shoulder level.

Stopped for breath. Wedged my toe into another space but it gave way under a clatter of falling rocks. Holding myself by three points, I searched wildly for a toehold. My legs and arms shook so violently, I was afraid they would give out. I dared not look down.

Just like climbing down from the yardarm, my inner voice said. *Concentrate and keep your wits about you. Down the ratlines now, one step at a time. Pretend your feet have eyes. Breathe.*

I breathed. Then lowered myself, reaching, stretching, finding a foothold. Finding a lower handhold. Another foothold. Just like climbing down the ratlines.

Slowly, carefully, I made my way down the cliff as cannonballs and mortars flew overhead. With each step down the sound of the surf grew more apparent, yet all I could see was the rock in front of my face. The surface was slippery now, glistening wet where waves had broken. I knew I was almost down.

"Ahoy, there!" a voice from the beach hailed me. An English voice, a sailor's jargon, and I trembled with relief at its dear sound. Letting go of my handhold, I dropped the last five feet, collapsing into a heap in the wave-washed pebbles.

"Who are ye—friend or foe?" the sailor demanded, his dirk drawn.

"I am Patrick MacPherson, surgeon's mate, British Navy," I panted, looking up into the grizzled, toothless face. "Of the *Richmond*."

His eyes showed his relief that I was not an enemy who he would have to stab with his knife. "I've got a jolly boat just there, sir. Get aboard and I'll take ye out to your ship.

Hurry now, before this whole bloody fortress comes tumbling down on our heads." The sailor put his dirk back in its sheath and helped me to my feet.

"We must wait for the gunner," I said, looking up at Morro Castle and shielding my eyes against the bright sun and falling cinders. "He's coming, he's right behind me."

"I don't see a soul," the sailor said, wading out into the water toward the boat. "And ye look right poorly. I've seen dead men look better, sir, with all due respect. Come on, let's quit this beach before one of these bombs falls short."

"No, wait!" I sputtered, my head pounding. "Just one more moment. He'll be here shortly, I know it."

I sank to my knees, unable to remain standing. Filled with remorse that I hadn't stayed with him. He who had risked his life to save mine. Sparks of light swam before my eyes, and the great black universe swept in, snuffing out my consciousness as if it were an ember.

ELEVEN

I came to my senses as the sailors were hoisting me over onto the *Richmond*'s deck.

"Put me down, lads," I insisted. "I have recovered. Just allow me a few minutes to catch my breath."

The sailors did not argue; they had plenty of work to do. Someone fetched me a dipper of brackish water, then left me standing against the rail in the waist of the frigate to fend for myself. I looked up at the smoking fortress, still valiant even in ruin.

The firing had ceased and a stillness had come over the harbor. The smoke and smell of gunpowder slowly lifted. In every warship across the harbor mouth ragged ensigns hung limp, forlorn in their victory.

Stevens, the bosun's mate, stopped to personally give me the news: the Spanish commander had been gravely wounded and a full surrender was expected. Though the ship's company was greatly relieved, no one had the spirit to rejoice.

My eyes searched the broken walls, the sea cliff, the shore below. The sun was harsh and I squinted against the glare. Looking for a trace of movement. Something other than rock and rubble.

"Shall I send for the surgeon?" Stevens asked, eyeing me with concern.

I said nothing. Held my hand up to shield my eyes against the painful brightness.

"Sir?"

"That won't be necessary." I did not take my eyes off the lone figure I now spied on the beach. Hope returned to me like a rising tide.

"See that man there on the shore?" My voice broke. "The man waving his arms, do you see him? He's one of ours," I cried, waving back with all the strength I could muster.

"Are you certain, MacPherson?" the bosun's mate persisted, eyeing me askance.

"Yes, that's him, all right. Brian Dalton. I'd know him anywhere."

"I mean, are you certain you don't need to go to sick berth?"

I laughed with relief, my knees buckling. The bosun's mate clasped me to keep me from falling. "Mr. MacPherson, hold on to the rail," he urged.

"Oh, I am much improved now, I assure you." Untying Dalton's bandanna from around my neck, I waved it overhead like a flag.

Sunlight poured down, baking the decks, warming my bones. The grizzled old sailor who had brought me to safety climbed back down into the jolly boat and gave us the ready sign. I cast off the boat's painter and watched him slowly make his way across the blue field to fetch our gunner home.

TWELVE

The next days passed slowly; we seemed stuck in the stream of time. The siege was over, Britain was victorious, yet there was little joy in the fleet.

More than eighteen hundred British soldiers and sailors lost their lives during the siege alone, and hundreds more died from illness in the days that followed. Of the enemy's casualties, I never heard a count, but we knew we had left many dead and wounded.

Everyone spoke of Commander Don Luis Vicente de Velasco, who had so valiantly defended the Spanish fortress. He had not surrendered, he had not fled, he had not taken cover behind the shield of his name and rank. De Velasco was mortally wounded during the final assault on the Morro, while Dalton and I were making our escape.

I wondered what happened to Captain Fernández, the

Spanish officer with whom I had played cards that night in camp. With any luck he survived his injury and was on a prison ship, to be exchanged for a British officer at the end of the war. I hoped he was well treated. I knew I would probably never see him again, just as I would never see so many other people who had come and gone. People I had cared for, if only for a short time. We all continued on our separate paths, paths that crossed but quickly diverged. Yet we all affected one another immeasurably. Like billiard balls colliding, our courses were altered.

Those of us aboard the *Richmond* were a bruised and battered lot. We took on provisions, mended our rigging, and prepared to set sail, as did the rest of the fleet. Though we had won for England the great prize of Havana, we knew at heart it was all for naught; Havana was but a chip to be traded in Europe's ongoing game.

We survivors were glad to be alive, yet each man wondered why he had been spared and not his messmate. It was the great unspoken question. There were so many empty places around the tables at mealtime now, and great holes in the conversations. Every man carried his grief on his face, and we recognized ourselves in each other's faces. We were brothers, triumphant yet beaten. The youngest among us looked like wizened old men.

Yet I did not feel old. I felt raw and ignorant as a newborn, my wrinkled red hands grasping at air. Stripped of all answers, I held no philosophies. I was starting over. I didn't know where we were going, or where I wanted to go— only who I wanted to be with for the journey.

THIRTEEN

We sat on the fighting top, our favorite rendezvous, delighting in our closeness. So near but not touching.

"Are ye well now?" Dalton asked, lighting his pipe.

"Well enough to climb the rigging," I said, still out of breath from the effort.

"I am glad of that. I was worried for ye." He drew his first puffs, savoring them, and I tried to catch the sweet, rich smell of burning tobacco before the wind carried it away.

His hair was growing back, a dark bristle. He had shaved it off shortly before the Spanish soldiers captured him. "Too bloody hot on land," he had explained with a grin. Dalton was not a man to wear a wig, yet I did not mind him hairless, not at all. I rather liked the shape of his head.

"Did they treat you well, your captors?" I asked.

"Aye. They were gentlemen. They were starving and in need of water, but they shared what they had with us."

"Their commander, de Velasco," I said. "He was a brave man."

Dalton nodded, his nostrils flaring. "He was."

"You were brave too, to do what you did. To rescue me."

He shook his head. "Nae. 'Tis only bravery when ye must force yourself to act. My instincts took over and I fled like a wild animal, Princess, taking ye with me. I feared we'd be killed in the crossfire or buried beneath the crumbling walls." He ran his hand across his head, fingering the new stubble of hair. "I surely did not want to die."

"I am grateful to you, beyond words. And I am sorry I left you alone with that Spaniard. He might have killed you."

Dalton flashed me his best smile. "But he didn't. And ye were in nae shape to help me—'tis a miracle ye got yourself down the cliff in one piece."

His eyes met mine and held. It was dark but I did not need light to see them shine.

"I would like nothing more than to take ye in my arms right now," he said.

"And I, you."

"The memory of that night on the cay, in the lagoon with you. It has kept me alive."

I felt a rush of pleasure, remembering. "So what happens next? To us."

"What do ye want to happen, Princess?"

"I don't know," I admitted. "I've worked hard for what I have. I cannot just reveal myself as a woman now. There would be embarrassment and shame—I couldn't bear it. And Freeman would feel betrayed." I shook my head and closed my eyes. "No, he'd be mortified. It would ruin our friendship."

Dalton squirmed. "Your friendship with Freeman, ye mean," he snorted. "It galls me."

"Jealousy doesn't become you," I said. "Besides, you needn't be jealous of Freeman. He is my comrade and has earned my respect, but I still don't like the man."

Dalton managed a chagrined smile. "But I *am* jealous. I am jealous of the time he spends with ye. Ye work together, eat together, play cards together—ye string your hammocks side by side. By God, that's hard to take!" He laughed, a short bark. "Well, I can live with it, I can. I am man enough if ye are, Princess."

"Besides, there's the money," I said. "If I reveal myself as a woman, I won't receive my wages when the ship pays off back in London, and I've worked far too hard to give up that. But most of all there's the satisfaction I feel in doing my job. I've told you, sir, I can never be an ordinary woman. Can you accept that?"

He looked at me with an open face and his eyes told me everything I wanted to know, though how it would work out remained unfathomable. There was nothing to do but wait, for we were living by the ship's bell. We had already waited so long and endured so much. I wondered how living beings could be at once so delicate, so easily destroyed, yet at the same time indomitable. I had said I could never be an ordinary woman but it occurred to me there were no ordinary women, or ordinary men. We're all extraordinary. And no matter what else it was, life was rich in possibilities.

"I have always loved ye for who ye are," Dalton said, "be it stowaway princess or another man's wife." His eyes twinkled and the corner of his mouth turned up. "Or a surgeon's mate in tricorn hat and breeches. But the real question is, what do *ye* want, Patricia? Can ye accept the man *I* am?"

I considered his words. At that moment my wants were few. Having just recovered from the fever, I was content to breathe freely and to move without pain. I was happy to go about my daily work, to have food and freshwater, to laugh with my messmates over our ration of ale. But love—how I wanted to love! My heart was full and ready to burst.

Could I accept him? My shipmate, my friend? No finer man lived, of that I was certain. More than anything I wanted to throw my arms around him, to offer my lips to his.

"Brian, I do," I said. "With all my heart I do."

Dalton held out his hand and we shook on it.

Someone, I tell you,
will remember us. . . .

———*Sappho*

(translated by Willis Barnstone; *Greek Lyric Poetry*)

Author's Note

In writing this story I wanted to explore what it might have been like for a young woman in the eighteenth century to live, work, and reinvent herself aboard a ship. Although it's a work of fiction, I have attempted to maintain historical accuracy.

Alexander Hamilton is said to have been born to Rachel Faucette Lavien and James Hamilton on the island of Nevis under circumstances similar to what I've portrayed. The *Richmond* was a real frigate, and Captain Elphinstone her commander. And British sailors were sent ashore to help the army take Morro Castle in the historic siege of Havana.

Eighteenth-century merchantmen and British naval ships did indeed carry women—wives, girlfriends, passengers, prostitutes, laundresses—even though the Admiralty had rules on the books prohibiting it. Children too were commonly found aboard ships. Some were born on the passage and some went to sea at an early age for the livelihood.

According to numerous sources, some women really did join the navy and army in male disguise. Several accounts tell of women who worked for months, and in some cases years, before being found out. These imposters carried out their duties, performed bravely in battle, and were only discovered to be female after being wounded in the line of duty. (The artifice may have occurred more often than has been recorded, simply because some women may have successfully carried it off.)

Though the work was hard and not without dangers, a ship provided room and board and a chance for adventure. In fact, it still does.

GLOSSARY

A

abeam (off the beam) A direction relative to the vessel, at right angles to the ship's centerline. If you were to stand in the center of the deck facing forward and imagine yourself in the center of a clock, abeam or off the beam would be in the direction of three o'clock on one side and nine o'clock on the other.

aft (after) Toward the rear of the ship.

aftermost The farthest aft.

amidships (midships) In or toward the center part of the vessel. (The naval term *midshipman* comes from the part of the vessel where the junior officers bunked.)

apoplexy A cerebral vascular accident, more commonly known as a stroke.

avast A command meaning to stop or cease the activity being performed.

B

beam 1. The extreme width of a ship at the widest part. 2. One of many transverse timbers used in constructing a vessel.

bilge The lowest internal part of a ship's hull.

binnacle A stand that holds the compass, usually near the wheel of the ship so as to be seen by the person steering.

blister To intentionally cause the skin to inflame and blister by applying caustic agents. This extreme practice was believed to encourage the removal of foul humors into the blister fluid. (See **bloodletting**)

block A pulley. Necessary to raise heavy sails, lift topmasts and yardarms, etc. Many hundreds of wooden blocks were needed to operate an eighteenth-century sailing ship.

bloodletting Cutting a vein and allowing a quantity of blood to run out. For many centuries, since Hippocrates first proposed the theory in ancient Greece, purposely bleeding patients was used as a remedy for all sorts of ailments. Draining a cup or more of blood was thought to balance the four vital substances called humors believed to be present in the body: blood, phlegm, yellow bile, and black bile.

boltrope A rope sewn around the edge of a sail for reinforcement.

bosun (bos'n) A contraction of *boatswain.* The officer who supervises the ship's rigging, sails, anchors, cables, and cordage. In the eighteenth-century British Navy, the bosun and his mate used pipes, or shrill whistles, as signaling devices to convey orders. *Swain* comes from Old English and means "attendant" or "assistant."

bosun's mate The bosun's assistant. A large naval ship might have a bosun and several mates.

bow The front of a vessel.

bower One of two large anchors carried at the bows of a ship.

bows The sides of a ship, at the bow.

braces A set of ropes and blocks that move the yards, allowing the vessel to change its direction of sail. To brace the yards is to move them to a different angle, to change course.

bulkhead A wall-like partition belowdecks, separating one cabin from another.

bumboat A small trading boat that did business with the bigger ships at anchor in the harbor.

buntlines Rope lines attached to the square sails used in furling the sail; can be used to give sails a fuller shape. (Pronounced BUNT-linz)

C

calomel (mercurous chloride) A substance used to induce diarrhea; thought to purge the body of toxins.

capstan A cylindrical winch to hoist the anchor, which required several people to operate by pushing on capstan bars inserted like spokes of a wheel. In the eighteenth century, such work as hoisting the anchor was done with a work song called a chantey.

careenage A place of shallow water where ships could be laid on their sides to have their bottoms scraped of barnacles or have repairs made to the undersides. From the word *careen,* which means "to tip over."

cat-o'-nine-tails (cat) A whip made of numerous strips of leather, used for punishment.

chain (chain-wale or **channel)** A strong piece of timber secured outside the ship's side, serving to extend the base of the mast for the shrouds, which support the mast. To stand "in the chains" is to stand upon one of the chain-wales.

chandlery A store that sells nautical supplies.

chantey A shipboard work song commonly sung by sailors as they performed specific tasks, such as hauling up the anchor, manning the pumps, or hauling on lines. There were different chanteys for different sorts of jobs. Chanteys helped people work together in rhythm, as well as helping to keep spirits up.

cinchona (Peruvian bark) The bark from a tree that contains quinine, used to treat various ailments, especially tropical fevers. Of all the eighteenth-century medications, this one actually had some effectiveness against the disease we know as malaria. In some cases quinine-based medications are still used to treat this mosquito-borne illness.

clews Either of the lower corners of a square sail. Also the lower aft corner of a triangular sail.

close-hauled Describes a ship with the yards braced and the sails set so that the vessel can go as far into the wind as possible. (Sailing vessels cannot sail directly into the wind.)

clyster An enema or suppository to clean the bowel.

collier A ship built for hauling coal.

companionway A ladder or staircase leading from one deck to another.

course 1. The two lowest, largest square sails: the fore-course and the maincourse. 2. The direction or compass point toward which the ship sails.

cox'n (coxswain) The helmsman in charge of navigating one of the vessel's boats. In a warship the cox'n is a petty officer responsible for the captain's boat.

crimp An agent who finds personnel for the navy for a fee, often by force or unscrupulous means.

cringle A grommet worked into the boltrope of a square sail at the outermost edge; used to reef, or shorten, the sail.

cro'jack yard (crossjack) The lower yard on the aftermost mast.

D

davit tackle A cranelike arrangement used to hoist small boats on and off the ship.

E

ensign The national flag of a vessel's country, flown at the stern.

exsanguination The process of bleeding to death.

F

fake To lay a rope in coils or figure eights so that it won't kink or foul.

fiferail The rail around the masts.

fifth-rate Warships of this era were rated from one to six according to how many cannons they carried. Most frigates were fifth- or sixth-rated, meaning they carried between twenty-eight and thirty-two guns. Although they carried fewer guns than the higher-rated ships, frigates were faster and could maneuver better.

fighting top (top) A platform above the deck where the topmast joins the mainmast. Serves to attach futtock shrouds and is also a place from which marines or sailors could fire muskets. There is one for each of the three masts, with the main one being the largest. On *Canopus* the main fighting top was five feet by four feet.

fireship A sacrificial vessel loaded with combustibles and explosives, ignited, and sailed into an enemy ship to destroy it. (The fireship's crew would make their risky escape on a smaller boat after setting sails, fixing the fireship's rudder, and lighting the fuses.)

flux Diarrhea, which could be fatal if its victims lost too much bodily fluid. Bloody flux was particularly dangerous, as it indicated internal bleeding.

fo'c'sle (forecastle) The foremost portion of the deck. The fo'c'sle was the sailors' domain, and for the most part the officers respected this. (Pronounced FOKE-sul)

fore (forward) Toward the bow or front of the vessel.

fore-and-aft Set or placed along the line of the vessel's length. Jibs, stays'ls, and spanker gaffs were fore-and-aft sails on a square-rigged ship.

fother To temporarily fix a hole or leak in the hull of a vessel by lowering an old sail or piece of canvas underwater, over the hole. The pressure of the water kept it against the hull and prevented water from rushing in.

four-pounder A cannon that fired a four-pound lead ball. Rather small, as eighteenth-century cannons went, but required fewer men to operate than larger guns.

frigate A three-masted warship designed for speed, maneuverability, and firepower. Generally rated fifth or sixth, which meant they carried between twenty-eight and thirty-two guns on the main deck. Though smaller than higher-rated ships and carrying fewer guns, they were fast and their crews generally highly trained.

furl To fold or roll up a sail on its yard or boom.

futtock shrouds (foot-hook shrouds) The part of the rigging that connects the upper mast to the lower. Here the shrouds and ratlines bend out and around the fighting top at a daunting angle for inexperienced sailors to negotiate.

G

gaff A wooden spar (pole) used to extend the head of a fore-and-aft sail that isn't set on a stay (one of the strong ropes that support a mast).

gasket Braided cords that are tied to secure the sail to the yard when furled.

glass 1. A barometer. When the air pressure drops, or "the glass falls," it indicates the approach of foul weather. 2. A telescope or spyglass for sighting faraway objects. 3. An instrument for measuring the passage of time.

grappling hook A small anchor for boats, also used in battle to board an adjacent vessel. Attached to a long line, the well-thrown clawed hook catches on the rigging or the rail of the other vessel, allowing the boarder to gain access.

grog A mixture of alcohol and water (1:3) issued to British sailors beginning in 1740 as part of their daily rations.

guaiacum The bark of this tropical tree was used to treat various ailments, including venereal disease.

H

halyard A line used to raise sails, flags, and spars.

hand 1. To furl a sail. 2. A crew member.

hawser A thick rope used in anchoring and mooring.

heave to To stop the vessel by adjusting the sails.

helm A vessel's steering apparatus. To be "at the helm" is to be steering the ship.

hold The interior cavity of a ship where cargo and supplies are stored.

hull The body of the ship.

hull-down Describes a ship so far away that its hull can't be seen because of the curvature of the Earth. Only the masts and sails are visible.

hull-up Describes a ship on the horizon but close enough that its hull is visible.

J ∼

Jack A nickname for a British sailor.

jolly boat One of the smallest of a ship's boats.

L ∼

langrel (langrage) Shot consisting of nails, bolts, and other hardware fired from a cannon.

larboard The now obsolete word for the port side of a vessel (that is, the left side when standing on a ship's deck, facing forward—the opposite of starboard).

latitude The distance north or south of the equator, measured in degrees. Parallels of latitude are imaginary lines drawn around the Earth parallel to the equator; the equator represents 0 degrees latitude, while the North Pole is 90 degrees north latitude and the South Pole is 90 degrees south. Each degree is subdivided into 60 minutes, and each minute into 60 seconds.

laudanum An opiate solution widely used in the eighteenth century for pain relief and a variety of other purposes, such as to treat diarrhea.

leeward Toward the lee, or downwind, side. The direction toward which the wind is blowing. (Pronounced LOO-erd)

lifts A system of ropes and blocks that reach from each masthead to their respective yardarms to steady and suspend the ends. They're used to keep the yards in equilibrium and to support the weight when a number of men are standing out on the footrope, furling or reefing the sail.

linstock A staff about three feet long with a forked head to hold a lighted slow match that is used to ignite the cannon's charge. Slow matches were made of rope impregnated with sulfur and resin, and when lit, burned slowly.

Lloyd's The name of a London association of underwriters that insured vessels and their contents.

loblolly boy The assistant to the surgeon and surgeon's mate, charged with the more menial duties of feeding the bedridden patients, fumigating the sick berth, and emptying buckets and chamber pots.

log A daily record kept by officers.

log line A device that measured distance traveled through the water. Combined with a timing device, it provided a means of measuring the boat's speed. The log line was basically a block of wood tied to a rope on a spool. The rope was divided by knots tied at set spacings 1/120 of a mile apart. One person "heaved the log" behind the vessel, playing out the rope and counting the knots as they passed. A second person used a sandglass to call the time. Knowing the time it takes the vessel to go a certain distance (as measured by the knots in the rope), its speed can be mathematically determined.

longitude The distance east or west of an imaginary line running from North Pole to South Pole through the Royal Astronomical Observatory at Greenwich, near London, England. Longitude, like latitude, is measured and defined in degrees. Knowing both longitude and latitude gives the navigator the ship's position.

lubber (landlubber) A derogatory term for someone not accustomed to shipboard life. An awkward, unseaman-like person.

lubber's hole The space between the head of a lower mast and the edge of the fighting top where one might pass without climbing the daunting futtock shrouds.

M

mainmast The principal mast of a sailing vessel. In a three-masted ship, the mainmast is the middle one, and the tallest of the three.

manifest An official inventory of the cargo of a merchant ship.

man-o'-war A ship of the Royal Navy, particularly a battle-ship.

mantelet A moveable defense used as a shelter in siege warfare.

mast A vertical spar for supporting sails.

master (shipmaster) 1. A warrant officer responsible for navigation and sailing of a naval warship. 2. The captain of a merchant vessel. 3. A man who owns the ship that he commands.

merchantman A privately owned ship used for trading. Often owned by companies or groups of individuals.

mess Any company of the officers or crew of a ship who ate, drank, and associated together. The sailors generally ate in groups of six. Dried salted beef or pork was the usual fare. The officers generally messed in the wardroom or someplace separate from the sailors. They often had their own wine or spirits and kept live animals at their own expense, to be used to supplement the standard navy diet of salted meat, dried peas, and old cheese.

mizzen (mizzenmast) The aftermost and smallest mast on a ship.

muster book The navy's official record of all crew members aboard a ship, used to determine issue of food and pay. While wives were not included, the names of dead men and deserters were sometimes kept on the muster books, to the gain of dishonest officers.

N〜

northing Progress made to the north. Though a ship might be pointed and steered in a certain direction, it usually drifts somewhat to leeward, and can also be affected by currents.

nostrum A cure-all, especially an ineffective or quack remedy.

O〜

oakum Fibers and bits of old rope picked apart to be used for caulking and stuffing.

Old Man Slang for the ship's captain. (But *never* used as a term of address!)

P〜

Peruvian bark See **cinchona**

pinnace One of a warship's boats, usually with eight oars.

pitch Tar and resin boiled to a sticky consistency. Used with oakum to caulk the ship and applied to the rigging to protect it and to make it less slippery.

post captain An officer holding a commission as captain, as distinguished from an officer of inferior rank to whom the courtesy title of captain was given. Courtesy titles were often given to temporary captains. Often lieutenants acted as captains in command of a ship on a particular voyage.

press (impress) To be forced into military service during wartime.

press gang A group of men led by officers that went through seaside towns gathering up idle sailors and unemployed landsmen, forcing them to serve aboard His Majesty's ships. Often sailors working aboard merchant ships would be pressed into military service. This system by which the British Navy secured sailors was called Impress Service.

prize An enemy ship captured at sea. Although technically the captured vessel belonged to the Crown, the Crown allowed it to be sold and its worth shared by the crew of the ship that captured it. As wages were low, this served as an incentive bonus, and all crew members were rewarded according to their rank.

pumps Hand-operated machines designed to pump out water that collected in the bilge or the hold.

purser The officer in charge of provisioning a vessel. A merchantman's purser might also be in charge of documents, accounts, and payroll. In the navy pursers were sometimes not liked or trusted, since they often made money on the provisions at the sailors' expense.

Q

quadrant A navigational instrument used to measure the altitude angle of a celestial body—that is, how high above the horizon it is. From this, the ship's latitude could be determined.

quarterdeck The aft or rear portion of the deck where the helm was located and the ship was steered. This was the officers' and gentlemen's section of the ship; sailors were only allowed here when duty required.

R

ratlines Small lines between the shrouds that formed rope "stairs," giving the sailors access to the upper rigging. It wasn't uncommon for the ratlines to break, and the prudent sailor always held on to the shrouds, which were much stronger. (Pronounced RAT-linz)

reef 1. To reduce the area of sail in windy weather by folding the lower section of it and tying it snugly to the yard. 2. A coral growth in shallow water that can sink ships if struck.

rigging The general term for the rope lines that support and operate the mast and sails.

roadstead (road) An anchorage outside of a harbor where ships may await orders.

S

sappers Those who dig saps, or covered trenches, in order to approach a besieged place without danger from enemy fire.

scuppers Deck drains.

shallop A boat used in shallow waters.

sheet A line attached to the sail, used on deck to set it.

shipwright A man employed in the building of ships.

shroud One of many thick, taut ropes supporting the masts.

Spanish fly Also called cantharis or blister beetle. A type of beetle (*Cantharis vesicatoria*) that was dried and crushed to make a remedy used chiefly as a blistering agent or counter-irritant. A caustic substance believed by some to be an aphrodisiac.

spanker Describes the supplementary fore-and-aft sail on the after side of the mizzenmast.

sprits'l (spritsail) A sail attached to a yard that hung under the bowsprit.

square-rigged Describes a vessel using primarily four-cornered sails on yards hung at right angles to the centerline.

starboard The right-hand side of the vessel, when you are on board and facing forward.

stays'l (staysail) A triangular sail that was set fore-and-aft between the masts, and which helped the ship to point up-wind, a difficult direction of sail.

stern The rear or aftermost part of a vessel.

stuns'ls (studding sails) Auxiliary sails set outside the square sails and used to gain speed when the wind was favorable.

sweeps Long, heavy oars used to propel boats. Sweeps could also be extended through the ports and used to propel the ship itself if the ship needed to be moved a short distance.

T

taffrail The upper part of the railing along the rear of the ship.

t'gallant (topgallant) The mast, yard, and sail above the topsail; generally the third sail above the deck on a square-rigged ship.

tiller Part of a vessel's steering mechanism. A smaller boat would just have a tiller, but a larger boat also uses a wheel, to reduce the amount of effort needed to steer.

topman An experienced seaman who was assigned to the more difficult work aloft.

topmast The mast below the topgallant mast on a square-rigged ship.

tops'l (topsail) The second sail above the deck, on each topmast.

trepan 1. A surgical instrument for cutting out small pieces of bone, especially from the skull. 2. To operate upon with a trepan, usually to relieve intracerebral pressure caused by a traumatic head injury.

V~

Victualing Board An office concerned with provisioning ships with food, especially ships of the Royal Navy.

W~

waist The middle portion of a ship's deck. Often, as on *Canopus*, it is a few steps lower than the foredeck or the quarterdeck.

wardroom A room in the afterpart of the ship, below-decks, reserved for the officers.

warrant officer The warrant officers included the ship-master and his mate, the bosun and mate, the gunner, carpenter, and in the mid-eighteenth century, the ship's surgeon and mate. The captain and lieutenants of a naval ship received their commissions from the king. Warrant officers could be hired and fired by the captain, but generally stayed with the ship to which they were warranted.

watch The period of time when each division of a ship's company alternately remains on deck and on duty; usually four hours, except for the dogwatches (two two-hour shifts), which serve to prevent the same watch being kept by the same men every day. For want of men, most eighteenth-century ships operated with only two watches, called the starboard and the larboard watch. (Later, the word *larboard* was changed to *port*.) With just two watches, a sailor never had more than four hours off at any one time.

weigh To pull up the anchor. *Aweigh* means that the anchor has cleared the bottom during hoisting.

whist A card game ordinarily played by four people, with the two players sitting opposite each other acting as partners. The precursor of the card game bridge.

windward Into the wind; toward the direction from which the wind is blowing. The opposite of leeward, the direction toward which the wind is blowing.

Y

yards Horizontal spars that support the sails of a square-rigged ship. Sailors stood on footropes suspended from the yards, which they leaned against as they furled or reefed the big sails.

yellow fever (**yellow jack**) An acute, often fatal viral disease of warm climates, now known to be transmitted by *Aedes aegypti* mosquitoes. The mosquitoes' role wasn't suspected in the eighteenth century, and remedies were not only ineffective, but in some instances harmful. Today, prevention is the mainstay of treatment.

ACKNOWLEDGMENTS

I would like to thank the officers and crew members of the *Endeavour Replica*, a working copy of the square-rigged ship that James Cook commanded during his first circumnavigation. Aboard this ship, on an eighteen-day crossing from Vancouver to Hawaii, I learned the rudiments of sailing an eighteenth-century ship and got a taste of an eighteenth-century sailor's hard—but in some ways rewarding—life.

My gratitude to Suzanne J. Stark for her insightful book *Female Tars: Women Aboard Ship in the Age of Sail* and to Joan Druett for her marvelous books, particularly *Hen Frigates, She Captains,* and *Rough Medicine.* Many thanks to my editor, Michelle Frey, for her enthusiastic vision and direction, to my agent, Laura Rennert, for her insight and her expertise, and to both of them for sharing my passion for the story. My appreciation to Kate Gartner, book designer, and to the illustrators Griesbach and Martucci, whose combined talents have produced such a visually compelling book. Many thanks to Michele Burke for her invaluable assistance during the editing process.

I'd also like to acknowledge Nancy Holder, who gave me advice and encouragement, and all the professionals and volunteers who *are* the Maui Writers Conference. I want to express my fond gratitude to *Topaz,* a Luders 36 sloop that has carried my husband and me across thousands of blue-water miles, providing me with experience and memories. Last but not least, I want to thank her captain, Bob Russell, for his support, his advice—and most of all, his love.

SELECTED SOURCES

Anderson, Fred. *Crucible of War: The Seven Years' War and the Fate of Empire in British North America, 1754–1766.* London: Faber and Faber, 2000. New York: Alfred A. Knopf, 2000.

Anonymous. *Authentic Journal of the Siege of the Havana. By an Officer. To Which Is Prefixed, A Plan of the Siege of the Havana, Shewing the Landing, Encampments, Approaches, and Batteries of the English Army. With the Attacks and Stations of the Fleet.* London: T. Jefferys, 1762. (I originally read parts of this journal on the Web site cubaheritage.com.)

Barclay, Juliet, and Martin Charles. *Havana: Portrait of a City.* London: Cassell, 1993. (Paperback edition, 2003.)

Biesty, Stephen, and Richard Platt. *Man-of-War: Stephen Biesty's Cross-Sections.* New York: Dorling Kindersley, Inc., 1993.

Bradfield, Nancy. *Historical Costumes of England: 1066–1968.* New York: Costume and Fashion Press, 1997. (First published in Great Britain 1938.)

Buckley, Roger Norman. *The British Army in the West Indies: Society and the Military in the Revolutionary Age.* Gainesville: University Press of Florida, 1998. Barbados: University of the West Indies Press, 1998.

Chernow, Ron. *Alexander Hamilton.* New York: Penguin Group, 2004.

Cohen, Daniel A., editor. *The Female Marine and Related Works: Narratives of Cross-Dressing and Urban Vice in*

America's Early Republic. Amherst: University of Massachusetts Press, 1997.

Cordingly, David. *Women Sailors and Sailors' Women: An Untold Maritime History.* New York: Random House, 2001.

Creighton, M., and Lisa Norling, editors. *Iron Men, Wooden Women: Gender and Seafaring in the Atlantic World, 1700–1920.* Baltimore: The Johns Hopkins University Press, 1996.

Druett, Joan. *Hen Frigates: Wives of Merchant Captains Under Sail.* New York: Simon and Schuster, 1998.

Druett, Joan. *Rough Medicine: Surgeons at Sea in the Age of Sail.* New York: Routledge, 2000.

Druett, Joan. *She Captains: Heroines and Hellions of the Sea.* New York: Simon and Schuster, 2000.

Earle, Peter. *Sailors: English Merchant Seamen 1650–1775.* London: Methuen, 1998.

Edwards, Fred. *Sailing as a Second Language: An Illustrated Dictionary.* Camden, Maine: International Marine Publishing Co., 1988.

Estes, J. Worth. *Naval Surgeon: Life and Death at Sea in the Age of Sail.* Canton, Massachusetts: Science History Publications, 1998.

Furneaux, Rupert. *The Seven Years War.* London: Hart-Davis MacGibbon, 1973.

Haeger, Knut. *The Illustrated History of Surgery.* London: Harold Starke, 1989.

Hubbard, Vincent K. *Swords, Ships and Sugar: History of Nevis to 1900.* Corvallis, Oregon: Premiere Editions International, Inc., 1998.

King, Dean, with John B. Hattendorf and J. Worth Estes. *A Sea of Words: A Lexicon and Companion for Patrick O'Brien's Seafaring Tales,* second edition. New York: Henry Holt and Company, 1995.

Lever, Darcy. *The Young Sea Officer's Sheet Anchor: Or a Key to the Leading of Rigging and to Practical Seamanship.* Mineola, New York: Dover Publications, 1998. Originally published in London by John Richardson, 1819.

Lloyd, Christopher, and Jack L. S. Coulter. *Medicine and the Navy: Vol. III, 1714–1815.* Edinburgh and London: E. and S. Livingstone Ltd., 1961.

Oxford English Dictionary, second edition (compact disc version). Oxford: Oxford University Press, 1994.

Porter, Roy. *English Society in the Eighteenth Century.* London: Penguin Books, 1991. First published by Pelican Books, 1982.

Rodger, N.A.M. *The Wooden World: An Anatomy of the Georgian Navy.* New York and London: W. W. Norton and Company, 1996. First published by William Collins in Great Britain, 1986.

Smyth, Admiral W. H. *The Sailor's Word-Book: An Alphabetical Digest of Nautical Terms.* London: Blackie and Son, 1867.

Stark, Suzanne J. *Female Tars: Women Aboard Ship in the Age of Sail*. Annapolis, Maryland: Naval Institute Press, 1996.

Vickery, Amanda. *The Gentleman's Daughter: Women's Lives in Georgian England*. New Haven and London: Yale University Press, 1998.

Williams, Guy. *The Age of Agony: The Art of Healing, 1700–1800*. Chicago, Illinois: Academy Chicago Publishers, 1986.